SAFE WITH ME

SAFE WITH ME

K.L. SLATER

Bookouture

Published by Bookouture

An imprint of StoryFire Ltd.
23 Sussex Road, Ickenham, UB10 8PN
United Kingdom

www.bookouture.com

ISBN: 978-1-78681-106-6
eBook ISBN: 978-1-78681-109-7

To my daughter, Francesca Kim
Thank you for your love and support
From the very beginning

So, they're tucked up in bed at last. You take a handful of matches and you light each one, watching the burn die to a powdery black dot.

The embers in the open fireplace are dying down but there's still the white hot core, deep in the centre, still powerful enough to help you set things good and straight one final time.

'Two squashy seat cushions piled on the floor, four squashy seat cushions piled on the floor.' It's fun to sing to the tune of 'Ten Green Bottles'.

You push the chair right up next to them so the fabrics are touching. You carefully extract two balls of molten coal from the ashes with the tongs, carefully placing each one in the middle of the cushions. Now you sit back to watch them melting in, deep down. The glowing balls sink greedily into the soft foam, and the scorched fabric cover of the cushion shrinks back as if it's trying to escape.

There is no noise and you enjoy the silence.

Entranced, you watch as the small flames start to dance, flicking their pretty, lethal tongues. The power amazes, terrifies and comforts you, all at once. You feel the layers of protection you have tried to coat yourself with over the years being stripped away. You needed them so you had a chance of getting through each day and drunken night but you are safe now. The flames will make it safe.

You have tried to tell them many times, of course, tried to ask for help. But they didn't understand what you were trying to get through to them. And now the rawness of your fear, your sadness – it's here for all to see in the sharpness of the thick, sulphured air.

You mustn't cough. You don't want to wake them, set the sillies screaming and crying. Leave them to their dreams, they will learn soon enough.

The flames grow larger, then fuse together. You know it's a sign that they are silently promising to help you and yet, for a second, you actually consider changing your mind. You could stomp down the flames and shout for help. You could wake them up.

Then you hear it.

'Let us do our work,' the flames whisper. 'Everything will be better in the morning.'

And that's when you decide to finally walk away.

CHAPTER 1
Present day
Anna

The small silver car coming the other way is moving far too fast, and as it takes the bend, the driver loses control and veers over on to the wrong side of the road.

Everything happens so quickly: there's no time for it to slow down or to even mount the kerb.

There is a hard, muted thud as the car hits the motorbike in front of me. The rider flies up into the air, sort of half-turns and lands face down in the road. As the metal bends and twists it whines like an injured animal, and my hand flies to my face, trying in vain to stem the acrid stench of burning rubber that starts to fill my lungs.

My foot slams down on to the brake, and I jump out, leaving the driver's door wide open and the car in the middle of the road. I stand there, swallowing down the sickly taste that floods my mouth.

Everything seems to freeze in time, and a silence descends. It has a deafening quality all of its own and, for a moment, I am lost in the empty roar that surrounds me.

Then the spell is broken as the door of the silver car opens and a woman of about forty, dressed in jeans and a short pink coat, staggers out and vomits onto the side of the road. She holds her hair away from her face as if it's somehow important to keep it clean.

And it is in that split second that I recognise her.

There is no mistaking that face.

I remind myself to breathe. My throat feels tight and dry, and my heart squeezes in so hard on itself I can almost sense it hanging in my chest like a dried-out apricot stone.

Twelve years ago, when I got out of hospital, even though I had met her only briefly on just a couple of occasions, I spent every spare minute I had trying to trace her again.

I was so young, desperate and naïve back then. With nobody to help me I hit a complete brick wall: she had simply vanished into thin air.

Eventually I was forced to acknowledge I'd lost her. Then all I could do was pray that karma really did exist and that she'd get what was coming to her for what she did to us.

And now she is here, right in front of me. Ruining yet another life.

I watch as the silver-haired driver from the black Mercedes that stopped behind me shrugs off his expensive-looking jacket and drapes it around her shoulders. He comforts her with a protective arm, murmuring reassuring words into her ear.

Something about her draws people in, gives them the impression she is a decent person.

So ironic.

Knots of people start to appear, seemingly from nowhere.

I think about getting back in my car, leaving the scene. Part of me is pulling to get away from her, but, of course, that's not going to happen.

I could never just let go of her again.

Amid the chaos my eyes are drawn to the long, broken shape lying in the road. Pieces of motorbike are scattered all around him like fragments of jagged chrome confetti.

I ignore the rapidly growing crowd on the other side of the street and crouch down beside him, feeling for a pulse. My hand shakes as I press his wrist gently and, for a moment, I think she's done it again, because I can't feel any movement at all under my fingers. No sign of life.

Then his eyes flicker, and I release my breath.

People pour out of the small, terraced houses lining Green Road, fingers pointing and mouths all frozen wide.

I look down at him again.

He is hanging on to life by a thread; I can sense it. If he slips away now, I will never be able to forgive myself.

That terrified young girl who didn't know what to do for the best is long gone now.

Maybe, this time, I can make a difference.

The rider has landed face down on his left-hand side. A thick pool, like ruby molasses, blossoms out from the underside of his head.

I reach down to stroke his face but I don't let go of his hand.

He looks about my age: early to mid-thirties, I'd say. His skin is smooth, lashes long and dark and twitching as if he is caught in a dream.

Over the other side of the road, where all the attention is, she is howling.

There is barely a scratch on her but then she was always so good at playing the victim, so I suppose I shouldn't be surprised.

I try to stop staring in case I give myself away, but I've no need to worry – she's oblivious to anyone but herself.

She hasn't got a clue who I am or what she did to me all that time ago.

Granted, I look very different now. It's been a long thirteen years; I'm much darker-haired and carry nearly four stones of extra weight. There is no trace of the naïve, slender girl who gave up her trust so easily.

See, people like her never really notice the insignificant people around them.

They go through life making their selfish decisions, leaving a trail of destruction in their wake, and never giving it a second thought.

Until it all comes back with a vengeance, that is.

Then they have to suck it up good.

I hear someone call: 'The ambulance is on its way.'

There are hordes of people standing around now, rubbernecking.

Their eyes are trained on the motorbike rider but I don't see much compassion, more a thinly disguised hunger for the gory details that might be revealed if they hang around long enough.

I move stiffly from my knees to my haunches and prepare to stand up, to walk away before the ambulance arrives.

I know I'll be able to keep tabs on her now through the local newspaper reports about the accident, and I can identify myself later to the police as a witness.

A big part of me wants to stay but I learned a lot from my therapist. Like how to stand back from my thoughts and evaluate a situation calmly and logically so I make the best decision.

If I stay, I don't think I can trust myself not to cause a scene. This time I need to make sure that every action, every step I take, is carefully planned and considered.

So that there are no mistakes.

I feel something brush over my hand and I glance down as the injured rider's fingers close around mine.

His slate-blue eyes are bloodshot and wide open now but he seems oblivious to all the people standing around, as if he can't see past my face.

A sharp intake of breath and he looks right at me.

'Help me,' he whispers.

CHAPTER 2

I've worked for the Royal Mail for just over five years.

Six days a week, I set the alarm for four a.m., and I drive to the delivery office in good time for the start of my shift at five.

My first job is always to organise the mail into postcodes according to the addresses on my round. Then I bag it up and deliver it to the residents of the Clifton housing estate, a sprawling mass of 1950s grey concrete on the outskirts of Nottingham that once had the dubious privilege of being the largest housing estate in Europe.

It sounds simple, but delivering mail correctly and in a timely manner is far from easy, and it isn't a menial task either. Most people place great value on their mail service.

For some of the other postal workers it's just a job but my view is that it doesn't take that much to make a real difference to people's lives.

Mrs Gray on Beck Crescent has ulcerated legs, so I always put her bin out first thing on a Friday morning. This summer, I cut Mr Bagley's lawn on my day off when his arthritis was playing up.

Now, when he catches me at the door he talks non-stop about his only son, who lives in Australia. I often feel like saying: 'And where's your precious son when the grass needs cutting and you need your prescription fetching?'

But, of course, I never do.

My colleagues at the delivery office are a good bunch really; they seem to know just to leave me alone and let me get on with my job.

People stopped trying to draw me in to their non-stop conversations about reality TV and *Coronation Street* a long time ago; although, I admit, by some kind of weird osmosis, I'd probably be able to tell you what's happening in each and every one of those programmes they discuss.

Everything had been going perfectly well at work and then, out of the blue last week, the situation changed. The management team decided we were to have a reevaluation of the delivery rounds.

When it was my turn, Jim Crowe walked over to my counter.

'You're not getting finished until way past three, Anna,' he said, consulting his clipboard. 'We think that's because the round might be too big for you.'

It was Jim who interviewed me after I'd applied for the position five years ago. I got myself so het up beforehand I caught the wrong bus and was a few minutes late arriving.

I remember how Jim repeated one or two of the questions when I got confused and told me to take my time when I forgot what it was I wanted to say.

He took a chance on me back then; he gave me a job. I suppose he's always sort of looked out for me a bit ever since. It's as if, on some level, he's always understood that I sometimes find things difficult.

He didn't know anything about what had happened to me before though; none of them did.

'I get the round all done, don't I?' I replied.

'With an hour or more overtime you do. But we can't keep paying it, Anna. Overtime's expensive, and I've got my orders to cut the rota.'

I watched as beads of sweat settled in the bald patches where Jim's hair was beginning to recede. I kept quiet and waited for him to meet my eyes but he just kept flicking through the papers on his clipboard.

In the end, Jim agreed I could keep my round for the time being, providing I didn't put in any overtime claims. Very gracious.

'We'll see how it goes,' he said. 'If you're struggling to get finished then we might have to put you on another round, possibly the Huntsmoor. I'm sorry, Anna, it's beyond my control this time.'

I shrugged my shoulders and sauntered off but, underneath, a blistering heat seethed deep into my bones. *Nobody* wanted the Huntsmoor round, which was precisely the reason they always covered it with agency staff.

The dreaded Huntsmoor; a sea of dirty concrete and boarded-up windows.

It was a miracle if postal workers could get past the banned-breed dogs straining at their leashes and the heckling, hooded youths who gathered outside the multi-occupancy council houses from dawn until dusk, whatever the weather.

It made my scalp crawl to think I could end up doing the Huntsmoor round if the management made big changes.

My job kept me on track, kept the days ticking on. It helped me escape the dark days, and I didn't want to go back there.

I made my mind up there and then that I would hang on to my delivery round at any cost.

As it turns out, I needn't have worried.

As of today, I have completed my round within my allocated time for exactly seven days and without the need to put in any overtime.

Now the management team have no excuse but to back off and leave me alone. They can go pick on someone else because I have found a way to manage.

Manage for now, anyway.

This morning, I finished bang on time and took the empty mailbag back to the office, making sure Jim saw me hang it up.

My customers depend on me and they don't like change. They wouldn't appreciate a new delivery person.

For starters, how would someone new guess that the Benson family of Buxton Crescent have all their internet shopping parcels delivered to number 86 across the road?

Who would tell the new delivery person that the immaculate Mr Staniforth, who commutes to Canary Wharf and is out of the house fourteen hours a day, likes his mail packaged together with a rubber band so it doesn't fly all over the hallway?

It's those kinds of details that count with people.

When I finished my shift this morning, I locked my bike up in the outdoor rack and set off back home in the car. I still wore my fluorescent jacket, and as it was still fairly mild for October I couldn't help sweating quite a bit.

I remember feeling eager to get back home, where I could throw on my comfies and chill out with my cat, Albert, a hot chocolate and a recorded episode of *Homes Under the Hammer.*

That's when I opened the car window a touch and turned the corner into Green Road.

It's only now, looking back, I realise that every single minute of the last thirteen years has been perfectly aligned to that very moment – to bring her back to me.

Despite the fact I lost hope a long time ago that she would one day be made to pay for what she did, the truth was now crystal clear.

I was always meant to find her again.

CHAPTER 3

In the morning, there is a cursory paragraph about the accident in the *Nottingham Post*.

Annoyingly, the driver of the car is not named; but, of course, I already know her real name. Before she changed it, that is.

I assume that's what she did, anyway. Months spent trying to find her and hitting constant dead ends smacks of someone getting a new identity and disappearing. But any anonymity she might have had has gone for good now, thanks to the accident.

Overnight, I've given the situation a lot of thought, and I think the most important thing I need to do is stay in contact with the motorbike victim.

So long as I can do that, I can be sure of finding out the important information right away. I'll have an indelible link to the driver so that she can't escape, however hard she tries. Not now that the police are involved.

Before I left the scene yesterday, a community support officer took my details. She said the police will be in touch very soon to take my statement, which will be my chance to put key evidence forward as an eyewitness.

I cut out the article and lay it flat on the dining table before clearing away my breakfast dish and mug.

Outside, in the car, I've just belted up when I remember I haven't checked the cooker. You can't be too careful when it comes to electrical appliances. It is always best to be safe rather than sorry.

I unlock the kitchen door again and stick my head round but I see right away that I have turned off the cooker *and* put the smiley-face sticker over the switch.

I lock up again and set off for the hospital, mulling the newspaper article over in my mind.

They gave the motorbike driver's full name, Liam Bradbury, stating he is in a stable condition, despite a head injury, and is currently receiving treatment at Nottingham's Queen's Medical Centre, known locally as the QMC.

This morning, when I rang the QMC, the receptionist sounded surprised when I told her I was the person who'd sat in the road and held Liam's hand until the ambulance arrived. She had given me his ward number quite happily after that.

There is not much traffic on the road and it takes me just under fifteen minutes to get to the hospital.

I drive by tired retail parks peppered with retired couples ambling from their cars. Young women stride along the pavements, absorbed with talking on their phones and pushing their ignored, sticky toddlers towards town in gaudy buggies.

I park up and stop by a small, overpriced shop in the hospital foyer to pick up a small basket of fruit and then head towards the lift.

Up on Ward Eight, they buzz me straight in without asking who I am, which I have to say, rather makes a mockery of the security system.

I ask a nurse at the desk where Liam's bed is.

'Are you a relative?' She peers at me over the counter. 'It's just that he's resting now and you're out of visiting hours.'

I explain who I am. 'I just want to make sure he's okay,' I say.

I follow her down the ward to a small, private room at the end. It almost takes my breath away when I see him.

Even though he is bruised, dotted with narrow, plastic tubes and an oxygen mask that covers most of his face, I can't help thinking he's quite an attractive man. That full head of brown hair shot through with sun-lightened gold, even dull and matted, promises to shine.

And he looks like Danny. Which sounds odd: putting the words 'brother' and 'attractive' together, but Danny was a beautiful person, inside and out, and Liam's square jaw and wide-set eyes makes me feel even more certain that this whole thing was meant to be.

I place the basket of fruit on a small table next to him.

'He suffered blunt trauma to the head but they've got him fairly stable now,' the nurse says, tugging the creases out of his bed covers. 'But how his poor gran is going to cope once she gets him home, I don't know.'

It occurs to me that he's a bit old to be living with his gran, but I suppose the price of property these days prohibits lots of people from getting a foothold on the housing ladder so I shouldn't judge.

I think about my own humble little terraced house. It is certainly nothing special but at least it's all mine. Been mine since. . . well, for the last thirteen years anyhow.

I wish the nurse would just leave us alone so I can replay yesterday's events in my mind.

Liam's flaccid hand lies pale against the powder-blue of the hospital blanket, and his eyelids are perfectly still now, not flickering the way they had been in the road.

When the nurse steps outside to speak to someone, I get my chance. I reach for my bag and pull out my phone. It doesn't take me long to get what I need, and it's a good job, because, in no time at all, I hear the nurse shuffling around behind me again.

'I suppose I've got to go now,' I say.

'Sorry, we have to treat everyone the same when it comes to visiting.' She looks at me and her face softens a little. 'Why don't you come back later, around six? His gran will be here then and

I'm sure she'll be very keen to thank you for everything you did for him.'

I look down at Liam's hand.

'It's no more than anyone else would have done,' I say.

I walk back to the car in the cold, grey drizzle.

Usually, if I'm at a loose end, for whatever reason, I go for a walk around Colwick Park, which is just a stone's throw away from where I live in Sneinton.

I like to sit watching the ducks bobbing around on one of the lakes; their lives seem so simple and unrushed. I used to take bread out on to the grassy bank most days but they'd all crowd in and go crazy for it, so I stopped doing that.

To keep things functioning properly, you have to keep a firm control. There's nothing else for it.

Today it is far too cold and wet for visiting the park, so I drive back home to wait until the official hospital visiting time starts at six. Before going inside the house, I pop next door to Mrs Peat's.

I tap at the small side window, and she looks up from her cross-stitch.

'Everything alright, Mrs Peat?' I call through the glass.

She smiles and nods, giving me a little wave with a fleshy hand.

We have a code: I tap on the window, and if she needs me to pop in she'll beckon, and then I go round the back and let myself in with the spare key which is hidden under the rusty milk-bottle stand by the door.

Sometimes, I just go in anyway whether she needs me or not. I'll often have a cup of tea with her to break the monotony of her day. I owe her that much.

'I wish you'd call me Joan,' she always scolds me, but I can't do it. I have lived next door to her all my life and some things, well, they stay sacred, don't they?

Mrs Peat will always be Mrs Peat in my eyes.

Between the two of us, me and her care assistant, Linda, we make sure she is well looked after. She isn't any trouble really.

Her useless daughter, Janet-Mae, lives over fifty miles away and visits once a month if Mrs Peat is lucky. But I'm guessing she will be over fast enough, though, the day one of us finds her poor mother stiff as a board in her armchair and it's time to sell the house.

Of course, I've never said as much.

When I get back home, Albert is sitting by the back door, waiting patiently. I always try to go straight home at the end of my shift so I can feed him at the same time each day. Albert seems to understand the value of routine.

People tend to think cats aren't social animals but they're wrong. Albert depends on me in every way. Naturally, I never let him go out at night; the thought of him wandering the streets is enough to stop me sleeping. I know how horrible people can be, and it's not always strangers that will hurt your animals.

I close my eyes and squeeze the painful memories back inside the imaginary box at the back of my head, like my therapist taught me. Now is not the time for dwelling in the past.

After I've fed Albert, I flick through the other local newspapers I bought to see if I can find anything else about the accident. There are a couple of mentions, just one or two lines, nothing like the *Nottingham Post* did. I cut them out anyway and file them with the other report.

I open a new folder on my laptop and make the first entries, noting down the time of my visit to the hospital that morning and Liam's condition. I make doubly sure to record the comments the nurse made about him living with his gran.

I'm not leaving anything to chance.

I put Albert out into the hallway so he won't disturb me. I open up the photograph on my phone; it has turned out much better than I expected.

I'd snapped it in a hurry when the nurse popped outside the room, and I couldn't even be sure the camera had focused properly. But the image is very clear and shows Liam lying pale and broken in his hospital bed, covered with tubes and monitoring pads.

I create a second file on my laptop and save the photo in there, once I've emailed it to myself.

It's such a shame I didn't think to take one of him as he lay injured in the road yesterday. I imagine Liam will probably be annoyed with me about that when he's feeling better.

Things haven't really turned out as I'd hoped or expected today.

I imagined getting to the hospital this morning and finding Liam sitting up in bed, ready to tell me everything the police have found out about the woman who mowed him down.

I look at the photo I took of him again and my heart feels heavy. He is still unconscious from the drugs they gave him.

He doesn't even know I exist.

I listen to the clock ticking and Albert scratching at the sitting room door to be let in again.

I'm beginning to regret ringing in sick this morning. What if the management gets someone else to do my round and that person does a better job?

I should have gone in. I can't risk them finding out the real reason I'm managing to get my round finished without putting in any overtime.

When I move from the table and sit down in the armchair, I glance down at the threadbare tweedy material where, for years, Mother's own forearms rested.

There is an intermittent low hum from the refrigerator but otherwise the house is silent. The air hangs thick and heavy, seeming to wrap itself around me like a cloak dripping with unpleasant memories.

When we were kids, no one was allowed to sit in Mother's chair. She knew if her cushion had been moved even an inch.

She liked things to stay just the way she left them, you see.

I close my eyes and feel the rough fabric pressing against the thin, pale skin of my wrists.

She can't do anything about me sitting here now.

None of them can.

CHAPTER 4
Joan Peat

She always stayed in the middle room until after Anna had left for work.

It wasn't necessary for Joan to sit by the window watching, though: listening was usually enough.

Their little side street was quiet. There weren't many cars that actually used it, particularly very early in the morning when her neighbour went to work.

Today, Anna had broken her routine and had left the house later than she usually would to go to work and returned way before her shift finished. And now Joan had just heard the back door slam – she was off out again.

Anna had parked her car at the front of the house. Joan watched her as she approached the driver's door.

She'd piled on weight over the last couple of years, Joan had noticed. She seemed to live in either her Royal Mail uniform, or jeans, boots and a grey oversized sweatshirt which made her look rather slovenly.

Joan had rarely seen Anna in make-up, and in recent weeks she had taken to wearing a rather unflattering dark brown baseball cap that only highlighted her pasty, slightly bloated complexion.

Still, Joan firmly believed that the Anna she used to know was in there somewhere; she was just hiding away, too afraid to come out. She lived in hope that someday there would be a glimmer of that enthusiasm for life that the young Anna had.

As soon as her neighbour drove away, Joan hoisted herself up from the armchair and walked into the kitchen to make herself a cup of tea.

Both Anna and Linda, her care assistant, were under the impression Joan was unable to move of her own accord. Joan didn't consider the fact that she could move was a full-blown fib; it was just that Joan hadn't furnished them with the truth. There was a difference.

Anyway, she often did have difficulty, and even on a good day she wasn't exactly sprinting around the house like Mo Farah.

So Joan preferred to think of it as a little white lie.

Generally, it was true that she could still get around without any assistance. Some days, she even made it upstairs, if she was careful not to push herself too hard and took the odd breather on the way up.

It was so nice seeing Anna and Linda regularly. If they thought Joan could manage, they'd probably stop coming round as often, and that was the last thing she wanted.

It was surprisingly easy to fool other people: even the district nurse, Jasminda, who called on her every couple of months to check her swollen, ulcered legs.

They were all so trusting of Joan and took her completely at her word. After all, why would she mislead them over something like that?

Well, loneliness was the reason why.

Joan thought it got used a lot, that word: 'lonely'. It got used by people who hadn't a clue of its true meaning. People who had no experience of the suffocating sheet of silence that attached itself to you like cling film from the moment you woke up.

It got used by people who had no concept of what it felt like to have to put the radio on in the other room in order to pretend family or friends were over to visit.

But, in Anna and Linda, Joan knew she still had real people to talk to most days and that helped her to breathe. It helped her to get through each long week, a day at a time.

All of the people who Joan saw on a regular basis came here because they thought she couldn't move and couldn't manage without their help. And, in a way, they were right.

The truth was, she really couldn't manage without them.

Joan felt lucky to have such caring souls around her.

And after all, she had always tried to do her bit in the past, helping others by doing what she could to ease their burden.

Take Anna.

They had been neighbours for nearly thirty years now, and Joan had virtually fostered her when she first came out of the hospital. Until she turned eighteen, anyhow.

Anna had no one else left in the world to turn to.

The way Joan looked at it, her legs might be on their way out but there was nothing wrong with her memory or her hearing, even if she was well on the wrong side of her seventies now.

Unfortunately, that also meant she was able to recall every detail of what happened next door thirteen years ago.

What a terrible business it had been.

She could remember just as clearly the day that the Clarkes first became her neighbours.

There had been a light dusting of snow overnight on the morning that Monica and Jack Clarke arrived next door with their little girl, Anna.

Joan and her husband, Arthur, had heard that Jack Clarke had been a faceworker at Annesley Colliery but he'd been trapped in a piece of machinery on a shift and lost his arm.

The Clarkes used the compensation to buy the little terrace next door to Joan and Arthur, to be nearer to the city so that

Monica could look for some part-time employment there, apparently.

Arthur had still been alive then, of course. Fit as a fiddle he was, cycling a thirty-mile round trip to the factory every day. That was two years before the pancreatic cancer got him, six weeks from the diagnosis to his death.

Joan placed her cup and saucer down gently on the coffee table and looked out onto the road.

Monica Clarke had been snooty and unfriendly from the start; although quite where her airs and graces came from, Joan couldn't imagine.

'A bottle blonde with no manners and far too much cleavage on show,' was how Arthur had described Monica when she first emerged from the removal van Jack had hired.

Monica had ignored them waving hello from this very window. Arthur had always been such a good judge of character.

Little Anna, though: she'd turned right around and given them the biggest smile.

Sweet little thing, she was. All fair curls and blue eyes, like a china doll.

Joan and Arthur's daughter, Janet-Mae, was at university by this time, studying for her business degree at Manchester. She came home when she could but that wasn't very often.

When Joan had set eyes on little Anna, her heart swelled with memories of when Janet-Mae was small and still needed her. It had been too long.

Joan stared out now at the space where the Clarkes had parked their van all those years ago. It had rained overnight and the gutter was filthy, scudded with mud and leaves and clusters of grit that stuck to the edge of the kerb like tumours.

She averted her eyes and recalled how Anna had stood out the front waving away at them until Monica came out and grabbed her arm, yanking her roughly away.

It wasn't long, of course, before they discovered Monica's penchant for alcohol and men.

As a regular churchgoer, Joan made a concerted effort to avoid joining in with the neighbours' whispered tales of Monica's colourful nightlife, whispered over garden walls and at the corner shop. But it wasn't easy.

From her upstairs window, late at night, Joan saw Monica on more than one occasion in the arms of a man who most definitely wasn't her husband. Far more likely someone else's.

The Clarkes had only lived next door for a year when Monica fell pregnant with Daniel.

Dear Lord, the arguments had gone on for weeks. With the help of an upturned glass against the joining wall, Joan could often hear what was being said virtually word for word.

Suffice to say, Jack Clarke seemed to be utterly convinced the child wasn't his, and within the month he'd left home. Leaving behind a pregnant Monica and his daughter Anna.

That was the last time the Peats saw him.

Six months later Jack Clarke was dead. They heard he'd had a drunken argument with an HGV in town and, predictably, had come off worst.

That was when little Anna first started visiting Joan and Arthur regularly.

It always amazes me how it is so easy to appear one way to the people around you but to live inside as someone else entirely.

You have to put the years of practise in first, of course. But in the long run, it is all worth it when you see someone unravel and you can stand back and think, 'I did that'.

You could say it feels a bit like dressing up in the brightest party clothes so nobody sees how low and lost you feel underneath. You'd be surprised how easy it is to hide your true feelings with a smile and a kind word.

Don't get me wrong, it can be irritating, pretending to be invisible. Letting them think that what you want and what you feel doesn't really matter.

The trick is to stay quiet and listen, absorb everything you can. People love to talk about themselves.

I tell them what they want to hear, watch them swallow my clever words like razorblades dipped in honey.

It doesn't occur to them they are being played like an old violin.

By the time they start to get suspicious, it will be too late. I will pull out that lethal ribbon of razorblades and they will suffer.

I know how it works because I have done it before.

CHAPTER 5

Anna

After my unofficial morning visit to the hospital, I end up pacing the house all afternoon, clock-watching and getting nothing done until visiting time comes around again.

However hard I try to blank my thoughts, I can't get her face out of my mind.

It is a face that hasn't changed that much over the years. No evidence left by the ravages of time; no deep lines that document the misery or regret but then that's probably because the misery and the regret is never hers. It always belongs to someone else.

If I wanted to be pernickety, I suppose she looks slightly different to how I remember her. The features seem more crooked than before, as if deceit has somehow skewed her face over time.

But then it's natural she would look different to me now. I was just fifteen years old when I last saw her: a gullible, very scared child.

Over time, the therapist helped me understand that she helped me remember who I was back then. She told me it was important to keep reminding myself I was just a child, that I did the best I could at the time.

Accepting that helped me to wrestle with the corrosive rope of guilt that had twisted and threaded its way so thoroughly around my insides I felt I would never be rid of it.

On difficult days, even now, it likes to pull a little tighter just so I know it's still there.

Waiting for information from the police about the other driver is torture but I can feel the comforting glow of payback drawing near.

When the details come it will be so tempting to just lash out and hurt her any way I can, but I am determined to take it steady, make it count.

And there is something else at stake now, too.

Liam, in his vulnerable state, needs to be made aware of how dangerous she is. I can't very well tell him too much at this early stage without appearing paranoid and exposing my own plans but, in a way, he needs protecting from her, too.

Even though he doesn't know it yet.

At last it is time to leave for the hospital. I have to go back twice to straighten the cushions in the lounge but, finally, I make it out to the car.

It is already dark outside and the rain drizzles heavy and re-lentless, reflecting the oncoming car headlights back up at me from the shiny wet road.

I drive slowly to the hospital, silently mulling things over in my head.

Work. The accident. Her.

My head is a maelstrom of thoughts that ebb and flow like a black tide but, slowly, my neck muscles begin to unknot as the hypnotic beat of the wipers vibrates around the car.

When I stop at traffic lights I conjure up pictures of what Liam's gran might be like. Perhaps a plump, homely woman who will take me into her arms, welcoming me into the family.

I expect she will be very pleased to see me and will no doubt try to make a thing over what I did for Liam but it wasn't such a big deal really. Some people would think me too modest but I'm not one for fuss. I just want to be there when he wakes up.

I stop at yet another red light and stare out at the rain as my heartbeat begins to quicken. Within seconds, the voice in my head begins its old tricks.

What if Liam's gran doesn't want me there at the hospital after all? What if they refuse to let me see him and I have no way of finding out what's happening with the police investigation?

Since my life fell apart all those years ago, I have found it easier to keep my distance from people than to reach out. It seemed the safest thing to do under the circumstances.

I mean, you can never be sure who to trust no matter how long you've known them, can you? You can't possibly know all the hidden sides to a person, not really.

I know that better than most people.

When I think about getting to know Liam and his gran it makes my hands tingle.

But this time it's not just about me; I have a new responsibility now. Liam asked me to help him at the roadside and I agreed.

What kind of person would I be if I let him down now?

Thanks to the hospital's inadequate parking facilities, it is well past six o'clock by the time I arrive.

The nurse I saw earlier is standing at the admin station in the middle of the ward. She smiles when she spots me.

'The patient's gran has just arrived, love. Bear with me one sec and I'll take you down; he's in a different room now.'

It turns out to be rather a longer wait than one sec.

The phone rings, then a doctor asks her to get him a patient's contact details. The poor nurse is run off her feet, and I feel bad because I'm just adding to her list of jobs but this is important. I have to see him.

My thumbnail carves its way into my index finger the way it often does when I get churned up about something.

I watch six thirty come and go, and I start counting my breaths to try and slow them down.

Visiting finishes at eight, and I want to have as much time with Liam as possible. At this rate I might not get to see him at all.

'You can't see into the future so stop telling yourself the story of how bad things are going to get,' the therapist's voice echoes in my ears.

So I do. I stop. I think about the accident instead, how Liam's hand felt in mine.

At last, the nurse appears and walks out from behind the curved counter. 'I'll take you down now. It's Anna, isn't it?'

I nod and follow her to one of the four doors at the end of the ward.

Every few yards along the main corridor is an oblong space running off to the side, housing six beds. Identical blankets frame pale, wan faces, most of them old with diluted eyes focusing sightlessly into the middle distance.

One feeble-looking lady is struggling to get out of bed, her hospital gown rucking up on one side revealing a scorched, marbled leg. I try to imagine her as a younger woman, with a husband, a job and perhaps raising a young family.

The thought of having to suffer curious eyes with no chance of privacy makes my stomach lurch. I feel grateful that Liam has a private room and doesn't have to endure the same indignity.

'Here we are,' says the nurse, slowing down.

She taps on a door, and I follow her into the room.

Liam is covered in a mass of tubes and breathing apparatus just like before. He looks even paler and more fragile, if that's possible.

I feel a pull inside and Danny's face flashes into my mind.

I want to sit with Liam without the others here.

Even if he is still unconscious, I want to tell him that I'm here for him.

'Ivy?' The nurse addresses the frail, elderly lady sitting by Liam's bed. 'This is Anna, the visitor I told you about earlier.'

Ivy looks up at me blankly. She is small and wiry with something of the vole about her. She twitches her nose at the air as if she's trying to get the measure of me.

'Anna is the lady who helped Liam after the accident,' the nurse explains.

Ivy tries to stand, but her infirm legs wobble and she sits back down again. 'You're the one who helped my grandson,' she says, as if Liam were still a helpless little boy.

The nurse gives me a conspiratorial wink as Ivy stretches out a small, wrinkled hand.

'Thank you so much. I do appreciate what you did.'

I squeeze her hand but my eyes are drawn back to the bed. 'How is he?' I ask.

Ivy shakes her head and presses her lips together, as if she doesn't trust herself to speak.

'No change as yet,' the nurse remarks, touching Ivy's shoulder. 'But that's only to be expected, considering what he's been through.'

'Have you got the other driver's details yet?' I ask.

'We've heard nothing,' Ivy replies. 'I suppose it's early days.'

'I'll leave you two to have a little chat.'

The nurse leaves the room, and Ivy fumbles around in her handbag.

'The doctor says it's the best thing for him at the moment – staying under, I mean.' She pulls out a tissue. 'He says it will give his poor body a chance to repair itself.'

I understand she's distressed and probably confused with all the information coming her way but her blind faith in the doctor galls me. It is vital that Liam has someone around who will ask the right questions of the medical staff.

'What about the woman, the other driver?' I ask. 'What are the police doing about her?'

'When they first called round to the house to tell me Liam had been involved in an accident, they said they'd be in touch again soon,' Ivy says. 'One of them gave me a business card with his telephone number on. It's at home somewhere.'

I walk slowly around the other side of the bed.

Liam's arm is uncovered and lying on top of the blanket. I touch him lightly on the hand and let my fingers linger there for a few seconds.

Touching a man's hand is bound to feel strange to someone who's never even had a boyfriend, I suppose, and I confess I am entranced by his large fingers and slightly weathered skin.

I stand for a moment and watch his chest moving up and down under the blanket. I wonder if this is how Danny would have looked at his age.

When I glance up, Ivy is staring at me so I move my hand away.

'They say you held him until the ambulance arrived,' she says faintly.

'I didn't hold *him*, I held his hand.'

People always get things wrong. You should never move people when they are injured; you could do more damage than good. Then again, I suppose not everyone has completed a voluntary first-aid course and got the highest mark in their group.

'You'll need to get the other driver's insurance details and her name and address from the police,' I tell her. 'The sooner the better; you don't want her trying to wriggle out of it.'

'As I said, they should be in touch very soon.' Ivy shuffles sharply in her chair.

I'm about to offer to liaise with the police on her behalf but then I reconsider. I suppose she might think it's a bit much, with us having only just met.

'He's a good boy, you know, but he would insist on having that motorbike,' she continues, looking at Liam. 'I told him, I said, "that thing is a killing machine", but you know what lads are like, they just won't listen.'

Liam is hardly a 'lad'.

That way she constantly talks about him as if he is still in his teens makes me want to grind my back teeth, and I don't want to start that habit again.

Never mind who said what before, Ivy should be chasing up the police to start proceedings against the other driver.

I feel a responsibility to both her and Liam to keep pressing for this. It's for their own good. But for now, I stay quiet.

I stand up and turn my back to her, moving over to the window to survey the car park from the high floor.

I watch as people scurry to and from their cars and the payment stations, all consumed by the dreaded wake-work-visit cycle that one has to endure when a family member is in hospital.

'There's just me and Liam at home, you see,' Ivy says quietly. 'To tell you the truth, I don't know what I'd do without him; he keeps me—' She suddenly breaks off what she is saying.

I turn around to see why she stopped talking mid-sentence, just as the room fills with her high-pitched shrieks.

Jumping back from the window, I gasp in surprise when I look at the bed.

Liam's eyes are wide open.

Ivy reaches for his hand, and I watch in silence, my heartbeat thudding so hard I can feel it in my throat.

'Thank you, God,' Ivy starts to sob quietly, pressing his hand to her face. 'He's OK; he's going to be OK.'

I wait for her to tell Liam who I am, that I'm the one who was there for him at the roadside, but she doesn't say anything about me.

I reach past Ivy and press the buzzer by Liam's head then I move to the other side of the bed and rest my fingers lightly on his hand.

He looks up at me but there is no recognition and no expression of gratefulness. There is no emotion there at all.

'He doesn't remember me,' I murmur.

'Where's the nurse?' Ivy shuffles to the door and peers out into the corridor. Then she steps outside the room.

I take Liam's hand in mine. 'Do you remember the accident, Liam? Did the police say anything about that woman, the other driver?'

He closes his eyes briefly as if he's sifting through a slide show in his mind. When he opens them again, he shakes his head slowly.

The door opens and two nurses walk in briskly, followed by an ashen-faced Ivy.

'Has he spoken yet?' one of the nurses asks.

I shake my head and let go of Liam's hand as they buzz around him, checking the various wires and tubes.

'We'll need to do a few checks,' the plump nurse says to Ivy. 'I've just paged Dr Khan.'

Ivy stands by the door but she doesn't say anything.

'He will be fine love, don't worry,' the nurse tells her despite the fact she can't possibly know this for certain. 'The doctor will be down very soon.'

The other nurse begins to speak, her voice loud and dramatic.

'Can you hear me, Liam? Can you say something?' There is no reaction from him, just that awful, non-comprehending stare. 'Liam, do you know where you are?'

'Speak to the nurse, son,' Ivy says. 'Just so we know you're alright.' She takes a few steps towards the bed. 'Please, Liam. Just say something.'

Slowly, Liam turns his head to look at her and in a broken whisper, he says, 'Who are you?'

CHAPTER 6
Thirteen years earlier

Carla Bevin had worked at the Cumber Meadows group of schools for just over two years, starting the job immediately after qualifying with the British Association for Counselling and Psychotherapy.

It wasn't that long in the scheme of things but certainly enough time to grasp the reason some kids found school beyond tough.

Often, there was no singular reason they attracted such misery to themselves, they just seemed to be a certain type and that fascinated Carla. She was determined to find a victim link and write a paper on it one day.

'Kids are cruel; they'll zero in on anyone who's even remotely different. Their parents should just transfer them to another school.' Mark had offered his esteemed opinion in a rare moment back when they talked about her work instead of how much money he was expecting to make from selling his art.

Her husband's 'art studio', as he liked to call it, was actually just a posh shed from B&Q at the bottom of the garden.

To a certain extent, Mark was right about the bullied kids but Carla happened to know that this certain type of young person could be transferred to a new school a hundred times over for a fresh start and the end result would probably always be the same.

It was as if some kids had a sign attached to them that said, 'Bully Me', visible only to other teenagers.

Carla couldn't possibly come out and just openly say something like that though, especially not in her current capacity as school counsellor. The PC mob would have a fit. After all, her most repeated phrase to her young clients was, 'It is not your fault'.

But the invitation to be constantly hounded and hated for the colour of their hair, the budget brand of trainers they wore or just for simply breathing was something some young people gave off like a bad smell that attracted the worst predators.

And Daniel Clarke was one of those kids.

In order to qualify for 'the minimum five hundred pounds' investment' that each counselled child incurred to the school budget, a pupil had to be considered virtually suicidal before the governing body would approve her involvement.

But they had recently approved Daniel, and rightly so. When he knocked on her office door that Monday morning, he was in a pretty bad way.

Young people reacted very differently during their first few appointments, but, generally, Carla had observed that they fell into three types:

Some were chatty – overly so, saying anything and everything in a thinly veiled attempt to cover up their real feelings.

Other kids said less and opened up slowly, over time, like a crushed flower.

Daniel was the rarer third type that Carla unofficially called 'a blanker'.

It wasn't that the boy said very little; rather, he refused to utter a word nor even give any visual clues in response to anything she said to him.

As soon as she opened her office door, Carla recognised the blanker expression pasted onto his face and immovable as a mask. Just what she needed.

'Please, Daniel, sit down,' she said brightly, sitting on one of the comfy seats she'd selected herself in a very pretty shade called periwinkle that resembled the colour of the sea.

The beige carpet (sand) and the chiffon lemon walls (sunshine) all merged to cleverly mimic a calming shoreline.

It was unfortunate the room was windowless but, even so, Carla had gone to the trouble of bringing in several smooth, flat pebbles and the odd bit of driftwood to heighten the serene effect and to compensate for the lack of natural light.

But it was all lost on Daniel Clarke; he didn't appear to notice any of it.

He sat down robotically, no shuffling in his seat to get comfy or glancing around the room to take in his surroundings. He stared straight-ahead at a blank stretch of newly plastered wall that she hadn't yet found a suitable framed print for.

Carla scribbled down her early observations on a piece of paper headed with Daniel's name and class.

'I'm Carla.' She lay down her pen and laced her fingers in her lap. 'Do you know why you're here, Daniel? Why you have been referred to me?'

Daniel did not move or blink.

He was a slight boy, but she thought malnourished rather than naturally petite in build.

Lank, dark blonde hair badly in need of a trim draped limply on his grubby shirt collar, and Carla noticed both outside edges of his fidgeting index fingers were red and looked sore as if he'd somehow sloughed off the first few layers of skin.

'I'm here to help you, Daniel; I think you might be going through a difficult time.'

No response.

'I want to reassure you that anything you say in here, anything we talk about, is strictly confidential. I won't repeat a word to anyone.'

Carla thought she caught a brief flicker of something in the boy's eyes but it was replaced almost instantly by the blank stare.

The day before, she'd met with Daniel's class teacher, Mrs Martin, who had fully briefed her. Apparently the teacher had noticed Daniel growing steadily more withdrawn since the beginning of the autumn term.

Through further investigation involving other staff, Mrs Martin had ascertained that Daniel had begun to use recognised avoidance tactics during the school day, such as sitting near the door to ensure he was first out of class when the bell sounded and making do without lunch most days in order to keep himself away from the dinner hall.

'One teacher even saw him taking a shortcut through the building between lessons, instead of walking outside with the other pupils.' Mrs Martin shook her head. 'I've spoken to the usual suspects in Daniel's year, Philip Naylor and his gang of thugs, but they're not owning up to anything and, for once, I actually believe them when they say they're not involved. But I can't get to the bottom of what's wrong because Daniel point-blank refuses to talk to me or anyone else about it.'

The Head of Year had become involved when possible signs of self-harm had been spotted on Daniel's arms by a Teaching Assistant during a recent PE lesson.

'We think the poor lad's been cutting himself,' Mrs Martin sighed. 'In twenty years of teaching I don't think there has been one quite as bad as this. He's fading away right in front of our eyes but he won't let anyone help him.'

The governing body had been made aware of all these concerns and the relevant agencies informed. But from previous experience, Carla knew it could be weeks before any action was taken by the city's hard-pressed social workers.

After a few minutes of complete silence, Carla poured two glasses of water from the jug on the low table and pushed one across the pale wood veneer to Daniel.

It remained untouched.

'I'm on your side, Daniel; I want you to know that. I'm not a teacher; you can think of me as a friend, if you like.'

'You work for the school.'

His clipped, cold tone took Carla by surprise and for a moment she was not entirely sure how to respond.

'It's true that I am employed by the school, Daniel,' she said, keeping her voice level. 'But my counselling work with pupils is entirely private. Whatever we talk about stays strictly between you and me.'

Daniel gave a derisory sniff and looked down at his hands.

'Can you tell me how school's been for you since the start of term?' Carla pressed.

Silence. This one was going to be a hard nut to crack.

The sessions were not nearly long enough, for one thing. Twenty minutes, once or twice a week, was no time at all to build up a trusting relationship with a traumatised child.

Nevertheless, Carla usually managed to get them saying something about their problems in the first session.

A lot more than the five measly words this boy had uttered, anyway.

'Are you afraid of someone, or has anyone threatened you?'

Her BACP-accredited counselling training had advised the therapist to speak as little as possible in order to allow the young client to divulge any concerns in their own time.

That was all well and good in relaxed one-hour privately paid appointments, but it didn't work too well in a cash-starved state school that constantly pressured her to deliver prompt results.

Carla was developing her own set of rules on the quiet, her own way to get the desired results, and it hadn't worked too badly so far.

She reckoned another couple of months and she might have enough successes under her belt to go for a well-paid job she'd heard was coming up at the prestigious, independent high school in the city.

Listening to affluent kids whose worst problem was whether to choose a pony or an activity holiday in the USA for Christmas beat the pants off the city woes she was trying to resolve here at Cumber Meadows.

And she saw it as a fast track to establishing an impressive reputation.

It followed that, before long, she'd be opening her own high-end private practice where she'd be entitled to charge top dollar to a plethora of harassed, wealthy parents who hadn't got the time or inclination to straighten out their own privileged kids' mixed-up heads.

It was also the key to freeing herself of the small mountain of debt in her name still remaining from Mark's doomed foray into the art world.

With mounting credit card balances that were a result of a too-ambitious monthly rental property in the prestigious leafy area known as The Park, a new job was the only valid path to keeping a decent standard of living.

Mark had liked to grandly describe his unfathomable splashes of muddy colours on canvas as 'contemporary abstract expressions'.

The only trouble being they were so abstract nobody wanted to buy one.

When she thought back to those days, she remembered only too well how the burden of their future security felt, settled as it was, so heavily and completely on her own shoulders.

If there was anything to be grateful for after their painful split, it was that she only had herself to support now, thank God.

It was true they'd had plenty of happy years but Carla was certain that if she had stayed she'd have ended up the same way as Mark: living in an elusive dream world that was never going to happen.

Carla shifted in her seat and brought her attention back to the room.

She remained quiet for a few seconds longer, but in this current battle of silence, Daniel was winning hands down.

'I think there's a reason you are always the first one out of class,' Carla said gently to the boy. 'I know you take shortcuts to lessons to avoid the other pupils, so who are you running from, Daniel?'

For the first time since he'd entered the room the child looked at her.

Creepily, his eyes seemed to focus just short of Carla's face.

'If you talk to me, I can help you. It doesn't have to be this way, you know. All you have to do is trust me; we have to trust each other. Is someone threatening to hurt you?'

The boy blinked rapidly; his eyes were big pools of olive-coloured misery in a bleached, impoverished face.

Carla caught an almost imperceptible nod.

'Who is it?' She pressed him harder now. 'Believe me, the worst thing you can do is stay silent: bullies rely on it. Nobody knows you're here, and nobody has to know one word you say to me today. It's strictly just between you and I, Daniel, do you understand?'

The boy shook his head, and Carla watched as he gripped his knees so tightly his knuckles turned white.

'He's always watching me,' Daniel whispered. 'He knows what I'm thinking. He knows about every single thing I do.'

CHAPTER 7
Present day
Anna

Dr Khan arrives and the room fills with medical staff.

'Is he going to be alright?' Ivy presses a fist to her lips.

'All will be revealed in good time,' Dr Khan replies without looking at her. 'Head injuries can be tricky things; no two are the same.'

'He doesn't seem to know me, Doctor,' Ivy says.

'Some memory loss can be expected under the circumstances,' Dr Khan mutters, studying a printout. He looks up sharply with raised eyebrows. 'Give it time, Mrs—'

'Bradbury,' the nurse supplies.

We are asked to move outside to the waiting area in the main ward. Ivy falls silent and sits with her head bowed, twisting her hands.

We wait for what seems like ages then a nurse brings Ivy a cup of tea, and I sit next to her without tea. The cup and saucer rattle in her hands, threatening to spill all over her lap.

I place my hand gently on Ivy's arm but she doesn't respond. It's upsetting for everybody but some of us try not to show it.

The nurse comes over and tells Ivy that Liam has been sedated again and won't wake up now until tomorrow.

'He doesn't remember me.' Ivy wipes her eyes. 'He doesn't remember anything.'

'Perhaps that's a good thing,' I point out. 'You wouldn't want to remember nearly getting killed, would you?'

Ivy doesn't reply but sets her cup and saucer smartly down on the floor.

'I'd better get off.' She looks out at the darkness beyond the glass. 'There'll still be plenty of buses running at this time.'

'It's silly you getting the bus,' I say, standing up. 'I can take you home.'

'No, I mustn't put you out, Anna,' she says firmly, gathering up her coat and bag. 'I'm fine, I always get the bus.'

'And what on earth would Liam say if I let you go home on your own when you're so upset?'

She looks at me.

'My car is parked quite close; it's only a two-minute walk from the main doors.'

When we get to the car, I open the door, get her settled in comfortably and make sure her seatbelt is securely fastened.

I imagine how pleased Liam will be that I'm looking after his gran.

'It's so kind of you, Anna,' she says again as we sit waiting at the traffic lights on the edge of the hospital campus. 'But I really don't like putting you out.'

'It's no trouble but you'll have to tell me where you live because I haven't got a clue where I'm going.' We both laugh at this and my breathing slows a touch.

It's natural, under the circumstances, that things feel a little strained. Soon Ivy will come to understand I only seek to help and support her in Liam's recovery. And to ensure he gets the justice he deserves.

It turns out they live in a semi-detached council house on the edge of the St Ann's estate.

I delivered on this very round a couple of times last year when they were struggling for staff – back when the management were still grateful to people willing to do overtime.

As with every housing estate, there are good and bad areas but Ivy directs me to Heath Close which is on the better side. Some people living here own their houses and generally they tend to look after them better than some of the Council's tenants.

'I've probably delivered mail to your house,' I say as we pull up outside the house. 'It's a small world, isn't it?'

'Our mail never comes now until the middle of the afternoon.' Ivy sucks in her soft, wizened cheeks. 'I'm always saying to our Liam it'd be quicker if I fetched it myself.'

'That's nothing to do with the delivery staff, Ivy.' I switch off the engine and turn to face her. 'It's the new policy. They've cut down on staff and stopped all the overtime.'

'Oh, I wasn't blaming the posties themselves.' She shrugs. 'It's just that we used to get it at a decent time and now it's always late afternoon.'

My heart rate ramps up a notch.

'But we *do* get the blame and it's not fair. Customers always seem to think it's our fault but we can't do anything about it.' I think of Jim Crowe, strutting around with his clipboard like the management team's puppet. 'I'd rather start early and finish early but do you think they listen? Do you think they care what *we* think?'

Everyone on my round moans at me for the fact their mail comes so much later now.

My head is thumping.

For some reason I start to think about what's in the spare room. There's this sort of bunching-up sensation in my throat that makes it difficult to swallow.

Ivy unfastens her seatbelt and reaches for the door handle. 'Thank you for the lift, Anna. I'd better get inside.'

When she slams the car door shut, I am shaken out of my thoughts.

I watch as she reaches into her handbag at the gate, pulls out her keys and then turns and waves.

She isn't going to ask me in.

I turn off the engine and clamber out of the car. She stops walking at the sound of the door slamming and turns around.

'I don't suppose I could use your loo?' I see her hesitate. 'I should have gone before we left the hospital but I wanted to get you home.'

'Of course,' she says, and I exhale. 'That's if I can ever find this blessed door key.'

It's one of those houses with a peeling, wooden porch that smells damp. I follow Ivy's lead and slip off my shoes.

Following her inside, I see that the front door leads straight into the lounge.

Ivy snaps on the light and reveals a predictably plain and dated room. The walls are covered in cream-painted woodchip, and a chipped, burgundy-coloured dado runs mid-height, all the way around.

There is a strong chemical smell of air freshener in here which I won't entertain in my own house, not least because it makes Albert continually sneeze.

'So, have you got family of your own, Anna?' Ivy asks as she slips off her coat.

After a few seconds she stops struggling to getting her arm free of the sleeve and looks over at me.

'Sorry, I'm desperate for the loo.' I hop from one foot to the other.

'Oh, the bathroom is up the stairs and first on the left.'

I nod and rush to the stairs.

Upstairs, it feels very cool and it's quiet.

Apart from Mrs Peat's, I can't actually remember the last time I was in someone else's house.

My chest flutters as if there is a tiny bird trapped inside.

The bathroom door is ajar, and there are two other closed doors leading off the landing.

I pull on the bathroom light cord and consider the other doors, wondering which room belongs to Liam.

I can hear Ivy clattering crockery in the kitchen downstairs.

I don't need the loo, of course, but I go through the pretence of flushing and washing my hands to buy a bit of time.

There are feminine toiletries in the bathroom cupboard and some tablets right at the back of the shelf prescribed for 'Ivy Bradbury, 11.9.37'.

I notice they use the same shampoo and toothpaste that I do.

As I walk back downstairs, a large ginger tom brushes up against my legs, and Ivy emerges from the kitchen.

'I see Boris has introduced himself.' She smiles as I reach the bottom. Her dated pink lipstick bleeds into the tiny lines that radiate from her mouth, bleeding out into her face like a wound.

I force myself to look away.

'He doesn't like me going out; he's not used to being on his own, you see,' she continues.

'My cat, Albert, is the same,' I tell her. 'Every day without fail he sits by the door waiting for me to come home from work.'

It's like I waved a magic wand.

Ivy starts chatting away like I've known her for years, giving me the low-down on the personality of every cat she's ever owned.

I try bringing Albert into the conversation once or twice, but she's far too engrossed in her own tales to listen to anything I might have to say. It's irritating but I expect I might well be the same when I'm her age.

'How long do you think it'll be before the police prosecute the other driver?' I ask.

'I've told you, Anna, I don't know.' Her tone implies that I shouldn't be asking. 'Soon, I hope. That woman could have killed Liam.'

I'm pleased Ivy at least seems to want justice as much as I do but I can't keep her interested in the subject of the accident for long.

Apparently, she tells me, Liam loves cats and has a special way with animals. That doesn't surprise me; I could tell immediately he's the sensitive sort.

She says that Liam came to live with her when he was just seven years old.

Someone ought to tell her he's grown up rather a lot since then but that would be a little callous under the circumstances. She's understandably upset and worried about her grandson. It'll just be her maternal instincts kicking in.

'His mother, Lynette, she left when he was two, so he never really knew her,' Ivy explains. 'She disappeared off to Spain one day with some rogue who sold secondhand cars. She was never any good, that one. I used to tell my Robert, "she'll be trouble, mark my words". But, of course, he never believed me. Until it was too late.'

Always the woman's fault, of course. Some mothers and their perfect, blameless sons.

I manage to work out that Robert was Ivy's son and Liam's father. Ivy has an annoying habit of dropping out names and assuming I'll know who's who.

She explains that Liam's father and his younger sister were killed in an accident some years earlier.

'That's terrible.' I press my hand to my mouth. 'What happened?'

She laces her gnarled fingers together and stares down at them.

I can see patches of pink scalp shining through her sparse silver hair. It is chopped too short at the back and shows a bony protrusion at the top of her spine.

'It was a long time ago.' She shakes her bent head. 'Best not to keep raking it all up.'

'Sorry,' I mutter.

'But you can imagine what I thought when the police came round to the house yesterday,' she says, looking up again. 'I thought history was repeating itself.'

'When I saw him fly off his motorbike and hit the road,' I say softly, 'I thought he was dead.'

CHAPTER 8

The conversation seems to dry up all of a sudden after that, and I get the distinct feeling that Ivy is waiting for me to leave.

There is more I'd like to ask her about Liam but the moment seems to have passed. I say goodbye and make my way out to the car.

The temperature has dropped much cooler outside now and I wish I had thought to wrap up a bit warmer.

It would have been nice to sit with Ivy a while, get to know each other and have a cup of tea together. Some might say she owes me that at the very least but I'm not the sort to think the worst of people.

Still, it seems so silly that we'll both be spending the rest of the evening at home, on our own.

As I drive home, I try and focus on the reassuring hum of the engine but it proves impossible.

The annoying thing is I know I can do it; I can easily cope with my delivery round. It's just going to take time.

Problem is, it's time that Jim Crowe and the management team isn't prepared to give me.

When you look at it like that, I suppose you might say it's the management team themselves who are forcing me to act deceitfully. I mean, what choice have I got really?

I unlock the back door, and Albert sweeps out past my legs without giving me a second glance. There are times I wish I could be as single-minded as he is.

I walk slowly upstairs without taking off my coat or shoes and stand outside the spare bedroom.

My hand hovers over the handle.

The last thing I ever wanted was to inconvenience the people who really value me, my customers. But sadly, I didn't get a choice.

Once the management cut the overtime, it was always going to end badly.

I remind myself I am simply buying a little more time until I can get things sorted and back to normal. It's just a necessary temporary measure, that's all.

I press my forehead against the door. It feels solid and cool.

Every day I come up here after my shift and open the door just for a few seconds. I'm always careful to make sure my head is turned the other way.

When the deed is done, I slam the door shut again and hurry back downstairs.

Today though, something is pushing me to face it.

To see it with my own eyes.

I take a deep breath and steel myself. It's only just over a week's worth, after all.

I grasp the handle and push hard. The door swings open and there it is, even worse than I imagined.

A gigantic heap of undelivered mail.

I snap awake at 3.25 a.m.

I started seeing the therapist in hospital, and after I was discharged, I carried on seeing her for the next two years.

She showed me some breathing exercises. I try to do them now but it's not working; I still can't get back to sleep.

I know the reason why. Today is my thirty-third birthday.

I have hated birthdays for as long as I can remember. That overbearing feeling that you really ought to be doing something special or going somewhere that you're not.

I remember the kids at school, their birthday parties and fancy trips out, and then, a few years on, it graduated to cinema outings in town. Mother used to say it was all a big fuss over nothing.

The odd invite I did get we'd always turn down, because if you accept someone's hospitality, they'll always expect something back.

There's this silly ritual at work. If it's your birthday, you're supposed to bring in cream cakes for everyone. Last week, Roisin turned forty over the weekend.

Monday morning, she bought a large box of sickly looking confections from the posh patisserie in the centre of town. She brought one over on a plate for me but I told her I had an upset stomach.

'Ah, come on, Anna, you have to celebrate with me.' Roisin grinned. 'It is the big four-oh, after all.'

'Oh go on then.' I chose a chocolate éclair just because those are the ones that tend to make the least mess. Roisin chose the same.

'Ooh that pastry,' she raved, licking her lips. 'So light it melts in the mouth, doesn't it?'

'Did you know that choux pastry is made by melting all the ingredients into a pan and then piping it onto a baking sheet?'

'I didn't.' She raised an eyebrow. 'You're a mine of information, Anna, so you are.'

I smiled in spite of myself, and Roisin nudged me and grinned back.

'We're still waiting for Anna to have a birthday and bring some cakes in,' someone at the back of the delivery office quipped.

I put the paper plate down and began to walk away.

'Anna,' Roisin called, 'you haven't finished your éclair.'

That's why I'm careful not to eat other people's cakes: so they can't throw it back in my face.

But all that doesn't change the fact it's definitely my birthday today.

I toss and turn in bed for ages, rubbing my tight chest and watching the red neon digital numbers on my bedside table tick through the minutes and eventually the hours.

Albert's warm bulk presses against my leg, and I try to breathe in time with the soft rise and fall of his chest. My restlessness doesn't seem to stop him sleeping at all.

Albert has a simple life, untouched by the stupidity of people and their narrowminded ideas of how one should behave.

My mind drifts on to thinking about the police and trying to figure out why they're so slow in keeping Ivy informed about the accident.

Surely by now they should have informed her of the other driver's full name and address; at the very least, for insurance purposes.

Her face seethes into my mind like a poisonous cloud and just sort of hangs there, clouding all my other thoughts. Those perfectly painted lips, those narrow, calculating eyes.

I toss and turn but, eventually, I must drop off to sleep because the next time I open my eyes it is beginning to get light outside.

I can hear Albert scratching around in his litter tray downstairs.

After visiting the bathroom, I walk downstairs and stop to enjoy the sight of the cards on the doormat.

One pink, two plain white and one card with a striped border scattered below the letterbox.

I gather them up and take them into the kitchen with me while I make my first cup of tea of the day.

Albert sits on my lap cleaning his claws while I open the envelopes and drink my tea.

There is one from Mary, a girl who'd been in my class at school.

I've seen her once or twice around the streets near my house, pushing her new baby in a pram. Although I can't say she was a friend back then, she was never mean to me the way some of the others were.

I tear open the other two envelopes and read the cards out loud to Albert.

'Happy Birthday, Anna.
Can't wait to see you Saturday night for the meal!
All our love Amanda, Dave and Sarah xxx

To Anna,
Have a great day. . . can't wait to catch up on Sunday!
Luv Suze X'

Later, when I'm arranging the cards on the windowsill, there is a knock at the door. This time I don't hide until the caller goes away.

'Delivery for Miss Anna Clarke.' The delivery man beams. 'Your lucky day, love.'

I smile and take the massive bouquet from him. Closing the door, I carry the flowers inside.

They're my favourites: tiger lilies, and these are going to be beauties. Massive pale-green buds with a pink tinge, full of dormant life.

'Let's see who they're from, Albert.'

I inch my fingernail under the flap of the small white envelope that is taped to the cellophane.

The front reads simply,

Anna '

with a single line scored underneath.

The card depicts a cottage garden in full bloom with fancy gold letters declaring,

'IT'S YOUR BIRTHDAY!'

Inside, the handwritten message reads,

'HAPPY BIRTHDAY ANNA.
THANK YOU FOR SAVING MY LIFE.
LOVE LIAM X'

CHAPTER 9
Thirteen years earlier

Carla had found it impossible to get Daniel Clarke out of her head all week.

It was unusual for this to happen because, despite the trauma and upset she witnessed in her young clients' lives, she rarely had trouble leaving it all at the office.

She relished the challenge of getting under a traumatised skin but Daniel's case was more than that. This child troubled her. There was something haunting about him.

But getting Daniel to open up wasn't the only thing that vexed her as she'd tried to get some sleep last night. Her mind had steadfastly refused to be relaxed by counting imaginary sheep or picturing an idyllic beach.

No, instead it insisted on reliving that fateful day two years ago when everything she thought was solid and real in her life began to crumble.

That morning, her first job had been searching high and low for her favourite china mug.

Like her gran used to say, there was nothing better than fine china for drinking your first cuppa of the day but, infuriatingly, it was nowhere to be found.

Mark had made an early morning trip into town to Borge's art shop to get more supplies. It hadn't escaped Carla's notice that, just lately, he seemed to spend more time selecting art supplies than he did actually producing anything that was remotely saleable.

He also had a terrible habit of making a drink in the house and taking it down the garden, never seeming to notice when numerous cups containing skinned coffee remnants began to pile up on the shed's work surfaces.

She'd had that mug for years. It held just the right volume of liquid and she swore blind, like Gran, that the tea tasted so much better in it.

When she'd looked in every cupboard, Carla finally deduced that Mark was definitely the culprit. He must have taken it down the bloody garden.

After rummaging in the kitchen drawer for the spare key, she pulled on an old cardigan and shuffled down the weed-strewn path in her flip-flops to the bottom of the garden.

The long, narrow lawn was bathed in sunlight. It was too early for next door's kids to be out screaming at each other before school so, for once, it was blissfully quiet out here.

Despite the cool breeze, Carla pulled her cardigan a little closer and stood for a few moments to enjoy the peace, turning her face towards the sun.

It had been months since she had ventured down into Mark's studio, mainly to save herself the ordeal of having to endure him showing her his virtually identical collection of paintings again. That, and telling her how much money he was going to make and how it was only a matter of time before some London gallery bigwig spotted his masterpieces online.

After the third year of hearing the same speech time and time again, of being told how they must be patient until he got his big break and in the meantime how she should pay all the bills. . . she found it all a bit too hard to keep nodding enthusiastically.

Carla continued her walk down the garden and unlocked the shed door. She snapped on the light and peered into the dim workspace.

Unfinished canvasses leaned side by side against a wall; others, strewn like discarded sheets of thick cardboard across the floor.

When Mark first got his shed, Carla went out and bought him a stack of plastic trays and specialised containers for his paints and brushes from Borge's shop. He'd bounced around his new studio like an excited puppy, promising her an opulent life.

'Once I'm established with the local galleries, you'll have diamonds in the soles of your shoes,' he enthused, grabbing her and planting a hard kiss on her lips. 'I promise you, baby.'

She frowned at her art shop purchases, now crusted up with dried-on paint and piled up in various corners of his workspace.

A stack of expensive sable brushes lay abandoned next to the overflowing wastepaper bin, their ultra-fine bristles rock hard and fused together beyond repair.

How Mark managed to produce anything worthwhile from this chaos, Carla couldn't begin to fathom. True, the creative mind probably wouldn't respond well to a neat, ordered space like her own office but this dump was seriously off the scale by anyone's standards.

Carla glanced around, her eyes scanning the jumble for a glint of the familiar duck-egg-blue china.

She peeked inside empty boxes, brushed aside screwed up newspapers and half-dried-out pots of paint as she searched. Nothing.

When she glanced down at the old armchair she froze, the air in the room suddenly thick and clogging in her throat.

The lilac mohair throw that her gran had knitted just a few months before she died lay slung carelessly over the back of the chair, its delicate skein trailing on the paint-spotted floor.

Carla had only used it a couple of times since her gran died because it was so very special to her and she was terrified of snagging it.

She didn't have that many beautiful things but those she did have were precious to her. She'd always been the same with things she cared about.

Her parents had struggled to scrape a decent life on a council estate in Lincolnshire. Luxuries were hard to come by for Carla and her sister, and she readily admitted it had probably made her overvalue material things. And Mark knew that. When they first met he used to joke that she had what he called the 'possessive gene'.

But with Gran's blanket it was different. It held a precious, emotive value that far exceeded any material worth.

Something wasn't quite adding up here, she realised.

In order to reach the throw in the first place, Mark must have gone to her wardrobe and purposely taken it from the back of the shelf.

Annoyingly, he would have also had to walk past the well-worn and slightly grubby cream faux-fur throws they used at night when watching TV and sitting on the two cold leather couches.

Why wouldn't he just use one of those?

The china mug now forgotten, Carla picked up the throw and sniffed at it. If it stank of brush cleaner, Mark was a dead man walking.

But it didn't smell of turpentine, it smelled of something else altogether more pleasant. Not perfume exactly but a musky skin lotion, perhaps.

It was not Mark's smell.

Carla tried to swallow down the sour lump that popped up into her throat, but it wouldn't budge.

She might be jumping to conclusions. Knowing Mark, he would have a perfectly acceptable excuse.

She held the throw up to the light to check for stains and something fine snagged around her finger like a gossamer thread.

It was a long, pale red hair.

Carla squeezed her eyes shut to try and stop the tears spilling down her cheeks.

She could overthink what happened two years ago as much as she liked but it wasn't going to change anything.

She remembered that the person she'd wanted to confide in, to talk to at that low point when she found the hair, was her sister.

But why should Carla expect her support when she had let her down so badly? When she'd needed her, Carla had left her at the club to go off with some random guy, and that's when she'd been attacked.

Her sister and her mother had never forgiven her.

When she came out of Mark's studio, Carla thought about picking up the phone and calling her sister. Holding out the olive branch. But in the end, she decided against it.

Different decisions made back then about her marriage might have led to different results now but wallowing in regret was going to get her nowhere.

She had no choice but to steel herself and move on with her life.

Carla stepped into the shower, and as she'd hoped the scalding darts of water did the trick. Within half an hour she had dried her hair, applied minimum make-up and was fully dressed.

Her broken heart was firmly disguised again for the start of another day.

* * *

When she got to work Carla avoided the staff room, dashed straight to her office and gulped down a steaming hot mug of extra-strength black coffee to give her fortitude.

Daniel Clarke's second counselling session was at nine thirty that morning and she hoped to make some headway.

She had invested hours of thought these past few days into her approach for the session. She was determined to crack him, and she didn't intend to wait for weeks on end, either.

His case would be the perfect one to illustrate – anonymously, of course – her expert counselling skills in her interview for the high school job.

She had taken time yesterday to avail herself of the contents of Daniel's school file and get the full overview of his domestic situation.

The father appeared to be absent from the family home, and as was so often the case, no reason had been logged in the school records. Daniel currently lived with his mother, Monica, and his fifteen-year-old sister, Anna.

Monica Clarke had little contact with school. She rarely attended parents' evenings, and there was a note warning staff that she did not generally respond to letters home.

In Carla's experience, single parents often worked more than one job. Also, they often worried more about putting food on the table and paying the bills than whether their children's education was on track.

Despite this, both Daniel and Anna were very bright academically with Anna being selected for the school's prestigious 'gifted pupil' programme last year.

Carla found another note on the file to say the school's requests for Anna to attend a summer school for one of twenty selected gifted pupils had been refused by Monica Clarke on the grounds she needed her daughter at home to help, with no further details given.

Repeated attempts to arrange a home visit with Mrs Clarke to discuss the matter had been declined.

By nine forty, Daniel had still not appeared.

When children were of concern to the staff, absences were a little more worrying than usual. The school had a responsibility to make sure the child was safe.

Carla locked her office door and walked over to Class 6M in the Key Stage Two building.

When she spotted Carla hovering in the corridor outside, Mrs Martin came to the classroom door.

'Daniel hasn't turned up for his session,' Carla told her.

'He's not in today,' Mrs Martin whispered while the seated children craned their necks to see who their teacher was talking to. 'He was at school yesterday though and seemed his melancholy self. Nothing unusual.'

The school office usually put a note in the class register if a parent had called a child in as being absent due to illness.

'There's no notification from the office but his sister's at the Comp, Year Ten, I think. Anna. I could probably get her over here at break if you wanted to speak to her?'

Carla thought for a moment.

It was imperative she gained Daniel's trust, and speaking to his sister without his knowledge at this early stage could seriously jeopardise that. Ringing home might have the same effect.

'I'll let it go this time,' Carla said. 'There's a nasty bug going around school, lots of kids are off with that. There's probably nothing to worry about.'

CHAPTER 10
Present day
Anna

I spend so much time enjoying my flowers and birthday cards, there is no time to take a shower or even bolt down my breakfast.

I have no choice but to just pull on my uniform which I know, from a quick whiff of the armpits, is badly in need of a wash.

I need to leave the house quickly, but I'm so tired from my restless night, my safety checks are taking twice as long. I do the kitchen plugs and appliances and then move into the sitting room.

Despite feeling so weary, my mind is already ticking over.

According to Ivy, the police don't have any details about the other driver yet. She might well have killed Liam; perhaps then they'd have shown a bit more interest.

It's all so frustrating but I can hardly walk away now and leave Liam and Ivy to work things out on their own.

They haven't got a clue who they are dealing with, for one thing. They don't know what she is capable of.

More importantly, they are my insurance policy against losing her again.

The plugs pass muster so I start plumping up the cushions and placing them in the correct order on the couch.

I feel as if I've known Liam for years, and I might be speaking out of turn but I suspect he might feel the same way.

I think of his hand grasping mine in the road; the way his hair flops onto his face, just like Danny's did. His broken whisper, begging me to help him. His instant trust in me.

Was it too much to hope for after all this time?

After conducting a final plug-check in the kitchen, I grab my bag and force myself out of the door to face the day.

At work, everyone has their own allocated section at the sorting counter.

There are shelves underneath the work surface and a vast lattice of light-oak pigeonholes on the wall above the counter where each postal worker organises the various postcodes of his or her round.

This process is important. If you get the address allocations wrong, you could end up backtracking on the streets to deliver a letter and that could send your timings right out.

I always leave my section of counter tidy before I leave after my shift, but invariably, when I get in the next day my area is scattered with other workers' elastic bands, unstamped mail and crumpled flyers.

Which is why I generally like to get to work a good fifteen minutes before my starting time of five a.m. It's important to start the day with some sort of order.

But this morning I arrive with only a couple of minutes to spare.

I unlock my delivery bike in the staff rack and walk inside the office, over to the main sorting area.

The usual huddle of staff are gossiping together in the corner but Roisin breaks away from the group when she spots me arriving at my counter.

'Jim's been looking for you.' Her pretty freckled face creases up with concern. 'He says you're to go straight to his office right away. Is everything OK, Anna?'

My heart lurches at the thought of what Jim wants with me, what it is he is going to say.

I can feel my face freezing so I duck down under the worktop and pretend to push my handbag further back on the shelf to give me a few seconds to recover. When I stand up, I have rearranged my face and I am smiling.

'I'll pop over and see Jim now,' I say brightly. 'I know what it's about.'

Before I can dash off, she presses her hand on the top of my arm.

'Let me know if there's anything I can do, love. I mean, if you fancy calling for a coffee after work and a chat, I'm always here.'

I picture me and Roisin sitting in the Costa café at Castle Marina. Sipping our drinks and chatting, laughing. Just like I've seen loads of other people doing.

Part of me wants to say yes to meeting up, I really do. But the old feelings flood in thick and fast before I can accept her offer.

'Thanks, Roisin, but I can't make it today,' I say. 'Maybe some other time.'

But as the words slide from my mouth I know it won't happen.

I can see Jim through the glass in his office door.

He is leaning back on his chair on a call. When he spots me, he beckons me into the small room.

Jim seems fairly engrossed in his conversation so I sit down on a peeling swivel chair and pick at the exposed yellow foam around the edge.

The desk is littered with brown folders, lidless ballpoint pens and crumpled delivery chits. I spot a framed photograph, placed on top of last year's hardback diary but it is facing away from me and I can't see the faces of the people in it.

A tall, thin man, Jim uses the long bony fingers of his free hand to stab at the air as he makes his point to the caller.

'I'm saying We. Need. It. Today. No excuses, Larry.'

I don't know much about my boss, just that he is married with a couple of grown-up sons. He, on the other hand, knows everything about me because he has full access to my personnel file.

After he finishes the call, Jim picks up a pen with a misshapen chewed tip and taps it on the desk.

'Thanks for coming in, Anna.' He rocks back in his chair. 'I'll cut straight to the chase. There have been a couple of complaints from the residents on your round.'

'Complaints?' The word comes out sounding normal but I'm battling to keep my hands from shaking.

He shuffles the papers in front of him and selects a sheet.

'Four days ago, Mrs Sheen, of 43 Briar Close, rang,' he reads aloud. 'Her daughter was expecting an acceptance letter from university which didn't arrive. She queried it and they sent another one out first class. She hasn't had that one, either.'

Jim looks up at me and opens his eyes wide in expectancy of a reply.

I shrug my shoulders and purse my lips, and I try to think what I should say.

He looks back down at the sheet.

'Then yesterday, Head Office took a call from a Miss Shelton, Flat 1B Cox Crescent.' He scans the typed script. 'Says here she's missed out on two jobs because she never got the letters inviting her for interview. Gave Head Office hell, by all accounts.'

'I don't know what to say, Jim.' I'm careful to keep my voice level. 'I always double-check the addresses before posting them through.'

Apart from the mail upstairs, of course. That stuff doesn't get delivered at all.

I wince as my thumbnail slices into my index finger.

Jim lays down the sheet of paper and pinches the bridge of his nose.

'Look, between you and me, I don't put much stock on these sorts of complaints. If folks realised the volume of mail that came through those doors they'd think twice about moaning.'

I nod and wipe the palms of my hands on my trousers.

'All the same, I have to mention it because the complainants are both residents on your round, which is unusual. Tell you what.' He waves his pen towards the papers, 'I won't write anything down on your file this time but just be careful, Anna. Double-check your deliveries.'

I walk out of Jim's office and stride across the delivery office floor to my counter. I'm trying to appear confident but it's all I can do not to run back outside.

People turn to observe me with interest from their various stations.

'Everything OK, Anna?' Roisin whispers as I pass her counter.

'Yep, fine,' I say but I don't look at her.

I can't wait to get out on the bike.

I sort my mail in double quick time and set off.

The early morning air has a bite to it that stings my face as I pedal all the way up Patchings Hill, but instead of pulling my cap down, I open my eyes wide and let the cold flood into them. It feels good to pedal on through the tingling hurt.

Once on the Clifton estate, I work hard and fast but my heart grows heavier when I see how slowly the bag is emptying. A glance at my watch confirms I am already halfway through my allocated shift time.

Half an hour before I am due to finish there is still a full bag of this morning's mail locked in the postbox near the high-rise flats that is waiting to be delivered.

I manage to make a start on it; I even work fifteen minutes over my shift but I daren't risk being seen working past my official finishing time.

That would be like admitting I can't cope, which is just what the management are trying to prove.

I transfer the undelivered mail into a bin bag and lock it back inside the postbox. Then I pedal back to base and return my empty mail bags to the office, waving casually to Jim when I clock out, as if I haven't a care in the world.

On the way back home, I collect the full mail bag from the locked postbox and transfer it into the boot of my car.

My chest feels tight and wheezy, as if I'm just getting over a bad cold.

Sometimes I think it would be so nice to just run away from it all, start somewhere anonymous and afresh.

Like she did, I suppose.

Difference being: if I disappear, a handful of people will get their mail late and that's about it.

Nobody's life gets ruined.

CHAPTER 11
Thirteen years earlier

Despite Daniel Clarke not turning up for his appointment, Carla's had a full roster of counselling appointments in her diary.

She accepted her pupil clients from a pool of six primaries and one comprehensive, all of them part of the Cumber Meadows family of schools for whom she worked.

Unless a child missed their session, like Daniel had that morning, she rarely had a spare session. She'd had more than enough to keep her busy during the day but Daniel's face loomed in her mind throughout all of her appointments.

Daniel's teacher, Mrs Martin, hadn't seemed overly concerned about his absence and so Carla kept telling herself neither should she be. But all day there had been a niggle at the back of her mind; it persisted even when she arrived home following the weekly staff meeting at just after seven.

She reached into the fridge for a bottle of Sauvignon and her mind raced over a multitude of possibilities of what might be happening in Daniel's life and why he hadn't come into school today.

Halfway down the glass, her worries about him began to fade and a new, far more dangerous, thought took its place. A very insistent thought.

'You promised, no more,' she hissed out loud to herself, taking another deep slug of wine.

She had tried so hard to fight the urge and it had worked for the last few weeks.

Right up until she'd gone rummaging in the bathroom drawer this morning for a nail file and found one of Mark's cufflinks zipped up in an old cosmetics case.

It was a silver cufflink with a solitaire diamond, one of his favourites. It had somehow survived her culling of anything that was remotely Mark when she moved to her new flat in Nottingham.

She slammed the drawer shut and left the cufflink where it was. But by then her resolve had all but disappeared into the big black hole that yawned inside her and the stirrings started with a vengeance.

She made a cup of tea but left it to go cold. She poured another glass of wine before flicking through around a hundred crappy TV channels to find there was absolutely nothing on that appealed to her.

She pottered around in the kitchen until she couldn't find the strength to fight it any more, at which point she walked into her bedroom and began to get ready.

She'd already decided. She would wear the white dress tonight.

CHAPTER 12
Present day
Anna

I get back to the house and that's when I first notice the smell.

Like rotting meat with a vile sickly sweet top note, it's a stench that clings to the inside of my nostrils from the second I walk through the door.

It wasn't there when I left for work this morning and there is certainly no rotting food in Albert's bowl or in the pedal bin.

I walk through the house, sniffing.

I even go upstairs but, curiously, the smell seems to remain exactly the same, neither weaker nor stronger, regardless of which room I enter.

I'm dragging my body around like it is something already dead but I suppose there is little wonder why I'm exhausted after so little sleep and working a full shift.

I'm desperate to rest, but instead, I pace around the house for what seems like hours, trying to identify the smell.

After I've padded around the entire house three times and searched each room, I'm still clueless as to what it could be.

Back in the kitchen I turn to the bulging black bin bag containing today's undelivered mail. It crouches by the back door, dark and menacing like a gigantic black spider that is just biding its time, waiting to sink its venomous fangs into me and finish me off.

I can't face dragging it up to the box room. Not right now.

I could stow the bag in the understairs cupboard or even in the dustbin outside perhaps; although even as I ponder this option I know it would be a sure-fire way of losing track of the mail and I would risk getting found out.

Besides, I have every intention of delivering it all. Soon as things calm down at work and they reinstate the overtime, I'll be on it.

But for now, if I want to keep my round, it's imperative I maintain the illusion that I'm coping.

For all I know, some of the other delivery staff might be doing the exact same thing because they are struggling to get their rounds finished too.

Nobody wants to take a drop in hours or get lumbered with the crappiest round if Jim Crowe decides they are struggling.

Perhaps if I got friendlier with Roisin I could find out how the others feel.

I could meet her for a coffee and chat. It's really no big deal.

A ripple of heat shudders through me and settles in my chest. I can't seem to shake it off.

I need to try and distract myself before I get sucked into the bad memories, but I'm there before I've even had the chance to redirect my thoughts.

I spent most of my school life watching others from the sidelines.

I'd managed to work out long before that most of my bad experiences in life had all come because I'd trusted someone and they had let me down in some way.

My logical solution had been to keep my distance from people as much as possible.

Generally, that worked quite well. But this one day, at the end of the summer term, I was stupid enough to be lulled into a false sense of security.

'Hey, Anna,' Ruth Metcalf called over to me at the end of one of the afternoon lessons. 'We're meeting at Cheatham's café after school. Fancy coming?'

She knocked me off guard.

Ruth was a member of the coolest group of girls in our year. I'd be an idiot to say no; this could be my chance to form some real friends.

This could be my chance to really change who I was and how others saw me.

'Great, see you there then.' She grinned before scuttling off to join the others as we piled out of class.

When I got to the café, they were waiting for me outside.

Ruth stood at the back of the large group of girls so I just sort of loitered near them, waiting for her to call me over.

'What the hell are you doing here?' The ringleader, Carol Taylor, turned on me. 'No room here for fucking freaks.'

'I. . . I thought—'

I tried to catch Ruth's eye but she turned to her friend, laughing.

Then they were all around me, poking and snatching at my bag and hair.

I screwed my face and eyes up tight so I couldn't see them all closing in on me.

I felt someone pull hard on my hair, a slap around the face. My bag was wrenched from my shoulder.

'Freak, freak, FREAK!'

They chanted in unison.

I heard a guttural cough then a thick ball of spit landed on my cheek, and the crowd erupted in laughter.

After that, it happened time after time, day after day. The minutes always felt like hours before a teacher came to intervene.

To distract myself while they tried to hurt me I'd think about our cat. Or Mum, when she'd had the first few drinks and would let me cuddle up to her.

But it didn't really work.

That's when I made up my mind to think of nothing at all, like a blank white wall.

Or being huddled up in the corner of a black room with no light, where nobody could hurt you.

It's something I still do now – on the worst days.

I start in the kitchen, emptying out all the cupboards and wiping down the shelves before putting stuff back.

I throw Albert's litter tray outside but I know he is not the smell culprit. Cats are extremely clean animals, unlike most humans. The mixed staff toilets at the delivery office are testament to that.

I mop the kitchen floor, and when all I can smell is acrid lemon cleansing fluid, I move on.

I clean room after room, vacuuming, spraying and wiping down endless surfaces.

As I work, it occurs to me to offer to help Ivy out with her cleaning, bearing in mind how poor her health is. Some days, I could go over to the house straight from work; she might like that.

I make up my mind to ask her later, at the hospital.

I find myself humming as I work, and I am astonished when I look at my watch to find I have been cleaning for nearly three hours. Visiting time starts in less than two hours at the hospital but I have to try and find just half an hour for a rest.

Staying home isn't an option. I know how much Liam will be looking forward to my visit, and he'll be gutted if I don't get to the hospital.

Last night, I offered to pick Ivy up before each visit and take her back home at the end of the evening. Initially, she seemed rather reluctant but I wouldn't let it go, and in the end, she accepted graciously.

'It's silly you struggling to get the bus when I've got time on my hands,' I told her just before I left. 'Friends should help each other out, don't you think?'

She blinked at me but she didn't answer. That's gratitude for you.

When I get upstairs, I lie on my bed and cover my legs with a soft fleece blanket. I feel the mattress bounce when Albert jumps up, purring and kneading around the bed in tiny circles until, finally, he settles and snuggles against my legs.

My eyelids feel heavy and sore but my arms and legs are still too fidgety to sleep so I lie with my eyes open and study the fine cracks on the ceiling. I know each line, each fissure.

The cracks radiate out from a central fracture in the ceiling that looks worse than it actually is. Some of the cracks are so fine you can't see them at first, but if you keep looking they slowly materialise in front of your eyes, creeping out like spindly insect legs into what you thought were perfectly smooth areas of plaster.

After a few minutes I close my eyes and do my breathing exercises but nothing seems to help.

I can still smell it.

I start to worry what will happen if the smell just won't go away, even if I clean and scrub every crevice in the house.

What if it gets worse and clings to my clothes when I leave the house and other people start to smell it?

My thumbnail begins to carve away and I make a conscious effort to breathe deeper to try and dispel the negative thoughts.

Still, somehow I manage to drift off because the next thing I am snapping awake with a start, which makes me feel queasy.

I only intended to doze, to hover in that restful place between wakefulness and sleep, but now I've gone and messed it up.

A glance over at the clock confirms it is five fifteen, and I'm supposed to be picking Ivy up at five thirty to take her over to the hospital.

I throw off the blanket and jump out of bed, and Albert yowls his objections, stretching fully out and yawning, extending his shiny black claws.

Last week he left me a small, wet mound of innards and feathers to clean up. I think it must've been a sparrow.

Maybe that's what the smell is: one of Albert's 'presents' that he's hidden somewhere.

I get dressed quickly and whip through my leaving-the-house checklist, not nearly as thoroughly as I'd like. But I remember to take the white box I'd bought the day before out of the fridge, and head for the car.

Ivy is waiting outside the house.

'I didn't think you were coming,' she says, making a palaver about lowering herself into the passenger seat.

I glance at my watch; it's only thirty-one minutes past five. I feel my scalp tighten.

'You've no need to worry on that score,' I remark. 'You'll find me reliable, if nothing else.'

Reliability. That's one box that has always been ticked in my annual onetoone appraisal with Jim at work.

'I've no doubt you are, dear, but there's no accounting for the traffic at this time, is there?'

Some people insist on having an answer for everything. I stay quiet and start the car.

Soon as we reach the main road, we hit traffic.

'You see, you don't get this problem with the bus,' Ivy comments. 'They rocket down the bus lane even in heavy traffic, like our Liam on his motorbike. He often whips straight down the middle if there's a traffic jam.'

Liam isn't going to be whipping around anywhere on his motorbike right now.

She frowns at the queue of vehicles in front of us. 'I'll never rest if he says he wants another bike.'

'Have you heard anything from the police yet?'

She shakes her head. 'I'll tell you when I hear anything.'

I hear the full stop loud and clear but I'm not going to let that put me off asking. It's far too important.

We drive a few minutes in silence and then I remember my idea.

'I'll come over to the house one day, if you like,' I say. 'Give it a good clean so you don't have to worry about getting it done.'

She turns to look at me.

'That's very kind of you, Anna.' I can tell there's a 'but' coming. 'But really, there's no need. I'm just taking things steady and I'm managing to get it all done so far.'

I bite down on my tongue.

'It's very kind of you to offer though,' she says again. 'I'm sure you've got such a busy life with lots of friends and probably a boyfriend, too?'

I keep my eyes on the road. See how she likes a taste of her own silent medicine.

We get to the hospital at just gone six.

I've managed to get us here in record time, weaving in and out of the back roads to make up a few seconds here and there.

'You've worked miracles behind that wheel, Anna,' Ivy beams. 'And it's so nice having someone to chat to, on the way in.'

I glow inside. Maybe I've got it wrong and Ivy does like having me around after all. Any luck, she'll completely relax before long and readily accept my help.

When we get up to the ward, Liam is sitting up in bed.

He still has a few tubes and pads attached to his chest and forearms but his improved appearance, compared to the day before, is astonishing.

Ivy rushes up to his bed and embraces him. I see Liam stiffen.

'Hello. . . Gran,' he mumbles awkwardly.

'Careful of his tubes, Ivy,' I say, setting down the white box I've brought in with me on the sliding table at the bottom of Liam's bed.

I sit down in one of the chairs next to him and wait for her to stop her fussing.

'How are you feeling, Liam?' I ask.

'I'm still aching but at least they've taken most of this stuff away now.' He indicates the remaining tubes snaking across his chest.

'You look more like your old self already.' Ivy stares intensely at him, stroking his hand. 'You'll be back to normal in no time at all, you'll see.'

Liam turns his head and stares out of the window.

'I won't know when I'm back to my old self,' he says vaguely. 'I can't remember who that person is. Or was.'

'Nonsense,' Ivy says. 'Another few days or so and it'll all start coming back. The doctor said as much, didn't he, Anna?'

'The doctor said his memory "might" come back but that we have to be patient,' I correct her. 'In the meantime, we're not supposed to be talking about it, Ivy.'

'But how is he going to remember, unless I help him?' She reaches into her handbag and pulls out a brown envelope. 'I brought you some photographs to look at, to see if that helps.'

She spreads a short stack of curling black-and-white photos out on the bed.

'Everything okay in here?' A nurse hovers in the doorway.

'Ivy has brought some photographs in to show Liam,' I say pointedly. 'I hope it won't upset him.'

'It won't upset me.' Liam squints briefly at the photographs. 'I don't know who any of these people are.'

'Oh but look, here's your grandad.' Ivy holds up a small, dog-eared print of an old man in braces leaning on a spade. 'Surely you must remember him?'

I wonder why she hasn't brought more recent photographs in to show Liam, perhaps of his parents or his friends. Surely he'd have a better chance of remembering more up-to-date events.

'It's best we don't rush this sort of thing, love,' the nurse says gently to Ivy, starting to gather the photographs together. 'It's not just for Liam's benefit; it can be very upsetting for you too.'

Ivy's face crumples. 'He was always so close to his grandad; they were inseparable until the day he died, and now he doesn't know who he is.'

I wonder when the photograph was taken. Looking at it, Liam must have only been a small boy.

Liam lowers his head back onto the pillow. 'I'm sorry,' he sighs. 'But the past is just a blank.'

CHAPTER 13
Joan Peat

Joan peered out of the window as Anna's car pulled away from the kerb yet again.

Just lately, she seemed to be constantly in and out. Their daily cuppa had dwindled to the odd rushed five minutes here and there.

Joan missed her company but the thought she might be getting her life together at last made up for it. It's what she had always wanted for Anna.

She sighed and sat down in Arthur's chair next to the window. She liked it here where she could watch the street from behind the nets; not that there was much activity these days.

People didn't seem to walk as much anymore. They'd rather jump in their cars and drive to the row of shops just around the corner.

If you believed all the news reports, children were only interested in playing in pretend worlds nowadays – virtual worlds, she thought they called them – on their computer screens. It was baffling.

Joan often thought that, had he still been here, Arthur wouldn't have known what to make of it all.

But her Arthur hadn't been here for years and now all she had left were her memories of how things used to be.

This was the very window from where they used to watch their five-year-old neighbour as she held one of her stuffed toys' tea parties out on the street.

Joan smiled at the memory. She was never one for dolls, was Anna.

She glanced back at the open lounge door where she could see straight through into the kitchen.

Nearly thirty years ago Joan had been standing right there, just inside the back door, the first time Anna came round of her own accord.

She could see herself now, humming to the little radio she liked to have on in the background as she worked; her hands immersed in a sink full of suds. Neat printed short-sleeved dress with her pale lemon apron tied around her middle. Jet black hair clipped up and a little bit of rouge and lipstick, even though she was in the house.

She'd always liked to make the effort for Arthur.

It had been a hot, muggy day soon after Jack Clarke, Anna's father, had left home.

The kitchen window was wide open but there was very little breeze and the air outside smelled of cut grass and scorched tarmac.

Joan had been pottering around all morning, and when she opened the back door to put the rinsed milk bottles out, there she stood: fair curls knotted and tousled, with a runny nose. Joan guessed there hadn't been a hairbrush near the child's head in days.

When Joan appeared at the door, Anna seemed instantly startled. She clutched a bedraggled soft toy closer to her chest and made to run.

'Do you like home-made lemonade?' Joan called.

The child had turned back then and nodded cautiously; her eyes darting around the yard.

Joan had brought her inside and taken her through to the front room. Anna leaned shyly into her leg when she saw Arthur, and Joan was reminded of Janet-Mae and how little affection her daughter had showed her, even as a small child.

'Who have we got here then, Mrs Peat?' Arthur peered over his paper at her. 'A pretty little fairy you found in the garden?'

Anna had giggled at that.

She stuck her thumb in her mouth and took a step towards him, still clutching what Joan could now identify as a ragged stuffed cat, colour unidentifiable.

'Now, when you visit someone's home it's customary to tell them a little bit about yourself,' Arthur said kindly. 'Let's see. What's your name and how old are you, fairy?'

'I'm Anna.' She beamed, her voice clear as a bell. 'I'm five years old next Tuesday.'

'Five years old?' Arthur exclaimed, dropping his paper. 'Why, you're nearly all grown up!'

From that moment on, Anna was sold on Arthur. Joan always told everyone the child worshipped the ground he walked on.

She had poured Anna a small glass of the cool lemonade she'd prepared that morning and taken it through to the front room with a malted milk biscuit.

Anna wolfed it down within seconds.

'You liked that, didn't you?' Joan remarked. 'Does Mummy make lemonade for you at home?'

Of course, Joan could already guess the answer to that, and she felt some satisfaction as Arthur witnessed Anna shaking her head, knotted curls bouncing.

'Does your mummy know you're here, dear?' Joan felt she had to ask but wished immediately that she hadn't. At the mention of her mother, the child quickly became fretful, twisting her hands.

'I think we can safely say her mother doesn't much care where she is,' Arthur muttered under his breath.

It was true. They'd seen Anna wandering around on the street on many occasions, playing with her stuffed toys alone at the side of the road for seemingly hours.

Arthur always stopped Joan from going out to see if she was alright though.

'Not our business, love,' he'd said sadly. 'Monica Clarke won't thank you.'

And Joan knew he was right.

Soon after the mention of her mother, Anna's bottom lip began to wobble. It was Arthur who'd put her at ease again.

'Come and sit here next to me.' He patted the sofa cushion. 'I've got something here that a little fairy like you might like to look at.'

He reached down by his seat and brought out his frame of pinned butterflies. He liked to sit in his chair with a magnifying glass, studying the specimens for hours.

Joan had thought a lot about that frame in the last few years.

It was packed into a box somewhere in the spare bedroom. She had never liked having it around; it troubled her.

The way that something so full of life and beauty could be captured, pinned down and changed for ever.

CHAPTER 14
Anna

I wouldn't consciously wish Ivy any harm, of course, but in the event she gets herself so upset about that old photograph and Liam's inability to remember his late grandad that she collapses.

Right there at the hospital, in front of us all. They take her off on a trolley to recuperate.

'Don't worry, she'll be fine,' the nurse reassures Liam. 'She's exhausted, that's all.'

When the nurse has gone, Liam says, 'I'm worrying that I'm *not* worried, Anna. I know I should be.'

My heart leaps when he remembers my name so easily. At last, I'll get to speak to him alone without Ivy rattling on about the past.

I sit down on the chair right next to his bed; the one Ivy usually commandeers.

'I feel guilty,' he says. 'That I have no feelings for my own gran.'

His slate-blue eyes bore into me.

I'm not used to people looking at me as closely. I can feel my face prickling up like it's covered in nettle stings.

But Liam doesn't look away, and I see that his eyes are kind and trusting and I like it a bit more then.

'Tell me a bit about yourself,' Liam says, still watching me.

'Me? Oh there's not much to tell.' I laugh, scratching at my wrist. 'Nothing interesting at any rate.'

'Come on.' He taps my arm lightly so I have to look up again. 'Don't be coy.'

For a second or two, I'm lost in those eyes, almost the exact shade of Danny's. And that hair, with its subtle threads of gold that keep catching the light.

I wonder if this is how Danny would look, how Danny would be, if he'd only been allowed to—

'Anna?'

'Sorry,' I mumble. 'It's just – I don't know, I don't really like talking about myself.'

Usually, I'd get annoyed if someone kept poking their nose in to my business but with Liam it feels different. It feels like he's genuinely interested in me.

'Good time to start then,' he presses. 'What do you do for a living?'

So I tell him the unimpressive truth; that I'm a postal delivery worker for the Royal Mail and that I live alone in a small end-terrace with my cat, Albert.

I can't dress it up more than that.

It feels as if an invisible hand is squeezing my windpipe and I stop speaking.

'When did you move there?' he asks, and his eyes slide from my face to my clawing fingers.

I glance down and see a cluster of angry red welts inside my wrist. I stop scratching and press my fingertips together in a stee-ple shape.

'I've always lived there,' I say. 'I mean, I grew up there and then when – well, the house just became mine in the end.'

'Not many people your age own their own home outright,' Liam remarks. 'That's impressive.'

'I wouldn't say that.' I pick at the edge of the blanket while heat channels into my cheeks.

'What about friends and stuff?' His forehead furrows. 'Is there anyone special in your life?'

I stand up quickly then, fanning my face with an NHS *Guide to Beating Infection.*

'Fancy a cup of tea?' I ask brightly. 'I could go and get us one from the machine downstairs?'

Liam shakes his head but he doesn't say anything. I pat the white box on the side table.

'I brought cakes in,' I say. 'To cheer you up.'

I open the box and peer inside, speaking as casually as I can.

'Have the police been to talk to you yet, about the accident?'

He shakes his head. 'Not that I know of.'

'That woman, the other driver, she nearly killed you. You can't let her get away with it, Liam.'

He shrugs his shoulders and looks down at his hands. 'I can't even remember what she looks like.'

'I don't want to alarm you but it is vital that you ask the police to come and speak to you soon, to tell you what they know about her,' I say. 'It doesn't matter if you can't remember anything about the accident. There were other people there who saw what happened that day.'

'Tell me *what* about her, though?' He yawns and watches as thin dashes of rain spatter the window.

'Her name, address, that sort of thing,' I say again, moving in front of the glass to get him to concentrate on what I'm saying. 'She mustn't get away with what she did. You need to make sure the police don't keep anything from you, that they tell you everything they know about her. For insurance purposes, you see. If you want, I could contact—'

I look up, annoyed, when I hear someone entering the room.

A young nurse I haven't seen before walks forward a little nervously and holds up a clear, plastic bag containing items I don't recognise.

'I've been asked to give this to Ivy Bradbury.' She looks at me.

'Thank you.' I take the bag. 'I'll make sure she gets it.'

'Looks like keys and stuff,' Liam murmurs, disinterested. 'Probably mine.'

I pop the bag into the pocket of my coat that is hanging over the back of my chair while the girl scurries out.

'I'll give them to Ivy later,' I say briskly. 'Now, time for the big decision. Chocolate éclair or vanilla slice, which is it to be?'

He looks at me, confused.

'My birthday.' I reach for the cake box. 'I thought I'd treat us.'

I think about those beautiful lilies and the joy of seeing several pastel-coloured envelopes on the mat.

I send myself birthday cards every year, but it was the first time I'd done flowers.

The drive back home seems to take forever.

I'm eager to scrutinise the contents of the bag the nurse gave me.

When I left the hospital, I decided to make myself wait until I got home to look and now I am savouring the anticipation of it.

In the end, although she had improved somewhat, the hospital staff decided Ivy should remain there overnight for observational purposes, seeing as she would be home alone if they discharged her.

I realised then that I couldn't possibly burden her with the bag containing Liam's belongings. It would only serve to upset her even further.

So I decided to take them home with me, for safekeeping.

When I get in, I snap on the lights and shut the lounge door behind me, ignoring Albert's mews of discontent. He's going to have to wait for his supper for once.

I take out the self-sealed clear plastic bag, which is about the size of a hardback novel. The contents take up only a third of it but I lay the items out in front of me on the coffee table.

There is a battered mobile phone, a few coins and a five pound note, a folded-up letter and a small bunch of keys on a leather Suzuki fob.

The letter is from a photographic studio, confirming that Liam is booked on to a course for instruction on how to use a wide-angle lens. I realise then that I haven't even asked him what his job is yet, and whether Ivy has informed his employer that he's in hospital.

I sniff the air. The smell is still here in the house, perhaps not quite as strong as before, but still.

Thoughts about that are swiftly dispersed when I pick up the bunch of keys and spot immediately that one of them is a pale gold Yale. It looks very much like a front door key.

Intruding on other people's privacy isn't something I'm proud of doing or that would usually occur to me, but there is a growing urgency to this situation. It is of paramount importance that I gather a little more information about their lives.

With Ivy reluctant to even discuss the accident or police progress and now that it's apparent that Liam has lost his memory altogether, albeit temporarily, someone has to keep an overview on what's happening.

Ivy mentioned something about a police contact number lying around in the house. Finding it would be a good starting point in getting things moving.

In that moment, I decide I am more than willing to battle through my own personal discomfort and use Liam's door key, if there's a chance I can help move things along.

I suppose that's just the sort of person I am.

It is still early evening, only seven thirty.

To my annoyance, the nurses suggested I left early to allow Liam to rest after the drama of Ivy's collapse. Obviously intimidated by them, he didn't object.

I can't seem to settle. Too antsy to watch TV, too tired to comb the house in search of the mystery smell again.

I try to put Liam's key out of my mind while I decide on the best course of action but I keep thinking about Ivy's cat, Boris, and how there is no one there to feed him tonight.

It occurs to me how much she'd appreciate me dropping by just to make sure he is okay.

And that's what decides it.

It is dark when I turn in to Heath Close and park up halfway along the street.

It's quiet here, everyone will already be tucked away into their warm, snug houses chatting about their day over a glass of wine.

A collarless dog of unidentifiable breed systematically sniffs and pees its way along the hedge on the other side of the road but, thankfully, that's the only sign of movement.

Heath Close isn't a long stretch and it takes me just a couple of minutes to saunter casually past two unlit lamp posts and a discarded bicycle frame to number fifty-three.

It is surprising how many people leave their curtains open at night. I get a good look inside a number of houses as I make my way down the street.

An old man wearing wire-framed spectacles pores over a small table creating some kind of structure from tiny sticks of pale wood. His light is provided from a single, stark light bulb.

There is something achingly desperate about the tableau that makes me look away.

I reach Ivy and Liam's house. It occurs to me I should go around to the back door to get in if I want to avoid walking straight off the road into the porch and be lit up like a Christmas tree.

The darkness folds around me as I walk down the side of the house. I can't see if there's another key on this keyring that looks like it might fit the back door.

If Ivy's neighbours are anything like mine, the nets will be twitching.

My visit is nobody else's business, but you usually find most people are far too interested in the lives of others for their own good.

There is no outside light at the rear of the house either and I fumble with the keys, trying to find the right one. Then I remember I've got a tiny little flashlight on my own keys.

I illuminate the lock on the peeling wooden door and my heart sinks. It requires a long key, like the one that opens the bike shed at work.

I shine the light on Liam's bunch of keys again and quickly sort through.

Nestling between his motorbike key and the Yale, a longer key glints. It turns easily in the lock, and I push open the door, wondering for the first time what I am going to do if an alarm starts wailing. But I needn't worry, silence remains.

I can't see him but I feel Boris soundlessly winding himself around my legs in a figure of eight.

I tap my fingers along the wall until I find the light switch, but before I snap it on I turn to look up at the row of houses that overlook the small back garden.

There are bedroom windows that look down directly on to where I'm standing.

I relax a little when I can't see any obvious signs I'm being spied on. I snap on the kitchen light, then close and lock the back door behind me.

I move quickly into the middle room, kick off my shoes out of habit and shut Boris in the kitchen while I have a quick look around to get my bearings.

There is a patterned carpet and a dark oak table with four chairs in the middle room. A picture rail runs around the walls displaying gaudy patterned plates, some of them chipped and cracked.

I have to say, it's a treat to be able to look round leisurely and take it all in. Anything that gives me a clue about Liam's life can only help him, after all, in the absence of his memory.

When I'd called in here to use the bathroom the night I dropped Ivy off, I had to be in and out. It was all so rushed and it had felt impolite to hang around but now I have the chance to see the house properly, to form an impression of how they live and how they might be able to use some help.

I take a cursory glance into the front room with its cold stone fireplace and greenandbrown patterned carpeting. The carpets don't have the feel of proper wool underfoot: they are cheap, nylon imitations.

The house looks tidy enough but it smells fusty, like it could do with a good airing. It feels very different to being in my own home but in a thrilling kind of way.

I place my hand on the handle of the door leading to the stairs and swallow hard, trying to relieve the dryness of my throat.

Strictly speaking, I shouldn't be here but I remind myself I'm doing it for the right reasons and that's what counts.

The stairs are steep and narrow, and the air feels even colder up here and smells faintly damp.

Strange as it sounds the house itself feels distinctly unfriendly, like it doesn't want me around. Similar to the vibes I sometimes get from Ivy.

I wonder if Liam is happy living here, holed up with an old woman who doesn't seem to know when to keep her trap shut and listen to the advice of people who know better.

I stand at the top of the stairs, in exactly the same place I had been two nights before, looking at the closed doors along the long, narrow landing.

I'd wondered which room belonged to Liam back then but now I'm free to look anywhere I please.

The first door I open leads into Ivy's bedroom at the front of the house, overlooking the street. I make do with the light shining through from the landing and peer in.

The room is decorated sparsely but in feminine colours. The pink candlewick-style bedspread is strewn with pulled threads, and mismatched pastel flannelette pillowcases poke out at the top.

Dusty bottles of what look like lavender water are clustered in a corner of the mirrored walnut dressing table. Damp. Lavender. Old.

I feel sorry for Liam. In the prime of his life but having to live with an old lady he doesn't know any more and suffering those smells.

He probably dreams of meeting someone around his own age and making a fresh start together.

CHAPTER 15
Thirteen years earlier

Carla opened her eyes, registered the relentless pounding in her head and groaned.

She reached over to her bedside table and pressed the home button on her iPhone. She immediately squinted against the brightness. It was 4.25 a.m.

Despite promising she wouldn't, Carla had gone out again last night.

It was just for a drink, she kept telling herself as the cab wound its way into the city. It was just to be amongst people again and enjoy a comforting buzz around her.

But Carla hadn't believed any of those things, not really.

She knew how it would end up. How it always ended up.

The Asian cab driver had barely looked at her apart from taking instructions of where she wanted to go when she first climbed in the car.

He spent the twelve-minute journey talking hands-free on the phone in his own language.

Carla was glad he did. She didn't want conversation, just the relief.

The cab dropped her off outside Lexi's just before eleven. It was too early to be completely lost and anonymous in a big crowd of people, as she would have liked. But unless she intended going into work the next day having had no sleep at all, she couldn't afford to leave it any later.

She huddled in close behind a group of squealing, laughing girls who'd reached the entrance just before her. She even shared a joke with one of them when the woman stumbled walking in.

Carla grabbed her arm to steady her.

'Bloody hell, I wouldn't mind but I'm the nominated driver.' She laughed to Carla as they walked past the two burly doormen who looked young enough to be Carla's sons.

Carla saw them check out a couple of the younger women in the group and then watched how their eyes just sort of drifted past her as if she wasn't there.

She knew the white dress looked good on her. She was still the same dress size as she had been in her twenties: a size twelve bottom and a size ten top.

Admittedly, it wasn't a result she'd gained through working out. Her lifestyle wasn't exactly healthy.

She drank way too much wine now and existed largely on ready meals because Mark had been the chief cook and bottle washer.

Beef stroganoff, creamy chicken pasta, green Thai curry and sticky rice. . . it had never been too much trouble for Mark to rustle up an amazing dinner at the end of a long day.

'It relaxes me,' he used to say. 'Must be my creative genes.'

Maybe he'd have been better training as a chef than an artist, Carla thought glumly. Even on minimum wage he'd still have earned more money than the paintings ever brought in.

Carla visited the hairdresser once a month to keep her glossy chestnut-brown bob neat and free of the annoying wiry grey hairs that had suddenly started appearing when she'd turned forty. And she had spent time tonight putting on her make-up; even making the effort to wear false eyelashes that enhanced the large, brown eyes that Mark had told her were "utterly incredible" the night they met.

But the two doormen noticed none of it. She might as well be invisible.

It was as if an inner sensor told them she was simply too old to be of interest, even without them having to check her out.

That was why she'd got into the online dating, although she wasn't interested in an actual relationship.

You could cut through all the silly games and hook up with someone for the evening.

Just long enough to touch skin to skin, to feel the warmth of another body and arms around you that felt like someone cared when you closed your eyes.

Just long enough keep the hurt at bay.

His name was Chad.

He was a medical supplies salesman from Kent, and he was working in the East Midlands for the week.

She was sitting with her third Pornstar Martini at the bar, surveying the dance floor, when she got the notification.

A message box popped up on the screen.

Fellow user nearby! Chad Brownlow is looking for fun and he is only 3 metres away!

She clicked on the photograph and a man – she'd guess in his late thirties, with salt-and-pepper cropped hair and a crooked but attractive smile – filled the screen.

She looked around her and saw him immediately – smiling back at her from a nearby table.

He beckoned to her and pointed to the empty chair next to him.

The budget hotel had been her suggestion.

* * *

It was just a five minute walk from Lexi's and the place she usually used.

Chad talked to her all the way there and as they checked in, too. He paid. He told her about his job and his kids. She wished he hadn't.

Afterwards, she couldn't remember much he talked about, at all. Only the longing to be held close, to feel his manliness, his warmth.

The room was minimal but adequate with a sterile bathroom that smelled like a hospital.

Carla pushed aside the voile net that covered the window and looked down onto the street.

A dishevelled man staggered across the Market Square, shouting. People laughed and walked around him, avoided him.

Chad came and stood next to her. He pulled her chin gently towards him and kissed her on the lips.

The walls were cast in a pink glow from neon lights on the building opposite. She heard a nearby siren wail louder and then gradually fade into the distance until it disappeared completely.

She lay her head against his chest and closed her eyes. Chad felt different to Mark, more cushioned.

When they undressed she saw his body was pale with a slight paunch and he had more body hair than she usually liked on a man.

But he was there and he was kind and afterwards, he didn't talk about his job or his kids and Carla had stopped feeling quite so alone.

And now here she was, back home and in her own bed. At least she'd managed that, this time.

She vaguely remembered hailing the black cab outside the hotel and falling into the back seat.

The driver had insisted she hand over the fare before he would even begin the journey. That had bothered her more than anything.

Carla snapped on the lamp and swung her legs out of bed.

Her eyes felt dry and gritty behind the lids and the pounding in her head was even worse now. She was desperate for water.

She reached for a torn slip of paper by her phone and squinted at the scrawl. Chad's number.

When she got to the bathroom, she screwed it up and threw it in the pedal bin.

CHAPTER 16
Present day
Anna

I leave Ivy's bedroom and pad down the long, narrow landing.

When I click on the light switch just inside the door, I immediately spot the computer and printer on a low table in front of the window.

Liam's room.

Posters of elaborately chromed motorbikes cover the walls. Piles of motorcycle magazines and manuals are stacked precariously next to his single bed and wedged into the shelves next to the computer.

The bed is unmade, and the floor is littered with dirty laundry. It looks like the bedroom of your average, messy teenage boy.

It appears that Ivy hasn't cleaned the room at all while Liam is in hospital. Even more annoyingly, she had instantly turned down my offer of help yesterday, claiming she could manage when she very clearly needs assistance.

I would like nothing more than to scoot around here with my cloth and lemon cleanser. Clearing out those dusty magazines and reorganising the furniture to maximise the space would make it all look a bit more grown-up.

I'm certain Liam would be delighted with the results.

But I can hardly take that job on this evening. I'm not even supposed to be here in the middle of all their mess.

Above the headboard is a poster taken from the middle of a magazine, complete with staple marks. Some slapper in a tiny pair of denim shorts, virtually showing what she's had for breakfast.

I had expected Liam to have better standards, if I'm honest, and I fight a sudden, inexplicable urge to tear it down.

I have to remind myself that he's in a difficult position. It's probably not his choice to live with his gran, especially since his bedroom looks as if it's caught in a time warp.

He probably doesn't even notice there are posters still up that have been there since he was an immature young man.

It goes without saying that Liam would obviously prefer his own place, if he had the chance.

I pull my phone out of my pocket and take a couple of photographs of the room from different angles, so I can study them later at home.

Over at the narrow window, I pull down the thin roller blind for a bit of privacy.

I notice the computer station is neat and organised, contrasting with the rest of the room.

A sign on a coiled, bouncy wire protrudes from the top of the monitor declaring,

'QUIET! GENIUS AT WORK!'

I run my fingers across the dusty keyboard and touch the buttons. I wonder if Liam used the computer on the morning of the accident.

Most people are obsessed with checking their emails or Facebook on at least an hourly basis. It was quite possible Liam had done just that before he left home on the morning of the smash.

His fingers might have touched the keys where mine rest now, and he'd have been totally unaware of the terrible danger he would soon encounter.

I sit down on the chair, trying to imagine Liam here, in this very space.

It brings home the sobering thought that none of us know what's waiting around the corner, what awful events fate may have planned for us.

Until tragedy drops on you like a ton of bricks.

I understand how that feels.

A tiny green light winks at me, indicating that the computer isn't turned off; it is merely on standby. I click a switch on the tower and it cranks into life. The monitor flickers, displaying a screensaver of a Harley-Davidson, peppered with numerous desktop icons.

I adjust the keyboard slightly to suit my seated position and a small white piece of paper slips from underneath it. I slide it out and peer closer to try and read the cryptic scrawl.

At first it means nothing, just senseless words and phrases. Then I realise just what it is that I'm looking at.

A list of Liam's usernames and passwords.

I've never really been a 'friends' sort of person. I just can't see the point in forging associations with people who take up all your time and want to know all your business.

Mother never allowed us to bring friends back to the house; it wouldn't have been right, what with her mood swings and all the other stuff.

The terrible stuff I didn't know about at first.

Don't get me wrong, part of me would have liked to get friendlier with others at school. Having people to sit with at breaks and lunchtimes would have made a nice change but let's face it, if you start getting close to others, you just end up saying stuff you wish you hadn't.

Stuff that people can bring up and use against you later on.

That's what I think about when Roisin tries to get chatting to me at work. She seems a perfectly nice woman but, of course, you never quite know.

I can see the appeal of Facebook in that it's perfectly possible to maintain controlled contact with people on your own terms. Still, even within that framework there is the potential for humiliation.

You can add people as friends all you like but it doesn't mean they *accept* you on to their friends list. No, you wait and wait until you realise they have quietly rejected your request. Then you have to go into work the next day and see them in real life and pretend it's hasn't happened or that you haven't noticed yet.

I don't know, maybe it's just me doing things wrong. I don't claim to be an IT expert but I can just about find my way around using the basics.

I click on a desktop icon and the Facebook login page comes up. I enter the email address and password that's written on the piece of notepaper, labelled 'Fb'.

I'm preparing myself for failure, but within seconds Liam's profile page loads in front of me.

I sit back and take a few breaths.

It's important I don't do anything rash. I don't want Liam to see that someone has been meddling with his information when he is well enough to come home, although I feel sure he won't mind that I've been concerned enough to take a look.

There might well be people on here who don't know what's happened to him, people that are trying to contact him and wondering where he is. I understand the importance that people attach to their social media, but Ivy wouldn't have a clue about it all.

A small box pops up to inform me that Liam has eighty-five notifications and one new private message from someone he doesn't know.

There is a link that must be clicked if he wants to accept the message.

Before I can overthink it, I click on the link and wait while the message inbox loads. When it's ready, and before I can change my mind, I open the envelope icon and take in a sharp breath.

The message is from *her*.

CHAPTER 17
Thirteen years earlier

Daniel Clarke sat upstairs on the bare floorboards of his bedroom, waiting for Father MacCarrick to arrive.

He had missed an appointment with the school counsellor this morning, and Daniel knew Carla was the sort of person who would definitely want an explanation as to why he hadn't turned up.

He pushed thoughts about school away. He had other things to think about right now.

His mother had drilled him in the sorts of questions the priest might ask and what Daniel's replies ought to be.

His mother didn't know this but Father MacCarrick had already talked to him about what the correct responses should be when he called him to the sacristy yesterday.

The priest called him to the sacristy a lot but Daniel tried not to think about that, either.

'This is your chance to put right all your wrongs, to repent.' His mother frowned earlier in the day, shadowing the sign of the cross on herself. 'God above only knows what Father MacCarrick sees in you. You'd better not let us all down.'

He didn't want to be an altar server for a number of reasons he couldn't discuss with anyone, least of all his mother. What if they found out at school? His life would be even more of a misery than it was now, if that were even possible.

'He won't make you a server just like that, you know,' John Peters had told him at church yesterday as Daniel sat praying. 'Only Father Mac's favourites get to be altar boys.'

John was a seminarian, a student of the church, and he was often rude about Father MacCarrick when the priest wasn't around.

'The priest has to really like you. I mean *really* like you,' John grinned, revealing furred yellow teeth. 'Do you know what I mean, Danny Boy?'

John's clawed hand slid down towards Daniel's crotch, and the boy swung his legs to the side to protect himself. John had grabbed his balls hard before and it killed.

Father MacCarrick *did* like him, Daniel felt sure of that. Otherwise, he wouldn't ask him to help file papers in his private office regularly or assist him in cleaning the vestments and sacred vessels in the sacristy.

Although why the priest needed his help at all puzzled Daniel.

Mrs Bream was the church's regular volunteer cleaner and she had a detailed rota pinned up in the annexe which included the dusting of the sacristy.

Daniel could hear his mother busying around downstairs.

For once, she wasn't lying on the sofa watching that American show that did DNA and lie detector tests on people who swore at each other and fought on stage.

He could hear plates and cutlery clinking.

His mother thought she was an important person at the church, but Father MacCarrick never let her do any of the special tasks, and the three ladies who arranged the flowers often whispered about her in the back when she sat praying in the front pews before service.

His mother thought she knew everything but she knew nothing. Nothing at all.

She was clueless about school, and she was even more clueless about what happened during the times Father MacCarrick called him to the sacristy.

CHAPTER 18
Present day
Anna

The next day I spend time recording the new information and photographs from yesterday's impromptu visit to Liam's house.

It gives me an overview of where we are and also ensures I don't forget anything. I can be prone to forgetfulness.

After the shock of discovering her Facebook message to Liam, I feel as though I'm running on go-slow. I am even a little late getting to the hospital for the start of visiting time.

It's hardly surprising but I've barely slept a wink.

The thought that she has hunted Liam down on Facebook in order to send him such a lying, conniving message beggars belief.

Leopard, spots. . . it just goes to show that people never change no matter how much time elapses.

She is calling herself 'Amanda Danson' now, so at least that's one mystery solved.

Before I left their house I neatly handwrote 'Amanda's' message word for word, and back at home, I printed off the clearest photographs of Liam's bedroom and filed them with the one I took of him in the hospital.

I was disappointed to discover I couldn't see anything more than her profile photo due to her high privacy settings. If that's not proof she's got something to hide, I don't know what is.

Still, I'm grateful I discovered the message before Liam had the chance to see it and buy into her seething lies.

Once I copied it out, I deleted it from his message inbox. What kind of a friend would I be if I left it for him to read when he's feeling at his most vulnerable?

Before I get into the car, I pop next door to check on Mrs Peat. My heart sinks when she beckons me: time is tight as visiting time starts in just half an hour.

'My legs are playing me up today, Anna, could you help me move over to my bed?'

Mrs Peat may be old but she's still quite sturdy, to phrase it kindly, and she takes some moving.

She suffers with chronic rheumatoid arthritis, has good and bad days. Linda, her care assistant, has set up Mrs Peat's bed downstairs, and she also has a commode in here.

She virtually lives her whole life in this one dreary room. I feel guilty complaining; the least I can do is stay for a quick chat.

I brace myself and hope my lower back holds up when Mrs Peat finally manages to get to her feet and lean heavily against me.

'You've been busy, coming and going a lot lately,' she groans with discomfort as we shuffle across the room at a snail's pace.

Mrs Peat might be old and sick but she doesn't miss much.

'Yes, I've been going to the hospital quite a bit,' I say between breaths. 'To see my friend, Liam.'

'Ah, a friend.' She smiles warmly. 'Sounds like things might be looking up for you, dear.'

'He's just a friend. That's all,' I say tersely. I don't want Mrs Peat getting the wrong idea.

When she is settled in her bed I make her a cup of tea and tell her all about the accident, how I sat with Liam in the road until the ambulance arrived.

'You're an angel, Anna,' Mrs Peat says. 'Always thinking of others. His gran must be so grateful you were there to help him.'

I let that one go. I'm not completely certain yet what Ivy thinks of me.

'I can still see you now, sat over there in the chair with Arthur, reciting nursery rhymes or drawing your pictures. Such a bright girl, you were.'

I make an excuse to go into the kitchen to wash my hands. At least until she stops talking about the past.

Once I am sure Mrs Peat is comfortable again, I head to the hospital.

On the way, I call at the cobbler's kiosk and get another copy of Liam's house key cut, just in case there is no one to feed the cat again.

And that's when I remember: *I didn't feed Boris yesterday.*

With the shock of finding Amanda Danson's toxic message to Liam, I forgot all about feeding the poor cat.

By some miracle, I find a parking space near the hospital entrance and manage to get a ticket just as a lengthy queue forms behind me.

I am a little late for the start of visiting but so is everyone else by the look of it.

I don't call in at the shop, and I don't wait for the lift. I take the stairs two at a time and then regret it when I have to stand outside the ward for a minute to get my breath back.

They buzz me in, and I walk briskly past the reception desk without speaking to anyone.

If you stand just outside the partial glass door, it's possible to see straight into Liam's private room from the ward corridor. I spot right away there is already someone sitting in there: a woman, with her back to the door.

I take in the blonde ponytail, the pink coat, and I realise, with a dizzy rush, that it's her. It's Amanda Danson or whatever she's calling herself these days.

My face and neck feel like they're on fire.

I decide I'm going to call her by this fictitious name for now, at least. I don't want to blurt anything out to Liam or Ivy about what she did yet. I have to keep my head clear and think rationally about what I'm going to do.

Amanda is busy talking, moving her hands animatedly.

Weaving her story, constructing new truths from old lies.

It is clear she has Liam's full attention. He is nodding and smiling.

I watch as she throws her head back and laughs raucously about something. Laughs! While the man she nearly killed is confined to a hospital bed in front of her, unable to remember and unable to move.

Something inside me seems to shrink, to pull tighter, and I have to steady myself by leaning against the wall.

'You alright there, love?' A passing nurse slows down.

Before I can answer her, Liam looks up and spots me.

'Anna!' he calls. 'Come in.'

I step away from the door, my head whirring. This isn't supposed to happen; I don't want Amanda Danson to see me. I need more time to plan, to think about my next move.

It kills me to abandon Liam to her lies but I can't blow my cover just yet.

But then the door opens and there she is, smiling in my face.

I ball my fists in my jacket pockets to stop myself from grasping her stringy neck.

'Hi,' she says, 'I'm Amanda.'

I have no choice but to stand still in the doorway and look straight at her.

I wait for the shock to register on her face. Wait for her conniving brain to bridge the thirteen-year gap and realise exactly who I am.

She glances back at Liam and then looks at me again. A couple more seconds pass and there doesn't appear to be any spark of recognition.

'Are you a relative of Liam's?' she asks.

'A friend,' I croak and swallow down a thickness in my throat that is threatening to choke me.

I can't bring myself to speak to her but I can't tear my eyes away from her face, either.

It seems she hasn't got a clue who I am but I am fully expecting it to click any moment now.

Her face is longer and thinner than I remember it but the features are identical. Roman nose, almond-shaped eyes that border on being sly rather than attractive. I remember she had a tiny mole on her chin but it looks like she got that removed. Her vanity doesn't surprise me in the least.

She stands aside at last and I move, trance-like, into the room.

Amanda pulls another chair round, as though *I'm* the visitor and she is Liam's good friend. 'There you go,' she says, brightly, before sitting back down in her own seat.

I wait for the, 'Hang on, don't I know you?' look that is bound to shadow her face any second now.

Only it doesn't.

She sits back, seemingly relaxed.

The sheer audacity of her takes my breath away. Why on earth didn't the nurses stop her from coming in? I can't imagine what they were thinking.

The first line of her message had been packed with lies.

'I just had to send you this message to say how sorry I am. One minute the road was clear, the next, there you were.'

She was driving too fast. And she doesn't look sorry to me, at all.

'Sit down, Anna,' Liam urges, and I realise I'm still standing frozen to the spot, near the door.

If by some miracle she really doesn't recognise me, the last thing I want to do is alert her there's a problem, so I sit down. Still, I can't stop staring at her. I can't.

With no make-up on and her hair pulled back into a severe ponytail she looks, to all intents and purposes, as if she is suffering too. But obviously, it's all part of the act.

She has to be at least eight years older than me but I think she looks younger, fitter. Liam is bound to compare us and I'll come away wanting.

Liam coughs.

'Anna, this is Amanda, the lady who—'

'I know who she is,' I say tightly.

Her face instantly glows red. She rubs hard at bony wrists protruding from beneath her cuffs as if she's surprised to find they are hers.

Liam opens his mouth to speak but then closes it again.

What was it that her message to Liam had said?

'I only delayed braking for a second but you kept on coming. I'll regret that second for the rest of my life.'

'I recognise you,' I say, and she looks up.

From thirteen years ago, I'd like to add.

'From the accident. I was there, you see; I saw it all. I helped Liam as he lay injured in the road.'

Silence. Liam clears his throat.

'I came here today to tell Liam how sorry I am,' she whispers.

She is putting on an impressive show but I've seen it all before. It's alarming, though, to see Liam looking at her almost pitifully.

Her message had been clearly constructed to garner his trust, his sympathy.

'I'll never get behind the wheel again. I could have killed you and now I have to live with that.'

Little did she know it hadn't quite gone to plan because he hadn't seen the message, thank goodness.

'You came to say you're *sorry*?' I repeat, in the vain hope she'll hear how ridiculously inadequate it sounds.

'Yes.' She stands up then and dusts down her jeans as if that might brush the problem away. 'I know sorry isn't really enough, I just wanted—'

She looks at Liam, tightens her lips into a small, straight line and her eyes glitter with tears.

It is quite a performance.

'It's okay, Amanda,' he says kindly. 'Thanks for coming; it took guts. I don't remember anything about the accident, but when I'm discharged you should pop round the house for a cuppa, like you said.'

Just as she'd planned:

'I hope we can be friends.'

Liam, in his vulnerable state, is playing right into her hands.

'I don't think it's going to be as simple as popping round and we can all forget what's happened, Liam,' I blurt out before I think better of it. 'The police are involved now, and I'm not sure you two should even be communicating.'

'Actually, the police haven't even been in touch with me yet,' she says in a notthatit'sanyof*your*business tone. Then she catches herself and softens her manner. 'They're giving me some space to get my head straight, you see. I've been in a bit of a state with the shock of it all.'

Only a few minutes earlier she'd been hooting with laughter.

I don't know how I manage it but I clamp my mouth shut and look away as she heads for the door. I'm afraid of what might happen if I let go of whatever is bubbling like acid in my chest.

She nods goodbye at me, which, of course, I completely ignore.

'Apparently, it's not the first time she's done this,' I say to Liam when I close the door behind her. 'She knocked a child off his bicycle, too.'

Even as the words tumble out, I don't know why I'm saying it. It's the sort of thing that can be checked out but someone has to bring Liam to his senses before she gets her claws into him.

Liam frowns. 'But she said she'd only just passed her test.'

'A woman of her age? I seriously doubt that,' I scoff. 'Besides, she's hurt a child all the same. I'm not supposed to know that so keep it to yourself but I think you need to be aware of what kind of a person she really is behind all that play-acting.'

'I can't believe it,' Liam says, staring out of the window. 'I can't believe she'd hurt a kid and not mention it, not after saying how much she loves her job.'

The back of my neck prickles.

'Her job?'

Liam looks up at me.

'She works at a private nursery, Little Bees or something, in West Bridgford, she said. She told me she really loves kids.'

And that's when my plans start to slide into place like a perfectly designed jigsaw.

CHAPTER 19

Just after three fifteen the following afternoon, I park the car up across the street from the Busy Bees Day Nursery on Melton Road in West Bridgford.

I don't know exactly what time she finishes but I do know most private nurseries stay open until quite late to cater for the sort of parents who insist on having children and then working all the hours God sends so they can pay someone else to look after them.

If I had a little boy or girl, I can tell you now, I'd cherish every moment with them. You can never be sure quite how much time you've got with the people you love; it's all too easy to take it for granted.

The street is mostly empty of people but there are a good few cars parked up at the end of the road. I'm guessing it is collect-the-kids-from-school time as there seems to be a definite lull in the foot traffic from earlier in the day.

At least getting here early, I have the best chance of spotting her when she eventually leaves work.

The sky is candy-striped with pinks and blues, apart from a smoky grey streak left from a passing plane that cleaves its way straight through the middle of the pastels, ruining the effect.

My thoughts are jumping around all over the place. It's sick that someone who causes injury and death is charged with looking after unsuspecting people's children.

There is movement at the main door. Two members of staff wearing the same silly yellow tabards embroidered with oversized bees step out and light up cigarettes, chatting and laughing.

Hardly a desirable image for a childcare establishment but, as it happens, neither woman is her.

Hanging on to her mother's hand, a small girl of about five stares into my car as they pass; the woman is busy talking on her phone and doesn't even notice me sitting there, watching.

It is impressive how astute children can be and how little most adults notice as they go about their daily lives.

I have always been observant, have to be in my job.

To Joe Public, a couple of pints of milk standing outside a front door late in the day means nothing. To me, the same thing could indicate that the elderly occupant has collapsed inside the house.

Thankfully, nothing like that has ever happened yet on one of my rounds but, all the same, I try to remain vigilant.

I've seen too many reports on the news where, following a report from a delivery worker or similar, the police have found a decomposing body that used to be someone.

Someone who had no one to miss them.

By four o'clock there is still no sign of Amanda Danson.

It occurs to me I could sit here waiting for hours yet, only to find she's left early today or it's her day off. That's when I have the brainwave.

I punch the number on the big Busy Bees sign into my phone. When the receptionist answers, I ask for Amanda Danson. 'I'm ringing from the accident repair centre,' I say.

I want to establish if she's actually in the building but my little ploy pays unexpected dividends.

'Amanda isn't working today,' the receptionist tells me. 'You could call her on her mobile, though.'

'I'm sorry, my notepaper is torn and half the mobile number is missing, which is why I rang her work number,' I sigh, my heartbeat quickening. 'I don't suppose you could give it to me again? It's just that I'll probably get into trouble if I can't contact her as I have some important information about her car.'

A moment's hesitation. Then: 'I'm sure that'll be OK under the circumstances,' she says. 'I know Amanda has been worrying about her car and if it's important—'

'Thanks very much.' I am hardly able to believe my luck. I lean over and rummage in the glovebox for a pen and a scrap of paper.

How typical: Amanda has been fretting about her car rather than the human cost of her negligent driving.

I hear the woman tapping on some keys at the other end and then she reads out the number, just like that.

And suddenly, my day doesn't seem so bad after all.

Back home, the first thing that hits me when I walk through the door is the fetid smell again. It has returned with a vengeance.

I look down at Albert happily rubbing himself against the edge of the kitchen cupboard. It doesn't seem to be bothering him and he's usually very sensitive to odours.

I'm beginning to wonder if he has dropped the corpse of a small rodent or bird in the house, somewhere inaccessible. I hope I won't have to clear up another of his nasty messes; tiny birds have a surprising amount of entrails packed away behind their feathery little breasts.

I walk from room to room again, trying to get a sense of where it's coming from. It's the mix of rotten sweetness I can't deal with.

I once watched a film with a scene that featured clouds of flies appearing inexplicably on the inside window of a closed-up room. Not for the first time, I wonder if the rottenness of this house and its miserable past are being purged from the walls.

The interior was in such a state back then, I thought the whole house might have to be knocked down. Social Services helped me make it new again.

They arranged for people to come in and replace things, to cover up the old and the damaged.

Despite this I often think that the trace of everything that happened remains under there. I know it will never go away.

I stroke my fingers across the smooth plaster of the long wall in the middle room. When the house became mine, I had more of it redecorated.

I knew it was just a flimsy coating, of course; a superficial veneer to attempt to obscure the sounds and memories that will be forever trapped in these walls.

I blink a few times to try and get my thinking back on track. This line of thought isn't helping me find where the smell is coming from.

Like before, it doesn't seem to get stronger or weaker anywhere in the house, it remains just as bad wherever I go.

I walk around the entire house again with a bottle of antiseptic spray and a cloth.

I peer behind furniture and into dusty corners. The only room I don't go in to is the box room.

I don't want to look in there.

Later, when I arrive at the hospital, Ivy is sitting next to Liam's bed.

'You're back then,' I say. 'Are you feeling better now?'

She nods and beams at Liam, obviously fully recovered after her funny turn. 'They're letting him come home tomorrow,' she says.

She is wearing a faded floral dress and a brown cardigan with worn knobbly bits around the cuffs. I notice she hasn't taken off her plastic hospital identification bracelet yet from her brief admission following her collapse. Some people crave attention.

Liam doesn't look quite as thrilled as Ivy at the prospect of being discharged, and I'm not surprised. Being holed up with an old woman you don't remember isn't really anyone's idea of fun.

'That's good news,' I say to Liam, sitting down at the other side of his bed. 'What time are they likely to discharge you? I'll make sure I'm around.'

'We don't know the details yet,' Ivy answers for him. 'Someone's coming to speak to us about it shortly.'

It feels like 'us' means just her and Liam.

A few minutes later a tall, plump woman with bright blue eyeshadow and tightly permed hair comes in clutching a clipboard. She wears ordinary clothes but an identity lanyard dangles around her neck and she bustles around like she has the most important job in the hospital.

'I'm Maureen, your Patient Care Coordinator,' she announces to Liam in one breath. 'My job is to make sure you have adequate arrangements in place at home when you leave the hospital.'

She asks questions and records his answers on a pre-printed sheet.

Does Liam have transport home, she asks and will he need a note from the doctor for his initial absence from work?

'I don't go to work,' Liam says quietly.

'You remembered that?' Maureen stops writing and looks up.

'We were just talking about it,' Ivy tells her. 'Before you came in.'

I glance at Ivy but she keeps her rheumy eyes fixed on Maureen.

'I can't work because—'

'He's in the middle of a career change,' Ivy interrupts. 'Studying photography at college.'

Maureen pauses and blinks a couple of times as if she is trying to focus on her questions again. Finally, she wonders if Ivy will require any home help for Liam while he recovers?

Ivy starts to babble about booking a cab and asking a neighbour to help her look after Liam for a few days.

'I'll take you both home tomorrow, Ivy,' I say firmly. 'And I can help you to look after Liam when he's back at home, too.'

'Nonsense, you've done enough, Anna,' Ivy says quickly.

I look at Maureen and offer her a small smile. 'She's only just recovered from collapsing with exhaustion herself,' I say. 'I don't mind helping out.'

'I see. Well, they'll need most of tomorrow to do any final tests and get his medication ready so it will be fairly late on in the day before he's ready,' Maureen says, jotting something down.

'We could take him at the start of visiting tomorrow evening if that's convenient,' I say. 'I can sort everything out; there's no need for you to worry, Ivy.'

'I'm not worrying,' she says tightly. 'It's just that—'

'I think you should take up your friend's kind offer,' Maureen tells her gently. 'It's hard work looking after an invalid, Mrs Bradbury, especially if you're not that well yourself.'

'But we'll be fine; Anna isn't really a friend, we only just—'

I shake my head slightly at Maureen to cancel out Ivy's protesting. 'I'll get them home, don't you worry,' I say. 'I won't let them struggle on without me.'

Later, on my way home, I call at the big Tesco Superstore in Carlton and pick up a cheap pay-as-you-go phone complete with a new SIM card and ten pounds of call credit.

I read somewhere that if you don't bother registering the handset with the carrier, your calls are completely untraceable. That sort of thing is always useful to know.

When I get back home, I call Amanda Danson's mobile number on the new phone.

It goes straight through to voicemail and I listen to her personalised recorded message, goosebumps popping on my arms as her voice drones smoothly on.

She sounds so polite and sensible. Like the kind of person you could easily trust.

I ring and listen eight times in all until I've memorised what she says and I have the exact tone of her voice in my head.

Then I close my eyes and imagine her pleading with me.

CHAPTER 20
Clifton, Nottingham

Colin Freckleton sat in his unmarked silver Ford Focus, waiting.

It was just before seven a.m. on a fine morning. Ideal weather for his task; nice and clear but not too warm. Colin opened the car window a touch to enjoy the birdsong permeating from the nearby hedgerows. Possibly a pied wagtail, if he wasn't mistaken.

Closing his eyes, he paused for just a moment to savour the anticipation of success he always got at the beginning of a new job.

From this vantage point he could see all the way down Patchings Hill, which made up a good section of this particular route.

Typically, he'd done a bit of a recce in his own time the previous evening to ensure the best position for his stake-out. Colin liked to think it was just one of the ways in which he stood out from the rest of the team.

On the passenger seat he'd laid out his usual kit in perfect order. He didn't mind admitting he was a creature of habit.

A pair of powerful mini binoculars, a digital camera complete with zoom lens, his tablet PC and phone and, of course, the always-reliable 12 HB pencil and Moleskine notebook. No batteries required.

Colin prided himself on his attention to detail and his track record of reliable, accurate surveillance. His record spoke for itself and was the reason he'd risen four full ranks from office administrator to Senior Officer of the Royal Mail Investigation Branch in less than five years.

He flipped open the notebook and scanned through his handwritten points again.

'ANNA CLARKE, POSTAL WORKER FOR FIVE YEARS.'

It was a familiar story. A good character with no previous indiscretions and then, bang, out of the blue, several complaints from customers relating to non-delivery.

Ms Clarke's manager had apparently spoken to her and got the usual complete denial that the RMIB saw regularly in these cases.

But in the last day or so, further serious complaints had been received from the local hospital. Several patients living on this particular delivery route had missed important medical appointments due to their mail consistently failing to get through.

In Colin's experience, it was almost never down to coincidence when the trace-back indicated that the errors had occurred on the same postal worker's round. Particularly when it was a worker who had already been spoken to about her delivery inconsistencies.

Consequently, Head Office had requested the involvement of the Investigation Branch, known as the RMIB, and Colin's team had been notified.

The first stage of the official process had already been completed with the RMIB dispatching several dummy letters.

Colin referred to his notebook and saw that of the ten pieces of mail sent recently, the non-delivery rate had been just sixty per cent. An unacceptably low rate of delivery.

It was now Colin's job to gather the practical evidence required for the subsequent suspension, dismissal and likely prosecution of the employee.

Providing there was sufficient evidence, then the RMIB had the power to enter an employee's home to recover any stolen or undelivered mail: legally, it was the property of Her Majesty The Queen.

In Colin's experience, the postal workers overwhelmingly always seemed to think they'd get away with it. As if they somehow believed they'd be able to catch up and eventually deliver the mail. Or in the worst cases, destroy it.

His eye caught movement at the bottom of the hill. Colin put down the notebook and reached for his binoculars.

The familiar fluorescent colours and Royal Mail lettering came into focus on the cyclist's reflective jacket. When she turned her face towards the road, Colin grabbed his camera, zoomed in and snapped a few shots for the file to prove a positive ID.

As he worked, he wondered fleetingly what had happened to the undelivered mail in this case.

Would this one be a destroyer or a hoarder?

They were always one or the other and it was Colin's job to find out which category Anna Clarke belonged to.

CHAPTER 21
Anna

Next morning, the weather is nice and dry with not much wind, and I manage to get a good two thirds of the mail delivered.

I dump the remainder in my car boot for 'processing', which is how I've decided to refer to it from now on.

Back home, I check on Mrs Peat, feed Albert, have a little rest and I'm back outside the Busy Bee nursery at three fifteen. There is a flurry of parents picking up at three thirty and then it quietens down again.

At four o'clock, movement at the side door catches my eye. This time it's Amanda but she is not alone. A man follows her outside, and they stand talking for a moment.

He is wearing navy overalls with brown steel-capped boots and clutches a short plank of wood and a rusty toolbox. His dark hair looks dusty and unkempt.

He leans forward, says something to her and she smiles and nods, and then he goes back inside and closes the door behind him.

Amanda glances briefly up and down the street as she rummages through her handbag and then walks slowly down towards my car on the opposite side of the road. Her hair has been tied back more carefully today, and she walks with her head slightly down, pressing buttons on her mobile phone. She has on flat pumps and has bare, tanned legs even though it's quite cool outside.

I'd been so distracted when I bumped into her at the hospital, I'd not been able to take a good, long look at her but I can take my time today. As I suspected, there isn't a scratch on her: no sign that she has been through any sort of ordeal at all. No crutches, no bruises, nothing.

Life is carrying on perfectly normally for this woman yet again.

You can tell she thinks a lot of herself. It shows in the way she's done her hair, all smooth and lacquered. Diamanté slides hold the style firmly in place and tiny coloured stones glitter at her ears and throat.

Certainly, she looks better put together than the gaunt, supposedly guilt-ridden wreck who begged Liam's forgiveness at the hospital a couple of days ago.

I think about the flippant comments in her online message to Liam. She doesn't look like a woman crippled with remorse and grief to me. She isn't that embroiled in a pit of guilt that she has been unable to tart herself up and reel off texts the moment she finishes work.

She has no idea I'm here, watching her.

But one day, soon, she will again know exactly who I am.

A cramping sensation pinches at my chest as I watch her walk down the opposite side of the road, straight past my car.

I'm trying to make up my mind whether to get out and follow her on foot but then she slows down, pushes her phone back in her handbag and stands at the bus stop at the end of the road.

It must inconvenience her not having the car.

I didn't notice to what extent her vehicle had been damaged after the accident, but after my phone call to her workplace yesterday, it's safe to assume she's getting it repaired and will be back on the road in no time, putting more lives in danger.

I'm trying to second-guess where she might be headed. I don't want to follow her to find myself stuck outside the shopping centre for hours on end, but if she is going straight home it could be the ideal chance to see where she lives.

That's something I'm definitely going to need to know, and the glacial pace the police operate at, I'm far better to rely on my own resources.

I manage to follow the bus, leaving several cars in front of me. I drive slowly so that when it stops I can see exactly who is getting off.

She alights just around the corner from Rowland Street.

I spot her turn in to the road, and I drive past her, parking up about halfway down the road, giving me a clear view of all the houses.

I take out my new phone and press the key I've pre-programmed with her mobile number. I switch it to loudspeaker so I can leave it on my lap out of sight.

A shrill ring begins, and as she walks, I watch as her hand dips into her bag and she presses the phone to her ear.

'Hello.' The car fills with her deceitful tones. 'Hello?'

I close my eyes and stay silent.

'Hello?' Her tone is more impatient now but I don't say anything, I just want to check again that I have the right number. That everything is in place.

I end the call, feeling reassured with how well my plans are going.

There are plenty of parked cars in front and behind me and she walks straight past, dropping her phone back in her bag with not even a cursory glance in my direction.

Another hundred yards and she turns in to a driveway with a small caravan on it. She lives in a standard semi tucked away in a cul-de-sac on Rowland Street.

I give it a couple of minutes and then drive by slowly so I am able to note down the house number.

I happen to know that this address is on John Burtree's round, and he's off sick at the moment with gout. He's one of those people who takes time off periodically and always makes sure it is foot or leg related, so nobody can argue that he could still come into work.

They've probably got an agency worker covering the area.

The house itself looks neat enough. It looks distinctly middle-aged territory, if such a thing exists. Nets and a shabby wrought iron seat under the living room window.

This house looks too big and well established for her; perhaps she lives with her partner, although I did notice there was no ring on her hand.

I've already managed to expose one of the lies in her message to Liam:

'I've stopped going out, I just can't face people, even my friends.'

Clearly, she has not stopped going out. I've just followed her home from work; she hasn't even had the decency to take a couple of weeks off.

Equally, she has managed to summon enough confidence to stroll unannounced into the hospital and upset Liam while he is struggling to recover from the injuries she has inflicted.

He had to take her on face value because of his circumstances but, luckily, he has me to act as his eyes and ears, and I'm not fooled one iota.

I shudder to think what might have happened if I hadn't walked in to Liam's room when I did. He had already issued an ill-judged invitation for her to call round which, in itself, illustrates he isn't in his right mind.

Liam might not think he needs protecting, but I know better.

I wonder what her ulterior motive is? She has to have one, or she wouldn't be going to all this trouble to visit him in hospital and construct a tissue of lies via her online messages.

No doubt it will have something to do with avoiding paying him damages or trying to dodge trouble with the police by getting Liam on side.

I can't be sure what is in her mind. I only know that, without the opportunity to be alone with him, she will find it very difficult to manipulate him further.

After stopping off for provisions on the way home, I've barely bolted down my sardines on toast when it is time to leave for the hospital.

It takes another twenty minutes to get out of the house by the time I've done my rounds. My essential checks seem to be taking longer but I eventually finish them all and still manage to arrive at the hospital punctually.

When I get up to the ward, I bump into Maureen at reception.

'Thanks for supporting Liam and his gran.' She recognises me right away. 'I don't think Mrs Bradbury quite realises the implications of Liam's head injury on his aftercare, although the doctor has tried to explain the difficulties several times.'

Ivy hasn't mentioned a word of this to me. If the doctor had any sense he'd involve me in discussions, too.

'Difficult in what way?' I ask.

'The possibility of mood swings and the memory loss, both of which can be hard for family members to deal with. He appears to have stopped taking his earlier medication, so the doctor has said it is imperative he restarts those tablets as soon as possible.'

I blink at her.

'Anyway, I shouldn't really be discussing it with you but just so you're aware of some of the issues.' She gives me a tight smile and waddles off without another word.

I wonder what medication she is talking about. . . His pain-killers, perhaps?

Trying to help Liam and Ivy feels like working in the dark.

The nurses have packed up everything Liam is taking home and, in total, I make three trips from his hospital room to the car.

Despite her earlier protests to Maureen, Ivy now seems quite happy to let me do all the fetching and carrying.

I can't help wishing she would make herself scarce for a few minutes, though. Time and time again, I try to speak to Liam and Ivy interrupts.

I see Liam's eyes flicker with annoyance, so I know he feels the same way.

No matter how much Ivy insists she can manage at home, I'm going to have to stick around for Liam's sake.

When all the stuff is loaded into the boot and I've collected his hefty prescription from the hospital pharmacy, all three of us make our way down to the car.

Liam has instructions to use a wheelchair loaned from the hospital until his leg has been checked by Dr Khan in a week's time. Ivy is too weak to push him much of a distance; she can't manage more than a few steps without struggling for breath herself.

So I push a sleepy Liam uphill and downhill through the seemingly endless hospital corridors until we reach the lift. It takes twice as long because I have to keep slowing down and waiting for Ivy.

'I'll bring him back in for his check-up,' I say, while we wait for the overworked lift. 'There's no sense in dragging you through all this again.'

'It's the palpitations,' she gasps, leaning against the pale-green glossed wall. 'Once they stop, I'll be fine.'

Ivy is herself now under hospital observation. It turns out she has a weak heart which can be aggravated by stress.

It's painfully clear to everyone but her that she isn't going to be much good to Liam under the circumstances. Still, she remains infuriatingly stubborn about keeping super-active all the same.

When we get to the car, Liam wakes up briefly and insists on standing up and shuffling out of the wheelchair and into the car himself.

'What medication have you stopped taking?' I ask him as he struggles into the car.

'What?' Ivy grasps the headrest from her seat in the back and leans forward to listen.

'Maureen said you'd stopped taking your medication, Liam.' I address him again, ignoring the old woman. 'Surely not your painkillers?'

'I don't—'

'Oh, that.' Ivy sabotages our conversation yet again. 'Yes, one of the tablets they gave him made him feel sick but they've swapped it now.'

'We can go through all his medication at home, Ivy,' I say when I finally get myself installed in the driving seat. 'Just so it's clear in your mind what he has to take and when.'

'It's already sorted, Anna,' she says. 'We'll manage fine, but thank you.'

When we get to the house, Boris paces up and down the path.

'That poor cat,' Ivy sighs. 'He thinks we've deserted him.'

'I popped over here while you were in hospital,' I say, choosing my words carefully. 'I looked around for him but I didn't like to leave food outside in case it attracted rodents.'

'That was kind of you but I rang my neighbour, Beryl, and she fed him for me.'

I hope Beryl didn't spot the lights when I spent time inside the house on my fruitless search for the police business card.

If Ivy is eternally grateful that Beryl has fed the cat, you'd think she would be ecstatic that I am here to help her with Liam's return home and his subsequent appointments.

But of course there is no evidence of that.

She has zero gratitude and, for some inexplicable reason, seems to be spending all her available time turning down my many offers of help.

CHAPTER 22
Thirteen years earlier

Daniel Clarke's hands were sweating and he felt so tired he could just lay down his head and sleep for the rest of the day.

He wished he could run next door to Mrs Peat the way Anna did the moment she got home from school. But Mother didn't like Daniel out of her sight; she didn't trust him not to do something evil.

He had been sitting waiting quietly in his bedroom for just over half an hour when his mother shouted up to him.

Father MacCarrick had arrived at last, and John Peters, the seminarian he knew from church, was here too. Daniel listened to their muffled voices as he walked slowly downstairs.

There were some marks on the top of his arms, hidden by his school shirt, and his throat was really sore but he wasn't allowed to tell anyone.

Mother had set the table with china teacups and matching plates. She had bought six French fancies from the bakery around the corner and arranged them neatly on the white porcelain plate that had a faded gold trim tracing the edge.

There was a proper teapot complete with a strainer, and the milk wasn't in a carton. Mother had poured it into a small white jug with a tiny chip on the handle.

Pride of place in the middle of the table was her heaviest, beeswax-polished mahogany cross complete with an impressively detailed suffering Jesus.

'Daniel has been excited about your visit all week, Father,' his mother told the priest. 'He's nervous but very keen to make a good impression on you.'

Her voice sounded higher than usual, and she didn't drop any letters at the end of her words.

Daniel stood in the doorway and studied his feet. He could feel John Peters watching him.

'*There* you are,' his mother said in her strange voice.

'Hello Daniel,' said the priest.

'Hello Father.'

'Hello Daniel,' the seminarian said.

'Hello John.'

'Well, don't stand back there in the shadows now, lad,' Father MacCarrick chided in his soft Irish accent. 'Come and sit with us. Look at this fine fayre your mammy has put together in our honour.'

His mother giggled like a young girl and refolded the napkin at the side of her plate again. When she poured the tea, she talked to Father MacCarrick about the East Coast trip that was to take place during Holy Week.

John Peters pushed a whole French fancy into his mouth and, while Father MacCarrick and his mother were in conversation, he slyly showed Daniel the chewed up fondant mess on his tongue.

Daniel was given his tea in one of the ordinary chipped mugs.

'Now, will you have a cake, Daniel?' Father MacCarrick offered him the plate where one fancy remained. Daniel had been told to refuse the cakes, if asked.

'No thanks, Father,' he said, breathing in the sugar and imagining the sweet, smooth fondant melting on his tongue.

'I don't mind another if there's one going spare,' John said, snatching it from the plate.

'Remarkable restraint, Daniel,' Father MacCarrick said with approval. 'A good quality to have, wouldn't you say so, Mrs Clarke?'

'We do our best to discourage greed in this house, Father,' his mother agreed.

'Very admirable,' the priest murmured. 'And what other qualities does young Daniel think a good altar server might require?'

A static noise filled Daniel's head. He knew all the right answers but they were lost in his brain fog.

'Come on, lad, we won't bite.' Father MacCarrick winked at his mother and she smiled but Daniel saw that her face was tight and pale.

Silence.

John Peters pulled a face at him over the priest's shoulder.

At last, Father MacCarrick spoke again. 'John, could you help our man Daniel out here? We're wanting to know the qualities of an altar server.'

'Don't stumble, don't fall asleep, don't yawn and work as a team,' John rattled off. 'Keep yourself smart and upstanding at all times, Father.'

'Perfect. Thank you, John.' Father MacCarrick smiled. 'I'm guessing you knew all of those qualities, Daniel. Am I right?'

'Yes, Father.' Daniel nodded and tried not to look at his mother's cold, incisive stare.

'Now then, I wonder if you might avail us of the duties of a book-bearer? See Daniel, this is to be one of the prestigious duties of our new altar server at St Mary Magdalene.'

Mother had said earlier what an honour it would be to act as Father MacCarrick's book-bearer in church. She had told him exactly what duties a book-bearer should carry out for the priest, and she had tested him several times. But now his head was as empty as a licked-out cereal bowl.

'Daniel?' Father MacCarrick tapped his long, slim fingers on the table.

Daniel watched the priest's fingers and began to feel light-headed. A hot trickle of perspiration slid down his back and he shifted in his seat.

'Carry the book,' Daniel whispered.

'Carry the book indeed.' Father MacCarrick laughed quietly but there was a brittle edge to it. 'It's a little more than just "carrying the book" though, am I right?'

'Yes, Father,' Daniel said.

'He *does* know all the answers,' Daniel's mother pleaded. 'I made sure he knows all of it, Father.'

'John?' The priest turned to the seminarian.

'The book-bearer holds the book of prayer for the priest at the beginning and the end of service,' John recited. 'He must ensure the book of prayer is open at the correct page and hold it at such an angle as is easy for the priest to read from, Father.'

'Quite.' Father MacCarrick nodded gravely. 'Thank you, John.'

The priest stood, walked around the table and stopped directly behind Daniel, placing his hands on the boy's shoulders. He bent forward to speak quietly into Daniel's ear.

'You're a bright lad; we all know that so let's have another go. Can you tell me the duties of an acolyte, at all?'

Daniel felt the warm pressure of Father MacCarrick's hands on his shoulders, smelled the priest's slightly sour breath on the side of his face.

Daniel's hands began to shake and he couldn't make them stop, even when he pressed his fingers into his thighs.

'Daniel,' Monica Clarke said, 'tell Father MacCarrick the duties of an acolyte this minute.'

Daniel heard the threat loud and clear that hovered under her reasonable tone.

'C-candles,' Daniel stammered.

He wanted Father MacCarrick's hands off him, but when he shrugged his shoulders the priest dug his fingertips in harder.

'Carry candles in pairs at the beginning and the end of mass and also during the gospel,' John offered.

But as he continued to speak, John's monotone voice drifted further and further away, and Daniel watched his mother's face contorting and her mouth opening wide but he was unable to make sense of her words.

John smirked at him, and he felt the pressure of Father Mac-Carrick's fingertips digging into his collarbone and the warmth of the priest's body behind him. Suddenly it became too much.

Daniel vomited all over the table.

CHAPTER 23
Present day
Anna

I have started waking regularly in the early hours. In fact, it is rather more than simply waking up.

There is nothing gradual about it, no coming-around sensation. My eyes just snap open from the depths of deep sleep like I've been woken by a loud noise.

Each time it happens I freeze and listen but there's nothing but silence. There is absolutely no reason for me to be so suddenly wide awake with a pummelling heart and painfully dry throat.

It's as though part of me has flipped back to being that terrified young girl again. The rehashed and counselled Anna seems to be losing her grip just lately.

I don't want to leave any room for thinking about the past or even what might happen in the future.

This morning it happens at three thirty a.m. and I am scared to move.

Scared of what? I haven't got a clue and that just makes it worse. Perhaps it is the silence, the shadows.

I can't move a muscle; I can barely breathe. I lie there in a state of terror, absolutely certain that something terrible is going to happen but without any inkling what it could be.

I think this is what it must feel like to slowly go mad.

I have lived in this house all my life, long enough to know all its noises. . . all those inexplicable little creaks and taps that you hear in the dead of night if you lie quietly and listen. But that isn't the sort of thing that is fuelling my terror.

It's more of an awful sense of certainty that the world is going to come crashing in on me in some indistinguishable way. I don't know how or when it is going to happen, just that it most definitely will, and there isn't a damn thing I can do about it.

All those years ago, I grew a little stronger each day by constructing a life of routine for myself. I had to put my head back together first and that took a whole year in the muted surroundings of the carpeted clinic with its crisp lawns and neatly bordered gardens.

I got better very, very slowly.

Eventually, within a few years, I had a life that just about held itself together.

I made sense of time mainly by doing certain things at certain times of the day. Nothing unexpected, nothing unusual. Just nice, reliable and simple tasks to drape each day around.

And when I was ready, the job really helped. My social worker had a contact at the Royal Mail and helped me apply. It was something else to hold on to: one of the few things I was good at and could take a pride in.

Now, it feels increasingly like there is nothing solid under my feet to keep me steady.

Once daylight floods the room and I am properly awake, the feeling slowly fades. By mid-morning, my heartbeat is normal and I'm not scared any more, just a bit bruised inside.

Still, after my shift I take myself down to Sneinton Medical Centre and join the seemingly never-ending sit-and-wait queue for those patients without an appointment.

For forty-seven minutes I sit there amongst the usual gathering of sneezers, coughers and squawking kids until, finally, it is my turn.

It isn't easy to open up to a stranger, but I manage to convey my disturbed sleep pattern to the peripatetic doctor. I try to describe how I often feel afraid for no reason.

'Anxiety,' he says simply and scribbles me a prescription.

I am to try the sedatives to help me sleep, he says, and if things don't improve he will prescribe something else, specifically for the condition. Happy pills, I've heard them called.

After seeing the doctor, I take myself off home.

I don't go to see Liam, and I don't take this morning's bag of undelivered mail out of the boot.

I take a sedative and I take myself off to bed.

I sleep straight through until the next morning when I snap awake at just gone three a.m.

I lie still, watching, as the red digits count me through to nearly four. Finally, I muster the courage to push myself up into a seated position.

My lower back is wet with perspiration, and when I unclench my fingers, my palms are clammy and tangled up with my own hair.

The thin curtains allow the street lights to illuminate the room with an eerie orange glow that seems to magnify my dread. I can see Albert's dark, curled form lying at the bottom of the bed, undisturbed by my movements.

I sit up and a dull ache creeps slowly up the back of my skull.

If I don't take some migraine tablets now, I know the ache will develop into a fullblown tension headache that could take days to go. Yet something stops me moving, and I feel flushed and uncomfortable despite there being no heating on.

I throw off the quilt and sit with my legs bent up to my chest, my arms wrapped around them. Resting my forehead on top of my knees, I rock gently.

Perhaps Liam is awake, too. The doctor gave him sedatives but said that sometimes the pain could be bad enough to still wake him up. Ivy also takes sedatives at night to help her relax and calm her heart down.

I wonder what might happen if Liam needs help and Ivy is in a drugged stupor, unable to raise the alarm. If it wasn't for the old woman's stubbornness, I would stay over with them and there wouldn't be a problem.

Should the worst-case scenario happen, I mean.

The hospital could have insisted on suitable home arrangements. They could have advised Ivy to let me stay over to help sort things out, at least for a few days.

To be fair, Ivy seems more grateful now that I am helping out with the daytoday tasks but she still fails to recognise there is a need for me to play a full part in their lives.

I'm tired of just being the woman who held Liam's hand in the road. I want to show him that I am a *real* friend. Someone he can trust and depend on, I mean. I could never hope that a man like Liam would ever be interested romantically in somebody like me.

I glance at the neon numbers on my bedside table. Just gone four a.m.

I become aware of pain in my jaw and realise that I'm grinding my back teeth together. It reminds me of the long weeks that drifted into long months after Danny died.

I wiggle my bottom jaw a little to free it up but I don't feel any better.

I think about how I am being really careful not to take any more time off work, so no one gets the opportunity to meddle with my round, but over the last couple of days I think I have probably delivered even less mail than usual.

It's really important that I don't draw attention to myself, give them reasons to look more closely at me at work.

Liam coming home from hospital was a distraction but he is depending on me to be there for him, and I plan to go over there this afternoon, when my shift is finished.

* * *

Later, when I am driving to work I decide on a new, more effective plan of action.

Instead of delivering the new mail each day, I'm going to refill the bags with the older mail that's been stacked upstairs. Then I'll deliver *that* mail.

That way I can be sure of falling only a few days behind at any one point, instead of the upstairs mail getting older each day.

When I get to the office, I head straight for my stretch of the mail counter.

'Morning, Anna,' Roisin sings as I pass her.

'Morning,' I say, slowing my pace a bit. 'How are you?'

'Oh you know, bored. Tired. The usual.'

I nod. 'I'm not sleeping very well,' I say and then clamp my mouth shut before I reveal more than I intended.

'I know the feeling; it's too much tea,' Roisin agrees. 'I get up to use the bathroom and then I lie awake for hours trying to get back to sleep.

'Don't forget that coffee,' she says as I walk away. 'Let me know when you want to meet up.'

I nod and smile and move away as quickly as I can without appearing rude. It would be a relief to have someone to talk to about my work problem. Someone who could help.

I pack up my mail bags quickly, not worrying about sorting the mail in order of streets. That detail ceases to matter when it is destined straight for the box-room mountain.

I've almost reached the exit doors when Jim Crowe appears and plants himself in my path.

'Morning, Anna.'

I swallow hard, and a ring of heat begins its crawl from the base of my neck.

Jim peers down at the bags I'm carrying.

'How are you getting on.' He pulls himself up to his full looming height. 'With the round?'

'Fine,' I say quickly. 'No problems, Jim.'

'You sure?' He lowers his voice and grins at me. 'You've only to say and we can split the round down for you.'

I don't want less hours or massive change. I don't want to let the people on the estate down.

Admittedly, I haven't been able to see most of my customers for a while because of my circumstances but that will all change once I put my new delivery schedule into action.

I shrug and keep my shoulders relaxed. 'Everything is fine.'

He flashes me a toothy grin and pats my shoulder as he strides past me into the main sorting area.

'That's what I like to hear,' he booms. 'Happy staff.'

I scuttle out of the doors, sweating under the weight of the filled pannier bags. I drag them over to the bike shed and drop them when I am out of sight and leaning against the shed wall.

The fine drizzle and dank air do nothing to alleviate my fuzzy head and pounding chest. Then a thick knot of panic pushes its way up from my stomach.

Deep breaths. Take some deep breaths.

I stand for a moment or two, looking at the bulging mail bags at my feet and thinking about the spare room back at the house.

The wall I'm leaning on feels soft and springy against my hand.

The scene of the accident snaps through my mind in short, jagged flashes. Liam's face, glass fragments on the road, a seeping ruby pool spreading out from his broken head.

I stand for a moment until the shed wall feels solid again.

But the sickly feeling won't go away.

When I get back to the house, I dump the mail bags just inside the back door and collapse down into one of the dining chairs in the middle room. I am too exhausted to go out delivering some of the backlog now.

I promise myself I will make up for it tomorrow. I will work really hard and deliver double the amount of mail.

Tomorrow, I will make a fresh, clean start.

CHAPTER 24

Later that afternoon after taking a rest, I drive over to see Liam.

I tap on the back door and walk straight in to find Ivy cleaning the oven. She never seems to sit still and relax despite the discomfort it obviously causes her. And she obviously isn't taking a blind bit of notice of the doctors telling her to rest after her recent funny turn at Liam's bedside.

'Hello, Anna,' she groans as she bends to spray cleaning fluid on the spattered oven-door glass. 'I'll make us a cuppa in a minute.'

I glance around the cluttered worktop.

'Did you come across that business card,' I ask. 'The one the policeman left you?'

'What? Oh no, it's around here somewhere though,' she says vaguely, straightening up and pressing her hand to her lower back, grimacing. 'You said you wouldn't mind doing me a couple of little jobs, so if you could carry that stack of towels upstairs and then—'

I zone out the remainder of the rather long 'little jobs' list she has saved up for me. I wait until she takes a breath before I speak.

'I've got a suitcase in the boot, Ivy,' I say lightly. 'Just a few clothes and essentials in there; enough to tide me over for the next few days or so.'

'Oh, are you going away somewhere?' She doesn't look up from her cleaning.

She's putting on a good show pretending she isn't fussed, but I know she'll be panicking inside at the thought of me not being around.

'Don't worry, I'm not going anywhere. Quite the opposite, in fact. I'm going to stay here at the house for a while, to give you a hand looking after Liam.'

Her head jerks up from the oven door, her eyes and mouth wide.

'Oh no, you can't possibly do that.' She takes in a sharp breath. 'I mean, you have your own life, your cat. . . and there's your work too, love. I wouldn't dream of imposing on you like that. Me and Liam will cope fine but thanks so much for offering, Anna, I'm touched.'

'I'll not take no for an answer, Ivy.' I keep my voice level. 'Liam and I have been worried about your health and the fact you're taking too much on. I can pop home when I need to, and I can go to work from here, it's no trouble, I—'

'The answer is *no*, Anna. It's just silly; a few days ago we didn't even know each other.' That comment stings and she sees it but she doesn't backtrack or apologise. 'It really isn't necessary and, besides, there's no spare bed for you to sleep in.'

I don't move.

I'm good enough to save Liam's life in the road but not good enough to be embraced in their home as a trusted friend. Unbelievable.

Ivy goes back to her cleaning, and a wave of heat rises from my abdomen up into my chest. I'm done kowtowing to Ivy Bradbury but my connection to Liam is key in keeping tabs on Amanda Danson. I will have to find another way in.

I walk out of the kitchen and into the lounge without speaking to her again.

I won't mention this exchange with Ivy or my work worries to Liam. He'll hardly want to be bothered by my problems when he has enough of his own.

His head is bent forward while he studies something on his knee so intently he doesn't even notice I'm standing there at first.

'Anything interesting?'

Liam visibly jumps and presses his hand to his chest. It's strange to see him in a T-shirt and tracksuit instead of his hospital robe. 'You frightened the life out of me, Anna.'

'How are you feeling?' I grin.

'A bit better today,' he says, standing up to prove it. 'Look.'

'I don't think you're supposed to be standing on that leg yet,' I chide him. 'You should rest it, like they told you to.'

'Everyone fusses too much,' Liam grumbles. He sits back down and sweeps his fringe out of his eyes just like Danny used to do. He needs a good haircut so he looks more like a man and not a boy. It's almost as though Ivy has kept him in a boyhood time warp since he came to live with her. 'My leg will be good as new in a week or two. It's this constant headache that is driving me crazy.'

'Are you taking your medication?' I ask him.

'Huh?'

His fingers start to dig into the seat cushion.

'They said at the hospital you'd stopped taking it and that you must start again,' I say. 'I just wondered, with you saying you had a head—'

'I'm taking it.' Liam stood up again. 'Why is everyone going on at me all the time? I mean why can't you all just fucking leave me alone?'

My heart drops like a stone, and I stare at him wide-eyed. I have never heard him swear before.

He starts limping across the room, shaking his arms as if he's trying to rid himself of something nasty that's crawling over him.

'Liam, I didn't mean to upset you.' I walk towards him but he turns his back and limps the other way.

'Blah, blah, blah. Yak, yak, yak.'

'Liam, seriously I think you should sit—'

'QUIET!' he yells and spins round to face me.

My whole body goes cold. He stands stock still and staring, and I take a couple of steps back.

'What on earth's happening in here?' Ivy appears at the door holding a glass of milk. She looks at us in turn as if she's trying to work out what's happening between us. 'Liam, sit down. Come on, everything's fine here, nothing to worry about.'

Ivy hobbles into the room and stands in front of Liam, pointing to his wheelchair. He seems to deflate in front of her and limps meekly back.

Ivy places the glass of milk on the coffee table, fusses around him a bit then turns to me.

'It's the mood swings that's all; they warned me this might happen.' She narrows her eyes, trying to get her breath. 'You shouldn't have got him upset, Anna.'

I open my mouth to defend myself but don't bother in the end. I don't have to justify myself to Ivy.

Liam flips over a piece of paper he is holding on his knee. It is a handwritten letter which he holds up to me. I frown when I catch the name signed at the bottom.

'It's from Amanda; she's written me a note to apologise,' he says, seemingly his normal self again. 'She said she sent me a message on Facebook but I never got that.'

I notice the computer then, behind his chair.

'Great, isn't it?' He grins. 'Beryl's son set it up for me down here.'

Thanks to Beryl's interfering son, Liam is now free to reply to Amanda Danson's messages all day long if he wants to.

I stare at Liam's pale face and weak arms. Despite being so upset a few minutes ago, he is now smiling and gazing happily at the note in his hand.

'How did you get that letter, Liam?' I keep my voice steady.

'Amanda brought it round to the house this morning,' Ivy cuts over me. 'She wouldn't come in. She was mindful that Liam gets his rest but she's calling round here again tomorrow.'

Liam won't meet my eyes.

I am struggling to process Ivy's stupidity.

Amanda Danson is trying to wriggle her way out of blame for causing the accident and this weak, stupid old woman is making it very easy for her.

'How did she get your address?'

'I gave it to her,' Liam says without looking up.

'You remembered where you live?' I ask.

'No.' He is silent for a few moments while he takes time to stretch his neck over to one side then the other. 'I found it on my copy GP letter the day Amanda came to visit me in hospital.'

I look straight at Ivy; my tongue feels all knotted up with so many things I want to say. But I speak before I think and choose my words carefully.

'How is he ever going to recover from this if she is bothering him every five minutes?'

'I don't know why you're so paranoid about Amanda.' Ivy turns to tidy a stack of magazines but her trembling hands make the task almost impossible. 'It's really not for you to worry about who visits us and who doesn't, Anna.'

The subtext is fairly easy to translate: 'Mind your own business.'

'You didn't even know each other a few days ago.' I can't resist throwing her own rude words back at her.

'It was a terrible accident for everyone involved but that's just what it was, an accident. She's suffering too, Anna.'

'She's not suffering like Liam though, is she?' I hear my voice rise up an octave and see the look on their faces but I can't seem to calm down. 'Why can't anybody but me see through her lies?'

I'm struggling to get my breath.

Liam and Ivy glance at each other but I don't care. How can Ivy be so gullible?

I snatch the letter from Liam's hands, and in the process, I catch his glass of milk and send it flying. It cracks on the edge of the coffee table.

Now the letter is torn, the glass is broken and there is milk everywhere.

Ivy shrieks and, without thinking, I snatch at a jagged piece of glass and a sharp pain prickles my hand. I unclench my fingers and let the glass fall to the floor.

'What on earth were you thinking?' Ivy shakes her head. 'I'll get you a bandage.'

'I'm fine,' I mumble, reaching into my pocket for a tissue to soak up the blood on my palm. 'I just called in to see how Liam was but I have to get back now. I have things to do.'

I hurry out through the kitchen door and run to my car, squeezing hard on my throbbing hand.

An hour later, I'm sitting in the car with my notebook and camera, watching Amanda Danson's house. It is time to refocus on what really matters.

The police told Ivy they would interview Liam at some point when he is feeling better. It is highly likely they will prosecute Amanda Danson for dangerous driving, and Liam's evidence will be key.

She will be perfectly aware of this, of course, cue her impromptu visits to Liam.

Ivy seems in no rush to enquire at what point they were at in their investigations and appears to have mislaid the officer's business card.

It's all happening again but nobody realises. Nobody but me.

I can't just stand back and watch Liam be destroyed and yet, the awful possibility is that if she starts visiting him regularly, she'll soon know him better than I do. And then there is a risk that I will find myself pushed out of Liam's life altogether and my plans scuppered.

Amanda has got a confident manner that encourages people to open up to her. I suppose it's the training from her previous job.

Some people might say she is attractive, although I can't see anything at all pleasant when I look at her. I hope Liam has more about him than to fall for anything as superficial as looks but women like her know how to get round men. They know what makes them tick.

It is misguided and foolish of Ivy to encourage their friend-ship, and she is bound to regret it. I can envisage the day she will come crying to me when it all goes wrong, expecting me to comfort her, but there will be nothing I can do about it at that late stage.

This nonsense has to be stopped right now.

Someone has to hit Amanda Danson where it hurts but it is vital I keep the past to myself. For now.

It is nearly five o'clock: the exact time Amanda got off the bus and walked home when I followed her from work the first time. Today, there is no sign of her.

Doubtless she will be out having fun with her friends or shop-ping for clothes and make-up.

I am just debating whether to sit here for a bit longer or go home when the front door of her house opens. A woman in her late fifties appears: petite, with hair that has been dyed too dark for her pale complexion. Still, the resemblance to Amanda is striking.

I watch as the older woman walks down the short driveway. She is heading for a small red Clio that is parked on the road and, as she turns from latching the small gate, her coat flaps open.

I have spent enough time at the hospital recently to recognise that uniform. She must be a nurse at the QMC.

I scour my memory for the faces of the nurses I've seen on Liam's ward and feel satisfied she isn't one of them but it's starting to become much clearer as to why her daughter had been able to stroll into Liam's private room unchallenged.

The red Clio pulls away from the kerb, and I start my own car, giving it a few moments to put some space between us and then pulling out behind her.

Ten minutes later, the Clio pulls into a parking space in the large rear car park of the hospital that serves both staff and the general public. I park up two rows behind and watch as she pops a permit in the window and heads for the main doors.

To get a ticket from the machine, I risk losing her so I slide yesterday's ticket on my dashboard and hope for the best.

I stay well behind her, and by the time she reaches the automatic reception doors, there is an elderly couple between us, also heading for the main entrance. She doesn't turn left for the main wards, as I expect, but turns sharp right and disappears through doors marked 'Accident and Emergency'.

When I see the sign, my head starts to pound as I remember but I don't slow down; I follow her straight through into the bustling reception area of the A&E department.

I try my best to ignore the sour lump that has lodged itself firmly in my throat. My head is pounding and fuzzy, trying to force the memories back again.

Not now. Please don't let me faint now.

Spotting the woman at the end of the corridor sharpens my senses again. She has taken off her coat and now carries a clipboard and a stack of record cards. She walks a short distance then disappears through a door on the left.

I walk up to the door past a line of sickly looking individuals with a variety of obvious ailments such as busted noses, bandaged hands and black eyes.

The sign on the door reads, 'Triage Nurse'. Underneath it is a name plaque: 'Nurse Emma Danson'. As I suspected, she is Amanda's mother.

An idea jumps into my head that is far too good an opportunity to miss.

CHAPTER 25
Joan Peat

Joan had the distinct feeling that all wasn't well with Anna next door.

Just little clues, things that didn't quite add up. There were the noises in the early hours; Anna pacing around long before it was time for her to go to work.

Then the other day, off she went to work just before five a.m., as usual. Joan had enjoyed her first cup of tea and was back in the kitchen about to butter a slice of toast when she heard Anna's car pull up again out the front.

She had scuttled back into the middle room at a breakneck pace, surprised herself how fast she could still move if she needed to.

But Anna hadn't tapped on the window or popped in. She'd just gone straight back into her house, and there had been silence from next door for the rest of the morning. It was tiresome because Joan had been limited to what she could do before Linda, her care assistant, arrived at twelve thirty. She couldn't risk Anna hearing her moving around.

Joan tried to think why she'd returned so quickly. Perhaps Anna had felt unwell when she got to work.

But those sorts of sounds in the early hours hinted at troubled thoughts. Joan had seen it all before when Anna had first been discharged from the hospital.

Her neighbour had turned into a creature of habit but it hadn't always been that way.

Young Anna loved to have a go at new things. Arthur would often bring her back the odd toy from one of the factory's production lines.

Just before she started school, he tried to guide her into experimenting with new things. He always said he'd been given the stuff at work, but once or twice Joan had found receipts when he'd chosen something in particular he thought Anna would like. He wouldn't have liked her thinking he was soft.

But it was when he came back one day with a large sketchpad and a long tin of slender pastels that the real revelation came.

Anna's eyes turned wide as saucers and, within moments, her fat little fingers were in the tin, grasping at the pretty colours.

'Careful now,' Arthur said, pulling the tin out of her reach. 'Nice things are worth looking after.'

When he pushed the tin closer again, Anna chose one carefully and looked around for something to sketch.

'Let's see if you can draw Mrs Peat.' He winked at Joan. 'Do you think you can do a nice big conk and two sticky-out ears?'

Joan had punched her hands onto her hips in mock fury as the two of them laughed.

When Anna started scribbling, Arthur went back to his paper and Joan picked up her knitting.

She kept glancing over and smiling at Anna, loving the way her eyes never left her face apart from to keep glancing down at the grainy white paper.

Anna selected new colours, always replacing the last one carefully as Arthur had shown her.

'Let's have a look then,' Arthur said at last, folding up his paper. 'Let's see if you've made Mrs Peat's ears big enough.'

Anna chuckled and handed him the pad.

His mouth dropped open, and Joan jumped out of her seat to see.

It was a portrait of her, alright. Detailed and wonderful.

That's when they realised that Anna could draw.

CHAPTER 26
Present day
Anna

I walk out of A&E and back down the corridor.

A few minutes later I arrive at the hospital café. I pay for a latte and sit down at a table in the far corner, where I can see all the customers. It isn't terribly busy, which serves my purpose well.

Outside the window people gather in a small group smoking, including a couple of the porters. You would think they'd have more sense working in a place like this, witnessing all that disease and misery. But there they all are, puffing furiously at their cancer sticks, one after the other.

Sometimes, there seems to be no justice at all in the world. Here are people who don't give a toss about their health, able-bodied and getting on with their lives, while Liam is stuck in the house and struggling to recover from his ordeal. All caused through no fault of his own.

I feel a biting heat in my guts, like red-hot coals are trying to expand in a space that is too small. I need to calm down and think about something else; the last thing I want is to draw attention to myself.

A bored-looking waitress comes over with a tray, picking up used crockery. She gives the table a cursory wipe without meeting my eyes. I watch her shuffle around the other tables, then make her way over to a long counter, next to the toilets.

I take a last sip of my coffee and stroll over to the toilet. Nobody so much as glances my way, and I am reminded that I'm in a hospital, surrounded by people either deep in worried conversation or staring into open space, not quite present.

The only eyes that meet mine are beautiful, honest pools of melted chocolate belonging to a guide dog that sits obediently next to its blind owner.

I get to the bathroom door and pick up a small glass as I walk past the counter that houses the dirty crockery. I slip it into my handbag and carry on walking.

Inside the toilets, I fish out a pair of nail scissors from the bottom of my bag and cut a flannel-size strip of white, absorbent cloth from the taut fabric of the hand towel machine.

I listen for a few seconds and, when I'm satisfied nobody is about to walk in, I drop the glass on to the hard floor from a height where I can be fairly certain it will break into several pieces but not shatter into smithereens.

I pick up a shard of glass that looks the sharpest and shunt the remaining pieces into a corner out of the way in case the woman in the café brings her guide dog in. Albert once came home with a very nasty cut on his paw that the vet said was almost certainly from a discarded broken bottle. The selfishness of some people is staggering.

I lock the cubicle door and inspect my palm. The earlier cut from the glass incident at Liam's house is very shallow and little more than a deep scrape, although my hand had looked in a bad state at the time because of the blood.

I trace the already fading lines with the tip of the glass, looking for the weakest area, then I clamp my teeth together and dig the broken glass in, raking it back along the earlier cut as hard as I can.

I steel myself but the pain still surprises me. The glass is like white-hot wire slicing easily through my palm.

I want to roar like a wounded animal, but I set my lips in a straight line and bite down hard on my tongue, closing my palm around the razor-sharp piece of glass. I grip it with my other hand and force the cutting edge deeper into my flesh.

Finally, I release my hand, take a few deep breaths and inspect my injury, feeling a bit light-headed when I see the mess.

Blood trickles down my hand, some bits already clotting like lumps of red gravy in the areas of the deepest cuts. I'm worried I've gone a bit too far.

A smell like boiled cabbage emanates from the café, seeping through the outer door into the toilet. I fight the unpleasant thickness that hits the back of my throat and wrap the piece of cloth tightly around my hand.

I tear off some loo roll and wipe up the blood from the toilet seat and floor with my good hand, then leave the bathroom, feeling a bit disconnected but nevertheless triumphant, my bandaged hand concealed behind my handbag.

Five minutes later, I am walking through the doors of A&E again.

Blood soaks through the white cloth on my cut hand, and I see one or two people glance at it with a curious concern.

When I reach the registration desk, a plump middle-aged woman wearing too much make-up pushes a form and pen on a clipboard across the counter.

'Fill this in, please,' she says briskly without looking at me.

Fortunately, it is my left hand I've damaged, so I manage to fill in the personal details without too much bother. Not that she's noticed.

'You'll need to see the triage nurse first.' She indicates the door Amanda's mum disappeared through earlier. 'Take a seat over there, please.'

I sit down on the next available plastic chair in the row outside the triage room. There are four other people to go before me.

My hand is throbbing hard now; I'm seriously beginning to fret I've cut too deeply.

'Looks nasty,' says the ripe-smelling, whiskered man who is wedged into the chair next to me. The chairs are spaced out fairly well but his shoulder still touches mine.

Some people assume a shared situation authorises them to be immediately familiar. I throw him a withering look and make a point of focusing on a poster about immunisation on the opposite wall. He doesn't say anything else.

The door opens and Emma Danson pops her head out. Glancing down at the form in her hand, she calls out, 'Tristan Peters?'

The young man on the first chair makes a big deal of clutching his elbow as he follows her into the room. Everyone moves down one chair, but I stay put. The whiskered man looks at me as if to say something, then changes his mind and studies his swollen foot which is encased in a grubby, striped slipper.

I've got a corker of a headache coming. My hand is pounding with an aching throb, and the vivid red blossom is expanding rapidly across the white cloth bandaging my wounds.

The sleeves of my jacket feel bonded to my arms. I pull at the cuffs in an effort to relieve the stickiness but to no avail. Why they have to keep these places bathed in a constant, near-tropical heat when the NHS evidently lacks funding is anyone's guess.

A full twenty-five minutes later, the man next to me limps into the room and four other people have joined the queue after me.

Sweat beads prickle on my upper lip. The ferocious pain in my head and hand seem to join up, until the whole of the left side of my body burns and aches.

I try to swallow but the dryness of my throat refuses to give and I splutter, coughing and groaning. My handbag slips, and I grab at it with my injured hand, sending stabbing, shooting pains all the way up my arm.

I yelp out in pain. The people sitting next to me all lean forward to watch the spectacle, and I want to scream at them to mind their own business.

Why am I even here? I have the most idiotic ideas at times, and yet I know I can't waste the chance to spend some time with Amanda's mother, to find out anything I can that might help me, might help Liam to prosecute her.

I get to thinking about my hand and what might happen if the wounds are so deep they can't be stitched. I pray I haven't severed a tendon because I could lose the use of my fingers, and whoever heard of a postal worker being employed who only had the use of one hand?

Thinking about my job drums up images of the spare room and the mail piling up. A fresh wave of heat and nausea starts up. I fan myself with my good hand and glare back at the woman next to me who is shamelessly studying the bloodied cloth.

After what seems like forever, the door opens and the man limps out and back down the corridor.

'Anna Clarke?'

I ease myself out of the hard plastic chair, grimacing, as my hand catches on my bag again.

I don't know why they have to say your full name out loud at these places; you never know who might be listening, nosing into your business. At one time, 'Miss Clarke' would have been sufficient but a formal courtesy is all but non-existent these days.

'Come on through, Anna,' Emma Danson says in a patronising sing-song voice I've noticed some of the other nurses have a habit of using with the patients.

The room is small but efficiently organised, with a pristine white-sheeted couch and various medical implements displayed on a table alongside.

Emma sits at her desk, and I take my cue to sit on the patient chair at the side.

'Looks like you've made a bit of a mess there.' She nods at my hand and turns her attention to the computer screen.

She is a small sparrow-like woman with the same black darting eyes as her daughter. I get the impression she's the kind of person who likes to go through the polite motions of conversation but isn't really interested what people are actually saying to her.

'I cut myself,' I say faintly, looking down at my hand.

'Very careless,' she scolds in a jolly voice. 'Let's have a look at you, then.'

She shuffles her chair closer and peels away the cloth bandage. I yelp as she tugs gently at a piece that has become quite firmly attached to the drying blood.

Close-up, I can see deep creases fanning out from the corners of her eyes and mouth. There are shadows under her eyes that she has attempted to cover up with a thick concealer, and her hair is overdue for a colour, judging by the fine grey wisps that speckle her temples.

I'm finding it increasingly difficult to move my fingers. The pain is steadily building as she presses on different parts of my hand, and her perfume is sickly sweet.

'I think I'm going to be sick,' I croak.

She grabs a kidney-shaped cardboard container from the edge of her desk, and I vomit into it.

CHAPTER 27

I reach for a tissue from my bag.

'Sorry,' I mumble, feeling another wave of heat ripple through me.

For the first time, she actually seems to focus and look at me properly.

'Let's get this jacket off.' She pulls at my sleeve. 'You're over-heating.'

She folds my jacket and places it behind us on the medical couch. Then she fills a small plastic tumbler with water from the small sink.

'Your hand looks nasty but it's really not that bad,' she says.

I sigh with relief and take a sip of the water. No severed tendons after all then.

Time to get back to the reason I came here.

She stands up and walks over to the table. 'You seem very anxious, Anna. How did you say you cut your hand?'

'I was clearing up some glass in my kitchen,' I tell her. 'I picked it up with my hands; I wasn't thinking. I've had a lot on my mind, you see.'

Emma returns with some wipes and bandages and sits down opposite me. 'Well, that's usually how these things happen.'

'My boyfriend has been in a very bad car accident,' I say. 'He was nearly killed.'

I'm surprised how easily the word 'boyfriend' trips off my tongue.

She stops fiddling with the pack of wipes and looks up at me.

'I'm sorry to hear that. Is your boyfriend here at the QMC?'

I shake my head.

'He's home now but he's very ill. There's not a single scratch on the driver that hit him.'

Emma starts to dab at my hand none too gently, causing me to gasp.

'Sorry,' she says but continues in the same firm manner.

'It doesn't seem fair,' I go on. 'Him in such a bad way, and the other driver free to carry on as if nothing has happened.'

Her mouth sets in a straight line and she blinks rapidly. When she looks up from my hand, I think I see a teary brightness.

'People seem to forget it can affect the other driver too.'

Like your fake-it daughter? Feigning guilt to Liam in her online message?

My heart is hammering and my hand is stinging terribly but I carry on. I've gone through this much pain, I might as well make it count.

'You sound as though you've been there,' I comment.

Emma sighs and puts down the wipes. She folds her hands into her lap and looks straight at me.

'It's usually a rule of mine not to discuss my personal life with patients,' she says. 'But, if it helps, my daughter was involved in an accident just over a week ago. So you see, I do understand.'

Involved in an accident? She caused the whole fucking thing!

'Is she badly hurt?'

Emma picks up the wipes again and shakes her head, sighing deeply.

'Not physically but mentally, yes. I worry she might never drive again. She feels like it was her fault, you see. She went to see the man she hit and says he's such a nice chap but she can't forgive herself.'

I can't think of anything to say without risk of blowing my cover, so I keep quiet.

'She isn't sleeping,' she sighs. 'It's not easy. An accident affects everyone in different ways and people don't always think about that.'

She means people like me.

Emma pours some liquid on to a piece of cotton wool and the stringent smell of pure alcohol fills the air.

I suck a breath in sharply between my teeth as she applies it to my palm. The sting feels like she is slicing my hand up all over again.

'Nearly finished,' she murmurs, dabbing at my wounds.

'Is your daughter in trouble with the police over the accident?' I ask.

Her face darkens. 'We're praying not but we just don't know yet; they're still investigating.'

Her tone has changed, become more formal, and I know she won't say much more about it.

'Prosecution or not, I guess your daughter will have to live with what she's done for the rest of her life,' I say.

She looks up at me.

'Strangely enough, it's as though the accident has brought them together,' she says. 'Her and the man she hit, I mean. He's been unbelievably forgiving.'

'Really?' My voice sounds reedy and thin.

Emma nods and smiles, unfurling the bandage.

'She's visiting him regularly now he's home; they're getting to know each other. Who'd have thought any good could have come from it all?'

I stand up, knocking over the bottle of antiseptic.

'Wait! I'm not finished yet.'

'It doesn't matter,' I say vaguely, grabbing my jacket and heading for the door.

'Your hand—'

I don't hear the rest. I storm out of the room and down the corridor.

I've got what I came here for: confirmation of Amanda's scheme to fool Liam into feeling sorry for her so he'll tell the police not to prosecute her. It's so obvious and yet both Ivy and Liam just don't get it.

What was she hiding? If the accident had been just that – an accident – surely she'd have no need to cover anything up.

Out in the car I swallow down two ibuprofens with bottled water and do my breathing exercises for a few minutes.

After that I Google a few things and then I make a phone call. When it is done I feel so much better.

Now I can enjoy the rest of my day.

The next morning at work, I volunteer to distribute the junk mail – the advertisement flyers that businesses pay us to deliver with the general mail – to everyone's workstations.

I meander over to the workstations, take out a wedge of flyers and glance around. Nobody is paying the slightest bit of attention to me, so it's easy to quickly rifle through the pigeonhole that contains Rowland Street's mail.

It takes longer because I'm trying to just use my good hand but nobody has noticed that. Until Roisin walks past.

'Anna! What happened to your hand?'

I snatch my hand out of the pigeonhole and spin around.

'I broke a glass,' I say. 'In the kitchen.'

I wonder if she's noticed I was looking through someone else's mail allocations.

'You OK, love?' She won't stop staring at me. I realise my eyes are open a touch too wide, and I've sort of frozen my arm in mid-air. I blink and shake my arm, letting it fall to my side.

'That's better, got a bit of cramp,' I say. 'Catch you later, Roisin.'

'Fancy a coffee after your shift?' she asks me yet again.

I take a breath and hear myself say: 'Yes, OK then. Where do you want to meet?'

Her face lights up, and I feel bad it's taken me so long to accept her offer to meet up. We arrange the time and place, and I can't help smiling as I walk away. This is a bit of a landmark for me.

I feel her eyes on my back, and I know she's probably thinking I'm a bit strange.

I slip out two official-looking envelopes for number 42 that I managed to slide in between my flyers before Roisin appeared. After a cursory check that she's not still watching me, I move over to the counter where Liam and Ivy's mail is processed.

Nothing of interest there, just an electricity bill, and a motorcycle magazine which I immediately bin. There's enough clutter as it is in that bedroom of his.

When I return to my own workstation, I fold the smuggled letters up and slip them into my trouser pocket. My mood brightens with the anticipation of reading them later.

I have a fairly good morning considering the challenges of my new delivery plan. I load up the mailbags, cycle home, dump the contents upstairs and refill the bags with the oldest mail I can find amongst the ever-growing mountain in the spare bedroom.

I cycle back and manage to deliver over three quarters of it, spilling over my shift time by just an hour.

I have the strangest feeling I'm being watched, but there's nobody around when I scan the street. It must be because Roisin was staring at me earlier.

My injured hand is sore and throbbing but I don't feel sick or hot anymore so I can just about manage to do my job, even though it slows me down.

The weather is fine for a change. The sun makes repeated attempts to break through the clouds and a pleasant breeze fans my efforts. The plan to get on a level footing with my deliveries is going to work, I'm convinced of it. I have proved today that it can be done.

I get to the coffee shop a few minutes early, and Roisin is already here. She smiles and waves me over.

'I got you a caramel cappuccino,' she beams. 'Hope that's OK.'

I'm not one for fussy drinks; I'd have preferred a plain latte or a normal coffee that tastes like the Nescafé I use at home.

'Thanks,' I say. 'How much do I owe you?'

She wafts my question away with a hand and takes a long draught of her own caramel-coloured drink.

I do the same. I watch her, try and mirror what she does so I get this meetfriendsforcoffee thing right.

'So,' she says, 'how are you?'

'I'm fine,' I say. She looks at me like she expects more words. 'I'm better now I've finished my shift.'

'Yeah, me too. That place, it's enough to drive you mad, right?'

'Yes,' I say.

'Yeah, crazy place. And they're changing the shifts and rotas, too. I don't know what's going to happen; I hope they don't reduce our hours.' She holds the handle of her long glass and wobbles it a bit so the coffee inside swirls around and leaves a ring of foam at the top.

I'd like to discuss my delivery round concerns with her but it's too early. Roisin seems nice but I don't know her well enough yet to let my guard down.

She looks at me and drops her head to one side.

'What dress size are you, Anna? I'm guessing about a fourteen?'

I nod, wondering where this is going.

'I have this lovely top I bought a few weeks ago. A nice salmon pink colour. Looks all wrong with my hair but it'll suit you, I'm sure of it. I'll bring it in for you to try.'

'Thanks,' I say. I can't remember the last time I had something new to wear.

Roisin looks pleased.

'Do you live near here?' I ask, getting into the swing of it now.

'Not right here in the city, too expensive. But not far away, in Lenton. I flatshare with another girl. You?'

'Sneinton,' I say. 'Park Hall Road.'

'Ah, I know it well.' Her face lights up. 'My sister works around that area.'

'Is she a postie?'

'Who?'

'Your sister.'

'Oh no,' she laughs. 'Linda's a care assistant. She calls on old people who need home assistance; I think she's got a client on that street, actually.'

I don't know whether the man who just walked by our table knocks my arm or if I just bring it up to my face too quickly but my coffee is knocked over and floods the table.

When I get back home, I feed Albert and have a quick scout around to see if the source of the smell has revealed itself. Thankfully, it isn't as overpowering as it was yesterday. Still, it is unpleasant enough that it makes me want to get out of the house as quickly as I can.

I take one of the vanilla slices I bought earlier and pop round to Mrs Peat's with the other still in its plastic casing.

'How lovely,' she says when I take the cake through with a cuppa. 'But Anna, what have you done to your hand?'

'It's nothing,' I mumble, dropping my arm to my side. 'It looks worse than it is. I cut it this morning clearing up some glass.'

Mrs Peat tuts her disapproval and sinks her teeth into the cake. The thought of all that cream and chewed pastry sticking to her dentures makes me feel quite bilious.

'Has Linda, your carer, got a sister?' I ask her, averting my eyes.

'I'm not sure, dear. I can't say as she's ever mentioned a sister. Why do you ask?'

'Someone at work said she has a sister who's a care assistant. She has a client on this street.'

'Well, Park Hall Road is quite long. It's true there are a few of us on here who need a bit more help these days.'

Mrs Peat is right. Lots of people have lived around here all their lives. It could just be a coincidence. I feel my neck and shoulders soften a little.

Still, it's a good opportunity to speak to her about privacy.

'You don't talk to Linda about me, do you?' She stops chewing and looks up. 'I mean I wouldn't want anyone knowing my business.'

'You worry too much, Anna. Drink your tea, dear.'

'I'm sorry I haven't been round for a couple of days,' I say. 'I've been busy with work and going to the hospital.'

'You're not to apologise,' Mrs Peat says firmly. 'I'm always grateful for you popping round here but I do realise you have a life.'

At last, I do. I really do have a life. Somewhere along the line, my solitary routine changed. Now, for the first time in a long time, there are other people in it.

I try this new realisation on for size. It feels a bit like wearing a new stylish hat to find it has a scratchy lining. I never expected it, and I'm not quite sure I want it.

It's only when I leave Mrs Peat's and go back home I realise she didn't reassure me that she doesn't gossip to Linda.

Come to think of it, she didn't answer my question at all.

CHAPTER 28
Thirteen years earlier

Carla Bevin sat opposite Daniel Clarke and poured two glasses of water from the jug.

If she counted the one he hadn't turned up for this was Daniel's fourth session, and Carla had to admit to herself that she was getting precisely nowhere.

Daniel appeared to listen to everything she had to say; he even shrugged now and then. Apart from that, he basically hadn't uttered a single word since that first session.

One more visit and he'd have had what they called a five-session bundle which meant his progress would have to be reviewed by the school leadership team before a further counselling bundle could be authorised.

It didn't take a genius to work out what their answer would be, unless something changed soon. Carla supposed she couldn't really blame them.

She literally knew no more about Daniel now than when he first walked through her office door four weeks ago.

At the end of the session he'd mentioned someone watching him, a man that knew everything about him, but when she'd tried to ask him about who it might be he had clammed up again.

So today when the boy took the proffered glass of water and said, 'Thank you,' Carla was blindsided for a second or two.

Would this be the session he would finally open up and share his problems?

'Thank you for coming, Daniel,' she began, careful not to appear too keen. 'Is there anything in particular you'd like to talk about today?'

'No,' he shrugged. 'Not really.'

There was definitely something different about him but Carla couldn't isolate exactly what it was.

His appearance was unchanged: still scrawny and pale with his nervous disposition plainly on display. She'd also noticed he winced slightly every time he made the slightest movement.

Carla didn't want to scare him off by sounding too interested or demanding, so she counted silently to five before continuing.

'The school staff are very concerned about you, Daniel. They think you are having some problems that are making you feel upset, maybe even afraid.' She paused to give him time to respond. After a few moments of silence, she continued: 'I wonder if you feel up to talking to me today about anything, anything at all that might be worrying you?'

No response.

'At the end of our last session you talked about a man. You said he knows everything you do. Who is that?'

The faintest ghost of a smile.

'He isn't a man,' Daniel said.

She suppressed a sigh. He was playing games with her so perhaps it was time to change tack, at least for now.

Carla watched the boy for a moment. She had never known a pupil sit as still.

'You seem very tense,' she remarked. 'Are you in pain?'

She watched as Daniel's hands curled into loose fists and pressed down into the seat cushion either side of his thighs. She was on to something.

'If someone is hurting you, Daniel, you need to tell someone. We can talk about it and work out a plan together. Just you and me—'

'Do I have to come to these sessions any more?' His clipped, clear words cut across her.

Carla closed her mouth and blinked at him.

'Sorry?' she managed.

He sat perfectly still and looked at her. Looked *through* her, almost.

'Do I have to come to these sessions or can I stop?'

His olive eyes appeared flat and seemingly without light, as if there was nothing behind them.

'I wouldn't advise that, Daniel. The sessions are here to help you, and if you would only—'

'But is it a *rule* that I have to come here?' he pressed her. 'Like we have to attend detentions?'

So that's how he viewed his visits to her office. As a punishment.

'Daniel, I want to explain something to you. Our sessions together are a privilege that most pupils don't get to experience.'

'Lucky them.'

He was on the brink of challenging her, and she realised that the change she'd perceived when he entered her office was actually a new attitude he'd appropriated. It bristled on him like a coat of spines.

'It costs the school a lot of money to facilitate these sessions, Daniel. Everybody here wants to help you. You're a smart boy with a bright future ahead of you and we want to make sure you make the most of that. Do you understand what I'm saying?'

'Yes,' he shuffled and winced. 'But it won't make any difference.'

'And why's that?'

'Because it just won't and that's why it's a waste of time me coming here.'

He broke eye contact and looked down at his hands.

Time to change tack.

'I understand your older sister, Anna, attends Cumber Meadows Comprehensive?'

Daniel looked up sharply and began to chew his bottom lip.

'Are you and your sister close?'

Carla watched as the chewing intensified, and she caught a gleam of vivid red bubble at the edge of his mouth.

This kid really got to her. One minute he pulled at her heartstrings, the next he twisted her up with his unnerving, blank stare.

More than anything, she wanted to be the one to crack him.

She knew she ought to stop the questions when his chewing drew blood. And she would, very soon. Just one or two more things to ask.

Carla consulted her notes for effect but she knew his circumstances well enough now.

'You live at home with your mum and your sister, is that right, Daniel?'

He nodded.

'Any pets?'

His jaw tightened. She pushed further.

'Cat? Dog? Goldfish?'

'We had a cat,' he said softly. 'But she – she went missing.'

'That's sad.' Carla pressed her lips together. 'I had a cat I loved, too.'

'What happened to it?'

'He was old, he died.'

'Death isn't the worst thing that can happen,' Daniel remarked.

Carla waited.

'Sometimes death doesn't seem that bad at all,' he said softly.

This boy was eight years old. She wanted to reach out and comfort him, but that was the worst thing she could do under the circumstances. It would break the new flimsy thread of communication she had worked so hard to build.

She must press on for his own good.

'It's true that bad things sometimes happen to good people but things can get better. People can find a way to get through the hard times.'

'You mean through God?' He looked up at her. His olive eyes filled with something that looked like hope or dread; she couldn't quite make up her mind which.

'Maybe,' Carla replied. 'Or just by talking to other people who care and who can help.'

'Bad things happen but it doesn't mean it's God's fault,' Daniel said sharply.

Carla looked at him and watched the expression slide from his face.

'It's true that sometimes people blame God for bad things that happen to them,' she said quickly, trying to pull his interest back.

'"People ruin their lives by their own foolishness and then are angry at the Lord," Proverbs 19:3,' Daniel recited.

It must have taken quite some practice to get that word-perfect.

'"Assume your own responsibility," Galatians 6:5.'

'My, you certainly know your—'

'"All of us will have to give an account of ourselves to God," Romans 14:12.'

'Do you go to church regularly?' she cut into his robotic quoting. 'With your mum and sister, maybe?'

He stood up and grimaced as he tried to shrug his school blazer looser.

'I know I don't have to come here,' he said, staring at the wall opposite.

'Daniel, I'm trying to help you,' Carla swallowed hard. 'It would be a mistake to just—'

'I don't want to come to see you anymore; I don't have to. The school can't make me do it.'

His eyes were focused on a space to the side of her face, and Carla knew that Daniel had stopped listening to anything she said.

Then it came to her, she understood why the boy seemed so different. Someone had got to him.

Someone had told Daniel Clarke exactly what to say.

CHAPTER 29

Present day
Anna

When I get back home after seeing Mrs Peat, I make a tuna salad sandwich and sit down with the letters I smuggled from the sorting counter earlier. Both are addressed to a 'Miss A Danson'.

I tear open the envelope to find it is a request from the police for her to contact them regarding the accident. This cheers me up no end because it means they are closing in on her. She won't be able to run away from the consequences of her actions as easily this time.

I decide to destroy the letter rather than taking it back into work to be delivered. Ignoring a police letter will make her look even guiltier.

The other letter is from the Busy Bees Head Office regarding details of a job she has expressed interest in. A senior position.

I'm about to tear it up when the Human Resources department address, top left, catches my eye.

I clear my plate and cup away and sit at the table with the laptop.

Next to me is a notepad with all the details I've found out so far about her and now the letter giving details of her employer.

Yesterday, I got things moving. Now I must keep the momentum going.

* * *

Late afternoon, I carry out my regular audit of the oven, microwave and kettle. I pull the fridge-freezer away from the wall. Then I put back the smiley-face stickers.

In the lounge, the cushions are correctly aligned. The television is off; the lamps are off. Stickers are on.

Satisfied it is safe to leave, I head out to the car.

When I arrive at Liam's house, I head straight round to the back door. I am surprised to find it locked.

I knock and rattle the handle to attract Ivy's attention then wait a few seconds. Nothing. So I knock again, louder this time.

'They've gone out,' a voice says, behind me.

I turn to see a stocky woman who I assume is their neighbour, Beryl, leaning over the small gate that separates the two properties.

Her face is bloated and pale, and I can smell stale smoke on her clothes, even here in the fresh air.

'Ivy said to tell you they won't be back until later, so not to bother waiting around.'

'Do you know where they've gone?'

She shakes her head and her chin wobbles.

'Went off in a taxi about ten minutes ago is all I know.' She holds up a canvas shopping bag. 'I'm off into town now myself. I don't suppose you'll be going back that way?'

I shake my head, startled at her boldness. I *do* actually drive past town on my way home but I have got no intention whatsoever of offering her a lift. Why on earth would I want to inflict ten minutes of senseless babble on myself?

I walk back to my car, heat flooding through my body.

What is Ivy thinking, taking Liam out in a taxi? He'll never find the time to recuperate from his ordeal if she is dragging him out of the house every two minutes.

I sit in the car, staring straight-ahead. I'm grinding my teeth but I don't care, it helps me think. The tap on the window gives me a start.

I lower it a couple of inches.

'Ivy said there was no point in you waiting around,' Beryl tells me again.

'I heard you the first time,' I snap and close the window again before she can answer. She glares at me and mutters something before waddling off down the street with her oversized shopping bags.

It occurs to me that Liam should keep his mobile phone turned on now he is out of hospital. If he needs help or needs to contact me for any reason it will come in very handy. I could have called him right now, for instance, to find out where he is.

It is so silly of Ivy, incurring the expense of cabs when I'm able to take them anywhere they need to go. Ivy seems to be making some very bad decisions for Liam's health in the process of trying to give him more freedom.

I'd decided it was fruitless to waste any more breath trying to convince her she needed my help but I can't help thinking I should really sit down and have a proper chat with her in an effort to make her see sense.

I become aware of a soreness on my scalp and realise I'm pulling at my hair again. My good hand clutches a wispy ball of it. I lower the window and release the hair, watching the breeze whip it off in the direction of Ivy's neighbour, Beryl. I imagine the ball of hair blowing down the street and straight into her big gaping mouth, choking her.

Chuckling to myself, I pick up the keys to start the ignition and then, like an epiphany, I remember the spare key. The one I had cut before giving back the original bunch from the hospital to Ivy.

I glance at the front door and imagine how it might feel walking through it and having the house to myself again.

There is a business card in there somewhere from the police. There was no sign of it last time but it's there. She will have tossed it carelessly somewhere amongst the clutter.

Ivy has been secretive with information the hospital has given her about Liam's progress, so who knows if she has had further communication from the police but not let myself or Liam know?

I glance down the street, wondering what time they will be returning in the taxi.

The old hag next door said they hadn't been gone long, and she was away now herself, off into town. I wonder, could I risk ten minutes in there?

A cursory look round the house could move things on a step if I manage to find the business card or any other important police communication that Ivy has kept to herself. That way, I could go straight to the investigating officer and get things moving.

I start up the car and drive a hundred yards back up the street, parking on the other side of the road out of the way and behind a large white van.

I lock my handbag in the boot so I've nothing I might leave behind if Ivy and Liam return. Should I need to I can slip out of the back door, unnoticed.

I take confident strides across the road and over to the small front gate. It's vital not to dither in these situations. People notice nervous, unusual behaviour; it breeds suspicion and interest. But someone who looks like they belong, like they are just visiting a friend? No one ever pays any attention to them.

By the time I get to the front door, my hand is shaking but I insert the key anyway and the door swings open. I close it behind me and stand still for a minute.

'Liam?' I call out to the still, silent rooms. 'Hello?'

I haven't a clue what excuse I'll come up with if it transpires that someone is home after all, but I have no need to worry.

The house is empty.

CHAPTER 30
Joan Peat

She heard Anna's car start up and hobbled over to the front window to watch the back end of the silver Astra disappear up the street.

Joan sighed and sat down in the chair next to the glass; the net curtain arranged just so, allowing her to watch the road without being seen.

It wasn't raining now but the thick covering of grey clouds looked as if it could very easily start again. If it did there would be nothing to see from the window, everyone would stay indoors.

Joan was tired of watching boring programmes on TV; she was tired of reading Linda's cast-off weekly women's magazines and, most of all, she was tired of the silence.

Right now there wasn't a soul around outside. Joan could hear the soft, intermittent hum of the refrigerator and the occasional click of the water heater.

That was it. That was her life.

Years ago, even after Arthur had gone, there was always noise, or rather what Joan regarded as comforting sounds. Especially next door once Daniel was born. Although, for some reason, he never spent a lot of time around at Joan's house like Anna did.

But if the two of them were playing out the front they'd always be popping in and out to show her something or other.

Joan had felt so wanted, important in their lives.

When Monica eventually called them in – always far later and darker than Joan thought safe – she could hear them running along the upstairs landing, singing or squealing in the front room.

She never minded the noise, liked it, in fact.

It was a kind of company for her that took the sharp edges off the unfillable black space that gaped inside after Arthur had passed on.

Sadly, she could also hear Monica shouting at the children quite clearly. Could sometimes hear the slaps and the cries, particularly of Daniel.

She used to take the glass away from the wall then.

Joan had always tried to avoid thinking about what Arthur might say but it never worked. She used to hear his voice in her head as clearly as if he'd been standing in front of her.

'That woman wants reporting, Joan. You've got to do it for the kiddies.'

But Joan knew that if the authorities got involved they would take Anna and Daniel away from their mother. She might well never see them again.

So Joan got quite clever at blocking out the thoughts by doing something else. Perhaps putting a bit of Neil Diamond on Arthur's old record player or turning on a television programme.

It didn't really matter what, just that it drowned out the noises from next door.

And when the crying stopped, Arthur's stern voice would fade away again.

Joan wiped her hand over the windowsill now and removed a layer of dust.

She used to be so fastidious with her cleaning. Arthur always said they could eat their dinner off the kitchen floor if they'd needed to, it was that spotless.

Years ago, she'd never have tolerated this thin layer of grey dust that now covered everything. Some days, she could feel it settling on her own body like a fine shroud.

Joan sometimes wondered if she might end up like that Dickens character, Miss Havisham, in *Great Expectations*; pale and dusty and covered in cobwebs.

It could easily happen if she lost her visitors, her lifeline.

In fact, it seemed she might already be losing Anna. She felt increasingly that Anna was keeping secrets from her, things she didn't want Joan to know. That gave her a sour twinge in her throat because Anna had always told her everything, had always seemed to value her advice, too.

Even as a child, Anna had confided in Joan. Told her some of the awful things that happened to her brother in that house.

At first, rather than judge her, she had tried to get to know Monica Clarke a little better.

Despite the things she'd heard, the things she'd seen, she had tried to do the Christian thing and reach out to her neighbour.

It was clear to Joan that Monica was a woman who had clawed her way through life relying largely on her own resources.

She never said as much and Joan never knew her background but she didn't need to. She could see it.

The lack of trust in the younger woman's eyes. The way she bristled on the odd occasion Joan popped round with a dish of lasagne or a wedge of Victoria sponge.

Joan could see, plain as the nose on her over-painted face, Monica had suffered a thousand disappointments in life, probably caused by other people letting her down. As a result, she shunned any offers of help.

In the end, and after Daniel's birth, the two women came to a sort of unspoken understanding that suited them both.

Joan used to keep Anna at hers a lot. In fact, when Daniel came along, Anna all but moved in with her and Arthur.

She had her own bedroom upstairs which Arthur let her choose the wallpaper for.

'Remember, it's our secret,' Joan used to whisper in her ear before she went back round to her mother. They both knew Monica wouldn't like it, and she didn't want to push her too far.

Monica Clarke was one of those women who didn't see why her kids should have more in life than she herself had been given.

Joan still thought of the spare room upstairs as Anna's bedroom. The same wallpaper remained although the bed had gone now and it was used mainly for the storage boxes full of Arthur's clothes and belongings that she still couldn't face giving to the charity shop.

She'd like to talk about those days with Anna again but Joan worried she might get upset. Besides, the rate she was in and out the house these days she'd be lucky to catch her in long enough to chat.

Joan stared out of the window. She thought Anna had said her friend was out of hospital now so she couldn't still be going there to visit each day.

Joan was curious to know exactly who this friend was. All these years, she'd never known Anna get close to anyone at all.

Things had started changing since the accident Anna had witnessed. Granted, this had included positive developments like Anna breaking out of her rigid routines at last, but other things were happening too that Joan found rather more worrying.

Anna pacing around in the early hours, although that seemed to have improved a bit lately. But then Joan had heard dragging and bumping sounds upstairs, and when Anna popped round today she had a bandaged hand with no real satisfactory explanation.

It would be nice to be a fly on the wall in Anna's house for a little while. It might give Joan a clue as to what was happening.

A long-lost memory fluttered and then settled in the forefront of her mind.

Joan had quite forgotten how she kept an eye on the house for the months Anna was an inpatient at the clinic.

She stood up and waited for the feeling to come back into her legs before she moved slowly into the kitchen.

People didn't ought to underestimate her just because she was old. They might be surprised. . . some of the things she could do if she wanted to.

Joan slid open the wide drawer next to the sink and lifted the clinking cutlery tray.

There it was. The spare key to Anna's house Joan had clean forgotten she'd had for all these years.

CHAPTER 31
Anna

The front door clicks shut behind me and I step fully into the lounge.

The front of Liam and Ivy's house is north-facing and so the room is cool and silent, despite facing on to the road. A faint damp odour persists; the smell of age and of furnishings that are years past their replacement date.

Ivy keeps the house relatively clean and tidy but there is just so much *stuff* here.

Neat piles, but nevertheless disorganised piles, of documentation lie dotted around, cluttering up every room. I've heard Ivy mumble numerous times, 'I'll read that properly later,' when she adds yet another letter or a leaflet to a stack of mail.

It's fairly obvious, looking at the towering backlog, that she never gives it another thought.

If the police have sent anything recently it will probably be 'filed' towards the top of one of her piles, so I sift through two or three stacks in the living room. My injured hand starts aching right away but I press on.

It is soon obvious there is nothing in here of interest to me but I stand for a minute longer, alone in the house without anyone knowing.

Granted, it is a shame I'm having to resort to such measures but I'm just going to have to force myself to do what is necessary for the good of Liam and Ivy.

I move to the doorway, deciding to leave the kitchen until last, and begin to climb the stairs beyond. I can't afford to delay, not knowing exactly how soon they will return.

I turn left at the top of the stairs and enter Ivy's bedroom.

The bed is made, the curtains open and a faint breeze wafts in through the scalloped nets, offering at least a little respite from the fusty smell that pervades the top floor of the house.

I am trying to work quickly but my bad hand is hampering me and my good hand is clumsy with jangling nerves.

I slide open the bedside drawer. Nothing here short of hankies, a pot of chest rub and a dog-eared Barbara Cartland novel.

The drawers under the bed hold only age-old bedding and towels. The dresser under the window boasts Ivy's dated toiletries and a fine covering of dust but when I turn my attention to the free-standing dark-oak wardrobe with its ornate coving, I spot the old-fashioned long brass key still in the lock.

Inside, the space is dark and deep, with Ivy's clothes nestling together in a clean line. I'm almost expecting to find fur coats, a sprinkling of snow and then maybe Narnia. But there are just more dresses here that surely belong to a time many years hence. A polka dot fifties-style halter-neck dress, a fuchsia-pink satin cocktail skirt complete with frivolous nets.

I feel a little softening inside despite Ivy's treatment of me but it's silly of her to keep such useless items for the sake of memories. I read somewhere that most people only wear twenty per cent of their wardrobe, eighty per cent of the time. In Ivy's case I think she wears a mere five per cent, *ninety-five per cent* of the time.

Shoes line the bottom of the wardrobe floor, the vast majority no longer suitable for Ivy's age and lifestyle but I am impressed with her organisational skills. At first glance, her bedroom looks as cluttered as everywhere else, but upon closer inspection I see it is actually quite tidy and arranged efficiently.

Periodically, I stop and creep to the top of the stairs, listening. The house remains deathly quiet so I am able to work methodically through the bedroom but there is no sign of anything that can assist with speeding up the police investigation.

I drop down on my haunches and peer into the back of the dark space beyond the rows of vintage shoes.

Although it might seem an unlikely place for anyone to store a business card, I remind myself there is no substitute for thoroughness.

Pushed right to the back are three shoeboxes, stacked one on top of the other and partially hidden by a pair of dated knee-length suede boots. I feel a flutter in the back of my throat as I slide the top shoebox from behind the boots and sit on the end of the bed with it.

It is half-filled with old letters, most of them yellowing and well-read, from Ivy's sweetheart – probably her husband – a serving soldier, back then.

The second box is more interesting. The documents look more official.

I'm primarily looking for something that might give me a head start on the police investigation but I'm not averse to discovering other information that might prove interesting.

I leaf through the neatly folded contents of the box. A stack of Liam's old school reports which I would like to read thoroughly, but can't risk doing so. Expired insurance certificates, old warranties and receipts.

Working one-handed as quickly as I can, I rifle through and find a padded envelope at the bottom. When I see Liam's name written on the front in black marker pen I wonder if this might contain information that Liam himself can't remember.

I sit very still for a moment and listen.

Silence.

I reach inside the envelope and extract the contents, spreading them out on the bedspread.

A handful of photographs and a thick wad of folded papers. When I open them out I find old correspondence from the courts regarding Ivy becoming Liam's legal guardian.

My eyes flit through the complicated wording. There is something strange here but for a few seconds I'm not sure exactly what, until I spot that only their first names are familiar.

I read through the details again more carefully. The surnames on the papers have been documented as Wilton for both of them, rather than Bradbury.

Perhaps Ivy changed both their names by deed poll because she was trying to forget the trauma of Liam's father's accident. After all, he had been her only son. Most people would want to preserve the family name for memories' sake but Ivy isn't most people. She'll go to any lengths to keep Liam exclusively hers.

There are five photographs in all. All are of Liam as a baby and small boy. Someone has written his name and age on the back of each one. In each picture, Liam is alone. In his push-chair, lying on a lawn in the sun, two at a play park and one standing on a chair at the kitchen sink, playing with the washing-up suds.

I set the photographs aside and slide a single sheet of paper out of a tatty brown envelope addressed to Ivy and marked 'Confidential'.

It's a shame Ivy has driven me to gather scraps of information in this manner. If only she could have been more open this unpleasant activity might well have been avoided.

I unfold the typed sheet. The old-fashioned typewriter print is faint and uneven and the edges of the paper yellowing but the heading, in rickety block capitals, is bold and clear:

'PSYCHOLOGICAL REPORT'

I scan the short sections, noting some quite startling words and phrases.

'*Delusional. . . a danger to themselves and others. . . psychopathic tendencies. . .*'

I take a gulp of air as I read the final line.

'*Recommended: Three further months of incarceration.*'

My eyes skip to the two signatures at the bottom of the page.

'*Psychiatrist: Dr A Meakin and Patient: Ivy Wilton.*'

CHAPTER 32

I'm about to go back to the beginning of the report and read it properly when there is a short, sharp knock downstairs.

I gasp, scattering the papers as I jump up off the bed. My arms prickle with goosebumps as I jolt upright and shooting pains zip across my cut palm. I stand there, frozen to the spot.

They are back.

It takes a second or two to snap to my senses with the realisation that I can't afford to wait until they come through the door.

I hastily stuff half the papers back into the envelope and pile the rest back into the shoebox. I then shove everything back into the wardrobe.

As I close and lock the wardrobe door, I realise it has gone quiet once more before a snapping and scraping noise has me on edge again. My mouth instantly dries out and I fight the building tickle in my throat to avoid a full-blown coughing fit.

I creep to the top of the stairs ready to face Ivy and Liam. I am trying and failing to come up with a convincing excuse of why I am trespassing in their home.

Searching for the police contact so Amanda Danson can get her comeuppance isn't going to cut it, I'm afraid. They don't even know I have a key.

All quiet and then another sharp bang. I prepare myself for the sound of the back door crashing open and being discovered.

Liam will be confused and upset and it will be difficult to explain to him that I am here only for his own good. So often, people just can't see what is best for them.

But the back door does not crash open. Everything remains quiet downstairs.

I creep over to the bedroom window and, concealed by the net curtain, I peer down to the road.

Two officers, a man and a woman, walk away from the house, back down towards the bottom of the street.

Dizzy and disorientated, I sit back down on the end of the bed to steady the hammering in my chest. The police must have called hoping to catch Liam in, to talk to him about the accident.

I had been so close to being discovered. My skin is crawling at the thought of what might have happened. My forehead feels really hot, but when I press the back of my hand to it I find it is cool and clammy.

Again, I go to the window and breathe a sigh of relief when the dark uniforms turn the corner and disappear.

I move back to unlock the wardrobe once more so I can restack the boxes properly, as I found them.

But I can't resist it. I have to pull out the third box.

I don't have time to look properly, of course, but a quick glance reveals it's just full of old newspaper cuttings anyway. Births and deaths no doubt – old people always seem obsessed with that sort of thing.

I rearrange the boots and shoes in front so that the boxes are partially hidden, as before. Then I slide the thick envelope stuffed with the interesting paperwork inside my fleece jacket and zip it up.

Downstairs, a white envelope sits on the mat, evidently the reason for the police officers' visit. Liam's name is written on the front.

I snatch it up and add it to the hidden depths of my fleece.

As an afterthought I walk into the kitchen and take a quick look in a couple of drawers. Nothing.

When I walk out I spot a pile of mail on top of the fridge-freezer. I lift the top few sheets down and there, sitting loose on top, is a Nottinghamshire Police business card.

There is an extension number written on the back in blue ink, and I am guessing this is the card the police left when they came round to inform Ivy that Liam had been injured.

Ivy has tossed it on to the pile like it's a piece of junk mail.

I pick it up and slide it into my jeans pocket. It certainly won't go to waste now.

Before I leave, I check the road both ways from the safety of the living room net curtain. When I am sure it is clear, I slip out of the front door, pulling it closed behind me until I hear the latch click into place.

I walk briskly but confidently up the road to my car. Only when the driver's door is closed do I allow myself to release a long sigh of relief.

I feel like I'm on fire inside so I open the window a touch and unzip my fleece. Both envelopes slide out and I hold them for a long moment before popping them out of sight into the glove compartment.

I sit back for a few moments, closing my eyes and taking a few breaths to try and clear the thick fuzz from my head. For all I had reservations on encroaching on Ivy and Liam's privacy, I have to admit that my sacrifice has paid dividends.

I have already started the engine and belted up when I spot the black cab coasting down the road. I turn the engine off again and sit back to watch.

The cab stops outside Liam's house, and the driver's door opens.

The driver gets out and takes several bags from the boot, offloading them at the front door. By the time he gets back to the vehicle, Ivy has managed to get her feet on the ground and is hoisting herself to a standing position with the aid of a stick.

It is painfully obvious that, far from improving, she is growing more unsteady on her feet each day. The fact she is obviously in denial about her own health makes a bit more sense to me now.

'Delusional', was the word the report used.

The driver removes Liam's wheelchair from the boot and unfolds it by the back passenger door, but Liam shakes his head and hobbles up the path himself, flouting Dr Khan's advice about resting his leg.

Although I'm surprised at Liam's range of movement, it still strikes me as a ridiculous scene. Two people that have trouble getting around, struggling for no other reason than being too stubborn to ask *me* for help.

Reality hasn't kicked in for them yet. They have people visiting, fussing around and asking if there is anything they can do. Let's see how much fun it is six months down the line when the realisation hits that Liam may well have to cope with lasting effects from the accident including his memory loss and mood swings.

Ivy will be out of her depth coping with the physical demands of caring for an invalid when she is already struggling herself both physically *and* psychologically.

I unbuckle my seatbelt and get out of the car. As I walk across the road I remind myself that I was Liam's guardian angel in the road as he lay bleeding and dying.

Metaphorically, I continue to hold his hand. Nobody can stop me doing that.

I knock at the front door but, predictably, there is no answer. I walk round to the back door and catch Ivy returning from putting the rubbish out. She looks surprised to see me.

'Hello Ivy,' I say. 'Lucky I saw the cab; I was just about to drive home.'

'Didn't you get the message I left with our neighbour, Beryl?'

She frowns and shuffles back inside with some discomfort, even slower on her feet than usual.

'Were you at the hospital?' I ask.

'No,' she says. 'Liam wanted to do a bit of shopping so we got a cab into town.'

She turns round and holds on to the doorframe to catch her breath before heading back into the house.

'Shopping?' I pause to absorb the sheer stupidity of the woman. 'In his current state of health? Dr Khan expressly said—'

'I know what he said,' Ivy snaps. 'But those doctors don't live in the real world, do they?'

And neither do you, by all accounts.

'Expecting a young man to be stuck in the house day after day is ridiculous. And anyway, he can walk quite well even though he's slow. Would you like a cup of tea?'

'Liam's in his thirties, Ivy,' I say, clamping my teeth together before I go the whole hog and ask her why she treats him like a kid. 'Hardly a young man.'

She doesn't answer me but shuffles off into the kitchen.

I follow her in, resisting the urge to rub my sore hand as I know it will only hurt more.

'The doctor also said he needs to rest for his mind to recover,' I point out. 'He might never get his memory back if he's got constant stimulation from shopping trips.'

'That might not be a bad thing.' Ivy shrugs, pulling mugs from the cupboard. 'Maybe a fresh start is what he needs.'

What Liam needs is a fresh start well away from *her*.

She has offered me tea but I feel certain she doesn't really want me to stay. I can feel her prickling, a static aura that buzzes around her.

I walk into the lounge, and there he is, emptying out the contents of three small carrier bags. Liam's obvious pleasure at my appearance nullifies the old woman's grumbling in an instant and serves as a timely reminder of why I keep coming back.

'DVDs.' He waves two plastic cases in the air. 'These are films I used to love and can't remember a damn thing about.'

I smile and sit down on the edge of the couch next to him. He presses his hand on mine, still cold from being outside.

'I wondered if we could swap mobile numbers,' I say shyly. 'So I can get you if I need you and vice versa.'

''Course,' he grins. He saves my number into his phone as a contact. It's embarrassing because he has to find it himself on my handset. I'm not very good with new technology. 'There, I've sent you a text and now you have my number.'

I open the text. He's written, *'Liam xx'*, and I feel my face flush.

Liam offers to save his number in my phone as a new contact.

'I'm glad you're here, Anna.' He looks up at me and my heart seems to melt like wax.

I don't know what to say. Even though Liam and I are just friends, it fills me with such a warm feeling when he looks at me like this it turns my brain to putty.

It's just silly and I mustn't lose focus on who I am really interested in.

'How do you know you liked the DVDs if you can't remember?' I change the subject and move my hand away even though I like it. I can't help it.

'Gran brought me this notebook down from the side of my bed. I started it as a kid,' he says, giving me back my phone and picking up an A5 spiral-bound pad. 'I suppose I must've been a bit of a geek really, writing down films I'd watched and what I thought of them.'

I'm surprised Ivy hasn't continued to buy him football sticker books and maybe the odd *Beano* annual. Liam must secretly ache to be out of here so he can breathe.

'How's the wheelchair?' I ask.

He pulls a face and shrugs.

'I just wanted to rely on my crutches but Gran insisted we take this thing. I hate it.'

'It won't be long before you can walk unaided, if you don't overdo it,' I say. 'Got anything good there?'

He hands me the DVD cases and takes another couple out of the carrier bag. The usual classic bloke-type adventure films, *Mission: Impossible, The Bourne Identity.*

I'm not a massive movie fan myself; I find it difficult to sit and keep my attention on them for an hour and a half when there always seem to be other important things that need doing.

'Good stuff,' I say, handing them back. 'That's you sorted for the next few days then.'

'Let's hope your friend likes them,' Ivy says from the doorway. 'I'm hoping we'll have more people around here soon to keep you company.'

'Friend?' I say mildly.

'She means Amanda,' Liam flushes, suddenly interested in his hands.

'She's coming over to see him later,' Ivy says. 'Now, shall I put the kettle on and make you that cup of tea, Anna?'

My teeth bite down hard on my tongue and a metal-like taste floods my mouth.

Tea, tea, fucking tea. The answer to the world's problems, according to Ivy. She scuttles back to the kitchen, obviously glad of the distraction.

'Let me get this right, the woman who nearly killed you is coming over to watch films?' My eyes are stinging, threatening tears, but I don't care. I can't stop myself from saying it.

'You could come over too, if you like?' Liam leans forward, urging me to agree.

I dig my thumbnail harder into my palm to stop full-blown tears from forming.

'I wonder what her boyfriend would think about her spending her evenings with you,' I remark.

'Boyfriend?'

'She's seeing the caretaker at the nursery where she works. Hasn't she told you?'

His shoulders drop and he looks at the floor. For a second I imagine slapping him.

'I saw them together when I drove by the other day.'

'But why – I mean, you never mentioned it until now,' Liam says.

'Why should I?' I shrug. 'I didn't think you'd be interested.'

'No,' he agrees. 'I'm not really, I'm just surprised.'

I soften a little, understanding. It's not that Liam *cares* about her, he is just surprised at how devious she is.

'Well, like I said, you're welcome if you want to watch the film with us.'

'I'm sure Anna's got other things she wants to do instead of coming over here, Liam,' Ivy reappears in the doorway.

'Actually, I haven't,' I respond tartly, looking back at Liam. 'But I'm not sure I want to be around someone like Amanda Danson.'

'She's not the wicked person you make her out to be, Anna. Amanda has been upset. It seems someone has got it in for her.'

Liam glances over at Ivy.

'Oh?' My ears prick up.

'Yes, she came home to a load of manure dumped in her front yard. And the company who did it without her authorisation are now demanding payment. Can you believe it?'

How I manage not to smirk I don't know.

I ignore Ivy and turn to face Liam. 'I think the police and her insurance company would be concerned to hear she's in touch with you.'

'Everyone is welcome here,' Ivy says lightly.

'Even someone who nearly killed your grandson?' The words spill out too loud before I can stop them, and Ivy looks alarmed. 'If it was someone on the street who attacked him would you invite them over too?'

All this time I've given Ivy the benefit of the doubt without knowing about her underlying madness. When I get home I'll be able to read the report in full but, for now, I've seen enough to know she's clearly unstable.

'It's hardly the same thing,' Ivy snaps. 'It was an accident; Amanda didn't mean to hurt him.'

No, 'Amanda' never means to hurt anyone. There's always a reason for her impulsiveness and lack of thought for the consequences of her actions.

I feel something shift inside me and I clamp my mouth shut before some choice words spill out. I have nothing else to say to Ivy.

CHAPTER 33
Thirteen years earlier

After school, Daniel walked home as slowly as he could. But when he reached the house, his mother was waiting.

'Go to your room,' she said coldly. 'Nothing to eat or drink; we will purge this evil from you one way or another.'

He had been in too much pain to sleep properly the night before and had been very uncomfortable in the dreaded afternoon session with Carla.

The counsellor never took her eyes off him. She looked as if she actually cared, and once or twice he'd been tempted to answer her. Then he'd remembered and kept his mouth shut. Today had been even worse; it took every bit of his energy during the session not to cry out at the slightest movement.

Now, he lay on his side on the mattress on the floor and drifted off. He woke up, shivering, to the sound of the door opening.

His body began to shake and he whimpered, shuffling back towards the wall.

'Danny, it's OK, it's only me.'

He breathed out when he realised it was just Anna.

She crept into the room and closed the door softly behind her.

'Mum's nipped to the shop for milk,' she whispered. 'So I brought you this.'

He took the slice of bread and cheese and wolfed it down. Anna passed him a glass of water and he drained it in one gulp.

'Danny, I need you to trust me. Can you do that?'

He nodded. His sister was the one person in the whole world he knew he could definitely trust.

'I need you to show me. I need to see how bad it is.'

He squeezed his eyes shut and shook his head.

'I'm not going to force you,' she said. 'But please, you have to let me see, Danny. I think it might be really bad this time but I'll find a way to help, you know that.'

He looked at his sister's eyes and saw that they reflected his own pain. He knew that, somehow, Anna would help him.

He gave a faint nod and began to undress.

Anna helped him peel off his school shirt as gently as she could, but on the lefthand side he could feel it was stuck fast with dried blood and so she left it hanging.

She turned him to the light and he heard the rush of shock catch in her throat.

Daniel twisted his head so he could see in the mirror. She tried to block his view but it was too late.

The welts on his back looked like strips of raw liver stuck on to his pale skin. Some were weeping and oozing.

He closed his eyes but that only seemed to make it hurt more.

'Danny, we have to get you to the hospital,' Anna whispered, and he watched salty channels slide down her face. She reached for him.

'I don't want to,' he whimpered and pulled his hand away. 'Please, Anna, Father Kilbride said—'

'We could go to Father Kilbride, Danny. He'll help you.'

'Anna, no.' He could feel his stomach rolling with the bread and cheese he hadn't chewed properly.

'Did he hurt you too?'

He couldn't get his breath; he thought this was what it must feel like to drown. He opened his mouth and tried to gulp at the air.

'Sssh, it's OK. Calm down.'

Danny rested the crown of his head on her arm.

'Are you scared of the priest?' she asked.

A coil of something ugly and slippery squirmed briefly in his bowel.

'Danny, has Father Kilbride ever hurt you?'

She waited, still and full of dread, but there was no response from her brother.

She pushed his head gently back and looked at him.

Daniel wouldn't lift his eyes to her but when she reached for his small warm hand, this time, he didn't pull away.

CHAPTER 34
Present day
Anna

When I get home I empty the big padded envelope from Ivy's wardrobe on to the dining room table.

My hand is consumed with a relentless dull aching, so I try to use only my good one, which means everything takes twice as long. I put the kettle on, feed Albert and, as a treat, place two chocolate shortbreads on my favourite glass plate I bought in the sale at John Lewis two years ago.

Occasionally I get a whiff of the sweet rotting smell but, mostly, today I can't smell it. Probably as a result of my vigorous cleaning campaign.

I take my tea and biscuits into the middle room and sit down at the table. I press my back against the rigid form of the chair and take a few seconds to glance around the room, feeling the tightness begin to seep from my bones as I go through my mental inventory.

There's the old dresser but Mother's ornamental china plates have now gone. The carpet is still the same one that Danny and I skipped across as kids and that Mother vacuumed and even scrubbed, many times, down on her hands and knees. It was threadbare in front of the door to the staircase and leading into the kitchen.

And this chair right here, where I am now, is where the priest sat.

That's as far as my mind will go.

On every stretch of bare wall in this room there had been a crucifix. Not just plain wooden crosses, either. Elaborate affairs, each one complete with a suffering Jesus.

I remember I used to stand in front of them and imagine how terrible Jesus's injuries would look in real life. I would press something sharp against my palm and try and imagine how it felt to be nailed up by your hands, your feet.

All the crucifixes are long gone now.

I suppose, in the end, I got my wish. I got to find out just how bad suffering could feel.

The cupboard under the stairs is just that again: a space full of junk, as it should be. No longer a place of fear and darkness.

It's not that I don't have the money to replace the things that remain from years ago. If I wanted to, I could kit the house out and hardly touch what's in the building society account. It is more a case of why bother when there is only me who will ever see it?

Things might change. It occurs to me that Liam might visit at some point. I could ask him over for tea and to meet Albert.

Upstairs, the walls are all the colour of the pages of an old, much-loved book. The thought of decorating up there has crossed my mind now and then but I'd only make a mess of it, and I certainly wouldn't want a stranger here in the house.

It had been my job back then to shovel out the cold ashes on a morning. Not too bad in the summer but in winter the frost would bite at my hands as I carried the dusty embers out to the tin dustbin.

I would come back inside and arrange the spindly iron bars of the solid fuel burner, long overdue for replacement. Mother would loosely plait newspapers to serve as firelighters and, if I didn't rearrange the grate bars right, the coal and paper would just slip through and the fire would fail. And then I'd be for it.

I haven't lit the burner since the bad things happened here. When everything was sorted out, the house became mine.

I can do what I like now; I am the one in charge.

Gates locked. Doors locked. Curtains closed.

I relish the warm feeling that spreads through my lower abdomen like a thick, comforting soup. Nobody can stick their nose into my business any more.

Nobody can see the letters I've got here in front of me.

If people knew I'd taken this stuff from Ivy's wardrobe, they would say it is wrong but other people don't know everything that is at stake. They can't possibly understand.

I always suspected something wasn't quite right between Liam and Ivy, that something didn't quite fit, and that report has proved me right.

With Liam's memory gone, he is relying on an old woman who has been medically certified as unstable. An old woman who is doing nothing to stop, even encouraging, a developing friendship with the woman who nearly killed her grandson. Plus, is neglecting to chase the police prosecution.

Thanks to Ivy, there is a real risk that Amanda Danson could escape justice all over again. That's something I can't face thinking about.

I wish I could tell Liam all this, so he understands my urgency. I think he would like to get to know me better but understandably he is holding back, not least because of my own nervousness.

It is a complication I didn't plan on.

After all this time I can't afford to let my focus slip. I won't do it.

I pick up the letter the police hand delivered when I was at Liam's house and slide a knife under the sealed edge, slitting the letter open in one smooth action. A shiver runs through my hands.

Unfolding the single white sheet of paper, I read the few lines quickly.

Finally, the police want to speak to Liam about the accident. They're giving him the choice of either popping into the station or ringing for an appointment for an officer to call on him at home.

I refold the letter and place it on the side to put into a fresh envelope later. In the morning at the delivery office, the letter will find its way into the correct delivery slot for Liam's house.

Next, I reach for the padded envelope. I lay the photographs out in a line, the baby ones first.

Liam won't remember anything from his childhood but what are memories, anyway? Part-fiction, part-real in everyone's head.

Past times are gone for good. They only stay alive and exist in the pictures in our heads. There are those who want to remember and those who'd rather push the memories away. Sometimes, people do both.

I sift quickly through the paperwork looking for Ivy's psychological report.

Soon papers are flying everywhere, and I realise with a burst of frustration that the report is not here. In my panic, I must have stuffed it back in the shoebox instead of in the envelope.

I thump the table. How could I have been so stupid?

CHAPTER 35

With a heavy heart I pack up the papers and photographs and stuff them back into the padded envelope.

I'll tuck it way in the sideboard for safekeeping until I get a chance to return it to Ivy's bedroom and unearth her psychological report again.

Until then I'll just have to put it out of my mind. There is nothing I can do about my clumsy error.

There is still one thing I can do that will make a big difference.

I fish out the business card from the police and tap the number into my new phone. When the automatic answering service begins, I wait for the relevant bit and then tap in the extension number of a PC Brixham who wrote his details on to the business card.

He answers the phone, stating his name.

'I'm Ivy Bradbury,' I say slowly, injecting a little quiver into my voice. 'My grandson was involved in an accident on Green Road recently, and I wonder if you can tell me what's happening with the investigation.'

'Ahh yes, I'm involved in this case personally, Mrs Bradbury. We're waiting to speak to the other driver and someone will be popping round to speak to your grandson soon,' PC Brixham says. 'I believe letters regarding this matter have gone out to both addresses recently.'

'Why has it taken so long?' I add in just a touch of distress. 'I don't want the other driver to get away with nearly killing my grandson.'

'I can assure you that all procedures will be followed, Mrs Bradbury. Unfortunately, there has been a spate of road traffic accidents in the area and we're trying our best to pull everything in with the limited staff we have.'

They need shaking up. Somebody has to get things moving.

'She's bothering us, you see,' I say softly. 'She came to the hospital and bluffed her way in to see my grandson without permission.'

'Miss Danson did?'

No, the fucking tooth fairy.

'Yes, she tried to get him to sign a statement saying he doesn't want to press charges.' I'm warming nicely to the role but I take care to sound a little unsure of myself, a little vulnerable. 'My grandson is very distressed about it all. She keeps calling at the house, insisting we talk to her. I'm sure you understand it is very unnerving for us, officer.'

'Absolutely. You did the right thing letting us know.' PC Brixham sounds far more interested now. 'We'll get someone out to you as soon as possible, Mrs Bradbury. Hopefully tomorrow.'

That suits me just fine. I have plans for the rest of the afternoon.

Later, feeling quite bold, I decide to send Liam a text before I go up to bed.

It's only eight thirty but getting up at four a.m. takes its toll, especially when I'm not sleeping very well.

'Just off to bed. Enjoy your evening,' I type. 'I'll pop over tomorrow'

His reply comes straight back.

'Thanks. Amanda cancelled so a quiet night for us, too X'

This is no surprise at all to me, of course, after my dealings this afternoon but it still feels good to read his words and realise that the early stages of my plan are having an effect. . . and to receive a kiss, which I decide to ignore in the end.

Focus.

All things taken into consideration, it has been quite a satisfying day.

CHAPTER 36
Thirteen years earlier

Carla had finally finished her last meeting and was making slow progress walking across the car park, weighed down by a large box full of pupil files.

A scrawny-looking girl of about fourteen or fifteen appeared as if from nowhere and stood directly in front of her. Carla almost dropped the box in surprise.

She was about to scold her when she saw her eyes, flashing and wild. The girl was wearing the uniform of the comprehensive. Her school blouse was smeared with suspicious-looking reddish-brown stains and her hair looked unkempt, as if she'd taken flight.

'Please, miss,' she gasped breathlessly. 'It's my brother. You've got to help him.'

Carla put the box down on the ground.

'OK, calm down.' She took a step back so she could properly assess the girl. 'Are you in trouble?'

She nodded vigorously.

'Well then, let's go back inside and you can tell me exactly what's wrong.'

'No, I can't. I mean you need to get help now, before it's too late. They're hurting him.'

'Let's start from the beginning,' Carla said gently, her heart beginning to thud. 'What's your name?'

'Anna Clarke.'

Carla took a breath. It was a name she recognised from the school file. 'Are you Daniel Clarke's sister?'

'Yes,' she nodded. 'He's in real trouble, miss. They'll kill him if you don't. . . oh God, please help him.'

The school office staff had left the building now. Carla would have to call the police herself if necessary.

'Who are *they*? Boys at school?'

'No. I have to get back, he's on his own, but I promised you'd help him. Will you help him? Tonight, miss?'

Carla shook her head and willed her thudding heart to slow down so she could think logically.

'There's a procedure to follow, Anna. Ask Daniel to come and see me in the morn—'

She stopped mid-sentence when the girl turned on her heel and ran away.

'Anna! Come back,' Carla called.

But Daniel's sister had already disappeared around the corner.

When she finally arrived home, Carla poured herself a large glass of white wine then sat at the breakfast bar and looked at it.

She gripped the stem of the glass between her thumb and index finger and twisted the glass round and round, watching, as the pale yellow fluid sloshed elegantly inside, its surface remaining smooth and unbroken.

The house was quiet and there was no sign of her neighbours coming in from work yet, which was unusual.

Carla was convinced that if her heart thumped any harder she'd hear it as well as feel it banging on the wall of her chest. She wasn't quite sure what to do about the girl in the car park. Should she take action now or wait until the morning? She knew the pupils could be unpredictable and dramatic over quite trivial matters, but there was something very desperate about Anna Clarke's panic that rang true.

Carla knew that the correct procedure would be to write up a full report and initiate the relevant agencies' involvement via the school's child protection officer. She could do all that in the morning.

Of course, if a child's life was deemed to be in danger, then the thing to do would be to call the police immediately. But she didn't feel as if she had enough information and somehow that course of action seemed inappropriate to her at this stage.

It occurred to Carla that she only had Anna's word for the fact Daniel was in trouble at all. Of course, she knew he had problems and that it was probably bullying but, although very unpleasant for the boy, it was highly unlikely to be life-threatening.

She would look really stupid if she got the police involved over something that turned out to be superficial. Plus, the governors would be furious if the school name became embroiled in something that could have been easily resolved with a little discretion.

On top of all that, after her earlier meeting today with the leadership team and her lack of results with the Daniel Clarke case, she was keen to show her involvement had come good after all.

If Anna Clarke's panic was justified, Carla's skills could be integral to sorting out a high-profile case. It would do wonders for progressing her application to the high school.

She pushed her untouched wine away and some of the pale golden liquid spilled on to her fingers. It would save until she got back.

CHAPTER 37
Present day
Anna

Recently, it has felt as if my routines are slipping away like a landslide but a little voice in my head reminds me that it is not unstoppable.

If I focus, I think I could still pull it back.

For once I sleep well and wake up with a new and welcome feeling of determination. Mercifully, this morning I feel calmer and more settled. This could be my chance to seize the moment and get as much sorted out as I can.

The first place to start is undoubtedly the mail mountain in the spare room.

It sounds a strange thing to say but it seems to cast a real shadow over the house and everything in it, leaving a silent threat that lurks behind.

Maybe, in the beginning, it would have been easier to admit defeat to the management at work. Told Jim, when he asked, that I was finding it difficult to cope. Swallowed down my pride and accepted reduced hours and a round on the roughest side of town.

Things have gone too far for that now. Too far to turn back.

Up until today I have felt powerless to tackle things upstairs but, today, I finally have the resolve I have been waiting for.

Ultimately, it is just a pile of paper, I remind myself. I am in control of it, not the other way round.

I climb the stairs. Paper and envelopes, this is just another problem that needs sorting.

Just paper and envelopes.

I place my hand on the cold, brass door handle and give it a push.

I've left the curtains closed in here so the room is in semi-darkness. The enormous mound in the middle of the room holds its own shadows, and I try to ignore the fluttering in my guts.

Before I can falter, I snap on the light and clamber over to the other side of the room to sit down.

Allowing myself to get so close to the terrible truth feels very strange. Ignoring it is always preferable, but now I am in here, I am facing first-hand the results of what *that* approach has done for me.

I nudge off my slippers and plunge my bare toes into the cool mass of envelopes, all shapes and sizes that are scattered around my feet.

My eyes take in all the different handwriting, inks, names and addresses. Each letter a secret little package, its contents meant for someone else's eyes.

Now they are mine.

There is a smell to all this paper, and I didn't expect that. A mixture of cardboard and a sort of outdoorsy, ripe kind of odour. Not altogether unpleasant but certainly another unwanted odour in the house.

The fluttering inside begins to ease at last. It is a big heap of paper, and paper never hurt anybody.

I can open every letter if I want to. Nobody will know, and no one can stop me.

I reach for an official-looking brown envelope nestling close to my knee. Before I can change my mind, I tear it open and unfold the letter within. A summons to appear in court for an unpaid parking fine.

'Oh dear, Stephen Trimble, you'll be in trouble for ignoring that,' I giggle, feeling a bit light-headed.

A small, white envelope with lovely bright blue, almost violet, ink is a note from a child to her gran, sending thanks for a recent birthday gift.

Doesn't feel as good opening that one.

I tear open a few more. Most are unimportant communications that won't be missed, nothing interesting or significant.

I'm beginning to wonder why I have attached such gravity and dread to it all.

It just goes to show what a waste most mail actually is. People generally are sending a load of crap and unnecessary words to each other that barely get missed at all.

Albert slinks in through the open door and sniffs doubtfully at the edges of the mail mountain. I watch as he skirts around it all and makes his way over to me, cautious and disapproving.

'We'll get rid of it all, Albert, don't worry,' I whisper. 'I'll make it all go away, and we can make a fresh start.'

Albert purrs and rubs his furry side against my outstretched legs. Where possible, his feet nimbly avoid the letters.

Albert obviously approves of this new plan, and it feels right to me, too. I need to get some normality back so I am able to think straight again.

I'm looking at the problem in a stark new light. It's too late to own up, and there is too much to deliver now. There is way too much to sift through and select earlier dates for retrospective delivery as I had originally planned. Besides, all of this mail is old.

The most sensible thing to do now is obvious: I must clear this room. A clean slate is required, so I have no choice but to dispose of it all and start afresh.

Before doubt creeps in, I reach for a handful of letters and begin tearing them into small pieces. I will fill bin bags with the torn bits and take them to the council dump for disposal. Quick, simple and anonymous.

Too soon, I discover the letters are often too thick to tear more than a couple at a time, plus the ache in my hand worsens almost immediately. The pieces have to be torn very small to ensure the addresses are unreadable. Nothing can be traced.

I have to use both hands, and after ten minutes my injured hand and wrist are throbbing, and I've barely made an inch of inroad into the paper mountain.

I shuffle backwards and lean against the cool wall, legs outstretched.

Years ago, this was Danny's bedroom.

His bed was over in the far corner. He kept his train tracks permanently set up in the middle of the room, right where the mail sits now.

We used to hide in the walk-in cupboard just behind me when Mother was looking for someone to take out her disillusionment with God on. That person was always Danny.

Sometimes I'd stand in front of him so she'd choose me. But it was always him she wanted.

He was the one who disgusted her, and he was the one who held all her hopes, too. I was no use to her.

My heart flutters like it keeps missing the odd beat.

Now the cupboard is full of Danny's old clothes, photos and toys, all packed neatly into boxes and bags and sealed with tape.

There is no space left in there. I've squeezed out all the badness so it belongs to Danny once more – a place where nobody can ever hurt him again.

I promise myself that, one day, I will sort through it all. But thirteen years after that terrible day I still don't feel ready.

It's vital I keep focused on the here and now, so I fast-forward through the painful memories and thoughts. My eyes snap open before the black cloud has a chance to descend.

I must stay strong and determined for Liam's sake. He needs someone sane and balanced who can look after his interests.

My tearing-up disposal plan clearly isn't going to cut it. It will take far too long with an injured hand, and I have neither the time nor the inclination to carry it out. There are far more pressing priorities.

At last, a perfect and simple solution presents itself to me. In fact, I marvel as to why it hasn't occurred to me before now.

The best way to completely eradicate paper is obviously to *burn* it.

There's nothing quite like the feeling of control for making you feel good.

Even better when a certain someone has no clue what you're up to. No clue that behind the kind words and considerate actions you are carefully setting them up.

Once everything is in place, once they trust you, it's too late to go back.

Best of all, they start to blame themselves for making the wrong decisions, for not recognising when things started to go wrong.

Sometimes, they even come to you for help, for advice.

It all comes back to trust. You have to have it and the way to get it is to keep plugging away without being overbearing.

Gently does it. Just a little more pressure each time until you start to feel them give way.

And then you're in and the real fun begins.

CHAPTER 38
Anna

The next day it turns out to be not such a bad morning at work, after all.

The weather is fine and, encouraged by my new plan to tackle the mail mountain, I make good progress on my round. I manage to deliver most of it with just one bag left over, which I lock in a postbox to pick up later in the car.

I drop the empty mailbags back at the office and, just as I'm heading back to the car, Roisin appears, brandishing a carrier bag towards me.

'The top I was telling you about.' She smiles. 'Try it and let me know what you think.'

'Oh, thanks. Yes, I will.' I smile back. 'Thanks, Roisin.'

'We're all going out for a drink on Friday night, if you fancy coming?'

'Friday? Can't, sorry. I've got something on,' I mumble.

'No worries,' she says and begins to walk away. Then she remembers something and turns around again. 'By the way, it is your neighbour. How's that for a coincidence?'

'Sorry?'

'My sister, Linda. I asked her, and she's the care assistant for your neighbour, Joan.'

* * *

On my way back home from the delivery office, I stop to pick up the surplus mail and throw it in my boot with the garden incinerator, lighter fuel and matches I purchased from B&Q earlier.

I'm going to have to reinforce my privacy message to Mrs Peat. The thought of all my personal business going back to Roisin via Linda makes me feel faint.

After grabbing a sandwich and feeding Albert, I gather a bag full of randomly selected mail from the spare room and take it out into the yard. I prop the incinerator up on top of a couple of broken bricks I find in the outhouse and dump the first lot of mail inside.

It is quite windy but the incinerator has air holes all around the base so stuff should still burn efficiently with the lid intact. I sprinkle some lighter fluid on top for good measure and strike a match. When the mail ignites, I fix the lid tight and stand back, watching the base holes fill with a bright, flickering light.

For the first time in ages I feel illuminated, like something is sparking inside of me, telling me everything will be okay.

In a short time, the spare room is going to be empty of mail. I can stop worrying about my job and focus on sorting out Amanda Danson and looking out for Liam.

When the light behind the holes dies down, I move back over to the incinerator and take off the lid.

Most of the mail has reduced to ash. I poke at it with a long twig and see that only a few stubborn pieces of paper remain right down at the bottom.

I calculate I can afford to burn far greater quantities than this first batch, which will enable me to get through the backlog much quicker.

Upstairs, I fill two bin bags and drag them separately out on to the landing one-handed. Naturally, as a postal worker, I'm already aware of the weight of mail but the average person would certainly be surprised by the hindrance of it.

Mail also carries an importance all of its own in that people value and attach high status to their mail. I feel a twinge in my stomach. It's regretful I've not been able to get these letters to the rightful owners.

I look back over my shoulder into the spare room and take some satisfaction in spotting a piece of carpet where there had only been cascading letters. Granted, it is a very small clearing but at least it signifies I'm making headway at long last. That feels good.

I haul the bags awkwardly downstairs and into the kitchen, leaving one by the back door and dragging the other over to the incinerator, piling fresh mail on top of the still-glowing embers. When it is half-full, I sprinkle on lighter fluid as I work to ensure the flames grab hold throughout.

With one last spurt of fluid on top for good measure, I strike a match and light the paper via the bottom holes. I replace the lid immediately and stand back. After just a few seconds, the odd spark spits out from the base holes of the unit and it's away.

As the light increases within and I hear the crackles and splutters as the flames take hold, the warm glow inside me builds too.

The wind whips up and there is even the odd spit of rain but the incinerator is a substantial piece of equipment and the flames continue their work easily, undisturbed by the elements.

After a few minutes, I retrieve a long poker from the unused ornamental set on my stone-surround fireplace and take it back outside. The flames seem to have died down again, judging by the disappearance of the glow and lack of noise from within.

When I lift the lid with a gloved hand, I see with relief that the bulk of the mail has reduced to a thick layer of ashes. I jab around with the poker, and it's gratifying to see there are no large pieces of unscorched paper.

I repeat the process. Half-fill the incinerator, stand back and wait and then check through the ashes.

It all seems to be ticking along nicely.

After I've dragged down another three bags full of mail, I make a cup of tea and stand cradling the hot drink outside, savouring the evaporation of my worries with each load of incriminating paper that burns down to nothing.

I finish my tea just as the third batch finishes. I figure I can probably do one more lot before letting it cool down completely and binning the ashes.

I half-fill it again with the contents of the second bin bag, packing the paper down firmly and sprinkling in the lighter fluid periodically to help the flames get a hold.

The incinerator is very full but the lid goes on easily, and I throw three lit matches in, just to make sure it stays alight.

Standing back, I wait for the comfort of the crackle and the glow and wonder why I hadn't thought about doing this before the mail situation got so bad.

Granted, it is taking a little more time than I had initially hoped, but if I can burn eight to ten loads a day, I should get through the backlog easily by the end of the week.

Thick tendrils of smoke curl out from under the incinerator lid and stream from the bottom. The crackling and spitting has grown quite loud but none of the neighbours are out as far as I can see and, apart from the hum of traffic and the odd dog barking in the distance, all remains quiet.

I'd better not pack the incinerator quite as high when I process the next batch.

I become aware of the sound of a car slowing outside. My heart begins to race but I take a deep breath and tell myself it's probably only Linda, Mrs Peat's care assistant.

The previously pleasant smell of burning now feels quite acrid in my throat.

Car doors open and then slam shut.

My head screams at me to go back inside, but my legs freeze me to the spot.

The cracking and spitting noises emanating from the incinerator seem louder than ever and smoke is puthering out now, top and bottom.

My fingernails dig into the fleshy mounds on both palms. 'Please don't let anyone come. *Please.*' I mutter the words aloud as if that might increase their power.

I hardly ever get visitors and the only unannounced callers are always canvassers who ignore my 'No Callers' sign in the front window.

My heart hammers out a frenzied rhythm which my mind immediately assigns words to.

If they come. . . they'll see the mail.
If they come. . . they'll see the mail.
If they come. . . they'll see the mail.

The phrase dances around in my head on a loop until I can barely think straight. And that's when I hear them.

Voices.

The gate latch rattles, and I peer around the corner of the house just as two uniformed figures appear at the end of the drive. I have failed to lock up the drive gates behind me in my eagerness to burn the mail. How could I have been so stupid?

My head feels light and airy, and the features of the two police officers walking slowly blur until everything about their faces looks wrong.

I glance, wild-eyed, at the overflowing bin bag that is propped up at the back door. I lurch forward, past the sputtering incinerator towards the mail bags. I must get them out of sight.

The lid of the incinerator dislodges and slides off completely, landing with a terrific clatter and echoing around the bare concrete yard.

The wind takes hold of its flaming contents and the whole yard suddenly fills with a maelstrom of seemingly millions of tiny grey cinders.

CHAPTER 39
Joan Peat

The arrangements for when Anna was first discharged from the hospital – or the 'clinic' – as that interfering social worker had preferred to call it, had been made while she was still receiving treatment.

It was decided that Joan would look after her – a sort of informal fostering arrangement – until Anna turned eighteen just over a year later.

That was the sort of thing you could do in those days. Joan frowned and reached for her knitting bag. You could cut through all the silly red tape and make decisions solely based on what was best for the child.

Joan had no hesitation when she was approached by social services. There was no question she was the obvious choice to support and temporarily care for Anna. After all, the girl was like a daughter to her. Up until that terrible day, she had spent more time at Joan's house than in her own.

But the authorities hadn't warned her that the person who would return from the clinic would be a very different person to the girl she used to know.

When the time was right, it was going to be very difficult for Joan to explain what happened to Anna. . . to reveal the horror Anna didn't yet know about.

Joan eased out the scarf she was knitting for the church's Christmas raffle and slipped a few key stitches as she began to click the needles.

She always got a bit het up when she thought about pretty, carefree Anna, as she used to be before the tragedy.

It was such an awful shame there was more to come.

CHAPTER 40
Present day
Anna

I rush through the thick cloud of smoke and grab all three bags from the doorway.

I drag them to the end of the small kitchen and throw a couple of tea towels over the top to cover the letters haemorrhaging out through the torn sides.

Coughing and hacking, I turn back to the door just as the uniforms appear.

'Hello, are you Anna Clarke?' The female officer offers her hand and bats smoke away from her face with the other. 'I'm PC Cullen and this is my colleague, PC Storer.'

They look mismatched. He is relatively short and on the plump side while she is taller and whip-thin.

'Hope we haven't caught you at a bad time,' he remarks behind a thin fog of smoke and bits. 'Looks like you're quite busy.'

Understatement of the fucking year.

'I'm having a clear-out.'

I stand by the still-whirling contents of the incinerator, my words slow and faint.

They glance around the yard and then at each other.

'Might we come in for a minute or two?' PC Cullen breaks the silence. 'It's about the accident you witnessed a few days ago on Green Road.'

My breathing steadies.

No one has reported me for burning undelivered mail. They don't know about the spare room mail mountain upstairs. They are here about the accident, probably as a result of my phone call to PC Brixham.

'I suppose you'd better come in,' I say curtly.

I'd already shut Albert away in the front room while I burned outside so we sit at the table in the middle room.

'Do you live here alone?' PC Cullen glances around the room like I might have stashed a husband or a lodger somewhere behind the furniture.

'Yes,' I say. 'That's not a crime, is it?'

She looks like the kind of person who plays squash after work on a Monday while everyone else crumples in front of the television with a glass of wine and packet of crisps.

She smiles. 'Of course not, just curious.'

'I'm trying to find out what that smell is,' I say. 'If you were wondering.'

They both sniff the air, and PC Storer shrugs.

'Can't smell a great deal apart from burning,' he says, and his colleague shakes her head.

He reaches across his puckering jacket into his pocket and pulls out a small notebook and pencil.

'We just want to go over a few details about the accident, Anna, if that's OK?'

I glance out of the window and see that the smoke seems to be dying down at last.

'Can you tell us exactly what happened that day?' he begins. 'Did you see the accident happen?'

I take a breath, trying to remember to take my time and make sure I don't say anything that I might later regret. I don't want to *lie* to them exactly, but if I tell the truth, then Amanda Danson is going to find it much easier to wriggle out of her responsibilities.

I am absolutely certain she mowed Liam down that day due to speed and lack of attention to the road. Yet the police refuse to deal with hunches and intuition. Everything has to have cast-iron proof, regardless of it allowing a low-life like her to escape justice.

I know how guilty she's feeling about not paying attention to the road but I can hardly say I've been snooping and read her Facebook message to Liam.

'The car was speeding and knocked him off his motorbike,' I say.

As I utter the words I see it happen in my mind.

He looks up sharply from his notes. 'You witnessed the moment of impact?'

I nod.

'Can you tell us exactly what you saw, Anna?' PC Cullen asks.

I have her full attention now. Her beady eyes have stopped their judgemental scan of the room.

'I saw the car approaching head-on. She was going far too fast and. . . well, the driver sort of bent down a bit and then it happened.'

'Bent down a bit?'

'As if she was reaching for something,' I say. 'That's what it looked like to me, anyway.'

They glance at each other, and PC Storer begins furiously scribbling away on his notepad.

This is probably the most exciting thing he has investigated for months. Kids shoplifting and people reporting antisocial behaviour are all that seem to happen around here.

'Are you saying she wasn't watching the road?' PC Cullen probes. 'How sure are you of what you witnessed?'

I shrug, careful to appear as though I'm reticent to point the finger of blame, yet hopefully remaining convincing enough to give Amanda Danson a massive problem.

'I was at a bit of a distance.' I'm getting into my stride now. 'All I know is that her face was there one minute then not the next. Her head seemed lower and near the middle of the wind-screen, as if she was bending forward to reach down for something. A phone, perhaps.'

PC Cullen widens her eyes at her colleague, as if to say 'told you so'. I'm beginning to warm to her after all.

At last, he stops making notes and asks me lots of boring technical stuff like how far away was I *exactly*? How many seconds between initially seeing the car and then witnessing the impact was it *exactly*?

I rub at my prickling face like my hand is a flannel. I really need to learn a lesson from this. I have had plenty of time to revisit the scene of the accident and get the story crystal clear in my head and yet I've neglected to do so.

I have been back there a couple of times but not to measure tyre marks on the bloody road.

I know for certain what happened that day. It doesn't matter that I didn't actually witness the bit about the phone.

I have other irrefutable evidence, not only from the past but from the here and now; Amanda's guilt-ridden Facebook message, her pathetic snivelling visit to the hospital and the fact she is still going to work and acting as if nothing has happened.

This is the *real* evidence that everyone else is missing.

'It's hard to say exactly what distance was involved. All I remember is that poor motorcyclist, flying up in the air then landing in a broken heap on the ground. It happened so fast, you see.'

'We understand that, Anna,' PC Cullen says gravely. 'But you are our only witness of the accident happening, so it's really important we get this right. What happened next, after the initial impact?'

I note with some satisfaction that, from what she says, the Mercedes driver behind me must have completely missed the accident actually happening.

I take a moment to recreate the scene in my head.

'Well, the driver got out of her car and stood looking at Liam lying in the road. She seemed more shocked than sorry.'

'Let's just stick with the facts,' PC Storer remarks. 'She got out of the car, then what?'

'It looked to me like she was thinking about getting back in and driving off,' I say. 'Then people started coming out of their houses and then she had no choice but to stay and face what she'd done.'

'How did you get that impression?' PC Cullen interjects. 'Did she physically start to get back in the car?'

I shrug. 'Not exactly, but—'

'We have to record *exactly* what happened here, Miss Clarke,' her colleague chips in again. 'Not what *might* have happened.'

Out of nowhere I start thinking about what's upstairs, directly above our heads. My neck tendons strain and begin to cramp my shoulders.

If all the undelivered mail falls through the ceiling now, I will lose my job and could be prosecuted. These two officers might even arrest me and take me to a holding cell.

My heart wallops away at my ribcage while my old therapist's voice appears in my head and tries to help me out.

'Calm down. The mail will not fall through the ceiling and in a few days it will all be gone.'

Still, I feel a desperate need to get them out of the house as quickly as possible.

'You OK, Miss Clarke?'

PC Cullen is watching me again with her mean little button eyes.

Then she says: 'Shall I make you a cup of tea?'

'No!' I almost jump out of my seat but just about manage to stop myself.

If she sees the bin bags in the kitchen they'll search the house. I realise too late that I've raised my voice.

I smile and cough. 'Sorry, I've not had much sleep since the accident. I find it hard to concentrate on conversation at times.'

'You do seem on edge,' PC Storer murmurs, tapping his pencil on his notepad and studying my face.

'It's because you're making me remember it all.' I feel irritated again. 'It was traumatic. I expect it's normal to feel on edge, isn't it?'

He gives a quick nod and glances back down at the notebook.

My breaths are getting shorter and quicker. I need to bring this to an end.

'Everyone was fussing around the driver of the car,' I say quickly. 'Liam was lying in the road; I didn't move him or anything. I just held his hand, comforted him.'

'You waited with him until the ambulance came,' PC Storer says.

I nod.

'Did he say anything to you?' He pauses his pencil eagerly above the paper.

I shake my head. There is no way I'm going to share the moment where Liam asked me to help him. His words aren't meant for some grubby police notebook.

'From what I saw it was entirely her fault,' I say firmly. 'Liam did nothing wrong; it was her. She was distracted; she shouldn't be on the road.'

The air in the room has turned thick and stagnant. My words seem to hang there, out of place.

'Take your time and have a think through what happened again,' PC Cullen says slowly, sliding a small card across the table. 'And if you remember anything else, anything more specific, give us a call.'

I nod and rub at a small scorch mark on the table top. They'll sit staring at me all day, if I let them.

'If that's all then,' I say, getting up. 'I'll show you out.'

They both stand, and PC Storer strolls over to the window.

'Bit windy for burning your rubbish today,' he says, arching his back and stretching. 'You'll have the neighbours up in arms about their washing if you're not careful.'

Out of the corner of my eye, I see PC Cullen moving towards the door at the staircase.

'OK if I use your bathroom before we go, Anna?' She points upstairs.

To use the bathroom, she'll have to walk past the spare room. I left the door open when I dragged the bags of mail down to burn. She won't even have to snoop to see the mail mountain in all its glory.

Instantly flooding with adrenaline, I fly over to the other side of the room and position myself between PC Cullen and the stairs door.

'No!' I bark. 'You can't.'

CHAPTER 41

I stretch out my arms and, facing her, place both palms flat either side of the door. I can tell from her face I seem like a crazy person. But I can't stop it.

She takes a step back, her smile falling away.

PC Storer turns quickly from the window at the commotion and moves towards us.

'Everything okay, Anna?' he asks mildly, like I'm a loaded gun that might go off any second.

I blink a couple of times, trying to get my thoughts together.

'I'm sorry,' I say with a nervous laugh. 'It's just that the toilet isn't working properly. It's broken, you see.' The skin on my face feels taut and stretched as if it might split with the effort of keeping my secrets in. 'I haven't got a body up there or anything.'

I giggle, trying to make light of the situation but they eye me suspiciously.

'I see,' PC Cullen says, turning to look at her colleague. 'We didn't mean to alarm you, Anna, I had no hidden agenda in going upstairs.'

'I know,' I say quickly, realising how ridiculous I must look. I allow my damp hands to fall away from the door and relax my rigid stance the best I can. 'It's just a bit – well, embarrassing, that's all. It's stinky up there at the moment.'

PC Storer nods slowly. 'Have you called a plumber?'

'Yes,' I say. Then, 'I mean no, I haven't called a plumber yet. I was just about to do that when you arrived.'

My shoulders relax a little as PC Cullen turns away from the stairs door but then she walks towards the kitchen.

'We'll leave you to it then,' she says, brushing down her uniform.

I feel like running past her and standing in front of the bin bags on the kitchen floor but, somehow, I manage to control myself.

'I'm sorry,' I say, following them out. 'About the loo, I mean.'

'No worries,' PC Cullen shrugs. 'We're going back to the station now, anyway, it won't kill me to hold on.'

PC Storer peers into the incinerator as they step outside, pausing for just a moment.

'You'd be better off with a shredder,' he remarks.

'Sorry?'

'The paperwork,' he says, nodding down into the ashes. 'Probably less mess to shred it than burn it.'

'Right you are,' I bristle.

Mind your own fucking business.

I watch them drive away before locking the gates top and bottom and going back into the house. I lock the kitchen door behind me and lean heavily against it.

The bottom of my back is wet; my heart is pounding.

I say a silent prayer of thanks they've finally gone.

CHAPTER 42
PC Cullen

Gill Cullen slid into the passenger seat of the police car parked outside Anna Clarke's house and turned to her colleague.

'What did you make of her?'

Jay Storer glanced in the mirror before pulling away. 'Pretty weird as far as weirdos go. Thought she was going to knock your head off when you asked to use her loo.'

'I swear she was lying or at least compromising the truth but why would she do that? As far as I understand it, she was just a random witness of the accident; she didn't know either of the drivers involved.'

'Let's face it, some people are just weird and there's no logic behind it.' He shrugged. 'She's probably just making the most of the attention. We've dealt with that sort before, haven't we?'

A couple of years earlier a child had gone missing and local volunteers organised a thorough search of the area.

One of the main organisers brought himself to police attention. He seemed to be everywhere at once, getting in the way and shadowing police activity. He even started questioning people himself and reporting what they said back to officers.

Happily, the little girl was found safe at a friend's house and only then did the man lose interest and make himself scarce.

It was enough to show Gill just how strangely some people could behave; seemingly, just to get themselves in the limelight of an investigation.

Gill stared bleakly out of the window as the car moved past rows of sooty-brick terraced houses and boarded-up shops.

She couldn't shake her gut feeling that there was more to Anna Clarke than first met the eye.

Eccentric was probably a kinder word than weird. After all, this woman held down a responsible job and lived quite independently and capably on her own.

To her credit, Anna Clarke had also stayed with the victim at the scene of the accident until the ambulance arrived.

Yet she had been very obviously spooked when Gill and her colleague had arrived at her house and proceeded to act in a textbook guilty manner for no apparent reason.

The last time Gill checked, it wasn't illegal to burn rubbish in your own backyard. Her own dad did it all the time, regularly infuriating neighbours who had just pegged out neat lines of damp laundry.

Despite all this, Gill still had reservations about the people involved in the Green Road incident. In fact, this whole seemingly run-of-the-mill accident left a bad taste in her mouth.

They hadn't been able to speak to Liam Bradbury yet because of his memory loss and trauma, and getting to see the driver of the other vehicle, Amanda Danson, was proving more difficult than it should be.

After posted letters were seemingly ignored, Gill had personally called at both houses with a colleague to hand deliver letters requesting that Mr Bradbury and Miss Danson make statements down at the station. Two days later, Gill was still waiting for a response.

No representative for Mr Bradbury, who had clearly come off worse in the incident, had been in touch as far as she knew, so Gill had no real reason to put the pressure on Amanda Danson.

Gill yawned and opened the window a touch.

Apart from the odd road accident and nuisance neighbours, her job seemed to consist of little else but community-relations bollocks. She hadn't signed up for that but it was now a major demand of the job.

Her Uncle George had been a detective for over thirty years, and his one consistent piece of advice to her was that she should trust her gut.

'You need to work to get noticed in this job, Gilly, or you'll end up a beat copper for the rest of your life,' he'd cautioned.

Uncle George told her how, over the years, he'd watched people who had begun their career with drive to subconsciously allow that drive to seep away, day after day. Dealing with small-time druggies and lost pets seemed to have that effect.

'Before you know it, the years just melt away,' he told her. 'Those once-ambitious beat coppers resigned themselves to the fact that it was now too late to do anything about it and just accepted their lot.'

Such pathetic acceptance was not in Gill's nature but she knew George was right. The only way to stop the same thing happening to her was to rise above the chaff and go with her gut.

She needed a way to win recognition from the management for being smart and using her initiative.

'Do you get the feeling there's more to this accident than meets the eye?' She looked over at Jay.

'Nah,' he murmured, raising a friendly hand to a group of hoodies as they passed the car at the lights. One of the lads responded with the finger.

'Cheeky bugger,' he chuckled.

Gill liked Jay on a personal level, but his lethargic and accepting nature of the job infuriated her. If ever there was a career beat cop, it was him. She wouldn't get tarred with the same brush.

It was time to put some pressure on the people involved in the Green Road accident to make their official statements. Maybe she'd invest some time of her own, dig around a bit.

CHAPTER 43
Anna

After I hear the police car pull away, I sink on to the kitchen floor with my face in my hands for a long time. I managed to fool them but my head feels swelled and fit to burst with the volume of stuff I'm worrying about.

My mail-destroying plan seems a very bad idea now but it's all I've got. It is the only way to set things straight and quick.

I glance at the wall clock and I'm astounded to see it's nearly four in the afternoon. I know Liam will be wondering where I am, waiting to have a cuppa and a chat with me after being holed up in the house with Ivy all day long.

I stand up slowly, feeling woozy like I've had too much to drink.

The three black bin bags hunker down in the corner of the kitchen, full of silent threat. They seem bigger, somehow, as if the mail inside is stealthily growing in bulk.

Much as I want to get over to see Liam, I know I have to clear up this mess. It won't do to allow any traces or clues to remain. I'm certainly not expecting any more unwanted visitors but it's only sensible to plan for the unexpected.

My mind instantly presents scenarios that would be out of my control. Someone could break in when I'm out. If I forget to turn off a plug and there was an electrical fire, the local fire brigade would have to force entry. I'll be discovered and nobody will believe I'm just having a temporary problem at work and that it isn't my fault.

Pulling myself together, I stand up and go back outside. Squinting against the wind, I begin to shovel ashes out from the bottom of the incinerator.

They aren't cool enough yet to pile into the wheelie bin so I stack them in a small pile in the corner of the disused coalhouse at the end of the yard.

There are a few larger unburned pieces of paper within the ashes that the eagle-eyed PC Storer somehow managed to spot.

I replace the lid on the incinerator and put that into the coalhouse too. Then I take the big brush and sweep up the tiny shards of paper that have fluttered out, escaping into the corners of the yard.

With the outside sorted, I go back inside and lock the door behind me. I feel so much safer with the gate and doors locked. I don't like surprise visitors.

I take hold of all three bin bags and drag them back across the kitchen floor into the middle room. My throat seems blocked up with what feels like cotton wool, and I have to pause for a few seconds to catch my breath.

The bags are heavy but I'd rather do it in one trip upstairs if I possibly can.

I've barely taken a few steps into the middle room when something stops me dead in my tracks. I let go of the bags and lift my chin, inhaling deeply to the left and then to the right.

The smell I thought I had scrubbed and cleaned away only two days earlier is back with a vengeance. That rotting, vile stench.

There is something familiar about it but I don't know what. There's something hanging around on the edge of my memory that I can't quite grasp.

I think I've smelled it before, not in the last week or so but years ago. A ragged lump swells in my throat and I take a few deep breaths to stave off the sickly feeling that's quickly rising from my stomach.

Standing by the kitchen window, I grip the worktop to steady myself.

I look out, almost expecting the two officers to appear again from round the corner with their little faux-friendly waves and smiles. They'll have to knock at the front door if they want to speak to me again and, of course, I won't be so silly as to answer this time.

I take a couple of sips from a glass of water and reach for the bottle of cleaning fluid and a cloth from the cupboard underneath the sink. I venture back into the middle room and sniff the air. Yes, it's there and back to its unbearable normal strength.

I move around the table. Is it my imagination or does the smell seem stronger on the side where the police sat?

I spray the tabletop and wipe around. Then I do the same on the chairs, including frames, legs and even the floral cushions, which are sodden with lemon cleaning fluid by the time I've finished.

I hear Albert yowling in the front room. I'd completely forgotten he was in there. When I open the door he stalks past, tail upright and refusing to look at me.

Albert hates visitors, too.

He makes a beeline for the table and proceeds to wind his way around the chair legs. He isn't purring or pleasuring himself from the rub, he's trying to eradicate the smell of the imposters. We both are.

Soon, the pungent sting of lemon cleaning fluid fills my nostrils and relieves the stench a little. Albert is none too pleased and within a minute or two he's sneezing and hacking. He brushes past me with barely disguised disdain, and I open the kitchen door to let him outside.

'Don't go too far, Albert,' I call before closing and locking the door again.

He'll come round and forgive me later when I tempt him with one of his favourite treats.

I grab the bags again and half-drag, half-carry them upstairs. By the time I get them onto the landing, the bags are badly torn and a trail of letters spills all the way back down the stairs.

I sit on the top step to steady my shaking legs and stare back down at the litter of white and brown envelopes and multicoloured flyers.

Part of me wishes I could just set the whole house alight and get it all done with in one go. I could start afresh then. Even that, given my current luck, would fail.

No doubt the authorities would put the fire out before it destroyed all the mail, or the water tank would burst and extinguish the flames.

Sharp pains shoot across my scalp. I lower my hands and release clumps of hair, wriggling my fingers so that the tangles flutter down and settle on top of the scattered mail.

I can't allow myself to get distracted like this or I'll never make it to Liam's house, and that would please Ivy and Amanda no end.

Ignoring the mess that is on the stairs for now, I stand up again and drag the bags along the length of the landing and into the spare bedroom, leaving them by the boiler cupboard until I can continue with my incinerator plan tomorrow.

I allow myself a little smile in the bathroom. I certainly outwitted the supposedly smart PC Cullen with my impromptu broken-toilet excuse.

I flush the loo and wash my hands at the sink. When I glance up at the small mirror a sharp cry escapes my lips.

My already sparse hairline has receded back very noticeably at my temples. Two large jagged patches of bare scalp are bleeding and inflamed.

I don't know how it got so bad so quickly.

CHAPTER 44
Present day
Anna

I glance at my watch and realise it is only an hour until Liam's check-up appointment at the hospital, and I am supposed to be driving him there.

When I arrive at the house Ivy is in an obstructive mood, giving Liam a hard time.

'There's no need for you to come,' I tell her as kindly as I can. 'You're struggling to get about as it is. We'll come straight back and tell you how it went, won't we, Liam?'

'Rubbish.' She struggles up from the couch. 'The Grim Reaper isn't knocking yet, you know.'

'Gran,' Liam says gently. 'Anna's right. It's silly you traipsing all the way to the hospital with us and back again when there's no need.'

It is obvious that Liam is looking forward to escaping her clutches for a short while and spending time with me. He hasn't said anything about the fact I didn't come over yesterday but that will just be him being polite and not wanting to upset me. I hope he didn't spend hours watching and waiting for my arrival, though.

If we manage to get some respite from Ivy this morning, we can have a coffee and chat in the hospital café afterwards or maybe even grab a spot of lunch.

'I'm fine,' Ivy insists between clenched teeth. Her voice is steely, despite her frail appearance. 'Anyway, he's been out all afternoon; be nice to see him a bit.'

'You've been out?' I ask faintly.

He ignores my question and gets to his feet. I am surprised by how much easier he seems to be moving.

'No, Gran, you stay here and rest. I'll go with Anna this time, end of.'

Ivy sighs and her shoulders sink down like a deflated balloon. It's well known that a troubled mind responds to firm direction, and that's told her in no uncertain terms.

I fetch Liam's jacket and crutches and shoot Ivy a look as I walk past her.

'We're trying to look out for you is all, Ivy,' I say. 'I want to help you in any way I can to make your life a bit easier.'

'I just feel so – so useless.' She wipes her eyes with the back of a liver-spotted hand.

The sooner Ivy realises I am a permanent fixture in their lives, the better off we'll all be. Putting up with this nonsense every time I come over is really getting on my nerves.

I'm sure she will feel more able to accept my help when I have moved in. If her health gets worse and she refuses to accept our help, Liam might even be forced to look for a suitable care home for her. I can only pray it doesn't come to that.

Once we are in the car and on our way, I notice my breathing gets a bit easier. Not least because Liam begins to talk to me.

'It's driving me mad being stuck in the house, seeing stuff around me that I don't remember anything about,' he says.

'It's bound to feel frustrating,' I agree. 'Hopefully, bits might start to come back to you soon.'

He shrugs but doesn't comment.

'I haven't been out all afternoon at all,' he remarks. 'I think Gran is losing her concept of time. I just had a walk to the park and back to get some fresh air.'

It seems Ivy is getting confused about everyday matters. And after having sight of the report that is currently hidden away in her wardrobe, it's no surprise to me at all.

'I'm worried about your gran, Liam,' I say. 'She's doing far too much, and I overheard one of the nurses saying she is a prime candidate for a heart attack.'

I didn't *actually* overhear those exact words but I'm certain it will have been said by someone at some point following Ivy's collapse.

'She's a tough old bird,' he shrugs. 'Trouble is, she doesn't seem to know when to put her feet up.'

Or keep her big mouth shut.

It doesn't take long to get to the hospital. I keep the conversation light for the rest of the journey. I don't want to pressurise Liam in any way before his appointment.

I can wait.

I sit outside the treatment room while Liam sees the doctor. I almost offer to go in with him but think better of it in the end. I'm not the sort to interfere.

Liam is seeing a doctor today who hasn't got a clue about his medical history or the trauma he has been through. Why you see somebody different every time you come to these places I don't know but it must waste a lot of time while each doctor gets up to speed.

Nevertheless, after just fifteen minutes in there he emerges from the room holding his crutches but not using them.

He's quite a bit taller than me, and I like standing next to him. Makes me feel safe.

'Doc says everything is knitting together nicely,' he grins. 'Next appointment is in two weeks, and I'll be starting physio soon.'

'It doesn't take long for them to lose interest,' I grumble loud enough for the receptionist to hear. 'Can't wait to get rid of you to free up the bed these days.'

Liam says he could do with a coffee so we head into the café, and I sit him down at a table while I queue for the drinks.

It's strange to think I was here myself only a few days ago when I cut my hand. The wound seems to be healing fine despite me rushing out of Triage, although it still aches and is very sore if I accidentally catch it.

I take the drinks over to our table on a tray.

'I've been thinking,' I say, as though the thought has only just occurred to me. 'I could move in to yours for a few days, if you like. To help you both out, I mean.'

He looks at me but he doesn't say anything.

My head starts to pound, and I can feel my face heating up.

'I'm just thinking of you and Ivy.' I'm trying to make it easy for him. 'She is struggling to look after you, and I'm sitting at home every afternoon with little to do. It seems the obvious solution.'

I realise he is probably just emotional and is finding it difficult to find the right words to thank me. I wait.

At that moment, a woman with bright red hair and lips to match stops at our table and beams at Liam. I stir my latte and try to ignore the furious itching at the back of my neck.

'Hello you, I'm Nurse Linda. Remember?'

Liam smiles at her politely but it's obvious he hasn't got a clue who she is.

'I was on your ward for a couple of days when you first came in. How are things?'

Liam is sitting here with crutches, looking far too pale and thin. How does she *think* things are?

She is dressed casually; obviously off-duty but still worryingly overfamiliar considering Liam is a patient.

I sip my coffee and busy myself looking around the café. I catch her glancing my way a couple of times, trying to draw me into the conversation but, of course, I completely disregard her efforts.

The two of them have a stilted conversation for a few moments and then finally she moves on, waving at Liam like an old friend.

Infuriatingly, the moment we had before her appearance is now lost, and Liam starts droning on about some wildlife series he's been watching on TV.

I've no doubt he is simply too embarrassed to bring up my offer again, even though it is what he wants.

When we've finished our coffee, I have to virtually force him to use one of the visitor wheelchairs again so we can move quickly through the hospital corridors and out to the car.

'I feel stupid stuck in here like an old invalid,' he grumbles, holding the crutches across his knees. 'A bad headache doesn't stop me from walking.'

'It isn't for long,' I scold, secretly wishing he was confined to a chair all the time so I could monitor his whereabouts and better assist him.

Once we are back in the car, I broach the subject again.

'As I was saying before, Liam, I am more than happy to stay over at yours for a short time until you get on your feet again.'

He looks out of the window and stays quiet. If we are to become closer as friends, he has to learn to open up to me.

'If your gran has a heart attack or, worse, dies, think how guilty you'll feel. Especially since it could all have been avoided by a simple arrangement.'

'Can I be honest with you, Anna?'

My heart is pounding but I try hard to concentrate on the road. His warm tone feels like he's confiding in me.

'For some reason Gran has this silly hang-up about us relying on you too much. You know how she values her independence, even though I agree she could do with the help.' He pauses. 'I just don't think she would entertain the idea of you moving in, even for a short time. It would be like admitting she couldn't cope, you see. She's always been the same.'

My head jerks round at him and then back to the road.

'You remember how she used to be?'

'Not as such.' He shrugs and shakes his head. 'I mean she's been the same since I had the accident.'

I have this overwhelming sense that we're at a pivotal moment in our relationship. It is clear to me that Liam is actually trying to say he's very fond of me and would accept my offer.

If it wasn't for Ivy being difficult about it. So I make an instant decision.

'What are you doing?' Liam yelps as I suddenly swerve the car into a lay-by.

CHAPTER 45

Once we are safely parked up, I turn off the engine.

Before I can properly give consideration to the best way to tell him, the words are spilling from my mouth.

'I know you've had an awful lot of stuff to take in the last week or so, Liam,' I begin. 'But I need to tell you exactly why Ivy is so afraid of me getting closer to you both.'

I turn my body so I'm facing him but he still won't meet my eyes. My breath quickens, and I think about reaching for his hand. But in the end, I just can't do it.

'You have to promise that this stays between us, for now.'

Liam shifts awkwardly in his seat, staring stubbornly out of the window.

I have no choice. I can feel the words stacking up in my throat, words that need saying.

'I don't want you to think I've been snooping because that really is not the case,' I begin. 'But when I took the towels and bedding upstairs at the house, I couldn't help but see that Ivy had left some documents out on the bed.'

His head whips round, and his eyes search my face as if he is trying to second-guess what I'm about to say.

'There were letters. Papers and things,' I falter. 'Obviously I didn't open anything but one or two of them. . . well, they were open anyway, and as I tidied them I couldn't help but get the gist of what was being said.'

I stare, fascinated, as his cheeks develop two dark pink spots of colour.

'What did you see?' Tiny spots of perspiration pop up on his top lip. 'Anna?'

'There's something you will have forgotten because of the accident and—'

'Just tell me!'

A muscle flexes in his jaw; his tense, broad shoulders turn towards me.

I don't feel afraid of Liam, of course I don't. That would be silly.

But I'm beginning to wonder if I have picked the right moment.

'I found an old report upstairs on Ivy's bed,' I say, looking past him through the car window. 'A psychological report.'

'You'd no right to go snooping.' He grabs the wrist of my injured hand, and I let out a yelp.

'Liam, please!'

He lets go, and I rub my wrist but it doesn't dissipate the bolts of sharp pain.

'Sorry,' he says, running a hand through his unruly hair. 'I didn't mean to hurt you, Anna.'

'It's fine,' I say but I stiffen under a growing urgency to just drive him home.

His fingers drum his knee urgently.

'You were saying. . . about the paperwork?'

I have no choice but to carry on now.

'It was a report about Ivy. Did you know she's had psychological problems?'

He laughs. 'I don't think so; hard to know with no memory but I seriously doubt it. I mean, she's a daft old bat alright but not proper bonkers.'

'She'd signed it off herself,' I say, carefully. 'The report, I mean. So the things it says must be accurate. An official medical opinion.'

Liam shrugs. 'I don't see what that's got to do with anything.'

His mood is all over the place. It must be the head injury messing things up.

'You're allowing her to make all the important decisions, that's my point.'

The ghost of a smirk drifts past his lips but he doesn't say anything.

He glances at his watch and lets out a long breath. I can almost feel the irritation prickling off him but I still can't let it go.

I keep my voice level. 'Ivy doesn't always know what's best for you, Liam.'

'What do you want me to say?'

I realise I have never noticed those silvery flecks in his dark blue eyes before. It's probably just the angle of the light but they shift and shimmer until I'm not sure of the dominant colour at all.

My heart performs little blips every few beats and, looking at Liam's dark expression, my big reveal about Ivy doesn't seem like such a good idea.

'I know it's hard to take in, and I know it's none of my business but I think you have a right to know.' I try again.

A swell, a kind of longing, fills my chest area.

I lay my hand gently on his arm, and he looks down at it. His face has lost some of its crimson colour, and his posture seems to have softened.

'Thanks, Anna,' he says, more like his old self again. 'You're a mate.'

My heart dips in my chest a little but then I have always known that's how he sees me. I'd be an idiot to hope for anything more. Then he speaks again.

'That's wrong, you're more than a mate.'

I feel like I'm holding my face up to the full sun under the heat of his words.

'You're special to me.'

'I think she's scared of being left on her own,' I start to babble, feeling my own cheeks inflame. 'After your dad and sister died in the accident, you were all she had left, and I think she's scared of you and I getting—'

He shakes his head in a strange, jerking fashion, and his colour comes back up.

'She likes Amanda,' he says vaguely, letting his hand fall away.

'Don't you see?' It feels like something is nipping at my stomach. 'Amanda is terrified the police will prosecute her, so it's her mission to befriend you. And with her mental health issues, Ivy is not the best person to be managing communications with the police.'

'You must've been mistaken, by the way,' he says, ignoring everything I just said. 'I asked the doctor and they haven't had a child in.'

'Huh?'

'You said Amanda had knocked a child off a bicycle. She didn't.'

'Oh, the nurse must have been mistaken when she told me that,' I say, swallowing hard. 'Amanda can't be trusted. Just a feeling but I'm quite intuitive like that.'

He is putting a cool face on: acting as though he isn't overly concerned.

'Amanda thinks if she wins you over, you'll speak up for her and the police won't take their investigations any further.' I decide to push this time. 'There's something not right about Amanda Danson. She isn't who she appears to be.'

'Who is she then?' Liam grins and his lips look sore, like the skin is stretched too far.

'Someone you would be well advised to keep away from. Trust me.'

He says nothing, and we just sit quietly but the silence isn't uncomfortable.

Then, at last, he turns to me.

'I'll speak to Gran,' he says. 'I'd like you to stay at the house for a while.'

My heart feels like it's going to burst, and I clasp his hand, hard.

CHAPTER 46
Thirteen years earlier

Carla Bevin opened the curtain a touch and watched as the cluster of reporters and TV cameras gathered outside the house.

Men and women, some with mobile phones trapped between their ear and shoulder, scribbling onto notepads. Others were looking around the street, eyes darting, brain working out new ways of getting the neighbours to talk to them.

She pulled the fabric back again, battling the lumpy knot that was trying to free itself from her throat

Two days earlier, on a stupid, stupid whim, she had paid an unauthorised, unscheduled visit to the Clarke family home.

She'd knocked at the door, picked off bits of peeling paint as she waited, thoroughly prepared to be given short shrift, when it opened.

'Yes?'

Daniel's mother wasn't what she expected. A petite woman, she was dressed in checked capri pants and a silky white blouse. An elegant gold cross nestled in the hollow of her throat.

She had a pert nose and full lips. Her make-up had been applied a little on the heavy side, but still.

'Mrs Clarke? I'm Carla Bevin from Cumber Meadows Comprehensive.' She held out her hand, and Monica Clarke shook it. 'I wouldn't normally just turn up like this but I need to speak to you about your son, Daniel.'

'Please, come in.' Monica showed Carla into the kitchen. 'I'll make us a nice pot of tea and then we can talk.'

Carla had been quickly made to feel both welcome and respected.

Monica took her into the middle room which, in contrast to the white kitchen, was dark and dreary. Lots of dark wood furniture lined the room and religious artefacts filled the walls.

Over tea and biscuits Carla gently began to talk to Monica about her children.

'So Anna approached you in the school car park?' Monica remarked.

Carla nodded. She thought Mrs Clarke looked concerned and a little upset.

'I'll have a chat with her. Young girls and their hormones; her imagination has been running away with her lately. It's difficult, you know?'

Carla did know. She remembered her and her sister at each other's throats at the same age Anna was now.

'So Daniel isn't in grave danger, Mrs Clarke?'

Monica put down her cup and saucer and gave a light laugh. 'Sorry, I don't mean to make light of the situation but Daniel in danger? He doesn't move away from his computer games long enough to be in peril in the real world, Miss Bevin.'

'Carla, please.'

Monica picked up her cup again and watched Carla over the top of it.

'At school, I've been trying to get Daniel to talk about any problems he might have.' Carla watched her reaction. Monica Clarke didn't seem to have any concerns about her son. Maybe he was hiding things from his mother. 'After speaking to you, I wonder if Anna might benefit from some counselling sessions, too.'

She had caught the brief flicker of shock on Mrs Clarke's face then and, at that moment, realised that Monica had been unaware of Daniel's sessions.

Moreover, Carla had to face the fact she herself had assumed Daniel's problems were confined to school when, in fact, she wasn't at all sure that was now the case.

Mrs Clarke excused herself and disappeared upstairs for a few minutes to speak to Daniel.

Carla looked around the room at the crosses. Dozens of them, large and small, dotted about the walls, on shelves, the dark oak Welsh dresser and even on the windowsill.

A shiver crept over her skin, and she wrapped her cardigan a little tighter.

A few minutes later, Monica reappeared at the stairs door.

'I'm afraid Daniel is quite sleepy. He's refusing to come down.'

'Kids,' Carla faltered. 'Perhaps you'd be interested in coming into school at some point, to attend some parent-child therapy sessions.'

'Sounds perfect,' Monica nodded. 'Just let me know where and when.'

This pacified Carla. The leadership team would no doubt be delighted she'd been able to persuade Monica Clarke to engage with the school at last.

She thanked Mrs Clarke and headed home, back to her glass of wine to toast this unexpected and very welcome result.

CHAPTER 47
Present day
Anna

Jim Crowe had mentioned an impromptu work meeting to me only that morning, and I agreed to go back into the delivery office early in the afternoon in order to attend it.

He didn't say specifically what it was about but, if it was regarding new round allocations, then I'd be sure to get myself there to fight my corner.

When I agreed, I calculated that I'd have plenty of time to take Liam to the hospital, have some lunch and drop him off before I had to go back in to work for two o'clock. But time whizzes by so quickly: I have to drop Liam back at home and get straight off again.

It is a fifteen-minute drive to the office and, despite nagging thoughts at the back of my mind about my problems at work, I feel euphoric at how well my discussion with Liam has gone.

Up ahead there is some kind of delay on the road; the traffic slowly backs up and then stops moving altogether. Instead of getting stressed I put the handbrake on and settle back to wait for the cars in front of me to move again.

I push work worries to the back of my mind and begin to plan my move into Liam's home. I wonder if he is already having the conversation with Ivy. If so, he may well be expecting me to bring my stuff over tonight.

I luxuriate in the warm feeling that is spreading through my bones. I can barely remember what it feels like to belong but I think it might feel like this.

Hopefully Ivy will allow me to help her at last. We can all help each other.

Then Amanda Danson will notice a difference when she feels like popping round uninvited. And she'll soon see justice moving along at a far quicker pace.

The driver behind me sounds his horn in one continuous blast. My eyes spring open, and I lurch forward in my seat, catching my arm painfully on the door in the process.

I look up ahead and realise that the cars in front have all moved on while I have been distracted.

I glance in the mirror and watch the driver behind as his mouth forms exaggerated words. He clearly wants me to see him openly cursing.

The warm, cosy feeling I had is swiftly replaced by an ice-cold bolt shooting through my body. I am sick and tired of people taking the piss out of me. The management at work, Amanda, and now this moron behind me. In that second, he seems to represent every single person who has ever disrespected me.

I open the car door and get out in the middle of the busy road to a blur of noise and the smell of hot metal.

I inhale the smog of exhaust fumes and everything comes into sharp focus. The gravel under my feet; the long line of drivers behind who are staring up ahead at me, their faces puzzled and wondering what is wrong.

The driver behind me cannot move. His vehicle is sandwiched in between my car and the one behind him.

I feel dizzy with bravado. My blood is buzzing around my body, urging me on.

His mouth stops moving. Several car windows slide open and the other drivers crane their necks.

I can't lose face now, and I don't want to give myself the chance to back down, so I let rip.

'What is wrong with you?' I scream, surprising myself with the strength of my reaction. 'Why do people like you always think it's perfectly okay to treat others like dirt on the bottom of your shoe?'

My body feels rigid with the fury and tension that's coursing through it.

His window comes down a touch.

'I wouldn't need to if you'd get moving.' His voice is calm and, I think, smug. 'The cars in front left five minutes ago.'

This is a ridiculous exaggeration.

'The traffic has been gone about ten seconds,' I hiss.

He returns my glare but I sense he is now feeling slightly unsure of what I might do. His fingers tap the steering wheel, and his lips twitch up at one side.

'A suit and tie and you think you can tell the whole fucking world what to do,' I say, reminding myself he isn't anyone I need to be afraid of or intimidated by.

'I have an important meeting to get to,' he says, his voice more reasonable. 'Just get moving, please.'

'And I am going to the hospital.' I raise my voice again, shouting loud enough that the following two or three drivers will be able to hear if their windows are down. 'My boyfriend is in intensive care; he nearly died in an accident.'

The injustice of it all comes flooding back. My eyes prickle until I'm barely aware of my flailing arms and hysterical shouting.

'He nearly died and all you can worry about is getting to work. He nearly died, you bastard!'

Half-shocked, half-exhilarated by my own use of foul language in public, I turn and glare at the other drivers before getting back into my car. Traffic is streaming down the other side of the road so it's impossible for anybody stuck behind me to get around my car.

This feeling that I am powerful enough to obstruct and inconvenience them all in the midst of their perfect little lives spurs me on. It all feels deliciously dramatic, as if I'm the director on a film set.

'You can all just bloody well wait,' I shout triumphantly.

I jump back in the car and flick my hazard lights on.

A cacophony of car horns begins blaring behind me, and I turn the radio on full blast.

Soon, the flow of traffic coming from the opposite direction ceases and cars behind start to drive around me – the obstruction. Some slow down right next to me and glare in but I keep my eyes straight forward with an IDon'tGiveaFlyingFuckadooWhatYouThink smile on my face, tapping my fingers on the steering wheel in time to the music.

I watch through the mirror as the idiot behind me reverses back a short distance and then swerves out like a rally driver. I turn to glare as he overtakes me but, disappointingly, he doesn't even glance in my direction.

The remainder of my journey into work is uneventful but my mind is racing with the realisation that I have kept my head down my whole life, accepting the views and actions of others – even when I feel angry or humiliated.

Today, my actions and words reflected how I was really feeling, and I can't believe the relief and the power it generated in me. What a refreshing change to see other people looking unsure and shocked, forced to listen while I voice *my* opinion.

It is an approach I intend using more frequently.

CHAPTER 48

The delivery office car park is quieter than I thought it would be and I find myself wondering how many other staff members Jim has asked to come in.

I have been so busy thinking about the disagreement with the driver that I have barely considered what the meeting might actually be about. I suppose it depends who else is here, too.

I realise I have been a bit naïve accepting an out-of-work meeting request without confirming all the details first.

I swallow hard, lock the car and walk slowly across the yard to give myself a few minutes to think over the possibilities.

It dawns on me there is a very good chance that Jim wants to speak to me regarding further customer complaints about missing mail. If that is the case, I won't panic. I will simply deny everything like I did last time he spoke to me. After all, I have managed to deliver a bit more than usual each day of my round, and soon, all of the backlog will be destroyed and I will have my long-awaited fresh start.

Even better, if I can get Jim talking about his grandchildren or his mindnumbingly boring fishing trips, he will easily be distracted and will more than likely just shrug off any complaints, like he did last time.

Then again, the meeting could easily be about the imminent round changes and could involve everyone. Jim has already spoken to us all individually about how we are coping on our respective rounds and has also flagged up possible changes to the rota organisation.

I realise that, for the first time, I wouldn't be totally averse to changing my round to doing something smaller. I have other things in my life now and work is not the be-all and end-all as it has been for the last few years. In fact, the possibility of a smaller round actually sounds quite tempting.

It would give me more time to spend with Liam, develop our friendship and help get him firmly on the road to recovery. At the same time, I could ensure that Amanda Danson is brought to account for her despicable actions.

I punch the security code into the keypad and enter the large, sprawling space. It seems eerily quiet compared to the busy working morning. As far as I can see, I am the only member of staff here.

Tremors shiver down my arms and legs.

'Hello, Anna.' Jim waves to get my attention from over the other side of the room. I begin to walk towards him but he holds up his hand in a stop sign.

'We're not ready for you yet,' he calls. 'Could you wait over there, just for a few minutes?'

'What's this all about, Jim?' I look past him, over his shoulder. Although the blind is drawn at his office I can still see movement behind the slats.

'Get yourself a coffee from the machine, Anna,' he calls again. 'We're just waiting for Mike Harvey to get here.'

Then he turns and walks back into his room.

I head blindly for the vending machine until I hear his office door close. A queasy wave rises up from my stomach but I swallow it back down and take a couple of deep breaths.

'We' are waiting, he said. Jim and who else, I wonder? And who is Mike Harvey? The name sounds familiar but I can't quite place it.

This meeting is starting to get a scarily official feel to it.

Jim had said to bring someone with me and now I wish I had. Although quite who, I'm not sure. I have nobody to call on.

I stand near to the vending machine and position myself so I have a clear view of Jim's office door.

I look around me. All the workstations stand empty and numerous canvas postal bags are scattered about the floor. I have spent most weekday mornings in this space for the last five years and yet, today, it seems both strange and unfamiliar to me without the buzz of other people around.

Overhead, fluorescent tubes flicker and buzz and I get an urge to run back outside into the fresh air and natural light. I close my eyes, try hard to calm my thoughts down.

Even if there have been further complaints, what can they really do apart from ask me questions about my round? They have no hard evidence, just their suspicions.

These days nobody can be sacked on mere suspicion; you have to have something concrete or an employee can sue the pants off you in a tribunal.

I silently curse the two police officers who inadvertently stopped me burning the letters by their impromptu visit. If I hadn't been interrupted, I could have destroyed a lot more of the backlog.

Still, once all the mail upstairs has gone there will be no more complaints because I will be delivering everything on time again.

I feel sure I can fend off one more meeting with Jim until I get to that position.

I conclude that the worst-case scenario will be if they are looking for a redundancy. I don't want to stop working completely, although I have substantial savings and no mortgage. But I need to get order back into my life again and work is a big part of that.

I am, however, prepared to talk about cutting my hours down so maybe that will placate them.

The seconds turn in to minutes. Long minutes.

I don't want a coffee from the bloody vending machine, I just want to get this meeting over and done with but there is still no movement from Jim's room.

I can't imagine what they are doing in there.

Perhaps my personal file is open on Jim's desk, the confidential contents spilling out. Some nosy clerk could be in there right now, sorting through the entries and making notes on how long I've worked here or how much money they might save by cutting down my hours to virtually nothing.

Sharp jabs of irritation start up in my gut.

I remember my courage on the journey in here, the way I refused to let that other driver intimidate me.

I believe that incident happened for a reason – to prepare me for this meeting. To remind me to stick up for myself and demand fair treatment as a loyal employee.

I drop my head on to my left shoulder, then do the same on the right, trying to stretch and relax my neck. I stand up tall and pull my shoulders back, try to look like someone who refuses to put up with their bully-boy tactics.

Jim's door opens and out he comes. I hear the outer door open and bang shut again and we both look towards the entrance.

Jim walks over to open the secure inside door and disappears through it. I hear discreet low voices out in the visitor area and, when Jim reappears, there is someone with him. A man.

I crane my neck in an effort to see more but I can't see who it is because Jim is nearest to me and blocking my view. They disappear into Jim's office and the door closes again.

It's ridiculous. They are obviously playing mind games, keeping me waiting like a naughty schoolgirl. Well, I refuse to let them think I'm in the least bit unnerved. I am determined to appear confident.

Jim's door opens at last.

'Anna, you can come through now.'

I assume my surliest look, snatch up my handbag and walk – slowly and calmly at my own pace – over to his office.

My flat boots clip the floor as I walk. With each step I silently repeat the mantra, *stay calm, stay calm*.

Before I reach the door I can hear people talking: confidential mumblings about me that I am not allowed to listen to.

I push open the door without knocking. A wave of heat sweeps over me when I look around.

There are four people in there, including Jim. Their heads remain down while they study notes and shuffle papers with some importance.

Jim's desk has been pushed forward to afford more room and they all sit in a line behind it, like some kind of formal interview panel.

The thought that this might actually be some kind of offer, an opportunity even, flits briefly through my mind. I have certainly heard of instances in the midst of office reorganisations where promotions have been offered to select, valued staff. Staff that have proven their loyalty and commitment.

'Anna, please come in,' Jim says, standing up and indicating the empty chair that faces everyone. 'Thank you for coming back in at such short notice.'

His formal tone instantly crushes any hope I might have had of a positive reason for the meeting.

I sit down, ignoring the line of faces and busying myself zipping up my handbag. If they think I am going to look at them in awe or fear I'm afraid they are going to be sorely disappointed.

'Anna, let me introduce everyone and then I'll tell you why we asked you to come in this afternoon.'

I keep my eyes steady and look back at Jim, ignoring the others.

'This is Colin Freckleton,' he indicates to his left. 'From the Investigation Branch. On my right is. . .'

Jim's voice fades out as the two words amplify and echo in my head.

Investigation Branch?

For a second I think I'm going to slip from the chair.

'Anna?'

I lift my head and look at Colin Freckleton from the RMIB.

'This is Mike Harvey from Head Office, HR department.'

I glance at the man who arrived late. He is sitting at the end of the line and, for a second or two, I actually think I'm hallucinating. Our eyes meet and we both hold the stare. His face doesn't flicker, doesn't even twitch.

I swallow, open my mouth and then close it again. I shake my head in an effort to dispel the roaring that fills my ears.

'Anna?' Jim's voice sounds as if it's coming from far away.

In the list of Worst. Possible. Things. That. Could. Happen. this tops the fucking board.

Mike Harvey is the driver who sat behind me in the traffic jam.

CHAPTER 49
Thirteen years earlier

The following morning, Carla pulled into the school car park just before eight.

She let out a cry as a dishevelled figure suddenly appeared from nowhere at her window.

Carla turned off the engine and opened the door. It was Anna Clarke.

'Please, Miss, you've got to help me.'

The girl's hair was tangled and her face filthy. Carla noticed she was shivering uncontrollably as if the damp cold air had seeped deep into her bones.

'Does your mother know you're here?' Carla asked.

Anna stared back at her, eyes wild and bottom lip trembling.

'Something bad is going to happen to Danny, I know it. Please, you've got to help him.'

Carla grabbed her handbag and locked the car. The girl was in danger of becoming hysterical. She'd have to come back out for the files later, after Anna had calmed down.

'Come on, let's get you inside and cleaned up and you can tell me all about it.'

In her office, Carla handed Anna a strong cup of coffee. Unlike her brother, the girl couldn't wait to offload her problems.

As Carla suspected looking at her, Anna had slept rough last night.

'Soon as you left last night she threw me out. I banged on the door twice in the night but she wouldn't let me back in.'

'Wasn't there somewhere else you could go?'

'Mrs Peat's, next door,' Anna shrugged. 'But I couldn't settle, I couldn't sleep. I'd have kept her up all night too.'

Carla felt heavy inside. Why had she broken regulations and gone to the house so readily? The last thing she had wanted was to make things worse for Daniel and Anna.

It was imperative she took the correct action from here on in.

'At eight thirty the office opens, and I'm going to have to get other staff involved in this Anna,' she said quietly.

'No! You can't miss, I—'

'Anna, I have to. I shouldn't have come over to the house like that last night. Now it looks like I've made things worse.' Carla glanced at her watch. They had twenty minutes before the school office opened. 'We still have a little time together. Can I ask you something?'

The girl nodded. It was difficult, and again, she was pushing the ethics but Carla asked the question anyway.

'In his first session, Danny told me there was a man watching him all the time. He said the man knew everything about him; he knew everything Danny did. Do you know who this person is?'

Anna thought for a moment, then gave Carla a quick, doleful smile.

'It's not a *person*, miss. It's God. *He* knows everything we do; *He* is watching all the time. It's what Father MacCarrick tells the kids all the time at church.'

CHAPTER 50
Present day
Anna

Jim looks first at me and then back at Mike Harvey.

'Is everything OK?' Jim blinks and clears his throat.

A strange lull takes over the proceedings as the other people on the panel look at each other, realising something is wrong.

'I didn't think I'd met Anna previously but I was mistaken.' Mike Harvey looks coolly at me now that he is the one in a position of power. 'We met on our way into the office today.'

'He beeped me for no reason in the traffic queue behind me,' I bluster before I can stop myself. 'So I got out and gave him a piece of my mind.'

'I see,' Jim glances at the others. 'That said, it doesn't have any bearing on today's meeting so I suggest we move on.'

'I'm surprised to see you here, Anna.' Harvey's jaw tightens. 'You said you were headed for the hospital to see your boyfriend in intensive care.'

'Boyfriend?' Jim said, raising his eyebrows.

My head is buzzing, threatening the mother of all headaches.

'Yes, well I *was* on my way to the hospital and then – for God's sake, what does it matter now? You're all just sitting here in judgement of me, anyway.'

'Right, well I'm going to press on here. I'm afraid there have been more complaints, Anna,' Jim continues, his face pale and lined. 'Serious complaints that have had to be formally investigated.'

Colin Freckleton coughs and reads in a nasal, robotic voice from a sheet of paper.

'We have carried out two brief covert operations and our investigations are still ongoing.'

'What does that mean?' I demand but he avoids my stare.

A rapidly growing sense of injustice is cancelling out the shock and embarrassment of facing Mike Harvey after our driving disagreement. They are ganging up against me; it's like the school playground all over again.

'Where's your proof?' I try but fail to stop my voice rising and it fills the small office. It feels like I'm listening to someone else, someone confident and unafraid. 'You need proof before you throw accusations at your employees.'

Jim pushes an A4 envelope across the desk.

'The RMIB report and associated findings are in there, Anna,' he says in a regretful tone. 'We'll be calling a formal disciplinary meeting next week, and I strongly suggest you find someone to accompany you who can properly support you this time, ideally your union representative.'

Jim knows full well I'm not a member of the useless union. The subs are considerable, and the days when the union had any teeth are over.

'We've called you in today to inform you that you are officially suspended from duty pending our further investigations into suspected serious professional misconduct,' Colin Freckleton drones on.

I stand up, heat gushing through my body.

'How dare you?' I scream, sweeping my arm across the desk and knocking off papers and plastic cups of water.

The woman squeals and jumps back as water splashes her expensive clothing.

'All my loyal service and devotion to this job and you try and treat me like a common criminal?' I grab my handbag and storm from the room, slamming the door so hard the sound ricochets throughout the whole building.

As I stomp through the delivery office I pull bags and junk mail from pigeonholes, sweep ink pads and envelopes from the surfaces on to the floor.

Finally, when I reach the exit door, I smash the fire alarm glass and let loose a deafening wail that heralds my departure.

CHAPTER 51
Thirteen years earlier

Carla reeled from Anna's explanation. All this time she'd assumed Danny had referred to a man but he'd been talking about *God*.

Her mind joined up the dots.

'Anna, this is important. Do you know if the priest is hurting Danny?' Carla said softly.

The girl looked away, her jaw sagging. Her blue eyes glittered with emotion, her cheeks flushing with two hot red spots on a pale background.

'Is that a yes?'

Anna shook her head.

'Father MacCarrick isn't hurting Danny, Miss. He spends loads of time with him at church to try and get him to open up about Mother, but Danny won't. He won't say a word to anyone.'

'Does the priest know your mother is abusing Daniel?'

'He knows something is wrong at home but he hasn't got a clue how bad it is. Danny told him he was seeing a counsellor at school and Father MacCarrick told him to stop going, that he should talk to God instead. He even tutored Danny on his altar-server duties so he didn't get into trouble with Mother, but Danny still messed it up.' Big fat tears plop into her hands. 'Only I see what she does to him. She whips him raw to purge the bad out of him, miss, but I daren't tell the priest in case he tries to talk to her about it.'

Carla shivered. She sat very still.

She could see Anna clearly wasn't a nurtured and cared for child but she seemed to be escaping the harsh treatment Monica Clarke reserved for her son.

'Why, Anna? Why Danny and not you?'

'She didn't want my brother; she got pregnant by mistake and that's why Dad left home. Every time she looks at Danny he reminds her of how everything went wrong, and she blames him.' Anna looked down at her twisting hands. 'She thinks Danny stands between her and God and that he must be cleansed.'

Anna stood up suddenly.

'I have to go, have to see if Danny is OK.'

'Just a few more minutes, Anna, then we can get help. Let's sit down and—'

Anna ran, wrenching the office door open, and disappeared down the hall.

By the time Carla reached the doorway to call her back, Anna was already out of sight.

CHAPTER 52
Present day
Anna

I drive straight to Colwick Park.

It is a dull, overcast day and there aren't many cars in the gravelled parking area. I manoeuvre the car over to the far corner, overlooking the water and facing away from the path.

The Trent thunders past, grey and choppy. It seems to pull the dark, heavy clouds down to meet it, reflecting my misery. I sit mesmerised by the strength of the current, tugging and straining non-stop against the flow.

I turn off the engine and something – the bravado, the rage – suddenly snaps into pieces. My whole body fills with a liquid panic that feels powerful enough to dissolve my insides.

The acidic sensation in my stomach and throat gets worse and then it seems to explode up and out of me. I manage to get the car door open and vomit on the gravel outside but the last dregs drip inside the car and over my jeans.

Tears roll down my face, partly from being so violently sick and partly because of the black, empty space inside of me.

I rummage in my handbag on the seat and find a small packet of dusty tissues. I mop up most of the lumpy splats although there's nothing I can do about the smell.

A couple walk by and their stupid terrier comes bounding towards the car.

'Go away,' I scream at it.

The man scowls and calls the dog back, and the black space inside gets a little bigger.

I close the car door, wind the window down and take a few breaths. I need to get home. It is the only place I will be undisturbed and I can think properly. But I can't quite bring myself to move yet.

I have a vague sense of time passing. The light is changing outside, dimming. I drift in and out of a strange calmness, like I'm watching from a distance.

How dare they accuse me of – what was it Freckleton had quoted. . . 'Serious professional misconduct'?

I admit I have had some difficulties with my recent delivery obligations but I'm pretty certain there is nothing in that mail backlog that can be construed as terribly important.

Most of the stuff I have burned has been useless junk mail that people are better off not having in the first place. It serves no purpose but to clog up their dustbins and harm the environment.

My customers would probably thank me if they realised I had spared them the small mountain of crap my employer pays me to shove through their letterboxes day after day. The management don't seem to realise that, in reality, the mindless crap usually finds its way into most people's dustbins within minutes of dropping through the door.

I recall Colin Freckleton also said the investigation was 'ongoing'.

They still haven't humiliated me enough. They still have more lies to peddle about the way I do my job and carry out my round, uncomplaining in all weathers.

Despite this feeling of disconnection, I know instinctively I need to get home and burn the mail backlog as soon as possible.

I turn the ignition and pray silently for help from someone, somewhere. From anywhere at all.

But there is nobody. Nobody I can confide in or share the worry, the panic or the terrible sense of injustice with.

Then the realisation hits me that, finally, I'm not really alone after all.

I have Liam. Liam will help me.

CHAPTER 53
Thirteen years earlier

Anna ran faster than she'd ever run before. She barrelled around the corner of the street, and as she swerved into the driveway, she collided with Mrs Peat.

'Have you seen Danny?' Anna gasped, trying to suck air in. 'I'm scared. I thin—'

'Anna,' Mrs Peat's voice was calm but her face looked drawn and more lined than usual. 'Come next door with me, we need to talk.'

'No – I have to check on Danny.'

'Anna, please.' Mrs Peat grasped her arm as she tried to pass. 'The door is locked, dear. I've been knocking but there's no answer.'

'Let me try.'

Anna broke free and ran to the back door. She banged on the glass until it rattled. She'd asked her mother for a spare key many times but Monica had always refused.

'I don't want you bringing boys back here. I know what girls your age are like,' she'd hissed last time.

'Danny,' Anna called, looking up to her brother's bedroom. 'Danny, come to the window.'

'Anna—'

'The letterbox.' Anna dashed down the drive to the front of the house. 'Danny! Danny!'

But there was no answer at all from the house.

CHAPTER 54
Present day
Anna

I intended on driving straight home but find myself turning right instead of left at the main junction leading into town.

By the time I arrive at Liam's it is nearly five p.m. I have been sat at the park in the car for over an hour and a half, slipping in and out of a strange stupor and going over and over in my mind the awful truth of what just happened at work.

I know Liam won't mind me calling. In fact, I feel confident Liam would *want* me to turn to him in my hour of need as he did with me on the day of the accident.

I walk down the side of the house, tap on the back door and walk in. The kitchen light is on, and I can hear bursts of canned laughter from the television in the other room.

I walk through the kitchen and into the hallway, and I see Liam standing there in the gloom, shrugging off his leather bike jacket. As if he's been out somewhere.

'Anna!' He spots me, freezing in surprise, one arm still caught in his jacket sleeve.

'Sorry to just turn up like this but—' I try to finish but tears tip down my cheeks.

'What's wrong? Come here.' He casts off his jacket and throws it on the stairs then puts his arm around my shoulders.

'Have you been out?' I manage.

'Never mind that now; you look awful. What's happened?'

I rest my head on his shoulder. All the dark bits inside finally roll out in wet, bucking waves. I can't stop it.

I feel so grateful when Liam just holds me and says nothing at all. It's such a relief to release everything without first having to explain all that has happened.

The lounge door opens and Ivy appears looking tired and in pain.

'Hello, Anna.' A flicker of concern hovers in her eyes. 'What's wrong?'

'Don't worry, Gran,' Liam says above my head. 'Go back to your programme, I'll sort her out.'

'Has Amanda gone?' She looks around.

'Amanda?' I repeat faintly.

'She was going to call round earlier,' Liam shrugs. 'Just for a cuppa and a chat, but she couldn't come over in the end.'

'You shouldn't let her in here.' I glare at Ivy. My breaths become ragged again. It feels hard to get enough air in.

'Calm down, Anna.' Liam holds my shoulders and looks at me. 'Let's get you sorted out.'

I close my eyes and start to count.

I hear Ivy shuffle out, muttering something about my negativity. She pulls the lounge door closed behind her.

'Why don't we go back to your house,' I hear Liam say softly. 'We can have a nice cup of tea there and you can tell me all about it.'

I open my eyes.

Fifteen minutes later, Liam opens the gates and I park up on the drive.

Liam has remained quiet and thoughtful during the journey.

'Concentrate on your driving,' he said when we set off. 'We can talk when we get there.'

I'm grateful for this, and I do feel a little calmer by the time we arrive.

It feels very strange bringing Liam to my home; I can't remember the last time I actually had someone I trusted here in the house.

When we were kids we never had visitors. I just don't feel comfortable having people in my home, trying to find out my business.

My eyes are swelled and blurry and every so often I let out an involuntary little sob. Liam stays really quiet. Out of the corner of my eye I see he is twitching a lot, like someone is giving him tiny electrical shocks. I don't mention it though.

I unlock the back door and snap on the kitchen light. The bad smell hits me immediately, and I wait for Liam to comment but he says nothing.

'Go through to the lounge,' I tell him. 'I'll put the kettle on.'

I open the cupboard and take down two white porcelain mugs that I keep for best and busy myself making the tea.

Despite everything that has happened this afternoon, I feel calmed by Liam's presence in the house. I can't help but imagine how it might feel if Liam came to live here.

We'd probably watch television together, and I'd make his favourite meals for tea each night. There wouldn't need to be anything smutty about it but perhaps, in time, we'd grow closer.

I take the drinks through. Liam sits on the settee leafing through the local newspaper while Albert sniffs suspiciously around the hem of his jeans.

'He doesn't usually like visitors,' I say. 'But I can tell he's warming to you.'

'He can probably smell Boris on me.'

I hand Liam a mug and sit down in the chair.

'Can you smell anything?' I ask him. The stench seems particularly strong in here.

Liam inhales and shakes his head. 'Like what?'

'It's hard to say: like a sweet, rotten stench. I can often smell it in the house but it seems to come and go.'

'Nope, I can't smell anything.'

I sip my tea and wonder if you can actually imagine smells that don't exist. I don't want to think about it.

'So, now tell me why you're so upset,' Liam says at last. He doesn't seem as jumpy.

Should I shrug off the whole sorry incident now I am feeling a little better or seize the opportunity to confide everything in Liam and share the burden?

A rush of dread grips me and the tears start to spill again.

'Anna?'

I look up from my hands.

'Please, tell me what happened.'

I feel as if my head is about to explode with the screams that are building inside my skull. I hear this low moaning sound. I think it might be me.

'Anna!'

Even through my distress I hear the panic in Liam's voice.

'My tablets,' I gasp. 'On the worktop.'

Liam jumps up, and I gulp in deep breaths, desperately trying to stem the rising panic.

He runs back in clutching the small brown bottle filled with my prescribed sedatives. They're fast-acting, and God knows, I need them now.

I shake three tablets out into my hand, and rather than return one to the bottle, I knock them all back with a swig of tea.

Liam sits down awkwardly on the arm of my chair and holds my hand for what seems an eternity. Slowly, I begin to calm down.

'Take it easy,' he soothes. 'Whatever it is, we can sort it out together, Anna.'

I realise then that there's no shame in admitting my failings to Liam. I take a deep breath.

'I got suspended from work today.'

There, I've said it.

The words are out now, although I can't say I feel an instant lifting of mood, as I had hoped.

Liam blinks. 'You lost your job?'

'Not exactly,' I say. 'They have to have proof to sack someone and they haven't got it yet.'

'Proof of what?'

'That I haven't been doing my job,' I explain. 'And I have. . . been doing my job, I mean. Most of the time, anyway.'

Liam sighs, runs his hand through his hair.

'Start at the beginning,' he says. 'The last I knew you were working on your delivery round as normal.'

'I was; it's all a terrible shock.'

'They must've given you a warning or something, though? They don't just suspend people for no reason.'

'They said there have been complaints,' I falter, wondering how best to phrase it. 'From local hospitals and places like that. One or two bits of mail haven't been getting through.'

'But that's ridiculous,' he says. Then he gives me a look. 'You have been delivering your mail, right?'

'Yes,' I say, tapping my fingernails together. 'I won't lie, the last few weeks haven't been without problems. I admit, I did get a bit behind at one stage but I was starting to catch up. There's just the undelivered mail, I—'

I feel the sedatives spreading fingers of soothing calm through my body and thoughts.

'Anna?'

I open my eyes.

He says, 'what did you do with the mail you couldn't deliver?'

'It's upstairs,' I hear myself whisper. 'In the spare room.'

CHAPTER 55
Thirteen years earlier

At Carla's request, the school office contacted various agencies; child protection, social services.

Nobody was available to speak this early in the working day. Messages were left for relevant staff to contact her as a matter of urgency.

Carla herself rang the police, who went straight to the family home. What they found there brought them back to the school.

Principal Turner called Carla to his office.

His secretary showed her in, and Carla stood frozen in the doorway.

Bill Turner's face was ashen. He didn't get up from his chair. He didn't move.

'What's happened?' she whispered.

'Sit down and close the door, Carla,' he said finally.

Her skin felt scalded; the very air seared her. She closed the door and sat down in one of the comfortable chairs opposite his desk but found herself looking around for something she could be sick into if the nausea continued.

'Carla, I'm very sorry to have to tell you that Daniel Clarke and his mother, Monica, were found hanged at their home by the police this morning.'

Blood rushed to her head and she gripped on to the sides of her chair to keep from sliding down.

'But last night she said she'd come into school to talk about it.'

She tried to pull in some air but it felt as if her whole head was wrapped in plastic.

Mr Turner buzzed through for a glass of water.

'Last night?'

'I – I went to the house, last night,' she faltered. 'Just for a chat.'

'You know the rules, Carla. You should never—'

'I know,' she swallowed. 'I thought – I just wanted to avoid any drama. I did it for the school, Bill. I just wanted to make it better.'

She thought about Anna.

'Does Anna know? She stopped me in the car park this morning; she was afraid something bad was going to happen to her brother.' Carla squeezed her eyes shut and covered her mouth loosely with her hand. 'I made her wait. We might've been able to save him – I could have helped her.'

But even as the useless words slipped from her mouth, Carla knew she hadn't helped Anna Clarke at all.

In fact, she couldn't possibly have made it any worse.

CHAPTER 56
Present day
Anna

When I wake up, Liam is walking back into the room. He looks tired and sort of puffed out.

'What time is it?' I croak, pushing myself up into a seated position.

The light looks different outside the window and the room feels cooler.

'You've been asleep for a few hours,' he says, placing a glass of water on the floor beside me and sitting in the chair opposite.

His jeans are fashionably torn at the knee and his gold-flecked hair falls messily over one eye just the same as ever, but he looks different. . . stronger, somehow. His fingers tap a beat on the arm of the chair.

'I'm sorry I've taken up your evening, Liam,' I offer. 'I feel much calmer now. You must've been bored out your mind while I've been out of it.'

'Nah, I've kept busy.' He shakes his phone at me.

He has probably been talking to Amanda Danson but I push the thoughts away as fast as they appear. He has been here for me today and that is what matters.

'I worry how you're going to manage, Anna.' His lips disappear into a tight little line.

'Manage?'

'If you don't get your job back,' he says. 'How will you manage financially?'

He sweeps his arm round to take in the house.

'Oh, I see what you mean.' I take a sip of water. 'Well, I haven't got a mortgage so that's something, I suppose.'

'You own the house outright?'

I nod.

'I've lived here all my life. When my family – well, let's just say it became mine, paid for years ago.'

'That must be a relief under the circumstances,' he says.

'I'm lucky. I've never spent a lot and when—' I hesitate but I know there is a decision to be made. Do I open up to Liam, trust him? 'When my mum and brother died, there was an insurance policy.'

Liam stares at me.

I can't make up my mind if the way he's looking at me makes my toes curl or my heart sing. All I know is he's the first person that's ever looked at me that way and it makes my head hum.

'You're amazing, Anna. I was worrying about how you'd manage if you lost your income but it seems you're all sorted.'

My cheeks are burning up now. Still, I can't say I'm displeased with Liam's assessment.

'I'm far from amazing,' I mutter.

'It's still a worry though,' he says, cutting into my thoughts. 'It's so easy to get into money problems before you even realise it.'

I look at him but he averts his eyes. I want to know what exactly he means but I'm getting vibes off him that will me to stay silent. It sounds like he's speaking from experience but that can't be so because he can't remember anything.

I jump slightly when a shrill ring starts up. We both look down at Liam's phone on the seat cushion next to him. 'Amanda' flashes up on the screen.

He picks up the phone and I feel like snatching it off him and smashing it against the wall. She still manages to intrude even when she's not physically present.

But the twist in my throat straightens out when Liam clicks a button at the side and cuts off her call. He places the phone back down next to him.

Albert jumps up on to my knee and allows me to stroke him while he calmly appraises Liam.

'He's got his eye on you,' I laugh but he ignores my quip. Still, a warmth is spreading through me at the way he just rejected Amanda's call.

'The thing is, Anna, depending on the outcome of this disciplinary action, they could sue you.'

'Who?'

'The people who didn't get their mail. Silly as it sounds, they could come up with all sorts of stories, claiming they've lost wages or suffered ill-health through not getting important letters through. We live in a blame culture society.'

I consider this.

'But they would have to have proof,' I say. 'It would be hard to make something like that stick.'

Liam nods. 'I agree, but still.' He sits next to me on the couch, lays his hand on mine. 'I'd hate to see you lose everything you've worked so hard to get.'

With a spare hand he tickles Albert's ear but the cat moves away and jumps down to the floor.

A beep signals the arrival of a text. Before Liam reaches for his phone, the message flashes up on-screen.

'Call me when you can. Need to talk. A'

She just never gives up.

'Think about it,' Liam says, stuffing his phone into his jeans pocket without answering her message. 'I read stuff about this kind of thing in the papers all the time. Ordinary people, sued privately for just doing their job.'

'I don't want to think about it.' A chill shivers through me despite a brief burst of glee over Liam's dismissal of Amanda's attempts to speak to him. 'There's nothing I can do about it if people decide to be so vindictive.'

Liam smiles and crinkles appear around his eyes and the top of his nose. Just like they used to with Danny.

'That's where you're wrong,' he says. 'There's a really easy step you could take to make sure everything you own is safe for good.'

I look at him.

'See, if you sign your assets over to a relative, nobody can touch anything at all. Everything you've worked for can be safe.'

'Assets?'

'You know, the house, the insurance money. The stuff that someone unscrupulous might want to get their hands on.'

'That sounds complicated.' I shrug. 'Besides, there *is* no one. I have no relatives.'

A weight settles on my chest as I say the words.

'A really good friend then,' Liam suggests. 'Someone you can totally trust?'

'Nope. There's no one.'

Voicing my utter isolation makes me want to run upstairs and pull the quilt over my head. I want him to drop it now, although he's set alarm bells off in my head. Is it possible things could get so bad at work they'll try to take my house, my savings?

'There must be someone, Anna. Think.'

Then, out of nowhere, a face pops into my head.

'Mrs Peat next door.' I brighten. 'She's known me from being a child. She'd always want the best for me.'

'But you'd have to explain the situation to her,' Liam frowns. 'And she's old, Anna. It's a horrible thought but she might not have long left herself.'

He's right but it's not something I want to think about. I might only pop next door for a few minutes here and there to chat with Mrs Peat but it's a company of sorts.

'Well, there's nobody else,' I say, studying my hands. 'The only other people I see regularly are the people I work with and that's it. Apart from—'

I snap my eyes up.

'Anna, what's wrong?' His selfless eyes search my face, eager to see how he can help.

'You!' I wonder how it took me so long to realise. 'I trust *you*, Liam.'

'Oh no, I couldn't.' He rubs his forehead. 'I mean it wouldn't be right.'

'Why not?' I'm seized with the idea. 'You're my friend; I know you want what's best for me.'

'Of course I do but what would people say?' He pulls his ear. 'I'm sorry, Anna. It just wouldn't work.'

'It would work perfectly. No one needs to know. It can be just between us. Our secret.'

Before I even realise, I've reached for his hand. His fingers feel warm and dry next to mine. He doesn't move them away.

'Say you'll do it, Liam,' I say, aware of my heart thudding relentlessly in my chest.

'I should think about it,' he falters, squeezing on my fingers.

'There's nothing to think about,' I reply. 'I've never been so certain of anything in my life.'

'Well, if you're sure—'

'I am,' I say firmly. I feel lighter inside, like we've moved closer in some way. 'I just need to know what to do next.'

'I suppose there's no time like the present.' Liam pulls his hand away and offers me his mobile phone. 'There'll be nobody in the solicitor's office at this time but leave a message asking for an appointment tomorrow afternoon, and we'll make absolutely sure nobody can take anything away from you ever again.'

CHAPTER 57
Thirteen years earlier

Somehow, in that way they do, the press had got hold of the information that Carla had taken it upon herself to carry out a home visit to the Clarke house despite it contravening all ethical guidelines.

Now everyone was blaming her. *Everyone.*

She had been suspended from her position at school by the governors and had been asked to withdraw her application from the high school. Her career was as good as finished.

Carla couldn't find out any details about what was happening; nobody would speak to her.

Where was Anna? What had happened to Anna?

If she'd had a phone number for her mother or her sister, she would have called either one of them right away.

All those silly years of feuding meant nothing now. She wished she had made the effort to stay close until they'd forgiven her for what she did; theirs was a special bond that should never have been broken.

But the same senseless pride that had stopped her offering the olive branch had now drained away, together with any glimmer of hope that she could set things straight for Daniel Clarke and his sister.

Carla opened the packet of extra-strength painkillers the doctor had prescribed after her minor leg op eighteen months earlier. She would just take a couple to ease her pain a little, help her to zone out.

Perhaps she would fall into a peaceful sleep, and when she woke up, she could try again. Leave the area and start afresh.

Become someone else entirely.

CHAPTER 58
Present day
Anna

When Liam has gone – typically unselfish and insisting he got a cab to save me driving him home – I walk into the kitchen and take out two small fancy sherry glasses from the back of the cupboard.

A drinker I am not, I hardly touch the stuff. But today is special. The most special day in my life so far, and I want to mark it in some way.

I fumble around at the back of the cupboard before I find what I've been looking for. A bottle of port, never opened; a raffle prize I won at work last Christmas.

Two minutes later, I tap on the window and let myself in to Mrs Peat's.

'What a surprise,' she beams. 'I was only thinking about you this morning, wondering how you were, Anna.'

I feel a weight settle on my chest as it dawns on me I haven't visited her for a while.

'I can't think of anyone better to celebrate with,' I chime, setting down the glasses. 'I've lots to tell you, Mrs Peat, about Liam, my friend. Everything is just perfect.'

'Are you okay, Anna?' she says slowly, watching me.

'I'm fine, absolutely fine.' I grin. The words tumble out of my mouth before I can properly think them through. 'I've never been better to tell you the truth. Even though they're trying to get rid of me at work, it's all going to be okay. Liam is going to move in, and we're going to see the solicitor tomorrow and then nobody can take what's mine.'

'Your head looks sore,' Mrs Peat says gently.

I touch my temple.

'It's not sore,' I say. 'Not really.'

'Anna dear, remember when you were small? Myself and Mr Peat used to tell you that you must always keep yourself safe. That you could come round to us day or night if you needed help?'

I stay quiet because I don't want to talk about the past, not now. But she still carries on.

'The same applies now, Anna. There are people who will try to take advantage of you, who might try and get their hands on what's yours.'

Mrs Peat wasn't making any sense at all.

I hand her a glass of sherry.

'To happier times,' I say. 'For all of us.'

We clink glasses and I take a sip.

'You've not known this man very long in the scheme of things, Anna. It's far too soon to—'

'I know she's up to something,' I say curtly.

'Who, dear?'

'Amanda Danson. The woman who knocked Liam off his moped.'

'You haven't mentioned her before,' Mrs Peat frowns.

'Haven't I?'

I feel sure I must have; poor old Mrs Peat is probably losing her mind. I start giggling and, bizarrely, can't seem to stop.

'Anna, I've known you a long time and I'm worried you're not feeling well again.'

'I'm fine.' I don't know why she's raking up the past.

'If you're having a bad time like before, you should go and see the doctor. There's no shame in it, dear.'

I tap my glass with a fingernail.

'You've been through an awful lot.' Mrs Peat's on a roll now. 'I don't know how you—'

'Don't mention anything about what happened in the past to Linda. I work with her sister.'

'Roisin?'

I look at Mrs Peat.

'She came here with Linda just yesterday,' Mrs Peat beams. 'She popped round to surprise you, but you were out. Gone ages, she was. She says you're good friends.'

My mouth is instantly dry.

'She's just a colleague,' I say faintly. 'I don't want her to come to the house. I don't want her knowing anything about me.'

Mrs Peat frowns as if I'm being unreasonable.

'I have to go.' I stand up suddenly. 'I'll come round again tomorrow or the next day.'

I hear her call out as I close the back door behind me but I don't go back.

I like Mrs Peat but it seems even she wants to put a dampener on my newfound happiness.

Back home, something white under the table in the middle room catches my eye.

I stoop to pick it up and find it's a letter addressed to a Mrs Dodds on the Clifton estate.

I thought I'd been extra careful but it must've escaped the bin bags when I lugged them upstairs after the police visit. Funny I've not noticed it before.

Who'd have thought that such joy and good feelings about the future could come amid such trouble at work?

With hindsight, I feel certain I'll look back on my job catastrophe as a new chapter in my future with Liam.

* * *

On a stroke of luck, I find a local solicitor working late in the office. He says he can arrange the process for my assets to be transferred into Liam's name.

I make an appointment for the following afternoon and text Liam to tell him. He insists he wants to come with me for moral support.

For the first time I allow myself to acknowledge I am not alone any more.

For the first time in my life, I have someone special who cares about me. I feel a glow in my chest; I never want to go back to a place where I feel so isolated from other people again.

Ignoring the now familiar stench in my nostrils, I lift the tiny sherry glass I've carried back round with me. The dark-amber fluid shimmers in the lamplight.

Albert eyes me curiously from the doorway as I take a sip of the port.

The drawers in the dresser catch my eye. Both are slightly open, and I always keep them closed: it is one of my pet hates. How odd.

I walk over and slide one open. I frown in at the muddled contents.

I keep my important papers in here: the house deeds, my bank statements and the like, filed and in order. I open the other drawer and it is in similar disarray, as if someone has rifled through it.

Perhaps Liam had to look for something when I was resting. Someone has been rooting around, I'm sure of it.

Just as I'm about to swallow the remainder of the port, a group of dark uniformed bodies appear from around the corner like a bunch of soldiers. One moment the yard is clear, the next it is filled with official-looking people.

I drop the glass and run into the middle room, the sounds of scattering shards filling my ears.

CHAPTER 59

Someone bangs hard on the back door. I catch a flash of Albert's back end as he disappears upstairs.

'Miss Clarke?' The glass in the kitchen door rattles. 'Open the door please, we have a warrant.'

A warrant? You can't be arrested for failing to deliver a letter or two.

'Liam,' I whisper, balling my fists in an effort to stop my hands shaking. 'Help me.'

I look longingly through to the kitchen at the small brown bottle of sedatives that sits on the worktop.

The banging at the door grows louder.

'Miss Clarke, please open the door. We are at liberty to force entry to your property if you do not comply.'

Sometimes they have those battering rams that just take the whole door down. I've seen them on the television. I jump as someone knocks at the front door too.

I imagine what the neighbours are thinking. If everyone around hears the shouting at my door, I will be the subject of spiteful gossip in the whole of the area. I have to put a stop to it.

I take a deep breath and walk into the kitchen. Standing at the door, I watch the distorted shapes of the uniforms standing on the other side of the fragile textured glass.

'What do you want?'

I hope my voice sounds strong; I won't give them the satisfaction of seeing me shaking and terrified. They are bullies, all of them.

'My name is Len Dichmont, Miss Clarke. I'm a Senior Officer with the Royal Mail Investigation Bureau, and I have a warrant to search these premises for stolen mail.'

'Stolen mail?' My voice is too faint for them to hear.

Referring to it as 'stolen mail' is just plain ridiculous. The mail upstairs is simply undelivered; nobody has stolen anything.

'I don't know what you're talking about,' I shout, swallowing down the rising bile in my throat. 'I don't have to let you in.'

'I'm afraid you do,' the disembodied voice retorts. 'We have a warrant, Miss Clarke, and the two police officers accompanying us here have the authority to force entry if necessary.'

I run back into the middle room and press my back against the cool plaster of the wall. If only Liam was still here, he'd know how to deal with them.

My impulse is to run, hide, but the problem isn't just going to disappear, not now. They'll end up battering the door down.

'Miss Clarke?'

Bang.

Bang.

Bang.

'Open the door.'

I take a deep breath and steel myself, try desperately to think logically.

I have Liam and a new life waiting for me. Despite the fuss they are making I am not a dangerous criminal; I have just got myself in a bit of a fix at work.

I know it will be the end of my job when they find the mail mountain, but so what? As I have already told Liam, I can manage without the income, at least for a while.

Slowly, I walk back in to the kitchen. I stand in front of the glass, take a breath and unlock the door.

'I've done nothing wrong,' I say, making a real effort to keep my voice steady. 'You're wasting your time.'

The man called Len Dichmont composes himself after an initial fleeting expression of surprise that I've finally opened the door. His tubby belly strains against the gold buttons of his official-looking black jacket, and he takes a long step forward into the house, sweeping a hand over his greasy comb-over.

'We have a warrant to search these premises for stolen mail,' he says again, swelling with his own importance. 'Please stand back, Miss Clarke.'

I feel a steady rage fill me as the all-male group tramp through my kitchen into the middle room. There are three RMIB officers with two police officers at the back. A bit overkill by anyone's standards.

'Isn't there enough crime on the streets to keep you lot busy?' I sneer at the police officers, following them into the room.

'Let's try and keep this as civil as we can,' Dichmont says, holding out a large brown envelope towards me. 'Here is the warrant if you wish to inspect it before we commence the search.'

'You can stick your warrant where the sun don't shine,' I snap back.

Dichmont reddens and places the envelope on the dining table, consulting his clipboard.

'I am required to formally ask if you wish to declare anything before the search takes place, Miss Clarke. Do you admit to withholding property of the Royal Mail on these premises?'

'No!' I scream, kicking the leg of a dining chair. 'I've done nothing wrong, you arsehole.'

Dichmont's jaw tightens.

'Please remain here while my officers perform the search.'

The two other RMIB officers split up. One walks through to the lounge, the other back into the kitchen.

One of the police officers pulls out a chair and, despite my anger, I collapse into it. They won't find anything down here but I'm damned if I'm going to make their lives any easier.

I rest my elbows on the dining table and cover my face with my hands. Despite my efforts to remain calm and level-headed, I can't help crying. Someone touches my shoulder.

'Get off me,' I scream, hitting out blindly at one of the police officers. 'Don't you fucking touch me.'

The officer backs off with raised flat palms. He shoots a look at the others, and I cover my face again.

I can hear cupboard doors opening and shutting, plastic bags rattling, drawers being purged of their contents. I feel raw and exposed, as if I'm sitting here naked in front of them all.

I desperately need my tablets to calm down but I know it will be a mistake to take any more. I have to keep my wits about me.

A RMIB officer emerges from the lounge and heads for the stairs door.

This is it. My worst nightmare is happening.

A strange sensation prickles through my face and arms. As I watch, he seems to move in slow motion. Then the speed snaps back to normal as he reaches for the door handle.

'No!' I yell, outraged and terrified. I jump up and lunge forward at him. One of the police officers grabs my arms from behind.

'Come on now, love,' he says. 'Calm down. Let's just get it over with, eh?'

The other RMIB officer comes out of the kitchen, and the two of them disappear upstairs.

Dichmont blinks. He opens his mouth and closes it again. This obviously isn't going the way he has imagined.

'I've done nothing wrong,' I say. 'You can't just come in here, tearing my home apart, you bastards.'

The rigidity of rage leaves me as quickly as it came and now I feel spent, all hope is draining away. The police officer lets go of my arms. Clumps of hair fall from my fingers on to the table, and I sweep them away on to the carpet.

Recent memories flip through my mind like a slide show. The delivery office, the undelivered bags locked in the postboxes, hauling them upstairs and dumping them in the spare room.

I hear creaking on the landing and recognise the sound of the dodgy floorboards just outside the spare bedroom. Any second it will happen. One of them will shout down their discovery, and Dichmont will march upstairs, all smug and accomplished.

I have already decided that I will not utter a word when they try to question me about the mail they find. I will bury my face in my hands and refuse to look at them, to make their job as hard as possible.

I silently pray they won't arrest me. Who will feed Albert and look after him? Liam doesn't even know I'm in trouble.

I throw my head back and release a wail, an explosion of frustration and regret.

'Miss Clarke—'

'Leave me alone,' I yell. 'Get out of my house.'

'Come on now—' a police officer starts to say and then stops as heavy boots begin to descend.

A strained hush settles over the room. Both RMIB officers appear in the doorway, and I brace myself.

The tall one shakes his head. 'Nothing up there, sir.'

'Huh?' Dichmont can't keep the disappointment out of his voice. 'Nothing at all, you say?'

'Negative search result, sir.'

I stand up from the table.

How can it be? Slowly, the invisible fist releases its stranglehold from around my throat and I start to breathe again. I feel my clenched fists slowly relaxing.

'Negative result,' I mumble to myself.

Dichmont's face floods crimson.

'I don't know how you've managed it,' he says through gritted teeth. 'We *know* you've been bringing mail back here, Clarke.'

His two henchmen shuffle their feet. It hasn't taken long for him to drop his fake show of being polite and calm.

I feel stronger already. The rage has returned but this time in a more controlled and focused way.

'Get out,' I hiss in Dichmont's face. 'And take your two monkeys with you. You'll be hearing from my solicitor.'

I haven't a clue whether I can take any action against them but it is worth the threat just to watch Dichmont's face drain of colour. I really do have a solicitor now, who I will be seeing with Liam tomorrow afternoon.

They file silently out of the room into the kitchen.

'So sorry for your trouble, Miss Clarke,' I shout as they walk past me. 'Apologies for being such dumb arses and wasting taxpayers' money, Miss Clarke.'

Nobody reacts, although one of the police officers has the audacity to give me a reprimanding look.

'What?' I challenge him, indignation seething from every pore. 'Tell me *you* wouldn't be completely pissed off, if it was your house that had just been wrecked for no good reason.'

He carries on walking and says nothing.

'Look at this mess,' I screech after them from the kitchen doorway as they tramp off down the drive. 'Who the hell is going to clean this lot up? Bastards.'

I slam the door shut and stagger back inside, shaking.

I've uttered more expletives in the last ten minutes than the rest of my life put together.

'And do you know what, Albert?' I say as he gingerly pokes his head around the bottom of the stairs. 'It feels bloody brilliant.'

Unconvinced, he glares at me and saunters past to investigate the mess and the strange smells of the unwelcome visitors.

The house has been violated. Strangers breathing in my private space.

I could get the matches from the kitchen door now and burn the place to the ground. Maybe that's the only thing that can really cleanse it after this.

I glance through the window at the houses overlooking my garden and see one or two nets twitching. Let them look; I've nothing to hide. The RMIB search has just proved that.

When I've locked the kitchen door, I dash into the lounge and watch them pile back into their vehicles. When the last one has pulled away and disappeared down the street, I take three sedatives again instead of my usual two.

In the lounge I sit down wearily on the settee. The bravado evaporates and I feel shaky and worried again.

How on earth could they have missed the mountain of mail upstairs? I had even heard the floorboards outside the spare room creaking. . . surely they must have gone in there.

I stand up and walk over to the stairs door. Climbing the stairs slowly, my heart races and the ever-present headache pounds in my temples.

I *have* to get rid of that mail today. If they come back again they won't miss it a second time.

Len Dichmont is the kind of man who does not like being proved wrong. He won't want to admit defeat and will probably press for another search as soon as he gets back to his office.

Several strides down the landing and I reach the creaking floorboards: the very same ones I'd heard only five minutes earlier as the RMIB officers reached the spot where I am standing now.

The spare room door is slightly ajar, which is unusual. I always close the door fully behind me without fail each time I empty mail in there. It helps me feel as separate as possible from the monstrosity concealed in the room.

So they must have opened the door. Yet if they had done so, how come they'd missed what was in there?

I push the door, and as it swings fully open I stagger back, my throat so dry and tight I double up coughing.

I have to screw my eyes shut, count to three and open them again before I can believe what I am seeing.

The room is empty. The mail mountain is gone.

CHAPTER 60
Thirteen years earlier

Carla did not fall into a peaceful sleep after taking the tablets.

Hounded by the local press and even by her neighbours, she packed a few things into a small case and fled to a bedsit the other end of the country, leaving her mobile phone and her name behind her.

There, she laid low, steeped in her misery.

Carla swallowed the sedatives the doctor had prescribed two at a time and washed them down with cold white wine.

She couldn't stop the banging in her head, the fractured thoughts.

She kept losing track of how many tablets she had taken. Then all the tablets were suddenly gone and the wine glass empty.

The walls of the room seemed to warp in and out around her.

She slid her legs to one side of the chair and tried to stand up but her body felt as though it were made of rubber.

Over she went, stumbling and falling headlong across the room, smashing her head on the stone fire surround.

For the last time, Carla Bevin closed her eyes.

CHAPTER 61
Anna

The undelivered mail *was* in Danny's bedroom. I am certain of it.

But then the horrid smell in this house seems real too, even though I'm the only person that can smell it.

It's true I've been in a bit of a bad way lately but I distinctly recall bringing the mail bags home each day and lugging them upstairs. And I remember burning the letters when the two police officers called unannounced to ask about the accident.

Surely, I can't be imagining the smell in the house. Its cloying, sickly sweetness sticks in my nostrils, making me gag. It is real. I can't explain why Liam cannot smell it, nor why the two police officers could not smell it the day I burned the letters.

Sometimes my memories get a bit blurred, good and bad ones together, until it is virtually impossible to separate them. But after all, what are memories but pictures in your mind?

There is no such thing as a memory-keeper, no entity exists that has the power to declare whether things really happened or not. All we have are the pictures and the short films we play over and over in our mind's eye. That's really all anyone can base their past experiences on.

A flurry of images surge into my head. Undelivered mail. The accident. Liam.

It feels almost impossible to separate them and determine which are true anymore.

It's so hard to watch someone I care about making such a terrible mistake. Having a blind trust in someone who would only hurt them seems to me like utter self-destruction.

Nobody will listen to me.

My whole life seemed transformed from the moment the accident happened. I'd thought of myself as a kind of fortress but something snuck up behind me and promised me the chance of happiness again. A real family connection that I thought I'd lost forever when Danny died.

And now that bitch Amanda is constantly calling Liam, trying to steal him away before my very eyes. He won't realise until it's too late, until he's been betrayed.

Past regrets wedge themselves like a hunk of gristle in my throat.

I've turned a blind eye once before in my life with disastrous consequences. Back then, I'd ignored my gut feelings and allowed others to take away the one precious thing in my life.

If I'd made different decisions, if I'd not trusted Amanda Danson, I could have prevented Danny's death.

What kind of a person would I be if I let it happen all over again?

Bang, bang, bang.

It goes again. It's coming from next door. Mrs Peat must be in trouble. I race round without looking through the side window, kicking over the milk stand and snatching up the key.

'Mrs Peat.' I burst into the room. 'Are you okay?'

She is sitting in her chair as usual, clutching a yard brush with the long handle aimed at our adjoining wall.

'Oh there you are, Anna.' She frowns. 'Linda gave me this brush in case I needed help in the middle of the night.'

'What help do you need, Mrs Peat?' I say quickly.

'Anna, are you feeling alright, dear? I heard voices, people were—'

'Everything is fine,' I say tightly. 'But I'm a bit tied up at the moment. Do you need something?'

'Let's have a cup of tea and I'll tell you all about it.' Mrs Peat remains infuriatingly unruffled despite me being so obviously on edge. 'There's something I want to tell you, something I should have told you many years ago, Anna.'

I sigh and go back into the kitchen and make the tea. I have two attempts before I get everything in the correct order. For some reason my mind just can't seem to slot things together.

It's no use trying to escape from Mrs Peat; I'll just have to stay for ten minutes or so to placate her. She has seemed hell-bent on living in the past just lately and I can do without it.

But as a concerned neighbour, after how Mrs Peat has cared for me better than my own mother in the early years, I've most certainly failed miserably.

I haven't seen her for days, haven't so much as given her a thought.

'Now dear, first things first,' she says when I go back in the room. 'Earlier, a young man came to see me. He sat in that very chair where you're sitting now.'

'That's nice,' I murmur.

Mrs Peat looks down into her teacup and frowns. She places it back on the saucer without taking a sip.

When Liam finds out everything that's been going on with the RMIB visit, he'll no doubt want me to move in almost immediately.

Unfortunately, I won't be able to see Mrs Peat nearly as often then. Perhaps I should tell her that now; it would be unfair and selfish just to stop my visits.

Ivy won't have a say in the matter because, if she objects, Liam will come here. To my house. To live. He is aware of her mental instability now; she can't hide it away any longer.

I swallow down the bad taste that fills my mouth and I wonder, fleetingly, why I can't just allow myself to be happy. Just this once.

'No, you don't understand, dear,' she says. 'This young man, he wanted to know about *you*. Although I've never met him, I believe it was your friend, Liam.'

My head jerks up from my thoughts.

'I saw all those cars and uniforms outside, Anna,' she says. 'And your hair, has it fallen out?'

'Who was he? What did he want?' I say faintly. It couldn't have been Liam; he didn't even know about Mrs Peat. Was this another official nosing around in my business, someone who was trying to get information from my neighbour? Surely the Investigation Branch weren't going to start interrogating Mrs Peat now?

That would definitely constitute harassment; I could mention it to the solicitor tomorrow.

'He asked me things like how long had you lived here, what had happened to your family and – this is the curious bit – did I know if you had any living relatives. He said you were taking a nap.'

Then it all made sense.

'Liam,' I whisper and some clarity returns to my thoughts.

'Yes.'

My guts cramp hard. 'What did you tell him about me?'

'I told him I'm not in the habit of gossiping about my neighbour, and if he has any questions then he needs to address them directly to you.'

I take a couple of seconds to regulate my breath again.

How does Liam even know about Mrs Peat? It must be something else I have forgotten I told him. What else have I blabbed out that I don't realise?

'He got quite agitated, and I ended up asking him to leave,' Mrs Peat scowled. 'Young whippersnapper, sticking his nose into your business. You should watch out, dear.'

'He's a good friend.' I scowl. 'He's only looking out for me.'

'You should be careful, Anna, you're too trusting by far. You must look after yourself, remember?'

She glances at me as though she is about to say more and so I look away.

Mrs Peat is mistaking his concern for something more sinister but she doesn't know how he feels about me. She doesn't know how our closeness has taken us both by surprise.

I plump up her cushions and tell her to use the brush handle to alert me if she needs the slightest thing. I'm not going to be here, of course, but she doesn't need to know that.

'But there's something else I want to talk about, dear. The most important thing. It's about—'

'Later, Mrs Peat,' I say, jumping to my feet. 'I'll call round later, and you can tell me then.'

I take her teacup into the kitchen and notice there is just hot water in the cup, which is very odd because I definitely remember using a teabag.

CHAPTER 62
Joan Peat

For years, Joan had been waiting for the right time to tell Anna what happened.

Today, when Anna called round, she'd actually stayed longer than a couple of minutes. But it was still too little time for Joan to gather the courage to finally unburden herself.

She sat in her chair now Anna had gone and closed her eyes.

She should run through it one more time in her head, in case Anna called round later like she'd promised. It was important Joan got the order of events just right.

The whole tragic episode was imprinted on her memory.

All the sights and sounds were as clear as when it happened, thirteen years before...

Joan turned down the television and listened.

There it was again, a sort of thumping, a dragging noise – then a child crying, hysterically crying.

Joan happened to know that Anna had gone to her drawing class after school. She'd popped around earlier to collect her pastels and notepad to take with her. Anna had looked pale and tired, her eyes wider and more haunted than usual.

'Is everything alright, dear?' Joan enquired.

Anna nodded and mumbled something about being late and, before Joan could say anything else, she was off out of the door.

Banging, yelling, sobbing. . . it was getting louder.

Joan jumped up and grabbed her listening glass from the table.

She headed for the dining room wall because Anna had once let slip that her mother sometimes shut Daniel in the understairs cupboard if he was misbehaving. But then another loud scraping noise told her that whatever was happening had moved upstairs.

Joan climbed up her own stairs and tiptoed down the long, narrow landing, avoiding the dodgy floorboards that would betray the fact she was eavesdropping. Although she needn't really have worried – the level of racket that was coming from next door.

She placed the glass on the wall and listened. For a few moments, all had dropped quiet again and then it started again.

Daniel was wailing, and Joan could hear his mother slapping him hard.

Dear God, the child was pleading with her to stop.

Joan pulled the glass away from the wall and wiped her own wet cheeks. She couldn't just carry on letting this happen without doing something.

It was clear Monica was getting more brutal with the boy, especially, she had noticed, when Anna was out of the house. Her only witness, or so she thought.

Joan rushed back downstairs and ran around the front of the houses to next door.

She knocked, but there was no response. She rattled the handle, but the door was locked. She banged on the glass with the flat of her hand.

Nothing.

Joan walked back down the drive and back into her own house again. Maybe her banging on the door would stop Monica Clarke now.

But minutes later there was more bumping and banging, more wailing and crying. Joan walked back around to next door. This time, in her hand, she clutched Anna's spare key.

She knocked again and again. When there was no answer, she slid the key in and unlocked the door, closing it softly behind her.

She looked down to see Monica's own door key on the floor. It must have fallen out of the lock when Joan banged and rattled the handle. She kicked it aside.

The kitchen was in disarray, dirty dishes and saucepans piled high. Joan wrinkled her nose against the sour smell and walked into the middle room.

She noticed the crosses on the walls in the dim light but her attention was firmly focused upstairs. The wails, the slaps, a sort of distressed gasping of air and then. . . oh, the silence.

Joan began to climb the stairs. She could hear someone moving about, but mercifully, Daniel had stopped crying now.

As she reached the top of the stairs, the air grew thick enough to choke her. There was what she could only describe as an *awfulness* hanging in front of her like an invisible cloud. It was all she could do not to turn and run back out of the house.

Joan didn't call out; she didn't speak at all. She simply carried on moving, light-footed and determined, along the narrow, uncarpeted landing.

Silence.

The odd floorboard creaked as she tiptoed along but she was past caring about that now. She had to find out once and for all what was happening to the boy, to Daniel.

A scraping noise alerted her to the middle bedroom. She knew this to be Daniel's room.

Joan swallowed hard, pushed the door and immediately staggered back.

'Dear God,' she gasped, holding on to the doorframe for support.

Daniel's lifeless body hung from the doorframe of the walk-in cupboard. Mercifully, his face was turned to the wall but he was swinging, very slightly, as if in a gentle breeze.

Next to him, Monica Clarke stood on a chair, a noose around her own neck. Her eyes wide open, tears streaming down her pale, twisted face.

'What have I done?' she whispered to Joan. 'Can you help me, Mrs Peat?'

Joan couldn't move, couldn't speak.

'Please,' Monica Clarke sobbed. 'He was playing a silly game, he slipped—'

Joan took a step forward. She watched Monica's eyes darting around the room, thinking of a way out.

'I told him to be careful. When I saw him, what he'd done to himself – I wanted to die myself. My son, he's gone—'

'He was crying; you were hitting him,' Joan said calmly. 'I heard it all.'

'No! I was trying to stop him hurting himself, you see, Mrs Peat.' Monica's feet shifted on the rickety wooden chair. 'I was trying to help him.'

Joan thought about the fear she'd seen in both Daniel and Anna's eyes at the mere mention of their mother.

'Please.' Monica clawed at the rope around her neck. 'You can help me explain to the police. Help me down.'

Joan felt herself walk forward.

And as she moved towards Monica Clarke, she thought about the bruises she'd seen on Daniel's upper arms. She thought about how Anna's hands shook when it was time for her to go back home.

She thought about the day Arthur tried to intervene when Monica dragged Daniel back round, and how she'd stuck two fingers up and told Arthur to 'Fuck off, you old twat.'

Joan stood in front of Monica now.

She tried not to look at Daniel, at his slight body swaying life-lessly on the rope. It was too late for the poor child, but it wasn't too late for Monica Clarke.

'Thank you,' Monica whispered, craning her neck to one side so Joan could get at the rope. 'I'll never forget this. If you could loosen the knot, I can slip it off my head?'

Joan stared.

'Mrs Peat?'

She looked straight at Monica Clarke and took a step back.

'May God forgive me,' Joan said out loud and then she kicked hard at the chair that Monica Clarke stood on.

Her neighbour shrieked as the chair tilted and tipped but it rebalanced itself and one of Monica's feet remained flat on the seat.

'What are you doing, you mad old—'

Joan kicked again, this time harder, and the chair skittled aside.

Monica Clarke gave a gasp as she bucked and twisted on the end of the rope she'd tied herself. Joan turned and walked out of the room, the guttural choking noise filling her ears.

By the time Joan reached the bottom of the stairs, all was quiet.

She picked up the door key on the floor and hooked it loosely on the inside of the lock. Then she used Anna's spare key and locked the door behind her.

Then Joan Peat went back home and put the kettle on.

CHAPTER 63
Present day
Amanda

Amanda Danson had no real evidence to support her suspicions so she hadn't actually mentioned it to anyone yet.

It was just a *feeling*. That was all.

As she kept telling herself: it was one thing knowing for certain you were being watched but another thing entirely to prove it.

Of course, it could be that she was simply going crazy but more likely it was just that, after what happened at work, she was feeling very nervous.

It had been a fairly uneventful day up to early afternoon but her stomach felt fluttery whenever she thought about seeing Liam later. It had been a long time since she'd felt like that about anyone; everything had changed after the tragedy. She had kept her head down, created a new, low-key existence.

It had all been so. . . final.

But this was supposed to be a fresh start, and she liked to think part of Carla was still alive. Through her, Carla lived on.

She had spent the morning actually looking forward to seeing Liam later and even planning to pick up a bunch of flowers for his sweet gran on the way over there.

At two fifteen, after ten minutes tidying the role-play area, everything changed.

Amanda had been just about to go up for her afternoon break when Carol Hartnell, the nursery's Business Manager, approached her.

Carol's partner, Susan, owned the West Bridgford franchise of Busy Bees but she basically left her to run the place and boy, did Carol enjoy wielding her power.

'Pop into my office when you've got a minute,' she said discreetly to Amanda as she whisked past. Her eyes darted everywhere at once, noting what tasks had been neglected by the staff.

'What did she say?' Sarah hissed from the carpeted reading area when Carol went back to her office. Obviously Carol hadn't spoken discreetly enough.

'She wants to see me.'

'Ooh, I wonder if it's about the lead TA job?'

Amanda shrugged but she supposed Sarah could be right. It might well be about the new position that was coming up in a couple of months at the Mansfield branch when Janis Lawton moved back down south. Amanda had indicated an interest in the lead Teaching Assistant vacancy but that was before the accident and she hadn't thought much about it since.

'You'll be set up if you get that,' Sarah gushed. 'A big pay rise, very nice.'

'I doubt they're going to just hand it to me like that,' Amanda laughed. And a big pay rise still wouldn't bring her salary anywhere near what she'd been earning before but there was no sense lamenting those days. 'There'll be interviews. Janis said that Karen Butler from the Mansfield branch was hanging her nose over it.'

'Ugh, she'd put parents off bringing their kids in,' said Sarah, blobbing out her tongue. 'Perma-tanned chav.'

Amanda couldn't help smiling; it was a good observation, if a little cruel.

She finished folding the mini police uniforms onto a hanger and left the other roleplay clothes for someone else to do later.

'Back in five.'

'Good luck,' Sarah called.

Amanda walked over and tapped at Carol's open office door. Carol looked up, smiled and beckoned her in but there was a tightness about her face that Amanda didn't like the look of.

'There has been a concern raised by a parent that I have to get to the bottom of,' she said as soon as Amanda sat down. Carol wasn't one for niceties.

Amanda felt the muscles freeze in her face. 'A concern about me?'

'I'm afraid so,' Carol nodded.

Amanda mentally scanned through her dealings with parents and children over the past week. Nothing untoward sprang to mind.

It had been a completely normal week with only the usual occurrences; the odd harmless scuffle between kids and one or two very minor first aid cases. That was it.

'So,' Carol said, finally looking up from a printed A4 sheet, 'a potential client emailed Mansfield HQ to report, and I quote, their "very bad experience with Miss Amanda Danson, at the West Bridgford branch".'

Amanda opened her mouth to protest but Carol raised a hand to silence her while she continued to read.

'"Miss Danson seemed distracted and disinterested when I came in to view the facilities with a view to my youngest child starting the nursery. Several times I had to repeat information that I consider to be key, and she took a personal telephone call in the middle of my appointment".'

Carol stopped reading and put the piece of paper back down on her desk. She folded her hands in her lap and leaned back in her chair, looking at her expectantly.

Amanda opened her eyes wide and shook her head.

'I swear nothing like that happened, Carol.'

She knew she sounded defensive and unconvincing but she was telling the truth. Her mind was still racing through the week, trying to match up anything that could be construed as negligent or unprofessional. She came up with a blank.

'Did the person leave their details?' Amanda asked. 'If I knew their name I could—'

'I haven't got that information,' Carol shook her head. 'Apparently, they told Mansfield they weren't interested in any involvement in an investigation but simply wanted to let this branch know about their experience as a new client.'

Amanda wrestled with a sharp niggle of injustice.

'But anyone could just ring up and say things about any one of us,' she tried to reason. 'They should at least be required to leave their names to prove they're genuine.'

Carol's face darkened.

'This is not the response I'd hoped to get from you, Amanda.' She slid a sheet of paper over the desk. 'Take this away with you and have a good look through it. It's a list of the appointments you've conducted with new parents for the past two weeks.'

Amanda took the list but she didn't look at it.

Of course she felt defensive, she was being attacked through no fault of her own. She couldn't deal with this happening, not after what had happened in the past. It was like history repeating itself.

'I already know there's no point in going through this list.' She glared back at Carol. 'I would never take a personal phone call in the middle of an appointment.'

Sure, her mum had called her at work a couple of times since the accident just to check she was OK. But she had definitely been on her break both times, never in the middle of showing a parent around.

'Well, I have to add there have been one or two comments made to me lately from colleagues, so it's not just this complaint that concerns me.'

Amanda was speechless. Who had been 'commenting' – code word for snitching – to their common enemy, Carol? Not Sarah, she was dizzy and thoughtless at times but surely. . .

'I realise you've had the accident to contend with and, if you recall, I did suggest you take a little more time off if you needed it,' Carol continued. 'People have noticed your attention span isn't what it was, and you seem to have lost interest in social activities that are important to the branch as a team.'

'That's just not fair,' Amanda said, fighting back tears.

Who had been talking about her behind her back?

She glanced out of the glass side panel of the office and saw Sarah looking over.

'I totally dispute what you're saying; I've tried not to let the accident affect my job but it has been hard.'

'I understand,' Carol agreed. 'Which is why I suggested you might not want to rush back to work when you did.'

Amanda folded her arms and glowered.

'We can't follow up on this complaint because there are no further details. Just take this as an informal chat. It's in your own interests to try and up your game from this point forward.'

'But what they said isn't true,' Amanda protested, not wanting to move until Carol believed she was innocent. 'Someone has obviously got it in for me; they're trying to make trouble.'

A flicker of impatience crossed Carol's face.

'I haven't got time to endlessly debate this,' she said firmly. 'Let's just agree you're going to buckle back down and focus properly on your role again. I have to say, I don't think you should be considering applying for the lead TA position at this point in time.'

Amanda found herself dismissed and drifted out of Carol's office like a zombie. Her heart bumped painfully against her chest, her breathing suddenly rapid and shallow.

She searched frantically in her head for a reason someone might complain about her. Perhaps the parent had got the wrong member of staff, surely that was possible? But no, according to Carol they had used her full name.

Maybe she had been a bit distracted with some of the parents.

The car accident had affected her, brought back horrible memories. . . but she definitely hadn't taken a call mid-conversation with a parent. That, she was certain of.

'How'd it go?' Sarah squeaked when she got back.

She snatched up her handbag and walked out without replying. She badly needed a break and some fresh air.

Somehow, Amanda managed to get through the afternoon.

When she returned from her short walk, she told Sarah straight that she didn't want to discuss her conversation with Carol. To her credit Sarah backed off and left her alone for the rest of the day.

The worst part was this new nervy feeling about who she could really trust. For all she knew, a colleague could have anonymously contacted Mansfield HQ and made an untrue complaint about her, simply to scupper her chances of getting the lead TA job.

But walking to the bus stop after work, she found herself turning around a couple of times for no other reason than a creeping sickness in the pit of her stomach.

Quietly, her brain had made a very faint link between the feeling someone was watching her and the fact that somebody was trying to cause trouble for her at work.

She scanned the pavement behind her and over the road but couldn't see anyone.

There had been two or three instances where she had almost seen something, mad as it sounded. You can't almost see anything: you either do or you don't, right? And yet that was the only way she could really describe it.

And there were the calls to consider. Numerous, silent calls where she couldn't hear anything at all but could *feel* the animosity trickling down the line.

Ten minutes later, she got off the bus and walked down the street. She felt OK now; maybe it was just a touch of anxiety through the stress at work today but then, as she turned into the driveway, she caught movement across the road out of the corner of her eye.

When she looked up there was nothing, nobody there at all.

At first she was convinced someone had dashed behind a parked car to avoid being spotted, so she waited for a minute or two at the gate but no one reappeared.

When she got inside the house, she had a cup of tea and a chat with her mum. She didn't mention anything about her concerns, and her mum was on the late shift so she'd have an early night.

Amanda texted Liam and said she was feeling unwell. She couldn't face having to go over there and act all upbeat.

He tried to ring her back but she ignored the call.

She couldn't face going out tonight. She longed for a relaxing bath and to catch up on the last couple of days' soaps on TV.

That would take her mind off things.

Two hours later, up in her bedroom, she'd almost forgotten about being creeped out earlier. Until she turned to close the curtains and saw that same infuriatingly quick movement just out of her visual range.

She turned the bedside lamps off and peered out of the window, scrutinising the churchyard and the path that ran parallel to the road. There were lots of trees and bushes and places to dash behind if someone wanted to remain hidden.

She closed the curtains but left a tiny gap through which she could stand and watch if the mood took her.

She really was starting to wonder if she was imagining things. After all, who would want to spy on or follow her?

CHAPTER 64

The next day, Amanda signed out and left work a full hour early. Headed for the bus stop, her eyes were stinging with humiliation and disbelief.

On her way out she'd had to endure people staring at her, whispering together and then studying the ceiling or the floor intently whenever she walked past.

She had shown some prospective parents around the facilities first thing and they had signed up their twin daughters there and then, which was a result that even brought a smile to Carol's face.

Amanda had managed finally to get the outdoor activity space reorganised, and instead of sitting in a quiet corner at morning break to read like she usually did, she joined the others and listened to some of the girls talking about a new bar in town they were going to, agreeing to join them for a drink later in the week.

But on her afternoon break, she popped upstairs to the small kitchen to find a tight huddle of people, including Sarah, and Pete Tooley, the maintenance man, talking in low voices over in the corner.

'What's wrong?' She craned over their heads to see what all the fuss was about.

Faces registered panic as she approached and the group fell apart, several people exiting the room in record time.

'I was just coming down to show you,' stammered Sarah, slapping down an A4 sheet on the table. 'It was stuck on the side door, and I didn't want Carol to see it before you knew.'

Amanda picked up the home-made A4 poster with the head-line:

'CHILD KILLER WORKS AT BUSY BEES NURSERY'

Underneath the headline was a paragraph written reporter-style, claiming that Amanda Danson was the hit-and-run driver of a toddler that had been killed by a car in the town just before Christmas. Police had not been able to trace the driver or vehicle to date but were apparently now investigating her after this 'second' accident – again, giving full details.

The bottom third of the poster was taken up with a grainy pho-tocopied black-and-white image of her. She recognised the pho-tograph immediately as being her profile picture from Facebook.

'This isn't true,' she said, quietly, sitting down and laying a hand across her forehead. 'It's a load of rubbish.'

'Don't worry,' Sarah said, suddenly a concerned friend again. 'We'll destroy this, no harm done.'

'Somebody has got a hate campaign going against me.'

It was the worst kind of campaign because it contained truth amongst the lies: the accident on Green Road. It seemed so much more plausible because of that.

Suddenly, the staff room door flew open and Pete Tooley burst in again.

'Amanda, you'd better come quickly.' He struggled to speak, panting heavily from bounding up the stairs. 'The posters are all over the High Street. Parents are bringing them in, and Carol is doing her fucking nut.'

One of Carol Hartnell's obsessions was keeping the profile of the branch squeaky clean in the local community.

'People will only leave their children with people they can trust,' was her catchphrase.

Before Amanda could get out of the building to begin tearing down the posters, Carol blocked her exit.

'Perhaps you should go home early today,' she said, her voice dangerously void of emotion. 'I need to investigate exactly what has happened here and get back to you.'

'Carol, it's all lies. Someone has got it in for me, I swear—'

'I'll see you in my office tomorrow at two p.m. Feel free to bring someone with you.'

So here Amanda was, an hour early out of work and waiting for the bus. Over the road from the bus stop, a quick movement caught her eye but, predictably, when she glanced up from her phone there was nothing to see. A sense of unease enveloped her. Who hated her enough to make up these lies?

The fact that the poster had included the Green Road accident that she was involved in, together with a complete lie – the 'awful truth' that the police still didn't know the identity of the hit-and-run driver of the vehicle that knocked over a little boy – implied she had something to do with a fabricated accident. But somehow it also helped to make her pleas of innocence seem empty.

Since her chat with Carol a couple of days earlier, things had seemed to settle down a little at work. Amanda had kept her head down and got on with the job, and after each appointment, she'd made a point of asking every parent she spoke to if they were happy with the way she had answered their queries and dealt with them. The answer was always yes.

She ended up confiding in Sarah yesterday that colleagues had apparently been whispering concerns to Carol about her but Sarah dismissed all that with a flap of her arm.

'Everybody knows what a bitch Carol can be,' she said. 'Bet she's just made that up to have a go at you.'

But after all that, there was now today's debacle to consider.

Someone was out there who hated her so much they'd go to great lengths to destroy her any way they could.

History was repeating itself.

She knew the nursery couldn't simply sack her because of a malicious poster; such accusations would have to be substantiated.

Unfortunately, she felt sure Carol Hartnell was creative enough to come up with another valid reason – that carried some weight – to get rid of her before the nursery's customers started to take a real interest in this very public hate campaign and wonder who was looking after their children.

It was shocking how easy it was proving to be to bring about someone's demise with no solid evidence at all.

Thinking logically, Amanda had to consider why on earth anyone would want to spend valuable time watching and following her. She had probably got the least interesting life of anyone around here. For her, it was just work every day at the nursery and then straight home – or sometimes to Liam's house – when she finished. There was nothing in between.

A police officer had called round to the house last night to take a statement about the accident. She was stern and virtually accused Amanda of ignoring a previous letter, which she had never received.

Amanda had felt her face flushing but managed to hold her nerve and answered all PC Cullen's questions. She said the police had been given witness information that indicated Amanda may have been distracted immediately before colliding with Liam. But, of course, they wouldn't divulge what proof they had.

Then PC Cullen began asking rather weird and vague questions about Liam and why Amanda had made contact with him and his gran after the accident. Had she tried to pressure them in any way?

That was a laugh: Liam had invited her over to the house.

It was all for show, of course. They could think what the hell they liked, they had no proof that she'd done anything wrong at all. He'd appeared out of nowhere on his motorbike, and she had no time to stop.

That was her story and she was damn well sticking to it.

You might wonder why I do it, what I get out of it.

Why plan and work so hard to get close to someone you loathe?

Well, I'll tell you.

It's the satisfaction.

I have nothing. Nothing. So why should anyone else?

People are so stupid. They surround themselves with material things because they believe those things matter. Things that make them feel 'more than' inside, things that make them feel their useless lives are worth something.

Yet it's that moment you take away the things they can't replace that you see the light in their eyes die. In that beautiful split second, they realise what has really mattered all along.

Trust. Love. Self-respect.

And once I take them, I make sure they can never take them back.

CHAPTER 65
Anna

Even though it's a while since I took the sedatives, I know I shouldn't really be driving yet.

But I have no choice.

I think about the safety checks but I don't do any.

When I have more time I will go back to the beginning and get everything straightened out again. I will sort out all the stuff that has got mixed up and in the wrong order in my head.

When I get to Liam's I haven't even reached the back door before I hear raised voices coming from inside the house.

'I'm not leaving, not before you tell me—'

The door is slightly ajar, and I see Liam first and then Amanda standing at the bottom of the stairs, yelling. When I step inside Liam rushes forward quite deftly, and I notice with surprise he doesn't need his crutches at all now.

'Thank God you're here, Anna.' He puts his arms around me and whispers in my ear. 'I'm trying to get rid of her but she won't leave.'

'Anna, I need to talk to you—'Amanda begins.

'I think it's time for you to go,' I snap, and Liam steps back from me to glare at her too. 'Your sad little game isn't working; Liam knows you're trying to wriggle out of prosecution.'

'It's got nothing to do with that,' she sighs. 'Anna, you need to know—'

'I know everything I need to know.' I watch her through narrowed eyes. 'About *you*.'

She runs rigid fingers through her hair.

'You don't know him.' She nods at Liam.

'I know *you*.' I take a step towards her. 'I know you very well. I remember everything that happened, everything you did, *Carla*.'

'Who's Carla?' Liam frowns.

'How do you know about her?' Amanda's face drains deathly pale.

I'm astonished that she has actually convinced herself that Carla is a separate person. She must have some kind of personality disorder.

'Look at my face.' I jut my chin out. 'Remember now, do you?'

'What are you two going on about?' Liam shouts. His arms cross over his body like an armour of flesh.

'I'll tell you everything, Liam,' I say walking over to her. 'Soon as I've got rid of her.'

I grab her arm, but she shakes it free. 'Get off me, you nutter,' she spits.

Before I can retort, she storms out of the house and slams the door behind her.

Then I hear banging on the floor upstairs.

'It's just Gran,' Liam says quickly. 'She's not well; the doctor says she has to stay in bed.'

Suits me. At least she isn't interfering down here when Liam and I need time to talk.

'Let's go through to the living room,' I suggest. 'And I'll tell you everything about so-called Amanda Danson.'

'Anna.'

I hear Ivy call weakly.

'Please. . . come up—'

I place my foot on the bottom step.

'Don't,' Liam says, pressing his hand on to my shoulder. 'Leave her to rest.'

'Anna—' Ivy's voice floats down again.

'She sounds distressed,' I say. 'I'd better just pop up.'

'I said *leave her.*'

Something in his eyes flashes, and I take my foot off the step.

'I need some thinking time alone, Anna,' he says looking away. 'Can you come back later?'

CHAPTER 66

I sit outside in the car a short while, thinking things through.

Liam was vague and confused just now. I wonder if he has stopped taking his medication again. I tried to convince him to let me stay and make him something to eat but he wouldn't hear of it.

Amanda, Carla, call her what you will, she is the reason for all this upset.

I just knew she would ruin everything given half a chance, casting doubt in Liam's mind about us, about the accident.

I blink a few times to disperse the murkiness that has settled in my eyes. I've noticed it happens after I take the sedatives. They dull my thoughts, untether them, as if they belong in someone else's head.

I start the car. I feel a bit woozy, and I want to get back home. If I take it steady I should be fine. When I get back I can take another sedative and go straight to bed.

Things often look different after a rest.

The sky is clouding over and it looks like there might be heavy rain soon.

I drive slowly down Liam's street and turn the corner on to Copthorne Way. It is a long road and when I get near the bottom I see a familiar figure turn the corner and then just as quickly she disappears from view again.

Adrenaline courses through my veins and a sense of anticipation grips me.

I turn in to the next street, and there she is, scurrying along like a dishevelled rat with her head down and eyes trained to the pavement.

The time is right. Confront her.

I drive slowly past her.

With a wet and swollen face, she is completely lost in her thoughts and doesn't notice me at all. She is probably replaying whatever argument she just had with Liam over and over in her head.

I turn the corner and pull in again halfway down the next street by the small row of shops where I know she uses a cut-through to get to her own road.

A few moments later, as she nears my car, I get out and stand directly in her path. She almost bumps into me by the time she comes to her senses.

'Sorry,' she mumbles, making to walk around me.

'Just a minute, *Carla*,' I say loud and clear, and her head jerks up from staring at the pavement.

'Oh, it's you,' she says, her voice flat.

'Yes. It's me,' I mimic. 'Haven't you been to work today? You're usually not back until gone five.'

She bristles, her face instantly flushing. Then she says slowly, 'have you been watching me?'

I smirk and take a step closer.

'I've been doing more than watch you.'

Her features twist up into a tight knot.

'It's been you all this time?'

'What are you talking about?' I mustn't let her distract me.

'You know what: the hate campaign at work. Why would you do that?'

Incredible. Despite ruining so many people's lives, she is still managing to keep up this indignant attitude and make up stories about hate campaigns. Not a shred of humility to be salvaged.

'I don't know what you're talking about, *Carla*.' I take another step towards her.

'I'm not Carla.'

She tries to push past me but I'm having none of it. I use my shoulder to thump hard into the side of her as she attempts to pass and she stumbles against a shop window.

'I need to get back home,' she raises her voice like she is in charge of the situation.

It is time to show her that's no longer the case. I move in quickly, using my weight to squash her against the shop's glass.

'For God's sake,' she cries out. 'What's wrong with you, Anna?'

People walking by slow their pace, and I can see customers inside the shop moving closer to the window to get a better view of what's happening outside.

'You have never fooled me for a second, do you know that?' I hiss. 'I always knew there was something strange about that accident but you've even managed to dupe Liam until now. Was that always the plan: to take advantage of his trusting nature?'

'What? Get off me.' She struggles to try and make some space around herself. 'I wanted to speak to you back at the house, Anna, there are things I need to tell you.'

I bring my face closer to hers.

'You'd better start talking then, *Carla*.'

'Who are you?' she whispers.

'Remember the eight-year-old boy you sacrificed? Daniel Clarke?'

Her hand flies to her mouth.

'What happened to that boy, it was nothing to do with me.' Her voice shifts up an octave. 'Leave me alone.'

'Is everything alright?' The shopkeeper sticks her head out of the door.

'Everything's fine,' I say pleasantly.

She makes another break for freedom, but I grab her arm and pull her roughly back.

'Not so fast, Carla.'

'I'm not Carla. Carla is gone,' she yells, her voice descending into a coughing fit.

Silence for a few seconds.

'She hasn't *gone* just because you changed your name.' I dig my fingertips into the top of her arm. 'You can't just conveniently forget what you did. It's finally time to face the consequences.'

I'm aware of a small number of passers-by starting to linger now, taking an interest.

I call out to them, 'I'm afraid we have someone here who caused the death of a young boy thirteen years ago. He trusted her and she betrayed him.'

Carla, predictably, starts to cry, her face a wet, shiny mess.

I look around the straggly gathering. Wide eyes blink back at me, unsure of how to react.

'She nearly killed my boyfriend too, knocked him off his motorbike two weeks ago. Her name is Carla Bevin.'

Shouting out her name like that feels like airing the truth. It is like a drug and I want more of it. Carla looks at me, her face twisted up, her eyes wild and desperate.

I begin to feel very hot, despite the chilly wind. I'd like to take off my fleece but I won't let go of her.

'You're crazy!' she cries out, turning to the onlookers. 'She's nuts. Someone, please just call the police.'

I turn to see if anyone is taking her seriously, and she pushes me hard, managing to twist from my grip and take off down the road.

I bolt straight after her, and when I'm close enough, I reach out and grab her arm again. I yank it to pull her back, and she screams out. Her arm makes a sort of snapping noise, and when I let go it falls away, hanging uselessly at a strange angle.

I grab her hair with my free hand and force her down to her knees on the pavement. She's sobbing in such a theatrical manner I start to laugh and can't stop.

The crowd of people seems to have doubled now and have followed us to watch.

'Leave her alone,' someone shouts.

'What's happened?' I hear another voice call out.

I ignore the crowd and Amanda's wailing and bend down so my mouth is close to her ear.

'Your nasty little game is finished,' I whisper, still tittering to myself. 'Everyone is about to find out what a conniving liar you really are.'

'I'm not Carla,' she utters stiltedly.

Her level of denial is staggering.

'You can't just say the words and make it true,' I scream. 'You *are* Carla, I recognise you. *You* killed Daniel and now you're going to pay.'

Something in the way she looks at me makes me freeze. She leans towards me and whispers.

'Carla was my sister. My twin. That's why you think you know me.'

'You liar.' I tighten my grip on her hair and she yells out.

'Carla died!' she gasps. 'After what happened to Daniel. She didn't want to live.'

I let go of her hair and watch her crumple dramatically to the ground.

I push my way through the crowd and head towards my car, disorientated by my thumping chest and shaking hands.

As I drive away, I look over my shoulder at people fussing over her.

She is lying. She is lying again, and I must not believe her.

She is trying to fool me like she fools everyone else. She just never stops.

And anyway, how can it possibly be that all this time I have been wrong? How could I have misjudged the situation so badly? I refuse to even consider it.

Focus.

Her little charade is over and she is fighting to the end. That's all this is.

CHAPTER 67
Amanda

She fumbled in her bag at the front door with her one good hand, almost dropping the keys when she finally found them. The door yawned open and she stepped quickly inside, slamming it behind her without checking the road for movement again.

She was safe now, it was OK. She could breathe again.

Her mum was working the late shift so there was no TV in the background and no rosy glow from the hall lamp. The house felt cold, dark and silent.

With difficulty, she shrugged off her coat, kicked off her shoes and flicked on the heating.

In the kitchen she poured herself a large glass of white wine and took a gulp, although she knew no amount of warmth or illumination would relieve the pain in her arm nor the tension that still coursed through her rigid body.

The altercation with Anna had left her shaky and tearful. In fact, the right word was assault, not altercation. She ought to ring the police.

Anna had assaulted her in the street in front of lots of witnesses, and she'd done something serious to her arm.

Amanda gingerly lifted it and a sharp stabbing pain radiated around her shoulder joint. When she kept it still, the pain reverted to a dull ache and she could just about bear it. Anyway, it would have to wait until her mum got back to have a look at it because there was no way she was leaving the house again tonight, not even for hospital treatment.

She rooted around in the drawer until she found a simple sling that formed part of her mother's formidable first aid kit. After a bit of a struggle, she managed to manoeuvre it into place and felt instant relief as the sling took the weight of her arm and kept it reasonably immobile.

That mad woman had bullied her in the street like a mean girl in the playground, and Amanda's toes curled in intimidation just thinking about it. At least a dozen useless people had stood and watched instead of calling the police.

Things had got so messy. First the accident and the police involvement. . . and now Anna knew about Carla, too.

Amanda couldn't face explaining it all to the police, not at this precise moment.

Aside from Anna's physical attack, the thing that had unnerved her the most was the fact that all this time Anna had known about Carla she had known about what happened to the boy.

How could that possibly be?

Amanda glanced around the room and her heart sank as she wondered how she had ended up living back here with her mum after leaving home and striking out on her own like a normal young woman in her mid-twenties.

It had been nothing whatsoever to do with her at the time, and yet what happened to Daniel Clarke had changed her life. It had changed *all* their lives. Anna wasn't on her own on that score.

Despite Amanda running and hiding from the stigma for thirteen years, Anna knew the truth.

She took another large sip of wine and closed her eyes. This line of thought wasn't helping one bit but it was hard to stay positive when you seemed to take one step forward and two steps back.

A relationship, travelling and all the normal things a woman of her age should be enjoying had proved beyond her. She just couldn't seem to finally get over the hurdle of the past.

Amanda had felt her life was fairly stable for a time, had foolishly hoped things would even improve. Then there'd been the car accident and now her life was unravelling at a rate of knots.

She picked up her glass and her hand jerked nervously, slopping wine on the kitchen table. A noise outside like a slap or perhaps something breaking had startled her. She held her breath and listened.

The soft hum of the boiler, a dog barking in the near distance and. . . there was nothing else. She released her breath and closed her eyes.

She must be going crazy, imagining she was being followed and now jumping at noises that didn't exist. She needed to calm down and get a handle on herself.

She glanced out of the kitchen window but could only see her own pale, worried face reflected back in the darkening glass. She stood up and flicked off the light switch and the garden came into focus.

Standing at the sink, she looked out. Past the glass at the dark cluster of sprawling bushes that scaled the fence, and the bare branches of the blossom tree that Mum had planted in memory of her dad in the bottom corner.

It occurred to Amanda that there could quite easily be someone crouched in there, watching her right now.

Some pervert or crazed stalker she didn't know but who knew everything about her.

She laughed out loud at her thoughts. She was going bonkers, it was official. Anyway, if there was someone out there, it was more likely to be Crazy Anna, as she had started to think of her.

Of course, she had realised from the start there was something definitely not right with the woman, that way she looked at everyone so slyly.

Every word that left her mouth seemed to carry an unspoken subtext that only Anna herself understood and now, today, there had been a massive escalation of that. Anna's aggression level had ramped right up and she had actually physically hurt Amanda in the street.

She couldn't let it go; she had to do something about it. Just not this evening.

They hadn't said as much but Amanda could tell that Liam and Ivy both thought Anna acted strangely at times.

The way she was always round at their house, else trying to wriggle into their daily lives with her offers of cleaning or taking Liam to his hospital appointments.

Amanda had read a real-life story once in some trashy magazine. A woman's account of her ordeal at the hands of a female stalker who pursued her for years after a minor disagreement at work.

Nobody, including the victim, took her antics seriously until the day the woman opened her front door and the stalker threw sulphuric acid in her face.

Maybe things could get even worse for Amanda than they were already.

Her eyes bored through the glass into the darkness beyond. Anna was quite a solidly built woman whereas Amanda was petite and weak. She was no match for her physically.

If Anna managed to get inside this house with ill intentions, there was no telling what she could do to her. And her mum wouldn't be back for hours. It sounded dramatic, even to Amanda, but ignoring Anna's behaviour today could prove perilous.

The back of her neck prickled. The noise, it was there again.

And over the other side of the lawn. . . a shadow moving by the fence.

There was someone in the garden.

Amanda's throat felt dry and rough; she had to battle the urge to run upstairs and hide under her quilt like she did as a child when it was Carla's turn to be the Bounding Monster.

A sharp rap sounded at the back door, and she gave a little cry out loud.

Amanda ignored the knock and crouched down in front of the sink so she couldn't be seen from the window. Her arm protested with a flash of pain in her shoulder.

Another rap. And another.

Whoever was out there seemed determined to get a response. Amanda balled the fist of her good arm to try and stop her hand from shaking.

What if Anna had finally flipped and had come to finish the job?

Amanda's heart sank when she realised her phone was still in her bag in the hallway. She should dash and get it right now. Then phone the police.

But then she might be seen from the window.

Another flurry of knocks on the door and then a voice she recognised. 'Amanda?'

She stood up carefully so as not to snag her arm. Taking a breath, she blew it out long and slow. She didn't want to speak to this caller but it was preferable to tackling a deranged Anna, and she had to face him some time.

Snapping on the light and sliding the bolt, she turned the key and opened the door.

'Liam.'

He looked a little wild-eyed and dishevelled, as if he'd been running.

'I just wanted a chat, you know, to get a few things straight,' he said.

She didn't really want him in the house. He was trying to worm his way out of her telling Anna the truth.

'I don't think that's a good idea,' Amanda said, praying he wouldn't hear the faint tremor in her voice.

'It is.' He pushed his way past her into the kitchen. 'Believe me, it is a very good idea.'

CHAPTER 68

Liam walked straight past Amanda and sat at the breakfast bar. He had never been inside the house before but showed no interest in looking at his surroundings.

'How do you know where I live?'

She waited for him to speak but he remained silent, staring at his hands. A small smirk played at the edge of his mouth. She was surprised at his boldness but she was the one in charge here, it was her home.

'Liam, why are you here?'

'What did you do to your arm?' He glanced at the sling. 'Is it repetitive strain from applying lip gloss?'

His voice was cold and sarcastic. He was like a different person.

'Why are you here?' She heard the tremor in her voice and hoped he hadn't.

'You should come out for a drink with me,' he said, his voice strained. 'You owe me, after all.'

'Owe you? For what?'

'For what you did. The accident.'

So, it sounded as if he did blame her for the accident after all. Up until now, he'd always brushed aside her apologies, never interested in discussing what had happened.

'Liam, I've said I'm sorry a hundred times; I don't know what else I—'

'You can come out for a drink with me. That would be a start.'

He had asked her out a few times when she had visited him at home but so far she had declined. She wasn't entirely sure why she'd always said no. There were times he seemed confused, frustrated. It made her stomach flutter and not in a good way.

'I said I would come for a drink when you were better.'

'I'm better now, better than I've been in a long time.' His thin, dry lips looked on the verge of splitting, and his blue eyes looked darker than she remembered. 'Thanks to Anna, my problems will soon be over.'

'I don't know what you've agreed with Anna but you should tell her about the debt. It's not fair to lead her on, Liam.'

'I don't know what you're talking about.' A sneer slid across his face. 'I lost my memory, remember?'

'Ivy told me everything. About buying the motorbike, the loan shark.'

She gasped as he grabbed her uninjured wrist, hard.

'You shouldn't listen to mad old women: they tell stories.'

'Liam, let go.' She pulled away.

Her breathing speeded up, like her lungs were trying to gulp in more air. She opened her mouth so he couldn't hear it.

He let go of her wrist and reached inside his jacket pocket, pulling out a small box of matches. He took one out, struck it and watched the tiny flame in fascination until it burned down to a powdery black head.

'Liam,' she wasn't sure quite how to phrase it so she just said it, 'you're scaring me. You're acting, I don't know – strange. Are you feeling OK?'

'It's not all about *you* and what *you* feel.' He looked up at her then, his eyes burning. 'It has never been all about *you*.'

She massaged her temples, trying to stop the buzz building inside her head. He was acting so weird.

Where had kind, understanding Liam gone? She was talking to a stranger. Even his voice sounded different.

He lit another match. And then another.

Her stomach fluttered when she remembered she was alone until her mum returned from work after midnight. She wished he'd just go. She should get rid of him.

'I'm so tired.' She gave an exaggerated yawn and tried to sound casual. 'I'm going to have an early night. I can pop over tomorrow, if you like?'

She was exhausted and just wanted him to leave.

Suddenly his face changed, as if someone had flicked a switch inside his head. The hard expression dissolved into a childish pout.

'I didn't mean to hurt them,' he said. 'It was the fire, it just went up. It was out of control, and there was nothing I could do.'

'We can talk about it tomorrow.' She guided him to the door. 'Everything will look better in the morning.'

She closed and locked the door behind him and breathed a sigh of relief.

What the hell was he talking about? Who had he hurt, and when had there been a fire? It didn't make any sense. Ivy said his dad and sister had died in an accident. Carla had assumed a road accident.

She walked across the kitchen and looked back just before she turned off the lights. Her eyes were drawn to the worktop.

There were dozens of spent matches littering the countertop.

CHAPTER 69
Anna

When I get back home from giving Carla Bevin what for in the street, I don't feel sleepy at all. I feel energised and powerful.

I feel like I am back in control, that I can do anything.

I pop upstairs and pull a few clean clothes together. Tonight I am going to stay over at Liam's for the first time whether mad old Ivy likes it or not.

I do what *I* think is right now; I don't give a toss what other people say.

But this smell. This smell just won't do but it will not beat me.

Starting in the kitchen, I rip out drawers, piling the contents on the floor. I sweep the shelves of the cupboards clean of their contents. When I find a claw hammer in one drawer, I use it to force the fronts from the mock drawer and corner cupboard.

I move on to the middle room and then the lounge, emptying, wrenching, ripping – it has to be somewhere. Wherever that stink is, I'm going to find it.

I see Albert slipping out of the back door, and I realise I haven't closed and locked it yet.

My head is spinning and my stomach is growling. I remember that I haven't eaten anything all day but there'll be plenty of time for that later.

When I finish in the living room I stomp upstairs. The house seems to be swaying around me, the walls of each room burgeoning out and then shrinking back again.

At the top of the stairs I sit down on the top step to take a breath. I can't think straight, can't fight through the pictures swarming in my head. Faces looming close and then fading away again. Liam, Carla. . . Danny.

'Anna—'

My breath catches in my throat. I heard my name, I'm sure. . . the faintest whisper.

The world stops turning, and I listen.

Nothing.

Did I really hear it or was it a noise from outside? The voice, it sounded just like Danny's. I sit for a full five minutes listening for anything else, anything at all. But silence prevails.

Something moves at the bottom of the landing and I jump up, my throat tight and parched.

'Albert?' I call faintly.

But it isn't Albert at all.

I recognise the distinct ginger markings and large white paws. It is Boris, Ivy's cat.

A tangle of awful possibilities presents themselves. Have I brought Boris back to the house with me by mistake?

I can't remember taking him; I wouldn't have. A cat needs his security, his home patch. Did Liam ask me to look after Boris?

I close my eyes and fight the queasiness pulsing in my stomach.

I had called back to the house because I wanted to get freshened up before racing over to Liam's to tell him what Carla Bevin did to Danny, so that he understands why I hate her so much and why she is a threat to our happiness as a family.

I feel angry I've let myself become distracted with finding the smell, and now there is the problem of Boris.

I have to somehow get the cat back to Liam's house without being discovered. Nobody will believe I had nothing to do with his abduction.

If I can only rest, sleep properly for a little while, my mind might straighten itself out and I will remember how the cat has managed to end up here.

A loud thudding noise on the wall puts an end to my thoughts. It is coming from next door. But I haven't got the time to go round to Mrs Peat's now.

I look down at the tangle of hair in my fingers; I don't even feel myself pulling at it any more. I shake it off and walk back downstairs, holding on to the walls for support.

By the time I get back in the kitchen I feel guilty. I slip on my shoes and rush next door.

I peer through the small side window and gasp. My hand flies up to my mouth, and in a whirl of confusion I trip, skinning my knee. The milk-bottle stand is on its side, and the key is missing. I try the door handle and it swings open.

It is quiet and still inside, even more so than usual. Mrs Peat does not call out.

She sits in her chair, her mouth slightly open. There is a clot of mangled skin and thick blood at her temple.

I cry out and touch her face, and then snatch my hand back when she blinks.

I think about the last time I saw her, how irritated I was with her.

How I felt confused and disorientated.

How Boris somehow found his way into my house without me remembering what happened.

Maybe Mrs Peat tripped and fell.

Something in my stomach shifts and I rush to the kitchen sink and throw up. I could never hurt Mrs Peat but someone else might have.

I have to call the police; I have to do it now.

I run back round to my house, snatch up my phone and call an ambulance. I ignore what she is saying to me and talk over her, repeating Mrs Peat's name and full address three times.

The operator is asking me what is wrong with Mrs Peat but I don't know what to tell her. The police might trace the call and put me in a cell and that can't be allowed to happen because I still have to tell Liam who Amanda Danson really is.

I end the call.

It is time to tell Liam everything.

CHAPTER 70

An ambulance sits outside Liam's house and a paramedic closes the back doors before getting into the vehicle. I watch it drive away.

My heart hammers at my chest and my throat is pulsing. Has Danny fallen or taken a bad turn?

No, not Danny. This is Liam's house.

Yes, Liam.

I jump out of the car and run across the road, straight down the path and round to the back door.

Liam is helping Ivy take off her coat. She clutches a bag of medication. The ambulance hasn't taken her away but has just dropped her back at home.

I feel quiet and shaky inside when I think about Mrs Peat. I don't think I should have just left her there alone like that with the door unlocked.

But I had to come here. I need to speak to Liam but there's something else I must do when I get the chance. Something really important.

'Where have you been?' Liam's voice is shrill. 'I called round at your house earlier.'

'You must have just missed me,' I say, watching him.

'Stay there while I get Gran settled,' he says but I follow them into the hallway. 'We've got to go in a minute or we'll miss your appointment.'

My appointment with the solicitor.

I completely forgot about it.

'I'll rearrange it,' I say, glancing at the wall clock and seeing there's only fifteen minutes to spare.

'No!'

I look at him, startled by him snapping.

'No, Anna,' he says more calmly. 'This is important for you. I'm worried about your job situation, about them taking what you have.'

'They can't do anything,' I shrug. 'They found nothing in the search.'

'Still, I think we should—'

The back door flies open and Carla Bevin appears, urgent and breathless. There is a bruise on her jaw, and her arm is in a sling.

'Anna, you need to leave this house right away,' she says from behind me. Her voice is shaky, and she stays back at the door.

I ignore her. 'Liam, I need to tell you all about her, about what she did.'

'Please, just stop,' Liam cries out. He clutches at his head.

For a few seconds there is a shocked silence. Then Ivy speaks in a tired, beaten voice.

'We've lost the cat but Liam can't get out and look for him. He's been having headaches you see,' she says softly. 'Haven't you, lad?'

Liam shakes his head.

'It's just silly little things stored up in here.' He taps his head, grinning wildly. 'Nothing important.'

'I need to rest,' sighs Ivy, shuffling towards the stairs. 'I'm going for a lie down but I don't want to stay up here all night. Hear that, Liam?'

'Ivy, I don't think you're well enough to go upstairs on your own,' Carla says.

Very clever. Playing the concerned friend.

'Anna and I have an appointment,' Liam says. 'We have to go.'

'Go where?' Carla asks.

'To the solicitors,' I speak up, smirking at her concerned expression. 'Liam is taking charge of all my personal affairs.'

Carla looks at him. 'Liam?'

My heart soars when Liam turns away from her and says, 'this is just between me and Anna.'

'Is it to do with you paying off the debt?'

'What the hell are you talking about?' I snap. 'Come on, Liam, let's go. I can tell you everything you need to know about her on the way.'

'Anna, don't do anything rash with your finances.' Carla turns to face me, actually touching my arm. 'I really need to speak to you in private for a few minutes; it's in your own interest.'

I push her hard and get in close to her face, ignoring her yelp of pain as the arm in a sling bangs against the wall.

'So you can get your story in first? Don't you dare try and say you care about me or Liam. Why don't you just tell him right now who you really are?'

Not surprisingly she isn't forthcoming with any information about herself.

'Anna, I told you, you've got it wrong—'

I take a deep breath and turn to Liam.

'Her name is Carla Bevin and she caused the death of my brother thirteen years ago.'

She looks straight at me, holding her injured arm protectively. 'I'm sorry for your loss, Anna, but you're mistaken. I'm not Carla, and she didn't kill Daniel, she – well, she made a terrible mistake.'

My head throbs with a dull ache, and I feel like I'm filled to the brim with sludge.

I want to slap her hard, discount her lies, but something about her words, her face, somehow rings true. It sucks the fire right out of me.

Liam doesn't react at all, doesn't even look at us.

He turns and walks into the living room. I follow and watch as he sits down with his head in his hands, rocking back and forth.

Carla fusses over Ivy, helping her off with her coat with one arm. Something is very wrong here, something doesn't fit.

I realise this is my chance.

'I have to use the bathroom,' I say calmly but nobody replies.

A couple of minutes later I'm in Ivy's bedroom, rifling in the wardrobe until I have the shoebox in my hands. There on the top lies the psychological report.

I unfold it and sit on the edge of the bed.

'Anna?' I hear Liam shouting to me. I haven't got much time.

I scan down the report. I haven't got the luxury of reading every word but I take a little more time than before so I can scan each line.

And there it is. The missing piece that I missed the first time around. The piece that makes sense of it all.

'The patient's guardian, Ivy Wilton, gives permission for her charge, Liam Wilton, to continue with his treatment at the clinic. . .'

'Anna come down, we have to go,' Liam bellows.

I flip to Ivy's signature at the bottom of the report.

'Signed below on behalf of the juvenile patient, Liam Bradbury. . .'

This report was never about Ivy. It was Liam's all along.

Back downstairs, I sit next to Liam. I feel light-headed as if I'm standing back and watching a different person. All the signs are there; I don't know how I missed them.

Liam is fidgeting and chewing his stubby nails.

'We have to go, we have to go,' he mumbles to himself.

I can hear Carla speaking to Ivy in the kitchen but she suddenly appears in the doorway and walks over to where we are sitting.

'Talk to me,' Carla says to him. 'Tell me the truth, Liam. Are you remembering stuff. . . important stuff? Your gran told me you had financial problems before the accident, do you remember?'

'What?' I say faintly.

'He took a loan out from a local loan shark. He didn't want you to know. That's why she didn't let you stay at the house.'

Liam jumps up and grabs my arm then, and Carla steps back in surprise. Every inch of my skin prickles.

'Let's go.'

He's acting so strangely, continually flipping tracks. The report is from long ago and people can get better but the accident. . . it must have unhinged him.

'Ivy told me about the fire, Liam,' Carla says. 'And how she changed your names so nobody knew.'

He reaches for the door handle but stops dead in his tracks.

'I don't know what you're talking about.' His voice is soft and low. His eyes are wide open but glazed, as if he's looking at something far away.

'Fire?' I say faintly but nobody answers.

'Are the memories coming back?' Carla says. 'You've not been yourself the last day or so. Do you want to talk about it?'

Liam stops walking and shrugs off her hand.

'I haven't got a clue what you're going on about,' he says, seeming to gather his wits again.

'Your gran told me about what happened,' she says. 'About the house fire when you were a boy, your dad and sister. . . you need help to talk about it—'

'She's lying!' he explodes. 'She's old and losing her mind, nothing like that happened.'

A noise at the top of the stairs makes us all look up. Ivy stands shaking and frail, holding on to the banister for support.

'Liam, it's time to talk to someone; they can't do anything, you were too young. I've tried to cover it up all these years but I've been wrong. You need help with your mind, you're—'

'*You're* crazy,' he shouts, his eyes darting over all of us. 'You're all crazy.'

He starts to climb the stairs faster than he ought to after an accident, his pain eclipsed by fury.

'Gran has got dementia. She's going to have to go into a home.'

'Liam, I can help you. We can talk.'

Halfway up the stairs, he turns and shoots me a vicious look.

'You're the craziest one of all, Anna. All that stuff you've done to Amanda, sending slanderous posters to her work, making anonymous complaints about her.'

'What are you talking about? I never did that.'

'Anna, you might as well admit it. You did,' she says quietly.

'I made some prank calls to your phone, and I had the ma-nure delivered. I admit that was me, you deserved it.'

'So if it wasn't you, who did the other stuff?' Amanda snaps.

Liam begins to emit a curious high-pitched laughter. 'You fucking stupid pair, who do you think did it?'

I press my hand against the wall to steady myself. Has his affection for me been nothing but an act? I start up the stairs, reaching out to touch him.

But Ivy's voice pierces my thoughts.

'It's all here, Liam.' In her free hand she clutches newspaper cuttings like those in the box in the wardrobe. She shakes them in the air, tears rolling down the soft, pale folds of her cheeks. 'You can't just pretend it never happened.'

'No!'

Nearly at the top of the stairs now, Liam lunges up towards the sheets of newspaper.

I'm not really sure what happens next.

CHAPTER 71

Absolute silence blankets everything. There is an invisible thickening of the air.

Ivy releases a terrible yelp and then she is tumbling, arms flailing out before her, wildly grasping at nothing. The scene freeze-frames before me and then speeds up again.

Ivy crashes and bounces off each step, plummeting past me, only stopping with a sickening thud when she reaches the wall at the bottom of the stairs.

I lose my footing and hear Carla scream out as I start to pitch down the stairs myself. I manage to break my fall by grasping the banister but still end up in a heap on the floor, right next to Ivy.

Silence.

The soft flutter of bits of newspaper floating down the stairs to rest on the bottom steps. I glance down at the headline.

'FATHER AND DAUGHTER DIE IN SUSPECTED ARSON ATTACK'

'Ivy.' Carla bends down over the old woman, rubbing her shoulder. 'Can you hear me?'

Liam limps back downstairs, grimacing now with the effort of the climb. His cheeks burn red, eyes badly bloodshot. He begins to gather up the scattered newspaper articles.

Carla wails, backing away from Ivy.

I move closer and follow her gaze. I can't see the old woman's face but her head is bathed in a sticky, ruby thickness that continues to ooze on to the wooden floor.

I look down at my own splayed hand and recoil at the awful splatters of her blood on my own skin.

Still, Liam continues to gather the cuttings. Carla and I look at each other.

A wave of nausea hits me, and I scramble to my feet, heading back towards the kitchen door to get some fresh air. Confused, I turn full circle.

Liam and Carla seem to blur into each other, their voices sound deep and slow, like an old record playing at the wrong speed. I collapse to the floor.

When I open my eyes, Liam crouches in front of me. His eyes are wide, his face pale. After what seems an age, everything snaps back into sight and my eyes focus on his face.

'What happened?' I say, struggling but finally managing to sit up.

'Anna,' he says, shaking my shoulders. 'Look at me.'

My head swarms and buzzes, full of pictures I'd rather forget. But I lift my chin and look at him.

'Anna,' he says. 'What on earth have you done?'

His voice sounds as if it's far away. So far away I can hardly hear what he is saying.

Like the flick of a switch, the words race closer and closer until his voice echoes painfully loud in my ears.

And then there is nothing.

CHAPTER 72

DC Gant clicks his fingers in front of my face. 'Anna, take us through what happened one more time.'

'I was trying to tell him,' I whisper. 'About her lies.'

'Whose lies? Ivy Bradbury's? What did you do with her cat?'

I close my eyes. I feel so tired, so utterly spent.

'Anna, you need to concentrate. We found your neighbour, Joan Peat, with a serious head injury, and the emergency call came from your phone. Did you hurt her?'

I open my eyes and look at his flabby, whiskered face, too close to my own.

'Where is Amanda Danson?' he asks.

All that has gone wrong is her doing. She tried to fool me that Carla Bevin was her twin sister, and it nearly worked.

He glances at his colleague. 'What do you mean, all her doing?'

Have I spoken out loud? I feel sure the words stayed inside my head.

'Anna, did you kill Ivy Bradbury and assault Joan Peat?'

I look at his hands. He has a wedding ring on, a thin gold band that is scratched and worn.

'Danny didn't tell me about the fire,' I say. 'I would have helped him.'

'Who's Danny?'

'This is hopeless,' the other policeman says.

'Did you get angry? We all get angry sometimes, Anna.'

'I just wanted Liam to know the truth,' I say.

DC Gant nods.

'I understand,' he says. 'You wanted him to know the truth but they made you angry.'

'Yes,' I say. 'Her blood is on my hands.'

I raise my arms to the light but I can't see the spatters any more.

'Liam told us,' he says. 'How you got angry and pushed Ivy down the stairs. Do you know where Amanda Danson is? Where did you take her in your car?'

'Her name is Carla Bevin,' I correct him.

He turns and whispers to the other man.

My mouth is a sour pit. My insides feel hollow and withered, as if my organs have been replaced with a tangle of dried-out rags.

'Carla was Amanda's twin sister, Anna,' DC Gant tells me. 'Her identical twin. Carla committed suicide thirteen years ago.'

Lies, lies, lies.

I close my eyes and try to remember. Did this all happen to-day or yesterday. . . or was it weeks ago now?

Climbing up the stairs, newspaper cuttings fluttering down, and Liam's pale face in front of mine. Ivy's crumpled shape lying at the bottom of the stairs, and the blood. So much blood.

'Do you remember?' He presses me as the other man slips out of the room. 'Pushing Ivy Bradbury down the stairs when she made you angry?'

'She held out her hands,' I say. 'Like this.'

I stretch out my arms far in front of my face. My hands are shaking and I see there are clumps of hair knotted around my fingers.

'You remember pushing her?'

Did I push her?

I remember climbing the stairs and seeing Ivy at the top. The newspaper fluttering down like big torn monochrome petals.

I think about the mail in the spare room: how it was there and then it wasn't. The smell in the house that nobody else noticed.

I bury my head in my hands. My elbows are tapping up and down on the table while thoughts slip through my mind like sand in an egg timer.

'I didn't push her,' I say.

The other detective comes back into the room.

'We know you had a scuffle with Amanda Danson in the street. Witnesses have come forward.' I hear the snatch of impatience in his tone. 'You attacked her. Where is she now, Anna?'

'She's gone to hell,' I whisper.

The two men huddle their heads again and then DC Gant stands up and sighs.

'Well, nobody can say I didn't try,' he says to his colleague.

When they've gone, I stand up and pace around the small floor space. I count my steps then I replace the numbers with words.

'Where – did – the – mail – go – where – is – the – smell – coming – from – what—'

'Anna?'

Two women have entered the room without me noticing. One is in police uniform; the other is dressed in ordinary clothes.

'I'm PC Cullen,' the officer says. 'We've met before at your house; can you remember?'

Paper burning, a million bits swarming in the air like white locusts. A broken toilet that was not really broken.

'And this is Dr Marsh.'

The doctor smiles at me and holds out her hand. She has short, neat nails and a perfectly round chocolate-coloured mole on her wrist.

'Where's Danny?' I say, sitting down.

CHAPTER 73
One year later
Anna

My favourite place to relax in the clinic is the sun room where floor to ceiling glass windows look out over the lawns.

On warmer days they open the folding doors and it's possible to sit reading a book while enjoying the gentle breeze.

It is also where the visitors come on Tuesdays.

Visiting lasts all day long but the rule is that one visit shouldn't exceed two hours. It's so the lounge doesn't get overcrowded with people.

Today is Tuesday, and I've been looking forward to visiting time all week.

I walk through the foyer into the lounge and pause for a moment by the door.

I smile when I spot him sitting by the window waiting for me, looking out on to the manicured gardens.

When I get closer I notice the sunlight speckling his face, his eyes crinkling up against the light.

'Hello, Liam,' I say, putting down the basket of fruit on the small table.

He looks up at me but his eyes are blank.

'It's a lovely day.' I sit in the chair opposite him. 'Albert and Boris have been lying on the balcony in the sun since eight o'clock.'

I even did a spot of drawing out there when I woke up this morning.

I like my small, neat flat. It feels good to have left the house behind at last.

It doesn't mean I have to forget my happy memories with Danny; it is more like I am allowing myself to finally leave behind the bad that happened there. I get that now.

Linda, the care assistant, contacted me a few months ago. We met up and she presented me with a beautiful framed cross-stitch of a little cottage that Mrs Peat had sewed for me in the care home.

She had included my name and even a picture of Albert. The picture was called *'New Beginnings'*.

I'm going to visit her next week. She sent a message with Linda that there was something very important she needs to tell me.

I doubt that very much but I'll humour her, of course.

I am keeping Liam's house maintained for the time being; it keeps me busy now I'm no longer working. Resigning from my job was the best thing I did for my health.

They couldn't prove that Ivy's death was anything but an accident, and consequently, her life insurance paid off the mortgage. Nobody knows when Liam will be well enough to leave the clinic, but when he does, I want him to have a home to return to, somewhere he recognises.

'Liam?'

He blinks, fixated on the glossy emerald lawn outside. His fingers are working into his thigh. I can see them scratching through the special mittens he has to wear.

I look up and see Nurse Janet waving to me across the room. I smile and return the gesture. All the staff know me here now; they're always saying how I've been such a great help to Liam on what will be his very long road to recovery.

It's not as if I do anything special. I just talk to him about this and that. I don't ask him any questions about unpleasant subjects.

If I learned one thing from my months of counselling sessions with Dr Marsh, it is that you can't push people to talk until they're ready to open up.

I study his profile in the sunlight, his long dark eyelashes and the way his hair curls into his neck. He doesn't really look like Danny at all. I can see that now.

He is still staring blankly through the glass but I remind myself you never know what's bubbling away in someone's head.

Who'd have believed he got his memory back just a couple of days after waking up from the accident? All that time he had us fooled.

They said the trauma of the accident had opened up a sort of crevice in his psyche and revealed a personality he had managed to cocoon away for years. Until the accident shook it all loose again like rotten apples falling from a tree.

It must be awful to burn your own family to death and then forget about it. As a young boy there was nothing they could do to punish him. He had psychological help for a few years and then the system just forgot about him.

Ivy had protected him all those years, moved away and even changed their surnames so it wouldn't follow him around. She'd kept him medicated and reliant on her, treating him like the little boy he used to be to try and keep things under control.

But in the end even she realised that Liam was losing his mind.

I have forgiven him for telling the police it was me who killed Ivy. It wasn't Liam who attacked Mrs Peat when she threatened to call the police, it was *the other one* as I like to think of it now; the other side of Liam we never knew was there.

When I fell into a drugged sleep, Liam discovered the deeds to the house and bank statements in the dresser drawer. He knew what I was worth before I even confided in him.

He must have realised it would scupper his plans if I got arrested for the mail backlog upstairs, so while I slept, he removed all the mail from the spare room with the help of Beryl's son. Apparently Liam had agreed to give him a cut of my money if he helped him.

But I'm not one to hold a grudge.

I have even forgiven him for saying I had abducted Amanda when it was him all along.

They found her curled up, barely breathing, in the wooden chest in Liam's front room.

He had used my sedatives to drug Amanda when she refused to go along with his plan to frame me for Ivy's death. Who'd have thought my old adversary would defend me like that?

And PC Cullen, who I'd got down as an interfering do-gooder, well thank heavens she was curious enough to do a bit of detective work herself and discover Liam's hidden past.

They arrested him, took him to the station for questioning and that's what caused his meltdown.

He admitted everything, even his plan to fleece me of the house and the lump sum I hadn't touched since Danny and our parents died.

It wasn't the real Liam that did all that, of course; the real Liam is gentle and kind. This time the bad stuff won but I believe that, one day, he'll be good as new again.

I'm going to be here for him when that day comes.

Later this week, I'm meeting up with Amanda for a coffee. Roisin is coming with me for a bit of moral support. It's so nice to have a friend at last.

Dr Marsh showed me photographs of Amanda and Carla as kids, looking like peas in a pod. All these years I thought she was living it up, she has been in the ground just like Danny. Amanda has had to deal with the fallout just like I have.

It took Amanda months to recover from her ordeal at Liam's hands but after everything was revealed, including Liam's vengeful actions at her workplace, the nursery stood by her and offered her a new position, a fresh start.

She is working in Derby now, in a new childcare manager job, but this weekend she's back in Nottingham.

She has been to see Liam a couple of times in here but she leaves me to look after him mostly, and it is an arrangement that suits us both.

People sometimes surprise you in good ways and you can never be sure how your life is going to turn out. Sometimes, there is no logic to it.

Your life takes a turn and, suddenly, everything changes and it just can't be put back together again the same way as it was before.

'Would you like a piece of fruit, Liam?'

He doesn't respond.

I sigh and look around the room at what everyone else is up to. Everyone has a visitor except for the boy who always sits alone in the same place by the French doors piecing together his jigsaws.

'I'll get you a glass of water,' I say and stand up.

The water dispenser is situated near the boy's table. As I walk by I look down at his half-completed jigsaw.

'You're doing well with that.' I smile.

I can't help but be thrilled with my new ability to talk to people. With Dr Marsh's help I have learned to start from a better place of assuming people are trustworthy and kind.

He looks up and his sombre face breaks into a grin.

'It's a level four puzzle,' he says.

'It does look difficult.'

'Sit down if you like,' he says. 'You can help me.'

I glance back at Liam but he is still staring out of the window; he's not even aware I have moved away. Nurse Janet is busying around talking to the patients and their visitors. There is nothing spoiling.

'Just for a minute or two then,' I say and pick up a jigsaw piece.

His name is Darren. He shows me where the piece fits when I have trouble.

'You're very good at this,' I say and he beams.

We place a couple more pieces and then Darren says, 'are you my visitor now?'

I look across at Liam.

Darren's face falls. His fingers begin to drum on the table edge.

'I suppose I am,' I say. 'For today, anyway.'

I take Liam a cup of water over and then come back to Darren's table.

'Will you help me do more of the puzzle?' he asks.

His light brown hair is floppy and falls over his eyes when he looks down, studying the puzzle. Danny had hair just like that. It used to drive him mad.

Once when Mother was out I put a girl's Alice band on him and we laughed and laughed as he danced around with it on.

I swallow down a scratch in my throat.

After a few more minutes, I decide it is time to get back to Liam.

'Don't go,' says Darren, placing his hand on mine.

I look down and slide my hand gently away.

'I'll come and sit with you next week,' I offer.

His brown eyes look sad, and with his floppy fringe, he reminds me of a forlorn puppy. I wish Liam was a bit more responsive when I make the effort to visit him; it is so nice to feel needed.

'Please stay,' Darren says again, chewing his lip. 'Stay and help me.'

I take a slow breath and look out over the lawns stretching out like a smooth, green carpet all the way down to the pond.

And gently, I extract my hand from his.

ACKNOWLEDGEMENTS

Firstly, huge thanks to Lydia Vassar-Smith, my editor, for seeing the potential in *Safe with Me* and for feeling so passionately about the book. Thanks also to Lydia for her expertise and guidance in the editing process.

I'd like to thank all the Bookouture team for everything you do, especially Kim Nash who is so giving of her time, advice and enthusiasm. Also, the other Bookouture authors who are so supportive of each other.

Secondly, a massive thank you to my agent, Clare Wallace, who worked on early edits with me and pulled out all the stops to submit *Safe with Me* just before embarking on her maternity leave. Now I have a book deal and she has Minnie, her beautiful baby daughter!

Enormous thanks to the rest of the incredibly hardworking team at Darley Anderson Literary, TV and Film Agency, especially Naomi Perry, Mary Darby, Emma Winter, Kristina Egan and Rosanna Bellingham.

Special thanks must also go to:

Angela Marsons, my writing buddy who encouraged me to give up the day job last year and to get *Safe with Me* out of the drawer and follow my gut . . . thank goodness it worked!

Julie Sherwin, for her early insight into the job of a postal worker. Any mistakes are entirely my own.

Carol Roberts for giving her time and feedback as an early reader.

Henry Steadman for designing such an amazing cover for *Safe with Me* which I loved the instant I saw it.

To my husband, Mac, for his unwavering belief in me in everything I do. For always being there through both the highs and the lows, for his patience and love and for keeping me well supplied with tea while I write. To my daughter, Francesca and my mum, Christine, who are both always there to support and encourage me.

To all family members and friends who show an interest in and are supportive of my writing – you know who you are!

LETTER FROM K.L. SLATER

Thank you so much for reading *Safe with Me*, my debut adult novel.

After many unsuccessful years of sending out my work to agents and publishers, I made the decision to go back to university at the age of 40 to give myself time and space to develop and focus on my writing.

'Safe with Me' began life as just a few chapters; the dissertation on my English & Creative Writing degree. It had another title and the story was slightly different in those early days but the voice of Anna, the main character, was just the same as it is today . . . and even after my degree was completed, Anna demanded her story be told. So I kept on writing the book!

I spend many hours alone in my writing room, so it has been wonderful to interact with lots of readers online and I would love to hear from you if you've enjoyed reading the novel.

I know you hear this a lot but reviews are so massively important to authors. If you've enjoyed 'Safe with Me' and could spare just a few minutes on Amazon or Goodreads to say so, I would so appreciate that.

You can also connect with me via my website, on Facebook or Twitter.

If you've enjoyed this, my debut novel, you might be interested to know that I've been working on my next psychological thriller. I think this one is going to keep you tense and guessing too, so I'd be really delighted if you could join me for book two!

Love and best wishes,

Kim x

 KimLSlaterAuthor/

KimLSlater

www.KLSlaterAuthor.com

Lightning Source UK Ltd.
Milton Keynes UK
UKHW020629231020
372100UK00010B/262